MW00443730

COPS,

CROOKS

AND

COWBOYS

ARL FARRIS

Copyright © 2019 by Arl Farris

Published by Dusty Saddle Publishing

All rights reserved. No part of this publication may be reproduced, distributed, or transmitted in any form or by any means, including photocopying, recording, or other electronic or mechanical methods, without the prior written permission of the publisher, except in the case of brief quotations embodied in critical reviews and certain other noncommercial uses permitted by copyright law. For permission requests, write to the publisher, addressed "Attention: Permissions Coordinator," at the address below.

Dusty Saddle Publishing

www.dspublishingnetwork.com

Ordering Information:

Quantity sales. Special discounts are available on quantity purchases by corporations, associations, and others. For details, contact the publisher at the address above.

Printed in the United States of America

ACKNOWLEDGEMENT

Cops, Crooks & Cowboys is a work of fiction. Names, characters, businesses, places, events, locales, and incidents are either the products of my imagination or used in a fictitious manner. Any resemblance to actual persons, living or dead, or actual events is purely coincidental.

The subject mater within this book is purely fictional. No part of this novel is intended as instructional or a guide for shooting, handling firearms or reloading of ammunition. Shooting sports can be fun, but should only be practiced under the watchful eye of a trained professional, not copied
from a work of fiction.

This novel could not have been written without the encouragement and support from many people. It would be impossible to list everyone, and I apologize to those persons I have mistakenly forgotten to mention, I'm sure there are many. I was privileged to work with some of the finest police academy firearms instructors in the world. Although I stood among them, I was never their equal. I will be forever be grateful for their friendship. We will never know the number of lives their teaching has saved. Thank you Rod Natale, Bill Murphy, George Zagurski, Michael Hall, Joe

Guarnera, Greg Nichols, John Krok, Cheryl Murphy, Randy Patrick, Greg Davis, and Chris Nesmith.

The Single Action Shooting Society is an outstanding organization and anyone who would like to participate in cowboy events or old west shooting, owes it to themselves to join the SASS. George Young, aka. Dusty Chaps, helped me with the cowboy shooting events for this book. Even with his help, I took some literary liberties for the sake of the story line.

Kathleen Cosgrove, Lily Wilson, Nina Slotkin Fortmeyer, Robert Mangeot and others from the Nashville Writers Meetup group as well as the gifted writers of Sisters in Crime, Middle Tennessee have helped me beyond anything I could have ever asked. Your friendship and guidance were second to none.

My editor Jaden Terrell, did more than dot the I's and cross the T's. She taught me how to write. She kept the story on track, my characters honest, and made the words fit together. She made me look better than I deserve. She is a one of a kind and a wonderful person.

A special shout out goes to Nick Wale and Bruce Bennett of Dusty Saddle Publishing. Thank you for believing in me and operating your business by The Golden Rule.

I am also fortunate to have a wonderful son and daughter, James and Emily. They read my manuscript and corrected the story. And only as your own adult children can do, freely gave me their advise.

Saving the best for last. I especially want to thank my wife. Nancy has always supported me when things were tough and celebrated my successes. She is the best looking and strongest person I have ever known. Without her, I would be a lesser person. She has made me the luckiest man on earth. I love you, Nancy.

This book is dedicated to:

Nancy

FOREWORD

All across this land of ours, members of law enforcement put their lives on the line every minute of every day, all too often with no thanks, or while facing criticism and disrespect. Why? Because they are not only sworn to do it, they are compelled by some strange force from within that pushes them to "protect and serve," even when they are "off duty." Yet, in spite of the constant criticism and mockery, challenges and accusations, they climb out of bed everyday and do it all over again.

On occasion, a rare author like Arl Farris pops up to provide us with an unusual look at the life of a lawman. I recently had the opportunity to read Farris' book, *Cops, Crooks, and Cowboys,* a fascinating story from a far different perspective than most of us ever consider. Written with a realistic eye toward law enforcement, and what happens when the system goes against the expected norm, Farris gives us a great *"What if..."* as that system turns on the very people sworn to protect and serve that system and the people it represents.

Someone once said, "There's a little larceny in us all." To me, this has always been a most appropriate phrase for members of law enforcement, as my experience has always been that the cop who can think like a crook will catch more crooks than the average cop. Farris incorporates that theme into this book, as the cops in this story use a bit of larceny to fight the system fighting them, and make some needed changes to it. Whether intentional or not, Farris also gives us a look into why, in every walk of life, sometimes "good people go bad."

I can't say more without giving away the plot, something I would never intentionally do. To do so would cheat both the reader and the author, and while I, too, have a bit of larceny in my heart, this is one of those tales that the readers must experience for themselves. At the end, readers might ask themselves how they would handle a system gone awry, what they would do if pushed into a corner while just doing their job. I trust you will enjoy *Cops, Crooks, and Cowboys* as much as I did.

Cherokee Parks

"There is nothing more exhilarating than to be shot at with no result."

– Winston Churchill

1

Did anybody see anything…

Two shots rang out at close range.

John dropped his water bottle and reached instinctively for the Beretta on his hip. His F-150 fishtailed and bounced onto the grass. He battled it back onto the gravel and skidded to a stop, sliding down in the seat, pistol pointed out the window.

"Yee-haw!" A man on horseback, holding a six-gun over his head and dressed as a cowboy, complete with boots, hat, and gun belt, galloped past, just off the gravel road.

"What the hell?" John holstered his pistol and pushed himself upright. A quarter-mile back, he drove under the overhead archway marking the Santa Ana River Shooting Complex. There were rules about where someone could shoot, even at a shooting complex, and shooting next to the road was strictly prohibited.

John had often seen shooters dressed like cowboys at the shooting complex, and occasionally they were on horseback. He thought they might be putting on a re-enactment, like groups commemorating Civil War battles. This guy was probably just an over-exuberant participant who'd ventured out of his designated shooting area. Dangerous behavior, but not criminal.

He blew out a slow breath as his adrenaline levels dropped. He'd report the event to the range office on his way out, to be on the safe side.

He arrived at the parking area, with dozens of cars scattered outside the pistol range. At the entrance, he parked in line with four other trucks, evenly spaced across the open gap of the range.

Built in the center of the Santa Ana flood control basin, the range consisted of several miles of open fields and areas with thick trees and underbrush surrounded by urban sprawl. There were close to two dozen tennis-court-sized ranges, each with dirt embankments or berms on three sides. A few larger ranges accommodated rifle shooters. North of the pistol ranges, an area for shotgun shooters had been established, with a sporting clays course and several trap and skeet fields.

In front of the trucks he'd parked beside, four other instructors, wearing similar red "STAFF" polo shirts, khaki cargo pants, and pistols, stood in a circle talking. They were a diverse group—a woman, a Hispanic man, a black man, and a white cisgender male. That was a perk in the current political climate. But beyond that, they were a top-notch crew.

Mano, the youngest of the four, said something that made the others laugh. Then Rebecca rolled her eyes, and Blakesley, the veteran, gave the younger man a high five. Scott, a little less gregarious than the others, turned away, smirking, and caught

John's eye. He nudged Blakesley with an elbow and raised a hand waving at their sergeant, John Chambers.

The range was nearly an hour's drive from the Long Beach Police Department, but outdoor ranges were hard to come by. Officers who worked the range were assigned day shift with weekends off. Their time at the range was paid at an overtime rate, but having a set schedule with weekends off was the main draw. That, and all the free ammunition they wanted, made for a very attractive collateral assignment.

John walked up to the group and asked, "Did anyone see anything strange driving in here?"

Rebecca lifted an eyebrow and waved a hand to encompass the group. "You're going to have to be more specific than that, Sarge. I'm surrounded by strange things."

"I saw some guy dressed like a cowboy, riding a horse and shooting a revolver next to the road. I didn't know if I was witnessing a crime or just looking at a kook."

Mano looked up and flashed a grin. With his Hollywood features and boyish charm, the young Hispanic officer was good-looking and knew it, but was too personable to dislike. "Yeah, I've been seeing those guys a lot. I don't know what they're doing."

John said, "If you run into any of 'em, watch yourself. The guy looked like a wacko. Now, let's get this group started. Are you guys ready?"

Blakesley made a tumbling motion with his hand. "Let's roll."

The police recruits wore black cargo pants, baseball caps, and royal blue tee shirts with their last names embroidered in two-inch white letters front and back. Around their waists were shiny-new, thick leather duty belts known as Sam Browne belts. The belts were organized identically with holster and gun on one side, T-handle baton, known as a PR-24, on the opposite, two extra magazines in front, and handcuffs centered in the back.

Looking over the group, John shook his head. They looked younger every year. Pushing the wannabe cowboy from his mind, John stepped away from the instructors and called out in a loud voice for all the recruits to hear, "I want the class sergeant, now!"

A fit Hispanic recruit who looked to be in his mid-twenties ran up and stood at attention. His head was shaved, he wore standard issue Oakley sunglasses, and tattooed just under his shirt sleeve was the combat infantry insignia of a musket over an oak leaf wreath.

"Sir, Class Sergeant Flores reporting as ordered, sir!"

"Flores, form the class up."

Flores barked back, "Sir, yes, sir!" He made a sharp about face, took three steps, and then yelled, "I need all recruits to form up into your squads."

After a minute of shuffling and shoving into perfectly straight rows, the class sergeant waited for them to become settled before calling out, "Class... Attention!" He turned to John. "Sir, academy class is ready for inspection, sir!"

It was obvious to John that Flores was chosen as the class sergeant for his military bearing.

John stood next to Flores. "At ease."

In unison, the recruits snapped their left legs eight inches to the left and moved their hands behind their backs to rest on their handcuff cases.

John looked out across the ranks and said, "There's a reason the department uses different staff officers for the range than at your regular academy. We're not here to gig you, have you do push-ups or make sure you're marching in step with spit-shined boots. Here at the range, there'll be no 'sir sandwiches.'" He glanced at Flores. "When asked a question, I don't want to hear, 'Sir, yes, sir.' I want to hear your honest answer. When you're back at the academy, those staff officers demand a certain level of discipline. We have another. If you forget to enter a victim's date of birth on a crime report, your sergeant can make those corrections with you. If you make a mistake in a shooting situation on the streets, there's no fixing it. Somebody dies."

He paused a moment to let that sink in, then said, "Let me see a show of hands. Who served in the military?"

Of the one hundred recruits, nine raised their hands, including Flores. John turned to Flores. "Have the class go to their cars and put away their batons. Then I want everyone to return wearing hearing and eye protection. The nine recruits who raised their hands, have 'em each bring a folding chair. Be back in formation in six minutes."

While the recruits were at their cars, John walked back to the group of instructors.

"Okay," he said. "Blakesley, you shoot the PPC course. The rest of us'll just hang back and look pretty."

Right on time, the recruits were back, standing at attention.

Flores and John took their places in front of the class and John addressed the class. "I want our veterans who served our country so valiantly and courageously to put their chairs along the safe area, to the side of the range. You're welcome to sit, relax and drink water while the rest of the class stands out here with me. Those recruits who stayed at home watching SpongeBob Square Pants and voting to legalize marijuana need to stand up and do something that just might benefit this country."

John saw several recruits attempting to suppress grins and hoped they were cartoon fans and not dope smokers.

He waved his arm for the other instructors to join him in front of the recruits. "If you've forgotten from my prior visits to the academy, I'm Sergeant John Chambers. I've been with the department sixteen years and teaching the firearms portion of the academy for eleven. I work patrol, and it's my job to teach you to shoot. Back at the academy, other tac officers see it as their mission to weed people out of this program, and they do a fine job. My mission is to make you successful."

The other range instructors were lined up next to John. In order, they introduced themselves.

With a welcoming smile on his face, Mano said, "My name is Manolito Torres. I've been with the department seven years and this is my third year teaching at the range. I work patrol, and for fun, I shoot action pistol matches and enjoy deep sea fishing." He paused for a moment. "Out here, you can call me Manolito or Mano for short, but when you start working the streets, I'm Officer Torres until you're off probation."

Next was Blakesley, a 47-year-old muscular black man with a shaved head and Tom on the front of his shirt. John was a little disappointed Blakesley had never attempted to promote, as he knew more than most of the lieutenants and captains combined. However, it was difficult to begrudge someone who loved helping new officers and was so adept at it.

After introducing himself, Blakesley said, "I started with the department after getting out of the army, infantry. I'm also in patrol and a competitive shooter. I have kids nearly as old as some of you, so I don't want to hear any complaining from anyone. Lord knows I hear enough of that at home."

Rebecca was next. "Well, let's see. I'm Rebecca Wells, and I've been with the department about eight years. I work patrol, and for fun, I'm a runner, do karate and also shoot competitively. I mostly like shooting sporting clays, but shoot action pistol to remain proficient. One more thing. A bullet shot from a woman's gun hits just as hard as one from a man's."

From Rebecca's business-like delivery, you would never guess how anxious she was about her upcoming court case. It was a bullshit case, a civil rights complaint that was more about politics than anything else. She'd confided her nerves to John and the rest of the crew, but John knew the recruits would see only a seasoned pro.

Scott was the last to introduce himself, pointing to the name embroidered on the front of his shirt. He was in his late thirties and, like the others, very fit. John had seen Scott deliver twin girls and shoot a machete-wielding madman all in the course of a single shift. Scott said, "Scott Smith, eight years, patrol. Just do what you're told, follow our direction, and you'll be fine."

"Okay," John told the recruits. "Officer Blakesley will demonstrate the Police Pistol Combat course of fire, or PPC. I hate calling it a combat course of fire because it's strictly a timed accuracy target course of fire." As John spoke, Blakesley stood at the 25-yard line, his shooting glasses and ear muffs on and his pistol and magazines loaded.

The recruits stood in silence as Blakesley fired ten rounds prone, ten rounds kneeling, and ten rounds standing. Without pausing, he moved up to the 15-yard line, then the 7-yard line, firing ten rounds standing at each distance. Finally, he stood at the 5-yard line and shot five rounds with his strong hand followed by five rounds with his weak hand, for a total of sixty rounds. It took him just over twenty minutes to complete the PPC course. When he'd finished, John said, "Holster your weapon."

The recruits looked suitably impressed. A few looked worried. Good. They needed to understand how far they had to go.

John pointed to the silhouette target Blakesley had shot. All sixty rounds were in the tenring. He said to the class, "If any recruits get a 600 score on the PPC course like this, I'll take you and your significant other out to any restaurant you want and happily buy anything on the menu, including drinks." The class cheered, and John added quickly, "Before you start making dinner reservations, just know, no recruit's ever scored a 600 on the PPC course."

He could see the mix of admiration and determination in their eyes. A few of them looked thoughtful, as if already planning their winning strategy. Well, let them plan. Maybe someday one of them would surpass Blakesley, but that day was long way off.

John pointed to the ten-yard line. "I want squads one and two on the line. Squads three and four stand behind them and help the other squads load their magazines."

For the next eight hours, they worked on basic marksmanship and weapons handling. At the end of the day, he assembled the recruits around him.

One of the recruits, whose hair was spun into a top knot that looked like she was concealing a coconut under her hat, raised her hand. John read the name across the front of her shirt. "Yes, Coleman?"

"Sir, Recruit Coleman, sir. Are you going to teach us how to clean our guns?"

"Absolutely," John said, suppressing a smile at her cockiness.

He pointed to a corner of the range. "Glocks over there." Pointing in the opposite direction. "Smiths on that end. Berettas with me and anything else with Officer Smith."

***

Rebecca looked up as a small group of men decked out in cowboy clothing, large-brimmed hats, vests, chaps, boots, and spurs gathered around. Each wore a double holster rig with a six-gun revolver on each hip. The spurs made a chiming sound each time one of them walked. It sounded like a bell ringing. The cowboys stood together listening as John spoke to the recruits.

The ranges were open to the public, and it was not unheard of for an occasional bystander to walk onto the safe area of the range and watch the recruit training. Still, seeing the men in their cowboy clothing, each wearing a pair of revolvers, Rebecca nodded in their direction and whispered to Manolito, "I think one of these guys might be the one who was shooting next to John's truck this morning. Come on!"

They edged to their right, approaching the men from their flank. As they passed behind Scott and Blakesley, she heard Manolito say, "Heads up, guys."

Rebecca glanced over her shoulder and saw Scott and Blakesley shift their focus from the recruits to size up the cowboys.

The cowboys were at John's back, and he seemed unaware of their presence. He continued speaking to the class. "At this point, all your weapons should be unloaded, but before we clean them, double check the chamber. Remember, no one here is an officer, so there should be no reason to be handling any ammunition until we are back here next week."

The cowboys nudged each other and laughed. One stepped forward, and Rebecca caught her breath. It was David Gaston, the prosecutor for her upcoming trial. He looked different in his cowboy garb, but beneath the broad-brimmed hat, leather gun belt and tough guy posturing, was the same arrogant sneer he'd worn during the pre-trial hearings.

He pointed at the recruits and jeered, "Not even cops yet? So cute in your little Gestapo uniforms!"

Rebecca clenched her fists. Nothing good could come from punching the smug little bastard, but that didn't mean she couldn't enjoy the thought. She glanced at John, who had turned toward the cowboys, scowling. He looked at class sergeant Flores and said, in a brittle voice, "Have the people who were in the military teach the others how to clean their weapons." Oh, boy, Rebecca thought. Her lips tugged upward in anticipation. Let the fireworks begin.

***

John spun around and walked up to the group of cowboys. He noted Rebecca and Manolito standing about fifteen feet to the cowboys' left, while Scott and Blakesley had walked in front of the interlopers and were standing between them and the recruits. He said to the cowboys, "I don't know what your problem is, but I didn't come onto your range to make fun of you. I'd appreciate if you'd leave."

"Or what are ya gonna do?" said a man whose full cowboy attire included a set of chrome Colt revolvers. "Your guns aren't even loaded."

John made a point of looking at Manolito and Rebecca to his left, then at Scott and Blakesley behind him. Rebecca raised her middle finger at the lead cowboy and stepped close enough for John to hear her murmur, "That's David Gaston. He's prosecuting my case."

The other cowboys' eyes followed John's gaze. He turned back to the cowboys. "If one of you puts a hand on a gun, you'll find out the hard way, if our weapons are loaded."

The other cowboys involuntary took a half step backwards. For a moment, Gaston looked uncertain. Then he recomposed himself and spat on the ground at John's feet.

John said, "I'm not the one who needs to play dress up in order to pretend I'm a man. Why don't you go off to your costume ball and leave our range?"

The recruits stopped what they were doing and gathered closer to hear what was happening.

Gaston said, "I'm known as 'Dusty Dave,' and you aren't shit. Tell you what. I'll have a shoot-off against you. If you win, I'll leave. When I win, I'm gonna tell your junior wannabes what a pathetic piece of shit you are."

"Well, Rusty Dick," John said, "I've got nothing to prove to you or your girlfriends. Why don't you just ride off into the sunset and pretend to be a tough guy somewhere else?" He turned away from the cowboys, raised his voice and told the class, "Class dismissed. I'll see you here next week."

The recruits slowly began walking away, looking disappointed that he hadn't accepted the cowboy's challenge.

☐

Cops, Crooks and Cowboys

2

…you should quit

From the range, John drove to the police department, where he took a quick shower and suited up in his uniform. Normally, thanks to his duties with the recruits, he'd have the day off, but a nasty strain of the flu had left the department short-handed, so he and Scott had volunteered to take an extra shift. Just as well. He was still on edge from the encounter with the cowboys, an energy he'd rather not take home to Jenny and the kids.

A quick call to dispatch told him he needed to be in three places at once. A jogger had discovered a body floating near Mother's Beach, students were staging a protest in front of the campus at Cal State, and a head-on collision had traffic in both directions on Pacific Coast Highway at a standstill.

The floater, if it was a homicide, would take precedence, but that didn't diminish the importance of the other calls. Any one of them could make it onto the front page of tomorrow's paper or be the lead story on the evening news. If he made the wrong call, some reporter would make him look like an idiot. But without clarifying information, the floater was the best bet.

He typed a quick message over his on-board digital computer telling Scott to take charge of the scene at Mother's Beach until he arrived.

John was trying to stay off PCH on his way to Mother's Beach when dispatch broadcast another call.

"Medical aid, 347 Magnolia Avenue. Unit to respond?"

Certainly, a medical aid was not the priority. But his captain had berated John's squad for slow response times and placed John on a performance improvement plan. If he didn't bring down the time it took officers to arrive at emergency calls, he would be replaced.

His on-board computer showed no available units. It could be an hour before another officer would be clear, and depending on the urgency, that might be too late. 347 Magnolia was just around the corner. Might as well take this one himself. Scott could keep a handle on things until he got there.

"How's this for response time?" he muttered, picking up the radio. "Sam 23—I'm in front of 347 Magnolia. I'll take the medical aid."

Dispatch responded, "Sam 23—See the man, 347 Magnolia, apartment 256, for a lacerated arm. Paramedics are en-route."

John hoped the laceration wasn't a bleeder. Like most officers, he tried to avoid going to medical aids. Policemen weren't doctors and only received basic first aid training. Unless a person was going to die without receiving CPR or some other noninvasive treatment, officers simply tried to clear the area around the injured person so paramedics could get to the patient.

There were no open spaces on the street, so John turned on his overhead light bar and left the black and white in the middle of the street. The building was a rat-infested complex that should have been torn down thirty years ago. The apartments were small one-bedroom units with kitchens smaller than most campers. And the residents didn't like cops. The only time they saw the police was when one of them was being dragged away in handcuffs.

As he navigated the second-floor maze in search of apartment 256, he heard doors slamming and people whistling, a warning to others that the police were in the building. At the end of the hallway, a small group of people hanging out in pajamas and baggy jeans watched him with nervous anticipation. After a short detour down the wrong corridor, it took John another minute to arrive in front of 256. He found the front door ajar and shouted inside. "Long Beach Police Department!"

He paused at the door and unsnapped his holster. Every year, policemen were ambushed on routine calls. In a typical ambush scenario, the police department received a call requesting an officer to counsel an incorrigible teen, check the welfare of an elderly person living alone, or go to a medical aid. When the unsuspecting officer showed up, assailants were waiting with sawed-off shotguns or AK-47s.

You never knew if, behind any given door, a room full of gang members were waiting to blow you away or if an elderly couple would be offering breakfast. The Long Beach Police Department had its share of officers killed in the line of duty, and John did not want to be next.

Keeping his pistol in the holster, he placed his right hand on the gun, ready to draw and fire. If this was an ambush, odds were he would be assaulted as soon as the front door opened. Pumped on adrenaline, he threw open the door and quickly looked inside. As his gaze swept the room, his mind filtered out everything except potential danger.

No gangbangers, no AK-47s, no one—as far as he could tell— hiding behind the furniture. Satisfied that he wasn't walking into a trap, he relaxed, snapped the holster closed and walked inside.

***

The apartment was filthy, with pizza boxes and hamburger wrappers strewn on a threadbare carpet that looked like it had not seen a vacuum cleaner since the first George Bush was president. Appearing out of place, an 88-inch plasma curved-screen TV, nearly as large as the wall it was mounted on, stood out in the living room, opposite a mustard colored couch. In the kitchen and away from the table, a wooden chair lay on its side. Beside it, a skinny, thirtysomething, shirtless man sat on the floor in a puddle of blood and broken glass. A shard of glass the size of a knife blade protruded from his left inner arm, three inches below his armpit. Blood trickled down the man's arm and pooled on the linoleum.

Shit. A bleeder.

The man looked up, eyes glazed with shock and pain.

John guessed the man to be three or four inches shorter than his own six feet, but it was hard to tell with the man sprawled on the floor. The man's ribs were clearly defined under pale white skin. John had a lean, athletic build, but next to the rail-thin figure, he felt like the Hulk.

John felt his empty pocket for a pair of latex gloves. Not that he planned on touching the man or getting anywhere near the blood, but he didn't want to touch anything in the apartment. He looked at his watch, hoping the paramedics would hurry up and get there so he could get to Mother's Beach and avoid the captain's criticism about not properly supervising his shift.

He stepped around the pool of blood and righted the overturned chair. "That's gotta hurt. What happened?"

The man looked away from John to the counter. "Getting a pitcher off the top shelf. The chair slipped."

"The paramedics are on the way," John said. "You can sit in the chair if you'd be more comfortable, but try not to move too much. Are you on any medication or anything I should tell the paramedics?"

"I take a cocktail of AZT and some other stuff. If I take the glass outta my arm, I think it'll stop bleeding." He reached for the shard.

"No!" John barked. "Don't touch your arm!"

He looked around the kitchen for a clean cloth, expecting to see hordes of cockroaches sizing him up for intruding on their domain. He didn't see any roaches, but he didn't see anything that could accurately be called clean, either. In a milder tone, he said, "It's possible you've lacerated an artery. If you remove the glass, you could open the wound. Are you HIV positive?"

The man looked at his arm. Ignoring John's question, he said, "I think you're wrong."

As he started to get up, John reached forward, grabbed the man's uninjured arm at the elbow, and helped him into the chair.

Wincing, the man said, "It hurts." He grabbed the shard of glass and, before John could stop him, ripped it from his arm. Blood spurted from the wound, and the man's eyes widened. Then he screamed, "I'm bleeding! Do something!"

A pungent, metallic odor filled the air as blood squirted on the wall and cabinet doors. The man spun around, waving his arm as blood sprayed in every direction. John raised his hands too late, and something wet and warm splattered across his neck and lower jaw.

Trying not to think of the virus in the man's blood, John clamped his hands around the man's wound and walked him to the living room couch. Blood pumped out between John's fingers as he looked for something he could use as a bandage to keep direct pressure on the hemorrhaging artery.

There. A balled-up tee shirt. Holding the arm in one hand, John picked up the shirt from the floor at the foot of the couch. A slice of pepperoni pizza clung to the shirt, and he tossed them both across the room in disgust.

The injured man gave a frightened little moan.

John wished he had a few basic first aid supplies, but he had nothing. Nothing useful, anyway. He had an AED defibrillator and small first aid kit containing the usual band-aids, aspirin, hand sanitizer, a few small bandages, and latex gloves in the truck of his car. Other than the defibrillators, the first aid kits were not for medical aid calls, but for the officers' personal use. After losing several malpractice lawsuits, police departments had stopped supplying any real medical equipment to officers.

Without direct pressure applied to the wound, the injured man would bleed to death in a matter of minutes. John's unprotected hands were still in the man's blood, but even though he'd read numerous training bulletins and briefed his officers at least a dozen times on the danger of blood-borne pathogens, it was a little late to worry about that now.

Above the couch, held in place with thumb tacks, John saw a rainbow flag. He reached out, placed his hand between two tacks, and gave the flag a jerk. Thumb tacks flew across the room, pinging off the TV screen. Quickly, he wrapped the flag around the man's arm, holding it in place and keeping direct pressure on the wound. Within seconds, a red stain spread beneath his hand.

After a minute, the bleeding slowed. The man's breath was still ragged with fear. John said, "Take it easy. Paramedics are on the way. I'm gonna get your medication so they don't give you anything that'll cause an adverse reaction. Where is it?"

The man drew in a startled breath. "You're not gonna leave me, are ya?"

"I'm just gonna get your medication." John adjusted his tone to convey understanding and support. He'd worked enough in the gay community to know how different—and how difficult—life was for many of its members.

Looking reassured, the man nodded toward the half-open bathroom door. "It's in there."

John took the man's left hand and placed it over the wound. "Hold the bandage tight. I'll be right back."

He had hoped to wash the blood off his face and neck while retrieving the medication but changed his mind when he saw the condition of the bathroom. What had once been a white porcelain sink was now greenish yellow and smelled of mold. The faucet leaked, a tooth brush lay inside the sink, and an empty tube of toothpaste with its cap off was on the backsplash. Razors, deodorant and an empty Sudafed box were scattered around the sink. A waste paper basket under the sink overflowed with tissues, bottle caps, and more Sudafed packages. John opened the medicine cabinet, reached between several more Sudafed boxes, and picked up two prescription bottles with their tops off.

As he read the labels, a scream from the living room interrupted him. The bottles slipped from his hand and bounced on the open toilet seat. The pills seemed to jump into the toilet and onto the floor.

Shit.

Another scream drove the pills from his mind, and he hurried to the living room.

The man—Nathaniel Freeman, according to the prescription labels—was still where John had left him, hand clamped to the makeshift bandage. He looked pale and shaken, his eyes wide with panic.

John tried to sound more like a big brother than the seasoned veteran who had spent seventeen years working downtown. "What's wrong?"

In a pinched voice, Nathan said, "I can't get a transfusion, I've got HIV. What's gonna happen to me?"

John suppressed a snicker. "You can get blood, you just can't give it." He hesitated a moment, then asked, "You using meth or just addicted to Sudafed?"

Before Nathan could answer, the paramedics arrived. Dressed in khaki turnout pants with navy blue T-shirts, they carried boxes of medical supplies and equipment. The crew chief looked at the blood on John and asked, "How bad are you hurt?"

Nodding toward Nathan, John said, "It's his blood, not mine. He lacerated an artery. I just tried stopping the bleeding... By the way, your patient's HIV positive."

The paramedics exchanged glances, then put on a second pair of protective gloves and face shields. With a cool efficiency, they placed the injured man on a gurney.

John stepped forward and clenched Nathan's hand. "It'll be okay. These guys are the best in the world."

As they maneuvered him out the front door, one of John's officers, Scott Smith, awkwardly squeezed his way into the apartment. He stopped short as if he'd stepped into an abattoir.

John frowned. The spit-shine on Scott's boots gleamed, and his uniform was a little too fresh. The sand should have dulled that shine. John barked, "What are you doing? Why aren't you with the body?"

Scott looked pointedly at John's bloody hands and neck, his forehead furrowed with concern. "There was no body at the beach, just an old sweat shirt stuffed with seaweed on a piece of driftwood. It looked real at first, but... are you okay? Why aren't the medics here instead of with the hype?"

"They're gonna clean me up as soon as I get downstairs. Help me lock up."

Securing the front door, Scott said, "That big screen costs more than my car."

John nodded. It would be gone in five minutes if they didn't lock the door.

The crowd from the apartment had gathered on the street, watching the patient being loaded into the ambulance. One of them pointed to the flag wrapped around the man's arm and yelled, "Gay basher!"

Other people started yelling, "We should wrap you up in a cop flag, see how ya like it." A thousand retorts warred in John's mind, but he knew better than to say any of them.

A paramedic who had been wiping the blood off John said, "If they only knew you just saved that guy's life."

John shook his head. "They only see what they want to see. I'm just glad his blood didn't get in my eyes or I didn't cut myself shaving this morning."

The paramedic took a box of latex gloves off his truck, held them up and asked, "You want some of these?"

John shook his head. "No, I don't think I'll be going on any more medical aid calls today."

Scott grabbed the gloves. "Those are a lot better than the ones they give us." He stuffed the box under his arm. "Hey, Sarge, you want me to get the names of some of the paramedics? Remember what happened to Buchanan after he arrested the tranny who hit him with her high heels? Even with the whole thing on his body camera, people packed the council chambers demanding he be fired. You don't have a body camera."

John looked at the angry crowd. "Good idea. All it takes is one complaint and the captain would be all over me."

The paramedic finished getting the blood off John's skin and laughed. "If the department gives you any shit for what you did in there, you should quit."

The crowd was moving closer and getting larger. Those who weren't yelling had their cell phones recording or were calling their friends to join them.

The paramedic put the names of his crew on a card and handed it to John. "You might need this. I'll be happy to tell anybody that guy'd be going to the coroner's office if you hadn't stopped the bleeding."

John stuffed the card in his shirt pocket. He hoped he wouldn't need it. "Thanks." He got in his car and waited for a break in the radio traffic. "Sam 23—Clear from the medical aid, subject transported to Memorial Hospital. I'll be en route to the station for a fresh uniform."

Dispatch radioed back, "Sam 23—clear."⧠

3

...it takes a lawyer to understand the law

David Gaston heaved a sigh and clicked out of the Single Action Shooting Society website. He had potential clients waiting, but sometimes he had to stop and take a break from all that whining. Not that he didn't sympathize with their position. He did. On one level, they had a common cause. He just wished they were less... loathsome.

Two-thirds of the officers in Long Beach worked in uniform. On any given day they each contacted roughly fifteen people per shift. If only a small percent of those were outraged, that was a lot of unhappy people. Should any of those decide to complain, what better way than through a lawyer, particularly a civil rights attorney who didn't charge any fees up front? Of course, if they'd read the fine print, they'd know that any money collected on their behalf would be split 70/30, said attorney getting 70 percent and the client 30. Any expenses preparing the case also came out of their percentage.

Gaston surmised he needed to filter through about twenty-five of these disgusting individuals before finding one he could mold into someone a jury might pity, and he set one day a week aside for interviewing them. This being a typical Monday, he had already listened to seven sob stories. His mind felt numb, and to top it off, he couldn't get the encounter with the cops at the shooting range off his mind.

I'm not the one who needs to play dress up in order to pretend I'm a man.

There was no excuse for a cop to talk that way to a citizen. The other instructors had been no better, smirking at him as if he were some kind of bug beneath their shoes. *I pay your salary,* he thought, heat rising in his cheeks. It was a paltry sum, but he resented it, and he damn sure resented being insulted in return. But he'd recognized one of them, a bitch he was prosecuting on a civil rights violation, and that meant he had them all right where he wanted them.

He thought about knocking off early and going to the Spearmint Rhino Gentleman's Club, where all his expert witness consulting fees incurred. Instead, he picked up the phone and called a former client. If anyone could help him nail those smug bastards at the firing range, it was Connie.

She sounded breathless when she picked up. In a hurry, as always. "Yes, David? What's up?"

"Got some cops I'd like you to dig up some dirt on."

Her laugh was warm. "That's a task I'm always happy to do. Especially for you."

Eight months prior, Connie Jones, a Happening Now News reporter, and her husband, Gordon, were on their way home from an evening with friends. They were each a little buzzed and had the bad luck of driving into a sobriety checkpoint. Gordon was charged with DUI and Connie was issued a citation for having her kid sister's Ritalin in her purse. When Connie called Gaston's office the next day, he agreed to represent both Connie and Gordon—for no money up front.

The last thing Connie wanted was to appear in court. She hoped to someday host her own cable news show or perhaps get a chance at being cast in a television drama, but her career would be over before it began if a network caught wind of her addiction to prescription drugs.

Gaston had pulled their fat out of the fire. At least, that's what Connie thought. But she didn't know the whole story. Unbeknownst to Connie and Gordon—and against their specific instructions—Gaston pled guilty to both charges. In return, the drunk driving charge was reduced to reckless driving and a four-hundred-sixty-six-dollar fine imposed. Gordon's driver's license was suspended for six months and restricted to driving during the course of employment.

Gaston had paid the fine, plus another one-hundred-seventy-three-dollar fine for a lesser charge on Connie's unlawful possession of another's prescription. It was a small price to pay for what he planned to get in return.

Afterward, he told Connie and Gordon that, although it had taken considerable legal maneuvering, he had gotten nearly everything dropped. He said the judge, fearing the Mothers Against Drunk Drivers might try blocking his re-election, had imposed a six-month restriction on Gordon's license. However, everything else had been dismissed by the court and they could put this entire unpleasant business behind them.

Everything he'd told them was a lie. But why not? What were the chances Connie or Gordon would ever see their own criminal histories? It would be years from now, if ever, and by then Gaston would have everything he wanted from Connie. Gaston would say he'd told them the truth, but they were too emotionally upset and had simply misunderstood. After all, it takes a lawyer to understand the law.

Gaston had been quick to suggest that, if Connie felt compelled to show a little gratitude, there was something she could do. He would call her whenever he needed to apply pressure against the city with a television crew on the courthouse steps, and she would call him if she happened upon someone claiming human rights violations against the police. So far, Gaston had been the one doing all the calling, but true to her word, the Happening Now News van had been present at the close of his last three cases and was scheduled to attend the one against Rebecca Wells.

Connie seemed to consider this arrangement a win–win. He'd gotten her out of an embarrassing scrape with the law, and she could use him to get even with those self-righteous cops who'd tried to ruin her aspiring acting career. Not to mention she was getting a possible link to any number of proverbial smoking guns.

"So," she said, "who are these miscreants?"

"Start with Rebecca Wells," he said. "There's a case pending against her. But aside from that, she's training a bunch of recruits at the firing range. I want anything you can find on her or the rest of the instructors—especially their supervisor."

"Is there a story in it?" she asked, which made him smile.

"Oh, I hope so," he said. "I really, really do."

They signed off, and he stepped out to wave in his next hopeful. A man in his early twenties wearing cubic zirconia stud earrings, thick gold necklaces with four-inch dollar insignias, and a freshly ironed white T-shirt shuffled in and sat down in front of Gaston's desk.

The man launched into his tale of woe, finishing with, "How'd I know the she'd tell the cops I stole her goddamn car? I had to spend the weekend in lockup, even after the bitch dropped the charges. So, can I sue?"

"I need to look at a few more details before I can answer that. I'll get back to you in a few days." As he watched the young man leave, a hopeful spring in his step, Gaston placed the manila folder containing the man's information on a stack of rejects.

Years before, a burned-out civil judge had helped Gaston fine-tune his current path. "There's plenty of money out there," Jarvis had said from his hospital bed. He was a few weeks from the graveyard, and he knew it. Lung cancer, forty years of smoking. The old bastard was estranged from all his kids, and Gaston figured he wanted to leave some kind of legacy. "But you won't find it representing rich frat boys. You need clients a jury can feel sorry for and defendants you can turn into monsters."

Tobacco companies. Firearms corporations. Big oil and fracking companies, and all those other assholes trashing the environment. It might take ten or twenty years collecting data and gaining an edge, but when the time was right, the judge said, he'd be ready.

And in the meantime, what was he supposed to do for money? Jarvis had an answer for that too. Police civil rights violations. That would pay off Gaston's student loans and give him enough time to build some expertise to fight the firearms industry or champion some environmental movement.

The icing on the cake was, it would be a public service, taking down the fucking cops. Gaston hated cops.

The judge's plan was brilliant in its simplicity. A true long game. "The best way to hurt these people is to join them. Get to know who they are and how they operate. Learn everything you can, and when the time's right, use what you've learned against them. You might even need to join the National Rifle Association. It's very powerful when a long-standing member brings suit against an organization. It shows consciousness on your part, and a group like the NRA can't say you're a kook, because you've been one of their members for a dozen years."

The real money was in changing an industry. If he could regulate the firearms industry and not just win a case because of a faulty gun safety, he'd be talking hundreds of millions of dollars in judgments. But to do that, he'd need to become an insider. Then, when he had what he needed, including the right plaintiffs, he'd be in a position to turn on the NRA and bring them to their knees.

And that was exactly what he was doing. Against everything he believed in, Gaston became a member the National Rifle Association, joined a shooting league and actually competed in shooting matches. To all appearances, he was as pro-gun as they came, but behind the scenes, he'd spent years compiling raw data on guns, gun companies and shooting clubs. For the last three years, he'd collected water and soil samples from the Santa Ana River, where it passed behind the shooting range. Every month, he submitted his samples to a laboratory for analysis of toxins and elevated lead particles.

For now, all he had was a jumble of information. He just needed the right combination of client and circumstances before being able to steamroll his opposition all the way to the bank. However, at this point, he had neither.

He took to heart what the old judge told him. He stopped pursuing petty trip-and-fall claims and built his practice on civil rights cases against the police. This gave him an outlet for his hatred of cops and enough time and money to pursue his real passion, to take on the firearms industry.

An image of Peter flashed behind his eyes, the look of surprise on his face, the spreading stain across his chest.

Pushing the memory from his mind, Gaston went to the door to greet his next possible client.

Go away, Peter. Please, just go away.   ▯

4

Suck it up, buttercup…

Officer Rebecca Wells watched as defense attorney David Gaston slowly made his way around the prosecutor's table. She had never been adrift on a life raft, but she recognized the look of a shark circling its prey. They were in the Superior Court of California, County of Los Angeles. Prosecuting attorneys called it 'the bank,' for the large settlements awarded by its notoriously generous judges. The irony of the courthouse being located on Commonwealth Avenue was not lost on her.

"Tell me, officer," Gaston said, "what does the term 'driving while black' mean?"

Rebecca glanced at the jury and saw two white women shifting uncomfortably in their seats. "It's a racially divisive term loosely used to describe profiling based on a driver's skin color."

"And were you taught to profile drivers based on their skin color in the academy, or was it something you came up with on your own?"

She looked at the defense attorney, hoping he would object to the question, but he seemed not to catch on that there was no way to answer the question without incriminating herself. It was like asking someone if they still beat their wife. "I have never stopped someone based on the color of their skin."

"Is that so? Well, then, how do you explain that, on November twelfth, you made two traffic stops along Shoreline Drive, one on a white woman in a Ford sedan and my client in a four-door Buick. You claimed in your earlier deposition that each was stopped for driving through a crosswalk with pedestrians crossing. Yet you let the white driver go and wrote a ticket to the black man."

Two black jurors made eye contact with each other and without speaking nodded in agreement. Another female juror nervously raised her hand to her mouth.

Rebecca exhaled. All she did was go out one day and scratch a few tickets because her sergeant said tourists were complaining about cars trying to run people over around the Pike and Aquarium of the Pacific. She made a few car stops, warned one person, wrote up another and somehow it turned into a federal civil rights case. She knew how she answered the next question could impact the rest of her career.

"Police officers have wide discretion when it comes to enforcing the law. The first person I stopped apologized for her mistake, and it was my opinion she would not do it again. When I stopped Mr. Roosevelt, he immediately said the only reason I stopped him was because he was black and demanded to speak with the watch commander. He said he did nothing wrong, and I felt he would not correct his driving from my talking with him, so I wrote the citation."

Gaston stood in front of the witness stand, leaning forward into Rebecca's space. She looked at him coolly, determined not to let him rattle her. She wondered what the jury saw when they looked at the two of them. The contrast between them must be striking. Rebecca's hair was pulled back in a tight bun. Her posture was perfect, her uniform immaculate, and she had on just enough make up to highlight her features. Gaston on the other hand slouched, wore a navy blue mock turtleneck T-shirt and black beaded necklace with a small cross that rode eight inches below his neck line, and had a ponytail held in place by one of the thick brown rubber bands used by the court to keep their file folders closed.

On the streets, Rebecca was an expert at being able to quickly size up a person and take the appropriate actions, but trying to read a jury remained a mystery. If they were able to distinguish between a professional police officer standing on the front lines, safeguarding its citizens, versus a sloppy, self-absorbed sleazeball out to make a fast buck, she should be okay. That, and it wouldn't hurt if the jury considered the evidence.

Gaston asked, "Did you get the watch commander like my client asked?"

She moved her hands from her lap to the podium in front of her. "No, I showed him the address of the police department on the ticket and told him he was free to see the watch commander after signing the ticket."

"Isn't it true you threatened to arrest my client if he didn't sign the ticket?"

"Signing a ticket is not an admission of guilt, just a promise to appear."

Gaston looked at the judge. "Your Honor, please instruct the defendant to answer the question."

"Please answer the question, Officer Wells."

She cleared her throat. "Yes, I did."

Gaston held a finger in the air to let the jury know he'd scored. He sauntered towards the jury box. "You denied my client the right to see your watch commander, just like you violated his civil rights not to be stopped simply for being a black man driving in Long Beach." Standing in front of the jury box, he spun around and pointed his raised finger directly at Rebecca. "Admit it. You're a white supremacist who would be wearing sheets and a hood if you weren't wearing that uniform."

Several jurors recoiled at the accusation, and this brought Rebecca's attorney to his feet. "Objection, Your Honor. That statement is speculation and not based on any evidence admitted."

Rebecca wanted to scream. Was that the best the city's attorney could do, object based on conjecture? This was about her reputation, and if her lawyer didn't do a better job, she would be labeled a racist and fired from the department. Not to mention the money the city would pay this guy and his conniving attorney.

Gaston dropped his outstretched hand to his side and smiled at the jury. "No further questions, Your Honor."

The judge looked at the clock, then to the city's attorney. "Your witness, Mr. Andrews."

He finished scribbling on a yellow legal pad, stood, and began reading his questions. "Officer Wells, at what point did you—"

The judge interrupted. "I don't know what they're teaching in law school these days, but I'm not gonna let you read your notes to the jury. Frankly, we don't have time and the jury's already bored. Just say what you need to say and let's get on with it."

He blinked at the judge. "Yes, Your Honor," and laid his yellow legal pad back on the table.

Losing confidence in her attorney, Rebecca placed her hands back in her lap and clenched her fists.

"Did you know the driver of the Buick was black before you pulled him over?"

She turned her head and answered to the jury. "I was behind the Buick and could only see the back of the driver's head. When

I made the traffic stop, I couldn't tell if the driver was a man or woman, black, white or Asian."

"You did in fact write other tickets that day, and you even made an arrest, is that correct?"

Rebecca felt momentum shift her way as the attorney was finally asking the right questions. "That is correct. I wrote two other tickets and arrested a parolee for violating the terms of his release."

Andrews handed her two traffic citations. "Please read the date on the tickets and the race of the violators."

She looked at the first citation. "November twelfth and Caucasian on this one." She scanned the second. "November twelfth and Hispanic on the second."

He handed her the face page of an arrest report. "I believe this is the arrest of the parolee you mentioned before. Please read the race of that individual."

"Caucasian."

"Thank you, Your Honor. Nothing further."

The case wrapped up that afternoon, but the jury deliberated two full days. On the start of the third day, they reported back that they were hopelessly deadlocked and unable to reach a verdict. By the time the judge called all parties back into the courtroom, Rebecca's calves ached from the extra miles she'd been running to relieve stress during the trial.

The judge lifted a hand to keep anyone from reading his lips and mouthed something to the bailiff, then addressed the courtroom. "With the jury unable to reach a decision, I am dismissing the case against Officer Wells and the Long Beach Police Department without prejudice. Case dismissed."

Gaston gave her a cool stare and pointed at her, index finger and thumb forming the barrel and hammer of a pistol. Bang.

She pretended not to notice.

As people filed out of the courtroom, Rebecca remained in her chair at the defense table while her attorney placed loose papers in a folder. She asked, "So, I won because they couldn't prove prejudice?"

He laughed. "Hardly. Dismissing a case without prejudice is a legal term. It means the prosecuting attorney can refile anytime he wants. But don't worry, I'm gonna make a settlement offer of thirty grand. They'll take it and this whole thing will go away."

She placed her hand on the folder Andrews was trying to shove in his briefcase. He stopped and looked at her.

"The hell it will," she said. "As far as the department's concerned, they had to pay out on a civil rights violation because of something I did wrong."

She moved her hand away and he picked up the file. "This has nothing to do with you. Legal bills the city four hundred and fifty dollars an hour for our services. Getting a case ready for trial takes thirty to forty hours, and I've already put in over sixty hours since the trial began. It's a lot cheaper for us to settle out of court than go back and win in front of a jury."

Rebecca's posture wasn't quite as straight-arrow as it had been on the witness stand. "What's my reputation worth? What am I going to do the next time I'm accused of violating someone's civil rights?"

Andrews closed his briefcase and stood up. "Suck it up, buttercup. That's the way it works around here. Just don't violate anyone's rights in the future." He turned and walked out.

She stared after him, blinking in disbelief. It was going to take a good six miles, maybe even a half-marathon to get this out of her system. ▯

5

Welcome to the big city…

John reached for the clock radio, shutting off the alarm before it woke his wife. It was hard enough getting up at 5:15 in the morning for work, but completely inexcusable to wake someone recuperating and on bed rest. Jenny had been injured by a tweaker out of his mind on meth at the hospital where she worked. She was healing, but it was a slow process and she needed her sleep. He left the lights off and silently put on an old T-shirt, shorts and tennis shoes before slipping downstairs and out the front door. Forty-five minutes later, he returned from his run and showered.

He dressed in the bathroom, quietly went to the nightstand by the bed, took out his 9mm, which had most of its bluing worn away, and eased it into the open-top holster on his right hip. Standing next to the bed, he softly said, "I love you."

Without opening her eyes, Jenny whispered, "Be careful, honey."

He kissed her gently on the forehead, then peeked into each of the two kids' rooms before he left. Leaving them was the hardest part of his day, every evening he made it home to them a gift.

Less than twenty air miles from the heart of Los Angeles, Long Beach had something for everyone. From its beautiful shoreline, the Aquarium of the Pacific, the Queen Mary, its own Grand Prix to the Pike Amusement Center. During WW-II, the Pike entertained and provided needed relief for sailors. After the war, the Pike died a lingering death until eventually closing in the 1970s. A few shops and restaurants tried at various times to make a go of it, but the once popular destination was never able to make a comeback. Starting in 2000, downtown Long Beach began to revitalize. Trendy restaurants lined Pine Avenue, and a light rail train system was incorporated, taking shoppers to boutiques, entertainment, and restaurants.

As was the case with many transitioning downtown areas, blight, crime, gangs and homelessness needed to be addressed. With 800 sworn officers and an equal number of civilian staff, the Long Beach Police Department made keeping the safety of visitors at the oceanfront developments a top priority. However, with violence spilling over from South Central Los Angeles and their own Carmelitos housing projects, the resources of the LBPD could quickly become over overburdened.

Despite the problems, John loved being a policeman in Long Beach. The department was the perfect size, small enough that he knew everybody, yet big enough that if he got on the wrong side of a lieutenant or captain, he could avoid them. In a thirty-year career, there were so many opportunities to work specialty assignments, he would never have time to work them all before retiring.

Briefing for officers who worked downtown began at 6 am. Afterward, officers inspected their black and whites and made their way to their assigned areas. Once on their beat, they began answering calls for service, or if it was slow, which it typically was until 8 am, they met with their area sergeant to see what was planned for their assigned beat. Generally, the sergeant let officers know if the gang unit might be working a surveillance in the area or if a narcotics or vice team were working a particular location. However, officers were frequently pulled out of service, booking prisoners, settling disputes, or being called into court to testify. Typically, the plans for an officer's shift changed several times during the course of the day.

Working downtown, John was responsible for twelve officers, the four who were like family and worked the range with him, and eight others. He picked up the microphone on his black and white.

"Sam 23—Lincoln units, channel 2."

After five seconds, he broadcasted, "Sam 23—Lincoln units, 10-87, 65 Cedar Avenue, second story, 07:15 hours."

65 Cedar Avenue was a public parking structure for the Pike. At 7:15 in the morning, the parking structure would be empty, allowing him to talk freely with his officers without the prying eyes of the public on them. And by having his informal briefing in

the field, if any officers received a radio call, they were already in their assigned area and could be wherever they needed to be within a few minutes.

When he pulled into the parking structure, several officers were already there. Their black and whites were backed into stalls and parked at odd angles to one another to allow them to speed away at a moment's notice. The sounds of racing engines and squealing tires coming up the concrete ramps let him know the others were on their way.

When all the officers arrived, he said. "All right, listen up. Auto theft is working a surveillance in Shoreline Village. Apparently, every Honda Accord, Toyota Camry and Toyota 4Runner parked down there's being stolen."

One of the officers chimed in. "Who knew?"

Ignoring the comment, he continued, "They'd like us to stay out of the area but will call us if they need a uniform to make an arrest. There's also some sort of convention in town at the convention center."

Another officer shouted, "Let me write this down, Sarge. There's a convention at the convention center."

John smiled. "We're getting an increase in the number of purse snatches off of Pine and Pacific Avenues. I'd like to see you get out of your cars and walk around. Maybe one of you crime fighters can catch a purse snatcher."

Rebecca shouted, "Don't you think calling 'em purse snatchers is sexist? Shouldn't we call 'em 'thieves of domestic handbags,' instead?"

Laughing, he said, "I don't have time for you guys. Go out there and catch some domestic handbags thieves."

As the officers returned to their cars, he shouted, "One more thing. We don't have air support today. If anyone wants a helicopter, I'll get hold of the Sheriff's Department or get one from Orange County."

Helicopters were fickle. Either the aircraft was down for maintenance or the crew was away at training. For the million dollars budgeted each year per helicopter, you'd think they could expect a little more reliability. After all, his truck hadn't cost nearly that much, and it worked every time he turned the key.

Leaving the parking structure, officers raced to get in front of each other. Seeing one of the officers cut in front of another black and white and slam on his brakes, John yelled, "Rodriguez, you drive like old people fuck."

Rodriguez smiled and hit the gas, then the brake, then the gas, rocking his car back and forth.

John shook his head. "Everybody's a comedian."

***

Tom Blakesley was the first officer out of the parking structure. He raised an eyebrow as he pulled onto the street, surprised to see another patrol car ahead of him on a traffic stop. The officer on the car stop raised his index finger and pointed to the curb behind him, signaling Blakesley to stop.

"Cocky bastard," Blakesley said under his breath. He jerked the steering wheel to the right, pulling in behind the first patrol car. He left his overhead emergency lights off but turned on the car's four-way flashers. "2 Lincoln 4—show me out on Ocean west of Pine," he called on his car's microphone.

"10-4," the dispatcher replied, "Ocean west of Pine."

Getting out of his car, Blakesley recognized the officer. Philip Gilespie graduated from the Long Beach Police Academy eight months earlier. Gilespie seemed a little too self-absorbed while he was at the range, but he was a hard worker. "What ya got, kid?" Blakesley asked.

"I was going back to the station and ran the license plates of the cars stopped at the light around me. This minivan came back with an active warrant for the driver."

Blakesley frowned. "Don't tell me you're out here poaching for misdemeanor warrant arrests?"

When officers wrote a ticket or made an arrest in another beat, it was referred to as poaching. Officers poaching too frequently found themselves subject to practical jokes. Talcum powder in their car's air conditioner vents or a harmonica duct taped to the underside of their car were popular deterrents.

"Hey, I can't help it if these people have warrants," Gilespie said.

Blakesley glanced inside the minivan. The driver's scarlet press-on nails tapped an anxious rhythm on the steering wheel, while behind her, a wide-eyed little girl peered out through the back windshield. "What ya gonna do with the kid in the back seat after you arrest her mom?"

"Not my problem. She should've thought about her kid before getting a warrant for misdemeanor theft."

"No kid," Blakesley said. "I'm not gonna get stuck babysitting. If ya hook the mom, you're responsible for the kid. Why don't you go up there and ask if she has a relative who'll come take the kid? Unless, of course, you'd rather drive the kid to social services."

"Ain't no fucking way I'm driving around with a kid in my car."

"Then you'd better tell the station to hold off abstracting the warrant."

"Fuck me!" Gilespie said, walking around to the driver's side of the minivan. He spoke into his handheld radio, canceling the warrant.

Going back to his black and white, Blakesley saw a homeless man to his left, sitting in the dirt and surrounded by shrubbery between two buildings.

Blakesley walked up to the man in the bushes. "How's it going, man?"

"I could use something to eat."

"What's your name, buddy?"

"Charles Riley."

The name sent a pang through Blakesley. His brother's name was Charles. Eighteen months older than Blakesley, Charles had been his little brother's protector. He'd introduced Blakesley to Shakespeare, Steinbeck, and Rex Stout—and made sure he knew better than to let the neighborhood kids know he liked to read. Then Charles had gone to Afghanistan, and Afghanistan had broken him, just like God-knew-what had broken this poor son-of-a-bitch in the bushes.

Blakesley took a deep breath. "Well, Riley, it's your lucky day. That officer up there is on his way to Denny's as soon as he's finished here. This month, our department received special government funding for feeding the homeless. He'll drive you to Denny's and buy you a Grand Slam breakfast, coffee and orange juice."

The man's eyes lit up, and he instinctively reached towards his stomach. "No shit! I haven't eaten in a couple days."

"Come get in the back seat of the car. You'll be full of pancakes before you know it."

Riley struggled to stand up, and Blakesley reached forward to grab his elbow. The homeless man reeked of stale urine and beer. Breathing through his mouth, Blakesley walked Riley to Gilespie's car and asked, "You don't have any guns or knives on you, do you, Riley?"

"No, man. I don't play that game."

Blakesley quickly ran a hand over Riley's oversized pants, checking his pockets and around the waistline for a gun. The front of Riley's pants was wet, and Blakesley forced a lighter note into his voice. "You must have really hung one on last night."

Riley laughed. "It happens. I like a drink now and then."

Blakesley unlocked the front passenger door of Gilespie's car, reached inside and opened the rear door, then helped Riley into the back seat.

All marked black and white patrol cars were equipped with a cage separating prisoners in the back seat from the officers. The cage took up a lot of room, and prisoners had little room for their legs. Once settled in, Riley folded himself onto the seat, his knees pressed into the cage in front of him.

Blakesley said, "You can lie down if you'd be more comfortable."

"I think I will." Riley curled up on the back seat.

Blakesley handed Riley a ten-dollar bill. "Make sure you give the waitress a big tip." He closed the door and stepped away, thinking, this rookie doesn't know the first thing about helping people or know what it's like to struggle in life. It was too bad he probably wouldn't spend five minutes talking with Riley. He could learn a thing or two. But you never knew. Maybe Gilespie would get the point. Either way, the ten bucks would buy Riley his pancakes.

Three minutes later, Gilespie walked back from the minivan and stood next to Blakesley. "The only person the mom can have come get the kid is her mom, but her car's in the shop."

"You know, not arresting someone on a misdemeanor theft warrant, especially a mom shoplifting to feed her kid, isn't such a bad thing. We don't always need to be arresting people to be doing some good out here."

Gilespie wrinkled his nose and looked at the sidewalk where they were standing. "What's that smell? It smells like a wino pissed himself around here!"

Blakesley said, "Welcome to the big city in all of its glory, kid." He motioned for Gilespie to follow him back to his patrol car. He reached inside, removed a bottle of hand sanitizer and squirted some on his hands. "You need any ghetto-be-gone for your hands?"

"No, I'm good."

"You know," Blakesley said, "there are people out here that absolutely need to go to jail. Our job's to solve problems, not necessarily make every arrest possible. Give it time. You'll get the hang of it."

Gilespie scoffed. "Yeah, but my sergeant wants arrests."

"Then your sergeant's an idiot. Arrests are all fine and dandy, but they're just one of the tools in your tool box. Making a lot of arrests doesn't make you a good cop. Solving problems makes you a good cop."

Gilespie looked away. "Whatever. I've gotta go."

"Hey, kid," Blakesley said. "Why don't you slow down, get yourself some breakfast and think about what I said?"

"See ya around." Gilespie raised his hand and pressed the back of it to his nose. "Swear to God, you really smell like piss!"

"Solving problems can be a dirty job. See ya."

Gilespie got in his patrol car and pulled away from the curb.

Blakesley walked into the street to get into his car. Standing next to the driver's door of his black and white, he looked up as John pulled alongside and shouted through his open passenger window. "What was all that about?"

"Hey, Sarge, just schoolin' one of the kids." Blakesley looked toward Gilespie's black and white, hoping the rookie would get the message.

***

As Gilespie pulled away from the curb, he thought, Geez, it smells worse in here! He rolled down his window and looked into his driver's door mirror while merging with traffic. He had just eased into the center lane when a movement in his rear-view mirror caught his eye. He looked up, startled, as a grizzled man in shabby clothes sat up in the back seat and said, "I like my eggs scrambled."

Gilespie gasped, slammed on the brakes, and skidded to a stop. Heart pounding, he yanked open the driver's door and rolled out of the car with his pistol in hand.

***

Hearing a car make a four-wheel locked skid, Blakesley looked up to see Gilespie rolling out of his car. Gilespie jumped up, keeping his pistol pointed at his passenger, and jerked open the rear door. Then he reached in, dragged Riley out of the car, and threw him down onto the street. Blakesley's muscles tensed.

Asshole. He'd have to intervene if Gilespie got too out of hand.

Gilespie knelt on top of the homeless man and began patting him down for weapons.

Riley screamed, "Hey, man, what about my Grand Slam?"

Blakesley glanced at John, then looked away, eyes narrowed, a muscle in his jaw pulsing. "These rookies outta east division are so jumpy when they're downtown."

John frowned. "Did you have anything to do with this?"

Blakesley hesitated. Maybe he'd been a fool to think his little prank would give Gilespie some perspective, but he wasn't fool enough to confirm his supervisor's suspicions. Still unable to meet John's gaze, Blakesley said, "Like I said, Sarge, just schoolin' one of our own."

John looked back at the altercation and snickered. With a twinge of guilt, Blakesley found himself chuckling too. It would take hours to get the stench out of Gilespie's car. Served him right.

As Gilespie finished patting down the old man, he looked back towards Blakesley. John and Blakesley smiled and waved. Gilespie raised his middle finger, flipping them off, then pulled the old man to his feet and sent him shambling down the sidewalk.

At least he'd get his Grand Slam—if he didn't blow the ten-spot on booze.

John looked at Blakesley. "I was never here." He checked his mirrors, made a U-turn, and drove away.

After a moment, Blakesley did the same.

Arl Farris

6

If you can imagine it…

It wasn't that Gaston didn't like cop bars, he just hated the people who frequented them. But he needed dirt on the officers he was targeting, so he agreed to meet with Connie at one of Long Beach's most notorious cop watering-holes, Joe Jost's, on Anaheim Street.

He spat on the sidewalk and slithered through the half open door, behind a red-faced man, with a mustache that only a cop or porn actor would have. He looked around and Connie was nowhere to be found. He'd strategically arrived fifteen-minutes late to avoid waiting and being there any longer than he had to, but she was not there.

He took a rear table, as far away from any bar patrons as he could, ordered a Heineken, and watched the front. He took a swig from the bottle, leaving the frosted mug untouched. Then fired off a text. 'You're late.'

He hit send just as the door opened and Connie dashed in. "Sorry, my producer called a meeting at the last minute."

Gaston looked side to side. "I've been here for thirty-minutes. You should've called."

Her phone chirped and she read his text. "Well, I think you'll like what I was able to dig up."

He grinned and took another drink.

She gestured at the mug on the table. "Why are you drinking from the bottle when there's a perfectly good mug, right there?"

He looked at the mug like he had x-ray vision. "You have any idea how many cop lips have been on that? Fuck…"

She flipped back her hair. "Hey, it wasn't my first choice to come here either, but I have a traffic commission meeting down the block that I have to cover." She slowly looked over her shoulder, then back to him. "Why do you hate cops so much, anyways?"

He smirked. "Why would you say that? I love cops. I love their names on subpoenas, love them at the defense table, and especially love them in civil court."

"Geez! What did they ever do to you?"

He exhaled and looked toward the ceiling. In his mind, he saw the look of shock on his brother's face, and the expanding crimson spot in the center of Peter's T-shirt.

Connie studied his face. "Who's Peter?"

The name jolted Gaston back to the present. He couldn't believe he'd said it out loud. He took a drink. "You're hearing things. Whaddya got for me?"

She removed a dogeared spiral notebook from her purse and placed it on the table. "First, tell me again what you're gonna do. You wouldn't believe what I had to do to get this."

He looked with revulsion at two detectives, with their pistols and handcuffs strapped to their dress belts and slacks, entering the bar. "You didn't put out for one of these swine for it? Never mind, I don't care how you got it, it'll be worth it, believe me."

She took the notebook off the table and placed it on her lap. "Are you going to tell me what you're planning, or not?"

"Oh, come on, after all I've done for you, this is how you pay me back?"

Her voice sounding more like a schoolgirl than a television reporter, she said, "I just want to know…"

He nodded. "Sure you want the answer?"

She cocked an eyebrow and stared back at him.

"Okay. Okay. It kinda depends on what you were able to come up with. I've got enough to file against two of the Long Beach range officers." He lowered his voice as the two detectives sat at a table across from them. "If I can get something, anything, on the others, I can file against the entire range staff as a whole. Combining each of the proceedings into one case would have the police department standing on its ear. Think of it, conspiracy, corruption, negligent training, and the code of silence for starters. The City would have no choice but to settle. I could write my own check…"

He saw her bite her lower lip, and quickly added, "Of course, your efforts wouldn't be overlooked. Have you and Gordon ever been to Hawaii? I have a little condo, right on the water…"

"You own it?"

He extended his palms. "If you can imagine it, you can own it. Now, let's see what you have. Then we'll talk about your reward."

She flipped open the book and stuffed several pages, which had torn free of the spiral wire spine, back into place. Finding the page she was looking for, she said, "Here it is. There are five range instructors. Sergeant John Chambers is in charge. He's been with the department for—"

"Damnit! I could pull that crap off the internet. I need a lot more."

She turned a page and the green lined paper crinkled in protest. "Did you know a complaint was filed against Sergeant Chambers after he went on a medical aid call and dumped a man's HIV medication down the toilet?"

Gaston shook his head in disgust. "Who do you think filed the complaint?"

"Oh!" She looked farther down the page. "That's all I have on him, but if anything else comes in, my source will let me know."

He twirled his finger in a circle, signaling her to turn the page. "What else?"

"Rebecca Wells used to be married to a deputy at the sheriff's department. They divorced after one had an affair. I'm not sure who."

He raised the beer to his mouth and stopped himself short from taking a drink. "If I can show her marriage ended because she broke their wedding vows, it's not a stretch to have a jury believe she would also violate department policy. Find me who she was sleeping around with and you'll be flying first class to Hawaii."

"And a limo ride to and from the airport."

He set down the bottle without drinking. "How 'bout the others?"

"Manolito Torres thinks he's the Casanova of Long Beach. He goes through women like most people go through TV stations. I haven't been able to find any of them who complained, but there has to be someone out there."

He grinned. "Yeah, find me one. I could get a lot of mileage out of a jilted lover."

She skipped more pages. "I have a couple things on Tom Blakesley, but I'm not sure they're worth anything."

"I can decide what's useful. Let's hear what you have."

"He had a brother, Charles, who fought in Desert Storm and came back totally screwed up. The family tried to help him, but it didn't work out so well. Charles lived on the streets here in Long Beach for years, before finally dying. I'm sure Tom must have come across his brother while working patrol."

He nodded. "Interesting…"

"And one more thing. Tom's in debt up to his eyeballs, but a few days ago, he bought his wife a new car with cash. No one knows where the money came from."

He closed his eyes in thought, then rolled a shoulder. "I might be able to do something with that. I don't know."

She slipped the notebook back in her purse. "That's all I got."

"Wait a minute," he said. "There's one more. What's his name?"

"Scott Smith." She shook her head. "He followed his dad onto the department, and as far as I can tell, he's squeaky clean. He's been involved in a couple shootings, but nothing controversial."

He grimaced. "Of course they were controversial. The families just didn't have the right lawyer representing them."

She shook her head. "I'm telling you, there's nothing out there on Smith."

"Did I mention there's maid service every day at the condo? Keep digging. I'm sure there's something. He's a cop, for Christ's sake."

She put an elbow on the table and rested her chin on her hand. "You're not trying to frame these cops for something they didn't do? I mean, I think they need a good comeuppance, but I'd never lie."

He sat upright and feigned surprise. "I'm an officer of the court. I would never even consider lying. I can't help it if I can put together a strong case where other attorneys find nothing."

Her phone chirped again with an incoming text. She looked at it and jumped up. "I have to go. My crew needs me for a breaking story."

He reached for his phone while watching her rush out and hoped she wouldn't be too disappointed that there was no condo.

He dialed the business number to the police department. "Connect me with internal affairs or the captain in charge of the patrol division."

☐

☐

Arl Farris

7

Attention all units…

Later that day, Rebecca drove south on Linden Ave from 6th Street. She noticed a primergrey Oldsmobile parked next to the curb with its hood up. A black man in a Raiders jacket stood in front of the car with his arms outstretched in front of him. He made no attempt to work on the car, just held his arms out between the engine and the raised hood.

Rebecca thought he was pretending to be working on his engine, but there was no one to witness his performance. He did not look under the hood, but kept swiveling his head around, as if trying to see down the street. The hairs on the back of her neck prickled.

She pulled her black and white to the curb, on the wrong side of the street, and continued watching. Something was definitely off. After a minute, she got out of her patrol car and crossed the street. Using the car's open hood as a shield, she was able to approach without being seen. When she got to the rear of the car, she stepped to the center of the street. The man was still in front of the car with his arms forward and his head turned, looking behind him.

As soon as he was in full view, she said, "How's it going?"

His head snapped around, eyes widened in shock. When he turned, she saw the handle of a pistol tucked inside the front of his pants. Shit.

She drew her pistol and the man lurched forward an inch, lowering his arms the same amount. "Don't do it, fucker!" she yelled. "Hands up. Step away from the car."

Coming up from behind the other side of the man, Rebecca saw another man running in their direction. He had a chrome pistol in one hand and a paper grocery bag in the other. A blue bandanna covered the lower half of his face. His attention was focused behind him, with an occasional glance forward to keep his bearings.

She side-stepped to her right, lining up the men so her pistol was pointed at both of them. "Move and I'll kill ya!" she said to the closest man, the one wearing the Raiders jacket.

The running man kept turning to look over his shoulder. He still didn't see her.

Rebecca knew she'd stumbled into the middle of something big, she just didn't know what. Maybe the tail-end of a home invasion robbery or a couple guys ripping off a drug stash house. The only thing she knew for certain, these were dangerous men and she had no backup. She hoped like hell they didn't have any more buddies coming to join them. She was already outnumbered.

She still had the element of surprise on her side, but if she didn't act quickly, things would get ugly. Her mind raced through the possibilities. If they started shooting, she would address the closest threat first, then take the second man. That was how she would have taught the recruits at the range to do it.

Bandanna Man skidded to a stop, breathing hard, eyes wide. He looked at his partner and said, "What the fuck, Derrick?"

She couldn't let them start talking to each other. She had seen enough training videos and attended enough shooting debriefings to know that when armed suspects started talking, they built each other's confidence, and the likelihood they would start shooting went up exponentially.

She shouted back, "Shut the fuck up! And get on the ground! I swear, I'll fucking shoot!"

Slowly, they knelt down. Then the man in the Raiders jacket turned toward the other.

Rebecca felt her throat close. She was losing control. "Move one more inch and I'll shoot!"

The tension in the men's bodies told her they were about to go off, which meant she was in serious danger. She wished she'd notified dispatch when she got out of her car, but she hadn't. She wanted to call for backup on her handheld radio, but if the two saw her calling for help, they might realize she was afraid and try to take her.

The radio on her belt sounded a high-pitched emergency tone, followed by the dispatcher's voice. "Attention all units. 211 bank—Bank of America, Elm and 6th. One suspect last seen running westbound through the rear parking lot. Described as a male adult, approximately twenty-three years of age, six-foot, medium build, dark skin, wearing a blue bandanna over his face, dark-colored slacks and a yellow sweat shirt, armed with a silver automatic. The loss was cash placed in a brown paper bag. Units to respond, please advise."

The radio filled with responding officers giving their locations and areas they planned to intercept the fleeing suspect. As the radio voices chattered on, Rebecca looked at the two men in front of her. The descriptions matched. No doubt about it. She had the robber as well as the apparent get-away driver. She was one block west of the bank. If she was lucky, one of the responding units would cut down Linden Avenue en-route to the call. There was no other chance for backup, since their helicopter was grounded again with mechanical problems.

As Rebecca's radio went silent, the man next to the car—Derrick—turned his head to the other. "What the fuck did ya do, man?"

The man with the mask over his face said, "What the fuck ya saying? I'll cap your ass right here."

Rebecca's stomach lurched as she felt her control of the situation slipping further away. She had to do something immediately.

She closed the distance fast and slapped her pistol across the back of Derrick's head. As he fell forward with a cry, she jumped on top of him, her shin across the back of his neck. Keeping her pistol pointed at the man wearing the bandanna, she said, "Set the gun down or I'll shoot!"

He laid the pistol on the sidewalk next to his knee and mumbled, "What'd ya hit Derrick like that for?"

For the first time, it dawned on her that both suspects were black. Not that she hadn't noticed; she'd instinctively registered a whole list of descriptors, such as height, build, dress, and skin color. But now the implications hit her hard. An unscrupulous attorney could easily twist what she was doing into something it wasn't. She imagined being back on the witness stand, with Gaston grilling her: "Tell the jury where, in the continuum of force outlined in the department training manual, does it describe bludgeoning a suspect with your weapon?"

She shook her head and pressed on. She might get mercy from the court, but certainly not from these two. "On your stomach. Keep your hands where I can see 'em."

With the masked man lying face down and his arms outstretched, she handcuffed Derrick, then took his gun and hurried to the second man. He grunted as she grabbed one of his outstretched arms, twisting it around to his lower back before cuffing him.

She breathed a loud sigh, removed the radio from her belt, and waited for radio traffic to clear. "2-Lincoln-12 to station. Two in custody for 211 bank. Request an additional unit to Linden street south of 6th for prisoner transport."

The dispatcher replied, "Confirming two in custody for the 211 at Bank of America. Are you Code-4?"

Code-4 was the radio code for no further assistance needed or signaling everyone was safe.

Rebecca responded, "2-Lincoln-12. Code-4, two in custody, requesting an additional unit."

The dispatcher said, "Sam 23 will be at your location shortly."

With his patrol car's overhead red and blue lights flashing and siren blaring, John skidded up to where Rebecca had the two men handcuffed and lying face down. She could smell the odor of hot tire rubber and brakes from John's car and knew he had driven hard getting to her. Any of the officers, without hesitation, would sacrifice themselves helping another. However, none were as fiercely protective as John.

A flood of relief rushed through her. Everything was going to be okay.

John pointed his pistol at the two on the ground and, without looking at Rebecca, shouted, "Have they been searched?"

"Yeah, their guns are in the front seat of my car. I patted them both down, twice."

"Great job!" He holstered his pistol and looked at her. "I'll have Blakesley go to the bank, get statements and write the report. I'll get Mano and Scott to transport your prisoners and start the booking process at the station. You just write up the arrest reports." He smiled at Rebecca and added, "Who knows? You still might be able to get out of here without racking up any overtime."

"Yeah, that'd be nice," she said, still uneasy about the possibility of being drummed out of the department. Never mind that the men she'd arrested had her outnumbered and had just committed a felony. There was a good chance her use of force would get her labeled a racist, and everybody knew that was the fastest way to kill a career.

Arl Farris

8

Nurses know stuff...

John had hung his uniform shirt in his locker and was peeling off his bullet proof vest when Lieutenant Jackson walked past him on his way out. "There you are. The captain's been lookin' for you." John reached for his shirt and the lieutenant said, "Metro tuxedo's fine. I wouldn't keep the man waiting."

The department had a policy prohibiting officers from wearing their uniforms to and from work. The officers who preferred to change at home wore their boots, dark navy trousers, a black basket-weave dress belt and a white T-shirt for their commute and finished dressing at the station. The contrast between the white T-shirt on top and the dark uniform on the bottom was referred to as a metro tuxedo.

John pulled at his sweat-dampened T-shirt between his thumb and forefinger. "If he doesn't mind the tuxedo..."

He took the elevator up to the third floor and found the captain's door open and the secretary gone. He rapped the back of his hand across the doorframe as he entered. "The lieutenant said you wanted to see me?"

Jason Dickerson looked up from his desk. "Yeah. Sit down."

Dickerson looked like he'd been in stasis for the past two decades. He had a pinkish complexion, and his flattened nose twisted to the right. He wore the same flat top haircut as in his college photos, and his suits were older than most of the officers on the department.

He'd been a lackluster sergeant who never finished first on any promotional exam. On his fifth, and what he told his buddies would be his final try, Dickerson's name appeared seventeenth on the lieutenants' list. That happened to be the same year the City of Long Beach adopted a new retirement package. The next day, nearly 180 officers filed for retirement and Jason Dickerson suddenly, at the age of forty-eight, found himself number one on the lieutenants' list. Three weeks later, he promoted.

The first year he tested for captain, he did not make the list. The next year, he managed to score just high enough. Like when he made lieutenant, there happened to be a large number of unexpected retirements, and he soon found two gold bars on his collar.

Dickerson could have retired twenty years ago. Officers referred to him as being retired on the job, but he didn't seem to care. If they didn't like the way he ran his division, they could always transfer out.

He was a big guy, six-foot, three inches, two-hundred forty pounds, who'd played defensive center for the Cal State Long Beach 49ers and kept an old football on the credenza behind his desk. According to the old timers, as an officer, Dickerson was a brutal street brawler. They talked about him going into bar fights along the docks, taking off his gun belt and challenging anyone to fight. If he won, they went to jail. If he lost... He never lost.

The higher up Dickerson promoted, the more he condemned any use of force. He regularly suspended and fired officers for things he had done on a daily basis as an officer. The man was a world class dick.

"Sure, Captain," John said as he sat down.

Dickerson pressed his stomach against the desk. "I've been tryin' to help you, givin' you my best advice, but obviously you're not interested in anything I have to say."

John frowned. He had no idea what the captain was talking about.

Dickerson scanned the top of his desk before lifting several sheets that had been paper clipped together. "I've received multiple complaints, and together, they show a pattern of bigotry and homophobia."

John looked surprised and hoped this had nothing to do with Rebecca. "Who screwed up?"

"You did," Dickerson said. "And I'm to inform you, Internal Affairs is preparing a major investigation."

"Excuse me?" John's pulse pounded in his ears. This couldn't be happening.

Dickerson handed the papers to John, then bobbed a finger up and down, pointing at the pages. "Some civil rights attorney alleges you went into a man's apartment, tore down his LGBT flag and threw his HIV medication into the toilet."

John looked at the bottom of the first complaint and saw the name David Gaston. He flipped the page to see what else he'd supposedly done.

Dickerson exhaled. "The second complaint states you verbally abused some period actors at the range. Called 'em cross-dressers and threatened to fight 'em."

So that was what this was about. Gaston's pride. John thought about standing up and making a show of wiping his backside with the complaints, but the captain didn't joke around. "You know this attorney is the same guy who tried turning Rebecca into a racist last week in court?"

Dickerson held up his hand, wanting the complaints back. "No doubt this clown's trying to make a name for himself, but he makes some serious charges and if they're true..."

John handed him the papers. "You can't be serious? These are baseless complaints and should have been rejected as soon as they came in."

Dickerson looked at his football on the credenza. "It's not 1974 anymore. You can't go around beating up the gays."

Exasperated, John gasped. "I'm not goin' around beating up anybody, and I certainly don't go around making fun of people, either."

"Well, that's not what it says here." Dickerson laid the papers back on his desk. "The chief is quite concerned that a sergeant in charge of a high profile unit is generating these kind of complaints, but this is the way policing is today. Even the slightest hint an officer's discriminating or violating the rights of blacks or gays, and you're out."

John repositioned himself against the backrest of his chair and forced a measured tone. "I've never discriminated against anybody, and I certainly haven't violated anybody's rights, black, gay or whatever."

"John," Dickerson said. "Let me tell you something. When I first started with the department, we had no gays. Now, every substation has a couple of 'em. By God, I'm gonna retire before being gay's a requirement for the job." He chuckled at his own joke.

John thought, if I told that to my guys, you'd fire me. Aloud, he said, "That's silly. This whole thing's ridiculous!"

Dickerson opened his hand and patted the two complaints like he was rewarding a loyal pet, then picked up another sheaf of papers. "I'll be honest with you, John. In the past few days, I've gotten more complaints about your unit than all the other ones combined. Rebecca's little escapade probably just landed her in a whole lot of hot water. I mean, what was she thinking, manhandling a couple of black men? And you know the media is going to be screaming about racial profiling."

"Are you kidding me? What was she supposed to do, ask them to come downtown pretty please for milk and cookies? Two guys with guns who just robbed a bank?"

"Then there's Blakesley. Did you know he just bought his wife a new car?"

"So?"

"He paid cash."

"He's been saving for two years for that car. He—"

Dickerson cut him off. "It looks bad, John. Civil rights complaints, suspicions of corruption... A squad goes bad, that comes from the guy in charge. That's you." He spread his hands flat on the desk. "You need to get ready for some serious discipline to come outta these, a transfer, suspension, maybe even losing your stripes. I can't say. But I can guarantee you this much, let another complaint come across my desk and I'll be tellin' you to clean out your locker."

John stared at a spot on Dickerson's tie. He didn't trust himself to speak.

Dickerson waved him toward the door. "Now, get outta here and give me some good old-fashioned police work."

John took in a long breath, still reeling from the shock. Slowly, he pushed himself out of his chair. "Thank you, sir," he said, and left, resisting the urge to slam the door behind him.

***

John found his son, Patrick, in front of the television and his daughter, Clara, on her computer doing homework. Determined not to let his resentment at the captain bleed into his home life, he asked Patrick, "Where's your homework?"

Patrick kicked his heels into the front skirt of the couch. "I didn't have any. Besides, we gotta leave for karate."

John picked up the remote and turned off the television. "Get changed. I'm driving."

Clara said, "Grams is driving us. Mom wants you to take her out for a romantic dinner tonight."

His eyebrows lifted. "Oh, she does?"

"Yeah." Clara twirled her wavy red hair between her fingers. "Can you wait 'til we get back and take me?"

He laughed. "That's not gonna happen. Where's your mother?"

Clara returned to her computer and without looking up said, "Mom's getting ready for your big date."

John heard his sister-in-law, Crystal, call out from the kitchen. "Aah, listen to her, what a sweetheart!"

John wandered toward the kitchen. "Crystal, I didn't know you were here."

Crystal and Jenny were sisters, but sharing the same parents and having natural ash brown hair was where the similarities ended. Jenny tended to be witty, reserved, and responsible, while Crystal was inclined to be chatty and flirtatious and seemed to always stir up trouble.

Jenny was smart and could think on her feet. She even made grocery lists by the way food was organized in rows at the store. When Crystal did the grocery shopping, she might return with McDonalds and a half-eaten bag of M & M's.

Jenny was tall and thin, with a swimmer's body, while Crystal, eight years younger, was curvaceous and six inches shorter. Her most dominant feature, or more precisely, her two most dominant features, were purchased on installments.

Crystal leaned over the kitchen table, adjusting the height of her phone to take a picture.

Seeing his police academy graduation certificate and Jenny's nursing license on the table, he asked, "What are you doing?"

"Guys think nurses know stuff, and they're always fantasizing about policewomen. I'm gonna Photoshop my name onto these."

He grabbed the certificates. "Think there might be a few laws about telling people you're a nurse or a police officer when you're not?"

Making a feeble swipe to get them back, she poked out her lower lip and pretended to whimper. "Why do you hate me?"

He laughed and looked directly at her boobs. Ignoring her question, he said, "If the guys down at Hooters aren't willing to tip you while staring at those, telling 'em you're a moonlighting nurse or a cop isn't gonna help."

Playfully, she slapped his arm, then glanced at the clock over the stove. "Speaking of Hooters, I gotta go to work. Tell Jenny goodbye for me."

She shoved the phone into the back pocket of her orange shorts but could only get it a quarter of the way in.

John suppressed a grin. "You should keep your phone in your purse or get some new shorts."

Sticking her bottom out, she said, "Ya think the phone distracts from my butt?"

He backed out of the kitchen, laughing through his nose. "I'll tell Jenny you left."

As he entered the bedroom, Jenny was slipping into a slim-fitting chiffon lavender dress. She hadn't worn it since the accident. With an admiring look, he said, "Wow, honey! You look amazing."

Three months earlier, during her shift in the emergency room at the Long Beach Memorial Hospital, the Signal Hill Police Department arrived with a patient who had overdosed on methamphetamine. As they transferred him from a gurney to an ER bed, he suddenly jumped up, tossed the two Signal Hill officers aside like they were rag dolls, and bolted to where the ambulances parked. Jenny had just come in from helping a group of paramedics restock their rescue vehicle, and the sliding glass door closed behind her as the patient stopped short in front of her, his addled mind apparently baffled by the closing doors.

Out of his mind and with superhuman strength, the patient picked her up and, using Jenny as a battering ram, shattered the glass doors and ran through. Then he dropped her in a shredded heap and ran on, leaving a blood trail in his wake. He ran into the neighborhood behind the hospital, the two Signal Hill officers giving chase. The first house he came to, he splintered the door frame and charged into the kitchen, where he picked up a bread knife and turned to confront the officers.

Three quick shots from the officers and the man lay dead on the floor.

Jenny suffered severe lacerations to the back of her head, right shoulder, hip and ankle. She'd lost so much blood that, if the attack had happened anywhere but the hospital, she would probably have died. She had yet to return to work.

Jenny looked up. "I didn't hear you come in. Did Clara tell you Mom's taking the kids to karate?"

"And she mentioned something about a romantic date?"

She laughed. "I'm feeling pretty good, and Mom volunteered to take care of the kids this evening."

He nodded. "I don't know what we'd've done if it weren't for Barbara and your dad helping out."

"When I'm better, we need to do something nice for them. Is Crystal still here?"

He shook his head. "No, and by the way, keep your nursing license and my academy certificate away from her."

"What did…?" She lifted a hand up as if to say stop. "I don't even want to know. I don't want Crystal to ruin another evening."

John stepped forward, putting his hands on her hips. "No one could ruin anything as long as you were wearing this dress."

She gently pushed him away. "How'd it go at work today?"

He thought about what the captain had said in his office, but there was no point in worrying Jenny when she was finally starting to feel better. He said, "Rebecca made a really good arrest on a couple guys who robbed a bank. She had 'em both in handcuffs before dispatch even broadcast the robbery."

Impressed, she said, "You really like her, don't you?"

"Yeah. I think we're all gonna be working for her someday."

She pushed him towards the bathroom. "Go take a quick shower and put on a sport coat. I made reservations at Gulfstream in Newport Beach."

He kissed her cheek and went to shower. He felt bad about keeping a secret from her, but with any luck, this would all blow over in a few days. He would tell her about it then. ◻

9

That's not what innocent people do…

John smiled ear to ear. A few weeks ago, Jenny's doctors had told him she might never recover from her wounds, and if she did, her quality of life would be greatly diminished. However, last night's dinner in Newport Beach proved them wrong.

Physically, her strength wasn't quite all the way back, but mentally, she was sharp as ever. The previous evening, when he finally broke down and told her about Dickerson threatening him over the absurd complaint where the man's medication accidentally spilled into the toilet, she surprised him by suggesting they hire a forensic accountant to get their affairs in order. "If the department's going after Blakesley for buying a car, it's only a matter of time before they come after his supervisor. That'd be you. I think it would be a mistake not to take this seriously."

John dismissed the suggestion. "That's not what innocent people do. Besides, we have ten years of tax statements to verify our income. The department would never go that far…"

After sleeping on it, though, he was ready to reconsider.

Driving to the range, he almost hoped Gaston would show up and poke his nose where it didn't belong. After seventeen years working the streets, he knew more than one way to put handcuffs on a bully. Most were legitimate, others, not so much.

He'd learned that when he started in patrol and got his first domestic abuse cases. All too often, women were afraid to admit to the abuse, which—at the time—meant the officers' hands were tied. John's partner had taught him how they could step on the ends of the tough guy's shoes and lean into the creep until he would grab at the officer to keep from falling over backwards. Then they would make an arrest for assaulting a police officer, allowing the wife a few days to pack her things and move out. John knew the shoe trick wasn't exactly ethical, but it was effective. And cowboy boots would be perfect with their pointy toes.

He parked next to the other instructors' vehicles and realized he was relieved there were no cowboys in sight. He was a better man than to stoop to Gaston's level, and it was up to him to set the example for the recruits.

After lining up the recruits and taking roll, he said, "We are going to the next level in your training, we are going to introduce the police shotgun. The shotgun is the most effective fight-stopper you will have in your car, much more than your pistol or M-4 carbine. Officer Wells will demonstrate the weapon."

Rebecca stepped up to the line. She was carrying a Remington 870, 12-gauge pump shotgun.

John said, "Officer Wells will demonstrate the effectiveness of the 12-gauge shotgun for police service. The shotgun can be your most effective service weapon. However, because most officers don't use a shotgun properly, it remains locked in their patrol car, instead of being used as the fight-stopper it is. Officer Wells will be shooting our standard buckshot load. She'll shoot one round at five yards, one at ten yards, twenty yards, thirty yards and then a slug at fifty yards."

The recruits circled behind her. She racked a round into the chamber and fired. At five yards, a tennis-ball-sized hole appeared in the center of the paper silhouette target. The recruits stared in awe at the large hole in the center of the target. The nine-pellet pattern from Rebecca's shotgun expanded in size across the silhouette target as she moved back and fired from distance. Each time she fired, an uneasy laugh escaped the class.

At the 50-yard line, she removed a rifled slug from her pants pocket and loaded it directly into the chamber. She raised the shotgun and fired.

John told the class, "That was one full ounce of lead. Let's walk to the target and see how it fared." The recruits were quietly talking as they walked to the target. When they could see the target, they went silent. The X in the center of the target's head had been obliterated.

John said to the class, "Not bad for a girl."

Rebecca gave John a sideways glance and carried the shotgun back to her truck.

Manolito Torres took his place in the center of the recruits.

On the far end of the range, fourteen round steel plates, each half the size of a frisbee with a flat edge on one side stood, flat edges down, on top of steel spikes in the ground. Forty feet from the last plate was a large metal wheel that looked like a starfish with steel plates at the ends of its arms.

The purpose of this course was to teach the recruits how to move and shoot at the same time. Far too often, officers were shot because they stood in place during a confrontation, making them easy targets for their adversaries.

John told the recruits, "Officer Torres will demonstrate combat action shooting. The skills you need for combat action shooting are the same skills you'll develop on the target range. Officer Torres has downloaded his magazines to only ten rounds each, requiring him to make several emergency reloads. He'll fire at each target until it falls to the ground, or he runs out of ammunition."

Manolito walked to the far end of the range, and the class followed. John told the recruits, "Take a few steps back. Small fragments of steel can fly off the steel plates when they're hit. Make sure everyone's wearing eye protection."

"Shooter ready." Manolito put on his ear muffs, quickly drew his 9mm Smith & Wesson M&P from its holster, and performed a press check, slightly moving the slide rearward just far enough to confirm a live round was in the chamber. He holstered his pistol, raised his hands into a surrender position, and said, "Ready."

John said, "You saw Officer Torres conduct a press check as part of his preparation. You'll all perform a press check prior to running each exercise here on the range and prior to the start of every shift before going into the field. We'll not have you raise your hands like Officer Torres is doing. In action pistol matches, shooters are required to start shooting from the surrender position, with their arms raised in the air, but for our purposes, you'll start with your hands at your sides, since that's how they'll be ninety-nine percent of the time. If you're starting a gunfight as a hostage, you're gonna need more than combat skills to survive. At that point, divine intervention might be your only hope."

From the corner of his eye, he noticed Gaston and a couple of his cronies watching from the edge of the range. Their horses stood beside them on loose reins, apparently habituated to the guns. The cronies seemed innocuous enough, but the attorney's presence raised John's hackles.

Pointedly, he turned his back to the men and their horses. With a whistle in his mouth, John said to the recruits, "Stand by," and gave a short blast on the whistle. Mano quickly drew his pistol and ran forward. Thirty feet in front of the plates, a rope had been placed on the ground. Mano abruptly turned to his right and followed the rope line. He began firing at the plates, and each time he fired, a metal twang sounded and a plate spun off its stand. The slide locked back on his pistol as his first magazine ran out of ammunition.

Just as quickly, he slid another magazine from his belt, slammed it into the weapon, and continued firing at the plates.

Twang, twang, thud, twang. Mano reloaded again and knocked down the last of the steel plates. He ran another forty feet and stopped in front of the starfish wheel. Swiftly, he removed a half-empty magazine from his pistol, put it in his rear pocket, and placed a full magazine into the pistol. As he shot the plates off the wheel, the falling plates caused a weight imbalance, and the starfish began to spin. Eight shots, and all eight plates were on the ground with the wheel still spinning. Mano looked over the top of his pistol, scanning the fallen plates. Satisfied all the plates were on the ground, he holstered his pistol.

John felt confident in his ability to take on almost any crook who might want to shoot it out with him. He was also grateful that he'd never had to face anyone as skilled with a gun as Mano. He glanced over at Gaston, who looked like he had a trout caught in his throat.

"The range is safe," John said, suppressing a smirk. "As you saw, we're not perfect. Officer Torres needed to shoot at one of the plates twice to knock it down. Other than that, his shooting was good and his reloads were excellent. I'm sure you noticed before he engaged the plate wheel, he went into it with a fresh magazine. He wasn't locked into standing in one place while he was shooting, yet his arms were in the same position for each shot and his grip on his pistol never changed."

He could see some of the recruits were still nervously rocking back and forth. He said, "Our marksmanship demonstration wasn't meant to intimidate or give anyone anxiety. By the time you're finished out here, our goal is to make each one of you as good or hopefully better than your instructors."

Several recruits gave apprehensive laughs.

John worked hard to match training at the range to actual events officers encountered while on the streets. He had officers practice shooting from radio car windows, shooting at night, having multiple adversaries, and shooting while moving. It paid off. Time and again, officers told him about shootings they were involved in and how their training helped prepare them. Those stories were his greatest reward.

It was the failures that haunted him. The times when officers froze, uncertain of what to do, or simply stopped fighting. He looked at the eager young faces in front of him and promised himself they would be ready for whatever life could throw at them when they left the academy. Even so, no amount of training could overcome bad luck. There were the officers who did everything right, and a bullet simply had their name on it. Like the officer who'd rolled up on a domestic dispute, and as she and her partner walked toward the apartment, a shot from inside the apartment ricocheted off a stucco wall and caromed across the metal handrail of the stairway before fatally lodging in her neck. No amount of training could have prevented her death, but it didn't make it any easier to take.

He told the recruits, "I need you guys to move all the steel plates and stands off the range and place paper silhouette targets in front of the berm."

For the next eight hours, the class worked on basic firearms manipulation and marksmanship skills. An hour into it, John glanced toward the reenactors and saw only the empty patch of grass where they'd been standing. Must have gotten bored. The muscles of his shoulders loosened, and he turned his focus back to the class.

This class was typical. There were some good shooters and others who were going to need more attention, like the two who insisted on closing their eyes as they shot and the one who dropped his gun while trying to draw it. John would have Blakesley work with those three, and in a few hours he would have them right up there with the others.

At the end of the day, John assembled the recruits. "Great work, everyone. When you get home, clean your weapons and practice drawing your pistols from the holster. Practice getting the proper grip on your pistol and work on your sight alignment. With your unloaded pistol, work on having a controlled trigger press."

He felt good about how the day had gone and even better about heading home to Jenny and the kids. Then he saw the 45-long Colt cartridge standing upright on the lip of his driver's side mirror. It could have been a prank or a careless oversight by someone who'd paused to load a pistol. It could have been, but he knew it wasn't.

It was a message.

He started to pick it up, then stopped himself and bent to look more closely. A pattern of ridges marred the smooth sheen of the metal. It looked like a perfect print.

John smiled. Then, carefully, he retrieved a small plastic bag from his glove compartment and, without touching the print, tipped the round into it.

Arl Farris

10

Who ya gonna call…

The next morning in the Pike parking structure, John paused before starting his briefing. "Is everyone here?"

The theme song from Ghostbusters began blaring through the parking structure.

They turned to see a black and white slowly coming up the parking ramp. The music blared from the unit's loudspeaker, and the overhead red and blue lights were flashing with no one inside.

John frowned. Squad cars didn't drive themselves. It was probably nothing, but he scanned the area for cover, just in case, and shouted over the music, "Whose unit is that?" The patrol car continued up the parking ramp with officers stepping aside warily, gazes trained on the vehicle.

The car stopped in front of them, and the music did too. Officer Barry Franklin raised up, grinning, and attached the monitor for the in-dash mounted video camera back on the windshield. He had been driving the car crouched down, using the mounted video camera to see where he was going.

The tension lifted, and the officers burst into applause and whistles as Franklin got out of the car and took a bow. John interrupted, "Very cute, Franklin. Just remember, if you'd hit one of these concrete pillars, we'd be giving you days off."

"What a killjoy, Sarge," one of the officers said.

Scott shouted out, "Before they suspend you, who ya gonna call?"

The officers shouted, "Ghostbusters!"

Everyone, including John, laughed. It felt good to ease some of the tension from the past week. Then he shook his head. "Just once, I'd like to be in control at one of my own briefings."

Manolito said, "Come on, Sarge, you know we all love you."

John looked at Mano. "And I love you, too."

Blakesley said, "That's not the way we love you, Sarge."

John and the officers laughed again. Then John put on his serious face. "All right, listen up. It's getting close to the end of the month. If you haven't gone to the range to qualify, get down there. Rodriguez and Franklin, why don't you guys go as soon as we finish here."

Rodriguez pointed his index finger and raised a thumb as if he were holding a gun, and mouthed to Franklin, "Lowest score buys lunch."

John said, "We had another purse snatch on Pine Street. I'd like to see someone walk the area and let the shop owners know we're out here."

Manolito said, "Otherwise known as community-oriented policing, or, as I like to call it, pressing the flesh."

John suppressed a smile. "And I'd like to congratulate Officer Wells on her timely bank robbery arrests from yesterday."

Several officers clapped, and Rebecca stepped forward to take a bow.

Franklin asked, "Is it true, you pistol-whipped one of 'em?"

She gave a mischievous grin. "It's a technique I perfected while dating."

Everyone laughed.

John said, "Don't make a practice of hitting people with your pistols, but if your life depends on it, knock the hell out of 'em." He hesitated, looking at the brave men and women in front of him. "Don't forget, we all have people at home who'd like to see us again. Be safe and let's put some assholes in jail."

John was the last to leave the parking structure. Radio traffic was picking up with officers making car stops and responding to calls for service. He had just crossed Ocean Boulevard and was turning north on Magnolia when he received a radio call regarding a citizen's complaint at the station.

He turned the car around.

Ten minutes later, John brought the complainant, a chunky woman in her mid-thirties with two-inch roots and a bottle-blond shag back to an interview room. He turned off the portable radio on his belt and began writing in his pocket notebook.

The woman said, "Every time I leave my house wearing a dress, I get pulled over. If I'm wearing jeans or a pants suit, I can speed or do anything I want and never get stopped. I'm being harassed by cops."

John returned the notebook to his pocket. "How do you suppose the officers can tell you have a on a dress when you're seated in your car?"

She thought for a second. "Cops have special machines that let them see inside cars."

"Is it one officer who keeps stopping you, or are there several?"

She unfolded a paper from her purse. "I wrote their names down." She read, "Blakesley, Torres and Wells," and slid the paper to John.

His cell phone beeped with a text message and he ignored it. "You do realize Officer Wells is a woman?"

"Women are the worst. Everybody knows all female cops are dykes."

***

Driving along the shoreline, Manolito Torres thought he would do as the sergeant wanted, and see if he couldn't catch one of the guys who had been ripping off woman's purses. He was on Ocean Boulevard, headed towards downtown, and stopped for the red light at Ximeno. Two young ladies—college freshmen, he guessed, or possibly high school seniors—were on the bus bench adjacent his car. They each had on skimpy swimsuit coverups. When they saw Mano, they started giggling and poking at one other.

After a few more giggles and nudges, they stood and walked over to Mano's passenger window. A girl with a white bikini top and a diamond stud in her right nostril said, "We've been waiting, like forever, for the bus. Can you take us to the beach?"

Manolito lifted a finger off the steering wheel and pointed to his left. "There's the beach. If you start walking, you'd be there before I could ask why aren't you in school."

The second girl, wearing oversized Dolce & Gabbana sunglasses, squeezed her head into the open window. Oil glistened on her shoulders. "Hey, you do Snapchat?"

The traffic signal turned green, and Manolito laughed, sticking his arm out the driver's window, waving the cars behind to go around. "Of all the people out here, why would you want to Snapchat with me?"

The girls howled with laughter as the one with the diamond stud in her nose also pushed her head and shoulders into the open window. She began positioning her phone to take a selfie. "Is it okay to take a picture with you?"

The girl with the sunglasses asked, "Ya wanna handcuff me?"

Mano took his foot off the brake and the car rolled forward an inch. Feeling the car move, both girls squealed and jumped back out of the car. Manolito winked. "Goodbye, ladies."

He looked in his rearview mirror and the girls were still standing in the street, smiling and waving as he drove away. He shook his head and thought, come see me in about five years...

He knew the guys thought of him as a ladies' man, often teasing he collected more women's phone numbers per shift than tickets he wrote. The thing was, he never went out of his way to get a date. He didn't have to. He loved women and considered each to be as lovely as a budding rose. He was not going to settle for a single flower, not when he could have the entire bouquet.

He couldn't help it if he was irresistible to women.

Crossing the intersection with Alamitos Avenue were two skinny black men, one with his right pant leg cuffed and the other wearing an L.A. Dodger hat tilted toward the right, obviously flagging themselves as Crips, each grabbing his crotch upon seeing Manolito's black and white. He gave each a hard stare and, when their eyes locked, raised his middle finger in slow motion at them.

For a moment, he was twelve years old again in Long Beach, standing in the sand at the water's edge at midnight with his father, waiting for high tide and the start of the grunion run.

Their summer ritual. They would fill a bucket full of the little grunion fish and later fry them up like French fries. He could still remember the taste of the grunion, the smell of grease, the way his dad could juggle six of the small fish in the air at one time. It was one of his best memories.

But not that night. That night, his dad said he was almost big enough that next year they could go out on a charter boat for albacore. Manolito insisted he was strong enough now. He took off his shirt, raised his arms, flexing his muscles as two members of the Rollin' Coast Crips happen to be walking by. The two laughed at Manolito, and his dad said something back to them in Spanish.

One of the men pulled a gun and shot his dad six times in the chest.

In his mind, Mano had rewritten the next part a thousand times. He'd single-handedly taken on the two gangsters. He'd pressed his T-shirt to his father's wounds until the paramedics came. He'd held his father's hand and told him that he loved him.

But none of that was true. Seeing his father fall face down in the water, Manolito ran. With his eyes filled with tears, he couldn't see where he was going or whether the men were still chasing him. The faster he tried to run, the deeper his feet sank into the sand and the more he kept falling.

Sobbing and breathless, he made it out of the sand and onto the pier parking lot. Then, too frightened to think, he bolted across Ocean Boulevard.

A passing patrol officer saw a frantic-looking boy running in traffic and pulled him aside. It took Manolito several minutes before he could speak, but eventually he was able to tell the officer what had happened. Thanks to Mano's description, his father's killers were caught later that night. It was small comfort, but it was comfort.

A couple of homicide detectives assigned the case took a liking to Manolito and started taking him out on half-day sport fishing excursions from the Long Beach Marina. It couldn't fill the empty space his father had left, but it gave him someone to look up to and a place to belong. He loved being around policemen and knew when he was old enough, he wanted to become one of them. It would not bring his father back, but perhaps he could save another twelve-year-old boy from having to watch his father being gunned down.

The Crips disappeared into the crowd, and Mano climbed out of the car and walked north on Pine Avenue, shaking it off. He strolled along the sidewalk talking to the tourists and shoppers that began to fill the many downtown boutiques and bistros. A few pretty women smiled and waved, and that made him feel better. Walking past King's Fish House, on the corner of Broadway, a couple seated at a table along the sidewalk shouted out to him.

The man, obviously a tourist, lathered in sunscreen, wearing a green Hawaiian shirt with brand new Maui Jim sunglasses, said, "I can't believe how quickly you guys got here. I just hung up the phone. My wife and I ordered a bottle of wine and poured a glass. We sat the bottle right here and these two punks came by and took it, right off our table. They ran across the street into the parking lot, over there."

He pointed across Broadway to a high-rise building and said, "They went down into the parking garage, not thirty-seconds before you got here. My wife said you guys wouldn't even come. I can't believe how fast you got here!"

Based on the couple's pale skin and looking like they were on their way to a luau, Mano guessed they were on vacation, living somewhere in the Midwest or maybe Canada. Probably, the only thing they knew about law enforcement was what their local Barney Fife, or Dudley Do-Right, told them. It was too bad they'd been targeted, but tourists were easy marks.

He asked, "What were they wearing?"

The woman said, "One was wearing a white T-shirt about three sizes too big and a white baseball cap worn sideways. The other had on black and gray plaid shorts that almost went to his ankles."

Manolito nodded. "Wait here. I'll go see what I can do. I'll be back in a few minutes." As he crossed Broadway and entered the underground parking lot, he called in on his handheld radio. "2

Lincoln 14. Show me out on the northwest corner of Pine and Broadway investigating a petty theft."

"Roger, 2 Lincoln 14. 10-6 Pine and Broadway," came the reply from dispatch.

Manolito considered calling for a backup officer, but the kids who took the bottle would probably be gone in the five or ten minutes he waited for follow-up. Besides, he could handle a couple of kids.

He removed his sunglasses, put them in his uniform shirt pocket, and stepped into the shadows of the underground parking lot. Almost without thinking, he ran his hands around his Sam Browne belt, feeling his equipment was in place and accessible. He followed the parking lot down to the second level. He could hear voices ahead of him and the sound of a bottle hitting concrete.

Not two voices. More.

Maybe he should have called for backup after all. He was outnumbered, and if these kids were old enough to be stealing wine off tables, they were certainly capable of a lot more.

He pulled his handheld radio off his belt and softly spoke into it. "2 Lincoln 14. Request a code 1 follow up to the underground parking lot, Pine and Broadway."

A code 1 backup was routine: get here when you can, no lights or siren.

His radio was silent. He looked at the radio in his hand and saw a small amber light indicating he had no reception. He muttered to the radio as if it could understand, "Of course you won't work underground. You only work when you want to."

He looked at the front of his Sam Browne belt and saw his body camera LED light was also amber. So, no backup and no camera. He took a breath and pressed forward.

He saw a spot with three open stalls and no cars. Inside the opening stood three young black men he guessed to be somewhere between sixteen and twenty years old. One was holding a bottle of wine and wearing an oversized white T-shirt with a white baseball cap turned sideways. The other two had their backs to Manolito. They had on baggy black pants below their butts, one with a wife-beater T-shirt tucked inside his underwear, the other with his shirt off. The two in the baggy pants were spray painting "Longo Crips" in blue script writing on the wall. Mano guessed the guy wearing the black-and-gray plaid shorts never made it down to this level.

Manolito had a visceral hatred toward people who spray painted graffiti all over the city, but he hadn't arrested anyone for the low-grade misdemeanor in over a year. The last time had almost cost him a night in jail. The judge dismissed all charges against the young vandal. Kids had the right to express their urban experience, he said, and doing it through art was a healthy way of expression. Manolito was threatened with contempt of court when he asked the judge if it would be all right if he brought a few kids over to his house to express their urban experiences.

Manolito ducked behind a parked car and tried to stay hidden as he approached. He knew he was on a limb, confronting three gang members without backup or radio communication. He briefly thought about backing away, going up to where his radio would work and calling for assistance. Just as quickly, he discarded the thought. In the seven years he'd been an officer, he'd made it through tougher situations.

He stepped around a parked car and stopped twenty feet away from the three teenagers. He stood upright. "Hey, guys," he said. "We need to talk."

The silence that followed his words seemed charged. The hairs on the back of his neck lifted, and he suddenly wished he'd called another officer. He tried shaking the feeling. These were just a couple of street rats and he had the drop on them. The worst that might happen would be one might run away, no big deal...

The two with their backs to him dropped their spray paint, and a metallic clang echoed through the garage. A voice from Manolito's side said, "The fuck we do!"

He turned his head to see the teen wearing black and gray shorts pointing an automatic pistol at him. He held it in one hand, gangster style.

The man in the oversized T-shirt, still holding the wine bottle in his left hand, reached under his shirt and pulled out a chrome-plated revolver. He said, "Slowly, pig. Hands up."

A memory flashed through Manolito's mind. He was a recruit, sitting in class at the police academy. The instructor would show PowerPoint slides of officer-involved shootings, and with every slide, ask the class, "What were the danger signs and what could the officer have done differently?" Manolito never wanted to be the officer studied by an academy class, but realized if he didn't do something quickly, that would be his legacy.

If he ever made it out of this alive, he would never doubt his instincts again. He took a half breath. "Wait a minute!" he said. "You want me to put my hands in the air?"

The guy in the shorts gestured with the automatic and said, "I'll cap your ass if ya don't."

Slowly, Mano raised his hands into the same position used at the start of an action pistol match. With his hands up, Manolito nodded in the direction he'd come from and said, "Here's my partner."

As all four turned their heads to look, Manolito reached down, drew his pistol, and in rapid succession fired two rounds, double-tapping Mr. Black and Gray Shorts. He turned and fired two more shots, double-tapping the center chest of the man wearing the baseball cap. The bottle of wine and the revolver clattered onto the concrete. Manolito turned to fire again at the man in the plaid shorts, but he had already fallen to his knees with a look of horror frozen on his face. Manolito spun back around just as the man in the ball cap crumpled to the ground.

Mano pointed his pistol at the two who had been spray painting the wall. "Lie down," he said. Both stared in wide-eyed disbelief. He yelled, "The ground!" This broke the momentary trance and the two quickly lay face down.

Manolito pulled his handheld radio from his belt to call for help, then saw the amber light. He put the radio back on his belt, reached into his pocket and pulled out his iPhone. Without taking his eyes off the teenagers on the ground, he sent a text to Sergeant Chambers.

'998 parking structure Pine & Broadway.' ▯

11

I have the Mona Lisa…

John's cell phone beeped again and he reached for it in his pocket, addressing the chunky woman across the table. "We have about three hundred female officers who work here and you're telling me…"

He reread the text, turned on his radio, and spoke quickly into it. "Sam 23 – Do we have a unit out at Pine and Broadway?"

The radio was silent. He looked back and forth from the radio to his phone. "Come on!" he screamed at the radio, gripping it tightly. The woman rolled her eyes, as if upset the sergeant was not paying closer attention to her revelation of harassment, when she was there to help him root out the bad cops.

Dispatch came back, "Sam 23 – 2 Lincoln 14 is at that location on a theft investigation. We're unable to raise him on the radio."

He barked into the radio, "Sam 23 – possible 998 Pine and Broadway in the parking structure. Roll all Lincoln units and start the area lieutenant."

998 was the radio code for an officer-involved shooting. It could go either way, perp or officer shot, or both. But Mano had sent the message, which meant he was alive—at least he was when he sent the text.

After making the broadcast, John went back to his phone and texted. 'Help is on the way. Are you hurt?'

He ran out of interview room with the woman calling after him. "I know my rights. You have to take my complaint."

Getting in his black and white, John picked up the microphone. "Sam 23 - roll paramedics, unknown status of the officer. All responding units use caution."

Hearing the call of an officer-involved shooting, half the detectives and upper brass scrambled out of the station. Between all the Lincoln cars, detective units and administration cars racing to the scene, more than thirty cars had their lights and sirens blaring. Downtown Long Beach echoed with sirens bouncing off buildings, and no one could tell where they were coming from. Traffic stopped as a parade of marked and unmarked police cars sped to the scene.

***

After texting Sergeant Chambers, Manolito handcuffed the still form in the black and gray shorts, the one who had been holding the automatic. The young man's body was limp and offered no resistance as his hands were twisted behind his back. Manolito wiped at his eyes. As his vision blurred, he moved as quickly as he could to handcuff the other man on the ground. The white cap slipped over the man's face as Mano cranked the man's limp arms behind his back. Like his friend, this one made no sound and offered no resistance. Mano flashed back to when he was a kid, running across the beach with tears in his eyes and it made it worse.

He picked up the guns off the parking garage floor. He knew that could be considered tampering with evidence, but he wasn't going to leave them where anybody could steal them, or worse. He was trying to survive. He would deal with the consequences afterwards, assuming he was alive.

Manolito reached into his shirt pocket and removed his sunglasses. In the underground parking garage, the glasses would make the dimly lit structure nearly black. But they hid the tears. Tears were like blood in the water for punks like these.

He pointed his pistol toward the remaining two. He couldn't see them clearly through the blur and the dark glasses, but they seemed to be lying still.

His Smith & Wesson M&P held seventeen rounds. After firing four shots, it still had thirteen rounds. Buying time until his eyes cleared, he removed a fresh magazine from his Sam Browne belt, loaded it and put his old magazine in his back pocket.

As he reloaded, the teen wearing the wife-beater pleaded, "Please don't shoot me. Please! I barely know those guys. I didn't know they had guns."

Manolito said, "Quiet."

He moved his wrist, so the barrel of his pistol waved back and forth in the general area where he thought the shirtless man was lying. He said, "And what's your excuse?"

The man said, "I just got here, man. I don't know nothin'."

After he spoke, Manolito knew where they were. He was afraid one or both might be armed like the others, and he needed to search them. He moved to where the first voice had come from and said, "Extend your arms over your head, then don't move."

Manolito didn't need to see someone to pat them down for weapons, but he did need to know where they were. He waited a half second, moved his left foot forward until it bumped the man. Then he knelt down, putting his knee in the small of the man's back and ran his hands quickly over the man's body, feeling for a gun.

He turned his head in the direction of the second. "You got a gun?"

"Fuck, man!"

Manolito moved toward the voice. He stepped on the man's ankle and stumbled. The man yelled, "Hey! Don't kick me. I ain't doing shit, man."

Manolito felt tears running down his face and knew his eyes were clearing, if only he could make it another minute.

He put his knee on the second man's back and checked his pants and around the ankles for weapons. Manolito opened his eyes as wide as he could and tightly closed them. Tears rolled off his face onto the back side of his sunglasses.

Manolito backpedaled and took off his sunglasses. Thinking he might be making a bad situation worse, he said, "Gimme your wallets."

The shirtless man Manolito had stepped on said, "Shit, man! First you shoot my friends, ya kick me, and you're gonna rob us, too?"

Collecting their wallets, he said, "We're gonna walk to the street. I know you won't run away, cuz I'm holding your wallets." He didn't say the obvious; he didn't have any more handcuffs and couldn't call for help.

Walking the prisoners up, the teen in the wife-beater asked, "Can't ya let us go? We didn't do shit."

Manolito said, "Don't forget about the graffiti."

His eyesight was definitely clearing, because he could see the bare-chested prisoner wince. "Geez! For real? Ya just shot Jamal and Marcus and ya want to talk about a fuckin' wall. Man, you're fucked up!"

Emerging from the parking structure, Manolito heard an electronic beeping tone on his radio. The tone was produced by dispatch during an emergency so officers not involved with the emergency would know to keep the channel clear.

He broke the radio emergency tone. "2 Lincoln 14 – Pine and Broadway. Requesting paramedics, two down, two in custody."

Dispatch came back. "2 Lincoln 14 – Paramedics are responding along with a shooting team. Advise your status."

The approaching sirens grew louder. He knew in less than a minute there would be more policemen here than they could possibly use. He told the two prisoners, "Sit on the curb."

Officer Rodriguez drove the first unit that screeched up. Manolito shouted, "Go across the street. Get as much information as you can from a man and woman sitting at one of the sidewalk tables. They're a white couple in their forties. He's wearing a green Hawaiian shirt and she's a brunette with a lot of personality." As he said personality, he moved his hands as if holding up a pair of large breasts.

Rodriguez started towards the restaurant and Manolito called out, "Give me your hooks before you go!"

Rodriguez helped cuff the prisoners, and Manolito shoved their wallets back into their pockets. The shirtless teen said, "I had a thousand dollars, better still be there. Fucking sticky fingers bastard."

Manolito said, "Right, you had a thousand dollars in your wallet like I have the Mona Lisa hanging up in my house."

Confused, the prisoner said, "The Lisa? What? Who's hanging on your house? Man, you're fucked up!"

Officer Rodriguez crossed the street, south towards King's Fish House. Black and white patrol cars and unmarked detective cars were flooding into the area.

***

A sergeant's primary role at an officer-involved shooting was to ensure the welfare of his officers. He was also accountable for protecting the scene and making sure the appropriate notifications were made. The longer it took to control the scene, the more likely evidence would be destroyed and witnesses lost. This scene was already a mess.

By the time John arrived, he had to park half a block away. Police cars were scattered all over Pine and Broadway, blocking both streets. A large crowd had gathered to see what happened.

The two handcuffed prisoners remained seated on the curb and were now yelling to the crowd. "That Mexican cop shot Marcus and Jamal when they weren't looking. They were just standing there, and he shot 'em. He didn't give them a chance. Killed Marcus and Jamal for no reason!"

John called to one of his Lincoln unit officers. "I need you to put the prisoners in your car and transport them to the station."

John found Manolito talking with two lieutenants who were wearing suits. He walked between them. "Where's the other two?"

Manolito said, "They're down on the second floor."

"Are they alive? Is anyone with 'em? Have the paramedics gotten here yet?" He fired off the questions without allowing time to answer.

Manolito shook his head. "Slow down a minute, Sarge. I don't know if they're alive. I hit 'em pretty hard."

John spoke on his handheld radio. "2 Lincoln 6 and 2 Lincoln 23 - go to the second floor and secure the scene. I need paramedics in the underground parking structure."

He looked up and saw a Happening Now News van setting up. He knew his job was about to become even more complicated, with reporters twisting facts to create a more sensational story. Not to mention how they would try to cross the yellow crime scene tape to get at witnesses or take photographs. "How do those guys get here so fast?" he said to no one.

He did a double take, looking at Manolito's face. John did not want a reporter seeing his officer's tear-streaked face and run with a story about an officer's remorse over a bad shooting. "Get with the paramedics and have them clean your face. You don't want the news crew getting a camera shot of tear stains on your cheeks."

Manolito recoiled, looking embarrassed. "Thanks, Sarge."

John reached out and grasped Manolito's arm. "Don't worry, we all react differently under stress. I've only been involved in one shooting, and my hands sweated so much I couldn't hold anything. A few tears is no big deal."

He looked over Manolito's shoulder and saw six detectives with sunglasses over the tops of their heads and carrying iPads. "The shooting team's here. Just tell 'em the number of rounds you fired and the direction you shot. Answer everything else at the station. I'm calling one of our department attorneys. Don't write any reports or answer any more questions 'til you have a lawyer."

Mano nodded.

John looked up to see Rodriguez returning from across the street.

"Hey, Sarge," Rodriguez said, "when I got here, Mano was really worked up about two people sitting in front of King's Fish House. I couldn't find 'em."

"Sergeant Chambers, Sergeant Chambers!" John heard a woman calling out from the street. He looked up and recognized Connie Jones, from Channel 9, trying to get his attention. She was in her late twenties with layered blond hair, and she was heading toward him, holding out a microphone. She wore an expensive olive pantsuit with a ridiculous-looking six-inch-wide black velvet bow cinched tight around her waist. Behind her, a cameraman jockeyed for position. "Sergeant Chambers, Connie Jones, Happening Now News. We're getting reports several minorities were gunned down by officers. What do you have to say about that?"

He said, "A press release will be forthcoming by our Press Information Officer at the station. You can get all current and relevant information there."

She shouted, "Sergeant, don't you want to comment on the excessive force allegations?"

John pointed his index finger towards the station. "P.I.O. at the station."

She shouted again, "Are you expecting criminal charges against your officers?"

He turned his back on the reporter and walked away.

***

Connie Jones placed her camera crew in front of King's Fish House and began interviewing people in the crowd. A woman said into the camera, "All I know is a Mexican cop shot Marcus and Jamal in the back when they wasn't lookin'. Marcus and Jamal wouldn't hurt anybody. There's only one reason a policeman would kill those precious boys in cold blood... Cops hate all colored folk."

Behind the woman, two adolescent boys were trying to push each other out of the way, so they wouldn't have to share being on camera. When one managed to shove the other out of the way, he would hold up his hands, forming the letters L B, before being pushed out of the way by his rival.

Connie smiled and stepped in front of the camera. "And there you have it, another senseless police shooting. Reporting live from downtown Long Beach. This is Connie Jones, Happening Now News."

Arl Farris

12

… Who did what?

Gaston was in his office creating an Excel worksheet that he titled 'Public Enemies.'

Sergeant John Chambers was listed as public enemy number 1, with complaint filed for homophobia after his name.

Rebecca Wells was number 2, with racist, adulterer, and assault under color of authority connected to her.

He had just entered Manolito Torres in the number 3 slot and sexual predator / pervert, when his phone rang. Caller I.D. showed it was Connie.

He was already grinning when he picked up the phone. "I'm glad you called. Tell me you tracked down one of Casanova's old girlfriends."

She was breathless. "Forget that. You aren't going to believe this. He just assassinated two people and stole money from the others."

"What!" Gobsmacked, Gaston pulled his mouse across the desk in excitement, causing the computer screen to jump to his subscription porn site. "Goddamnit, not now!"

She sounded surprised. "I thought that's what you wanted?"

He clicked at his mouse, bringing up a blank document. "It's exactly what I needed. I just needed to clear some important files off my screen. Now, who did what?"

"Manolito Torres. He disarmed two young teenagers, then shot them in the back. Unfortunately for him, there were a couple witnesses. He then steals their wallets with all their cash, at least a thousand dollars."

He couldn't believe this was being handed to him on a silver platter. "Was he on duty, in uniform?"

"In full uniform. He was out of his car, but never called in his location to dispatch."

Gaston's mind was spinning. He'd dreamed about cases like this, but to actually get the scoop on one was practically surreal. "How many were there, again?"

"Two. I mean four. Well, really two."

"That doesn't matter. You said they were handcuffed when he shot them?"

She was breathing into the phone. "They had handcuffs on when the coroner took the bodies away."

Gaston's fingers trembled with excitement as he entered information into his computer. "He really killed these kids?"

"And stole their money," she blurted.

"Geez! And you were worried I was trying to frame him. This is worse than anything I could make up."

She gulped air and tried to sound nonchalant. "My producer said the story is being picked up by the network. I will be seen across the country."

"It's a break for all of us. Well, maybe not for the children he executed."

"I know! I don't care what it takes anymore. I want to see the Long Beach Police Department taken down, and the range staff... I'll do anything you want, just tell me what to do. I see why you hate them so much."

He wondered if she might be so grateful after this was over that she'd leave her husband for a week and go with him to Hawaii. No, better make it Vegas. No piece of ass was worth renting a condo in Hawaii.

He snapped back to the assassination. "You said there were witnesses?"

"Yeah, that's who he robbed."

He stopped typing. "Wait. I thought he was taking lunch money or something from some kids, handcuffed the witnesses and shot them in the back of the head?"

"Maybe? That Sergeant John Chambers was at the scene trying to cover everything up when I got there. There's no telling what really happened."

He switched screens back to the Excel spreadsheet and typed assassin after Manolito's name. "Give me twenty-four hours. I'll be able to tell you exactly what happened." No matter what the evidence might say.

☐

13

Tolstoy was never a cop

Completing formal briefing to the thirty-three officers working day shift, Lieutenant Willie Jackson looked to the last row of desks where the senior officers and sergeants sat. "Sergeant Chambers, Captain Dickerson wants to see you."

Remembering his last conversation with Dickerson, John hoped the captain was having him stop by to say the complaints had been investigated and determined to be unfounded, but he knew better. He hid his concerns by joking with the officers around him. "I'm sure he wants to know how many third graders are working this shift. All the reports read like an elementary school book. 'See crook run. See crook in jail.'"

Blakesley laughed, but John thought he detected a note of bitterness in it. "Tolstoy was never a cop."

***

Still grinning at Blakesley's crack, John sighed and headed upstairs to talk to Dickerson. Might as well get it over with.

John took the elevator up two floors to Administration. Carol, Captain Dickerson's secretary, sat in her cubicle and looked up from typing. "Good to see you, John. How's Jenny?" He smiled. "She's nearly back to one-hundred percent. But her doctors say it'll be another eight to twelve weeks before she can go back to work."

She looked admiringly at him. "At least you're together."

"Yeah, Jenny likes to tell people methamphetamine is the secret to a happy marriage. Let a meth-freak nearly kill you, and it allows for quality time with your spouse."

"A little too drastic for me. I think I'll stick with Cosmo." She placed her fingers back on her keyboard. "You better go in. He's expecting you."

He heard an angry, "Goddamnit!" from inside the captain's office, followed by a desk drawer being slammed shut. The sounds within confirmed what John already knew. This was not going to be pleasant. He opened the door as Dickerson stood up, breathing hard. He looked like he wanted to throw something out the window. "Close the door and have a seat."

John had never seen Dickerson fired up, but imagined back in the day when he was fighting sailors and dock workers, he must have been a knuckle-dragging monster.

John nodded and sat.

Dickerson propped his elbows on the desk and steepled his fingers. "As you know, the department requires officers to be off work a minimum of one week after being involved in a shooting. At the least, seeing the department shrink and calming down takes a couple of days. We don't want officers returning to work with their minds screwed up."

John wondered where the conversation was going. "Sure, my guys know the drill. Twice a year during roll call training, we discuss what the aftermath will be if they are ever involved in a shooting."

"Well, this time it's a little different," Dickerson said. "This is coming down from the chief's office. Torres is to remain off work until the shooting investigation is complete and there's a final resolution in the case."

Until the investigation was complete? Shooting investigations took months and final resolutions took at least a year. Before he could stop himself, John said, "Have you people lost your minds? Torres' shooting was clean."

Dickerson leaned forward. "These things need to be investigated. You know that. "But like I said, it's not up to me." He shook his head in disgust. "I don't know what the hell Torres was thinking out there. He should've never contaminated the scene by picking up those guns. Our only witnesses say Torres shot those two because they were black, waiting until they were distracted and not looking."

John wondered if Dickerson actually believed his own twisted interpretation. "Was that the witness who claimed Mano stole a thousand dollars from him or the gang member who's on probation for narcotics violations? Oh, excuse me, they're both gang members on probation."

Dickerson's barrel chest rose several inches as he took a breath. "We've got to look at the seriousness of the charges. When officers don't record citizen contacts on their video systems and a complaint is made, I have no choice but to believe the complaint."

Outraged, John said, "The hell you don't!"

Dickerson pointed a thick index finger at John. "Watch yourself, sergeant!"

John understood the captain's veiled threat of an insubordination charge. He spoke in a more suppressed tone. "That's a bunch of bull and you know it. His body camera was on. If our damn equipment actually worked, we'd have a video of the entire shooting."

Body cameras were wirelessly tied to the officer's car. When an officer turned on his camera, the video feed was recorded on his video system located in the trunk of the black and white. The downside to this system was its limited range. When an officer was more than a quarter-mile from his patrol car or went into a steel-beamed building or an underground parking lot, it exceeded the capability of the system. Kind of like the helicopters—they were a good idea when they worked.

Dickerson placed a hand on a stack of papers. "I can't tell you how many times a day I hear officers complain about their equipment not being good enough. Hell, when I was an officer, we didn't have hand-held radios or expensive video recording equipment. We managed to get by without those luxuries, and people weren't coming in here every ten minutes complaining."

Yeah, John thought, and you walked to school six miles in the snow. Uphill both ways.

"All I know is what I'm being told from the chief's office," Dickerson said. "Your suspects' fingerprints weren't found on either of the guns picked up by Torres, and the two guns had been reported stolen. And I might add, the officer who took the stolen reports happened to be Torres."

This was bullshit. John felt his neck grow hot. "Of course there wouldn't be any clear fingerprints on the pistols," he said. "Torres tucked the guns into his pants when he walked the witnesses out of the parking lot. He couldn't leave the pistols lying in the parking lot for anyone to come by and take."

He and Dickerson were both leaning forward in their chairs like two pit bulls straining to fight. John could see Dickerson's desire to jump across the desk and kick his ass. Probably as much as I'd like to kick him in the balls.

"Look, John," Dickerson said. "I'm not gonna argue with you. It's coming directly from the chief's office and that's final. Besides, you have your own problems to worry about. Or have you forgotten our little talk?"

"I haven't forgotten anything."

Dickerson set down his papers. "Look, John, I know you care about your officers. But the days of Dirty Harry are over. The media is all over this thing, and we can't have rogue cops giving the department a bad name."

"Manolito's not—" John began.

Dickerson held up a finger. "I'm being very patient, Sergeant. Extremely patient. But that patience is wearing thin. Why don't you take the rest of the day off, before you say something you'll regret?" He gave John a hard stare.

John stood up, gritting his teeth. "Sure, Captain. Whatever you say."

***

Jenny tossed the paperback she'd been reading onto the coffee table and walked to the window. The early afternoon light slanted through the glass, and a light breeze ruffled the leaves, beckoning her to go for a run. She rolled her shoulders and stretched up on her toes. She felt good. Pretty good. Especially since two weeks earlier, she'd needed help going up and down the stairs. Her recovery was progressing on schedule, but not fast enough for her. She'd begun to feel like a prisoner in her own house and was spending more time in the backyard, sunning herself by the pool. Nice, but even that got old after a while.

Was it too soon to get back to her jogging routine? If she took it slow? Maybe just a walk around the neighborhood.

She was getting a water bottle out of the refrigerator when the door leading from the garage to the kitchen opened, and John walked in.

Delighted and surprised, she said, "Wow, you're home early!" Her mind raced ahead with plans for the afternoon. Maybe he'd want to join her on a walk. That would be fun. Then she saw the look on his face. Her smile faded, and she set the water bottle back on the shelf. "You feeling okay?"

He said, "I don't know how I feel. I think the captain's building a file to fire me."

It took a moment for his words to sink in. Despite her earlier warning to take Dickerson's threat seriously, she hadn't really thought anything would come of it. John was a good cop. And a good man. Surely his superiors knew that.

She laid a hand on the refrigerator door, suddenly unsteady on her feet.

He said, "In the name of political correctness, the department's trying to sacrifice Mano for his shooting and me for giving first aid to some guy on a medical aid call. Rebecca and Blakesley are in the cross-hairs too."

Her mind raced through the implications. This was bad, really bad. What if John lost his job and she wasn't cleared to go back to work? Or what if she was cleared and she wasn't ready? She hated to admit it, even to herself, but whenever she thought about going back there, she could hardly breathe.

But one of them had to work. If John lost his job... Would they have to sell the house? The kids would hate it if they had to move. They had friends here. Their school. Sports. Extracurriculars. Would they even be able to afford extracurriculars? And what about college? Sure, that was a long way off, but...

She took a long, calming breath and held on to the refrigerator door handle for support. She needed to be strong for John. To care for him the way he'd been taking care of her since the accident. When she finally spoke, her voice was steady. "What are you talking about, John?"

"Mano's been suspended, and internal affairs is gonna be looking into a couple complaints against the rest of us."

With a firm grip on the door handle, she said, "That's good, though, right? When they look at everything, you guys'll be fine."

"Sure. I know it will." His smile was strained. She'd first seen that smile fourteen years ago in the emergency room where she was working. He'd been writing a traffic ticket when a drunk driver slammed into his patrol car and sent it skidding into him, slamming him to the sidewalk. They'd brought him in, unconscious and concussed, and as he regained consciousness, he'd looked up at her and smiled. She thought it was that smile, somehow both stoic and vulnerable, that had made her fall in love with him. A year later, they were married.

He gave her a quick kiss on the cheek. "I'm gonna go for a run and clear my head."

"Before you go, sit with me on the patio. I want to hear some more."

She opened the refrigerator door, removed a pitcher of iced tea and handed it to him, placed a couple glasses on a platter, along with crackers, cheese and an apple.

Sitting next to the pool, under the shade of an umbrella canopy, she tucked her legs up under her and said, "Tell me, what's going on?"

He took a drink of iced tea, then asked, "In all the years we've been married, have you ever known me to be prejudiced or do anything to harm or insult anyone because they're black, gay or whatever?"

She frowned, sifting through memories. "There was the time we were going through the drive-thru at Taco Bell," she said slowly, "and you whistled at the poor Hispanic kid working the drive-thru window. That was very insulting."

"It wasn't," John said. "He was standing at the window with his back to us, texting on his phone and letting the line of cars back up. I just whistled to get his attention to get our food."

She nodded. "Yeah, but it was bad."

"Okay, other than whistling to get a kid's attention who was on his cell phone and not doing his job, can you think of any other time I did something that could possibly have offended someone?"

She pointed toward the front door. "Well, a couple nights ago, a teenager came by selling magazine subscriptions and you didn't buy anything. I think he was black?"

"My God, Jenny," he exclaimed. "It's a good thing wives can't be compelled to testify against their husbands."

"Come on, I'm only screwing with you, honey." She set down an apple slice and ran her hand across the back of his neck. He must really be rattled, to take her ridiculous examples seriously. "Of course you've never done anything to degrade or belittle anybody. You are the most ethical and conscientious person I've ever known."

He traced the top of his glass with a finger. "I'm getting so tired of the police constantly being blamed for everything that's wrong in society. They stop us from doing our jobs and are upset because crime is out of control. What would they do if the police were half as bad as they think we are? You know, if we wanted, we could show this city what real crime is. And we know how to get away with it."

Jenny stood and took John's hand. Humor hadn't worked, but she had an idea what would. "You're going off the rails, dear.

Come with me. I think I know something that will help you relax."

◻

◻

14

...a man walked into a bar with a parrot

The recruits clustered around John. A few hung back, and he wondered if they'd heard about the investigations into him and his squad. If they hadn't, it was only a matter of time. The media vultures Dickerson had mentioned would make sure of that.

"Diligentia, Vis, Celeritas is Latin," he said. "The English translation is Accuracy, Power, Speed. In a gunfight, those are the three things that will determine if you go home at the end of your shift or are driven to the mortuary."

He scanned the faces of the recruits, some worried, some with a cocky confidence that said they were sure they would never be among the latter. If he did his job right today, they'd end up somewhere in between. He went on, trying not to think about the possibility that he'd be leaving them before the job was done. "The department sets the standards for power. 9mm, .40 cal. or .45 ACP are authorized by the department and each have ample firepower to stop any adversary. If your life comes down to a speed and accuracy contest like it did for one of your instructors this past week, you'll be ready, provided you practice and are using good technique."

The recruits looked at Manolito, who put his index and middle fingers to his eyes, then pointed back at John. They turned back to John, but he could feel some portion of their attention still focused on Mano.

John scanned the group again, collecting his thoughts. For the first time, he doubted that this academy class was joining a world class policing agency. What kind of a department would rather investigate its officers than have them keep the city safe?

He pushed the thought away and continued. "I realize most of you were disappointed last week when the guys dressed in their cowboy costumes wanted to shoot against me and I refused. As you know, all your instructors are competitive shooters. However, what you saw last week wasn't a friendly challenge. Those guys were trying to see if they could take a policeman in a gunfight. If you only get one thing out of today, it should be this: you'll never lose a gunfight you're never in. Do anything and everything you can to avoid a gunfight. However, if you're forced into one, act with extreme prejudice."

A tall blond female recruit with "SANDERS" across the front of her shirt raised her hand.

"Yes, Sanders."

"Sir, Recruit Sanders would like to know what you mean by, 'with extreme prejudice.'

I'm not prejudiced against anyone."

Instructor Blakesley stepped forward. "Sarge, I'll handle this one, if you don't mind."

John extended his hand forward. "By all means."

Pointing at the other instructors, Blakesley said, "When we're working, Mano isn't Hispanic, Rebecca isn't a woman, Scott isn't white, and I'm not black. We're police officers and we wear blue. The people we contact aren't black, white, Asian, gay or whatever. They're people, victims, suspects, witnesses, or uninvolved parties. We don't judge people by the color of their skin, who they pray to, or who they choose to go to bed with. However, we're all judged by them as one. We're all cops. When you wear the uniform, you're blue. When you find yourself rolling around in some back alley at three-thirty in the morning with a meth freak trying to kill you, he doesn't care what your name is, where you grew up, or if you donate to the Red Cross after a disaster. He only sees you as the cop who's gonna arrest him, and he'd rather shoot you than go to jail. When you find yourself in that struggle, or some gangster's pointing a gun at you, acting with extreme prejudice is acting quickly, acting with confidence and striking back with everything you have. That's extreme prejudice."

John watched their expressions to see if they got it. As usual, there were a few who seemed unfazed by the thought, but most, he could tell, were processing Blakesley's words, considering what it would mean to strike another human being with everything they had.

His gaze fell on the class sergeant. "Class Sergeant Flores, have the class put up paper silhouette targets along the back berm. We're going to shoot our PPC course for score. After the targets are up, have the class use the restroom, get a drink of water and prepare for a full day of shooting."

Flores stepped in front of the class and called them to attention. "Class... give me twenty recruits to post the targets and the rest of you, load your magazines."

The instructors returned to their trucks, where they could keep an eye on the recruits and still speak freely, as long as they were careful to lower their voices. Rebecca asked John, "Think these guys can run the range for a bit? I'd like to talk privately with you."

"Sure. But first, Blakesley and I are gonna step away for a few minutes. Whaddya say we shoot a round of skeet during the lunch break? We can talk then."

She shrugged and glanced toward the recruits. "That'll be fine."

John followed her gaze to a line of recruits in front of three Porta Potties. As one recruit would finish using the portable toilets, the next one would enter. Recruit Sanders stepped out and quickly reached to her ears. "Oh, I forgot my earmuffs in the sink."

The recruits waiting in line laughed hysterically. Sanders looked confused.

Chuckling, John told Rebecca, "You better help her."

Rebecca walked over, put her arm around Sanders' waist, and guided her towards her truck. "Honey, there's no sinks in Porta Potties. I have an extra set of earmuffs you can have. You probably don't want to wear those anymore since they're in the men's urinal."

Sanders shuddered. "Oh, my God, I think I'm going to be sick! I've been setting them in there since last week."

John turned his head to hide his grin. Then, with the paper silhouette targets up, he called out, "Scott, I need you, Rebecca, and Mano to run the range for a while."

Scott nodded. "No problem."

John and Blakesley walked out of their shooting area along a dirt road.

John said, "That was impressive what you said back there to the recruits."

"Thanks. I really meant those things, but…" Blakesley looked away, the muscles around his eyes tightening. "I felt hollow saying them."

John chose his words carefully. "You know I value your opinion. That's why I wanted to talk with you. Mind telling me what you mean?"

"Sarge," Blakesley said. "It's hard to explain, but the department's changed. Hell, it's not even the same city anymore. There were always idiots out there, but now even little kids are asking if I'm going to shoot 'em or beat up their daddies." He kicked at a clump of gravel and several small stones went flying. "I'm not a bad guy, but everyone, especially the department, is treating me like I've done something horrible."

John nodded. "I still don't get why the captain ordered you to internal affairs. Buying your wife a new car with cash is a far cry from being corrupt."

Blakesley's fists clenched. "Sometimes I'd like to show them what horrible is. You know what I'm talking about?"

With an expansive gesture, John said, "We've got the crooks trying to hurt us. The reporters spinning the truth, the legal system's upside-down—and what's up with this attorney coming after us? The chief and Captain Dickerson are undermining us at every turn. I don't see how this ends well."

"And we're caught in the middle, being blamed for everything." Blakesley jabbed a finger in the air. "Let me tell you something. I ain't going down without a fight."

John laughed, but there was no humor in it. "Who do you wanna fight, the city, the department, who? And if we did go after 'em, we'd have to go outside the system. We'd be abandoning everything we've ever stood for as cops."

Was he ready for that? He wasn't sure, but he knew he wasn't ready to lie down and let Gaston and the department roll over him.

Blakesley said, "That attorney who accused Rebecca of being a racist and challenged you last week. He'd be a good place to start. And Captain Dickerson next."

John didn't answer. It was a nice thought, but career suicide. He suspected Blakesley didn't need anyone to tell him that.

They heard shooting on a range in front of them and continued walking towards the gunfire until they were standing at the edge of another dirt berm range, watching a group of cowboy action shooters. Both men and women were dressed in western clothing, with lever action rifles, double-barrel shotguns, and two single action revolvers strapped around their waists.

So, this was what those people who wore cowboy clothing did. They had their own shooting sport.

Blakesley nodded toward three men in elaborate western costumes and said, "I think they might put more effort in dressing up than they do shooting." He turned to John. "I'm serious. I'm gonna do something about what's going on. I've worked too hard to let some punk-ass attorney leave us out here twisting in the wind."

John looked at Blakesley. "Jenny and I had this very conversation. I felt the same as you, but she reminded me justice will prevail in the end and we don't wanna do anything we'd regret."

"You're wrong, my friend. If you can't see how the department's turned on us, you need to look again."

They stood in silence, watching the cowboys. After several minutes, Blakesley said, "Even my kids are embarrassed to tell their friends what their dad does for a living. Hell, Jaclyn stopped calling me Dad and now refers to me as Tom. Can you believe that crap? Then there's that TV reporter." He hesitated, the disgust on this face replaced by hurt and indignation. "She called the house a couple of days ago, implying I turned my back on my brother and left him to die on the street."

That was bullshit. Blakesley had pulled Charles off the streets a dozen times, and when his brother inevitably returned to his life as a homeless nomad, Blakesley had scoured the streets looking for him, armed with blankets and nonperishable food.

But before John could answer, an attractive, forty-ish woman wearing an Old Gus cowboy hat, a button-down long-sleeved shirt with leather cuffs, tight pants, chaps, and suede cowboy boots with spurs walked up from behind. Her suede gun belt supported two blue steel Ruger Vaquero .38 caliber revolvers.

She stepped between and brushed up against them. "Howdy, partners. Y'all thinkin' 'bout signing up with this here outfit? I'm Hurricane Heather."

"I bet you are. I'm John. This is Blakesley."

Hurricane Heather said, "Oh, that'll never do. You guys are real greenhorns. Let me tell ya about cowboy action shooting. First, you need to pick your handle, which would be your cowboy name. If you're with a group, you also need to name your posse. This here's the Lead Bottom Posse. I've been shooting with these guys for years and don't even know their real names."

John smiled. "That's convenient."

She laughed. "You're funny. You'd fit right in."

Blakesley said, "I've heard all his jokes. Trust me, he's not that funny. Have you heard the one where a man walked into a bar with a parrot on his shoulder?"

She looked Blakesley up and down. "Well, Mr. Tall, Dark and Handsome, we've plenty of room for two big strapping fellas. In cowboy action shooting, we shoot replica guns of the Old West." She touched one of the pistols at her hip. "We have stages in our matches where we only shoot double-barreled shotguns. Some we use lever action rifles and others we use revolvers. If you're really adventurous, we also shoot mounted matches, where we ride horses and shoot from horseback. Don't worry, ya don't have to buy a horse. There's plenty of outfitters who rent 'em."

John asked, "How's it I've been shooting at this complex for years and never run into you guys before?"

She shrugged. "That's the cowboy way. We don't like to brag. We don't show off and we keep to ourselves. If you hadn't walked onto our range, you might never've found out about us."

John said, "True. There's a lot of ranges out here."

"You don't know the half of it," she said. "Every few years this area floods. The county sends a bulldozer in here to reestablish the roads and build up any dirt berm ranges that get washed away."

She pointed southeast with her buckskin gloves. "Most people don't know there's a range hidden along the river. When it floods, the dozer clears out some of the brush and small trees, pushing dirt and debris up along the river, making a berm we call the river range. Since no roads go there, not many people use it, and it's deserted most of the year. We keep a couple plate racks and two Texas Star targets down there, but it's hard to find. To make matters worse, when it floods and they remake the river range, they never put it back in the same place."

She laughed. "I don't know if you've ever tried walking around by the river, but the trees and brush are so thick, it's nearly impossible to get though."

John raised his eyebrows. "Thanks for the geography lesson, but I've no plans on going there."

Blakesley pointed at the cowboy shooters. "Is this some kind of organized league?"

"Oh, darling," she said. "Ya gotta join the Single Action Shooting Society. If you shoot in three matches during the year, you'll qualify for the End of Trail match. That's where all the top shooters from around the country compete. You're in luck. This year, End of Trail will be here in four months. That'd give you one month to buy all your gear, shoot in three monthly matches, and qualify for End of Trail."

John listened intently. "This just keeps getting better and better."

Looking at the pistols on their hips, she said, "I hope you boys lose those funny-looking shootin' irons, get some real guns, and join us. I've gotta go. I'm up in a few minutes on the next range for my mounted shoot."

They thanked her, and she walked away, spurs jangling.

Looking at John, Blakesley said, "I know that look. What're you thinking?"

John shook his head. "I can't believe that attorney is a member of a cowboy shooting league. There's gotta be something else going on here."

Blakesley shrugged. "Everyone's got a hobby. Maybe he just likes dressing up and shooting?"

John didn't think so. "I'm gonna do some online research on cowboy action shooting and see what I can find." He looked at his watch. "We better get back. The recruits should be about ready to break for lunch. If we come up with a way to fight back, you might want to keep some of the details from Anita."

"You know I don't keep secrets from Anita, just like you don't keep 'em from Jenny." Blakesley looked up and watched a red-tailed hawk soaring overhead. "Do you wonder if they float up there in the wind currents for fun?"

John searched the sky for a second before seeing the raptor. "I think predators have a one-track mind. It doesn't matter if they have feathers or a Tom Ford suit, they're only thinking about their next kill."

It was now clear to John who was the predator and who was meant to be the prey. But this time, the "hawk" was in for a surprise. John was done being the mouse.

◻

15

…a Jeep and a Ferrari

They arrived back at their range just as Scott told Class Sergeant Flores to break the class for lunch.

John enjoyed seeing the enthusiasm on the faces of the recruits and their carefree horseplay as they made their way to their cars to retrieve their lunches. He hoped most of them would be well into their career before having to deal with the politics of the job. The idea of chasing crooks was what got officers out of their beds in the mornings, and the political correctness and higher-ups posturing for power was what ended careers. While they were still recruits, he could shield them from the nonsense.

John and Rebecca watched the other instructors pile into Scott's white Ford Excursion and head into town for lunch. Then, remembering his promise to Rebecca, John put a green canvas gun case into the bed of Rebecca's raised 4X4 Tacoma pick-up and she drove five minutes to a field with two skeet ranges. One of the fields was being used, and Rebecca said, "Perfect," as she parked near the vacant range. "I didn't want anyone to overhear us."

John sighed. He had a lot of officers confide in him after saying similar things. They never had good news.

When Rebecca graduated from the Los Angeles County Sheriff's Department police academy, she married another recruit. Even with over eighty-five hundred deputies working in the department, it became apparent there were going to be problems. The department had a policy prohibiting spouses from working the same shift, but that didn't stop deputies from comparing the two. The constant scrutiny from other deputies and never being able to see each other became too much, and after one year on the department, she transferred to the Long Beach Police Department.

Things didn't improve for the couple, though, and she saw even less of her husband. Eventually, they agreed on a one-month trial separation. John knew Rebecca had hoped they'd get back together, but one night after work, she went to their old apartment and found her husband in bed with a dispatcher. She filed for divorce the next day. She'd told John once that she was grateful they'd decided to wait before having kids.

Living alone and making a decent income, she put all her energy into the job. She attended classes in Administration of Justice at California State University Long Beach, took up karate and distance running. She had always been a shooter, going quail hunting with her dad and having a family membership at the trap and skeet range. Since her divorce, she'd bought a thirteen-thousand-dollar shotgun and joined a sporting clays league. John never knew her to take half measures. When she made her mind up to do something, there was no one better.

The two uncased their shotguns, Rebecca with an overunder Krieghoff K-80 Pro Sporter and John with his semiautomatic Benelli combat shotgun. They put on shooting vests, and each dumped a box of twenty-five shotgun shells into their vest pockets. John looked at his Benelli, then at Rebecca's Krieghoff. "This is like a Jeep and a Ferrari stopped side by side at a red traffic light. They're each really good vehicles, but neither has anything in common with the other."

She said, "True, but when you pull the trigger, the pellets going down the barrel don't know if they're in the Jeep or the Ferrari."

Standing directly under station 1, John extended his hand. "Ladies first." He held the push-button remote control thrower and took several steps back.

In skeet, the clay birds came from two stations, known as houses. There was a high house where the bird was thrown from a height of ten feet, and a low house, where the bird was thrown from three feet off the ground. Stage 1 was directly under the high house. There were a total of eight stages where the shooters progressed in a semicircle, shooting from marked stations as they moved around the semicircle.

Rebecca loaded a single round into her shotgun and yelled, "Pull!" The bird flew from the high house. She squeezed the trigger and the bright orange clay bird disintegrated into black dust. She broke open her overunder shotgun and the empty hull ejected up and out of the bottom barrel. She loaded another shell into the lower barrel and closed the gun. She put the shotgun to her shoulder and her cheek rested perfectly on the stock. She yelled, "Pull!" again and a clay bird from the low house streaked at them. She pulled the trigger and the bird shattered into a dozen pieces.

They lowered their heads as pieces from the clay bird landed around them. Rebecca ejected the empty round from her weapon and loaded both barrels. Again, she yelled, "Pull!" A clay bird from the high house and low house were thrown at the same time, in opposite directions, crossing each other in the center of the skeet range. She quickly swung the shotgun from one bird to the next, breaking each bird.

John recalled the silver medal Rebecca had won at last year's police olympics in sporting clays and knew he was in for a performance.

She opened her shotgun and both empty hulls sprang out of the gun and onto the ground. She blew into the barrels and grey smoke came out the end of the barrels. She balanced the open shotgun over her shoulder and took the remote thrower from John and said, "You're up, Sarge."

He stepped into the box for station number 1, chambered a round and said "Pull!" He shot as soon as the bird was visible above him, and the bird shattered. The empty hull was automatically ejected and the action remained locked to the rearward position, indicating the gun was empty. He put another shell into the Benelli, shouldered it and called, "Pull!" He waited until the low house bird was almost past him before firing.

The bird broke, and Rebecca said, "You might not want to wait for the bird to fly into the next county before shooting."

"Yeah, I guess I was a little late on that one." He loaded a round into the open chamber, ran the bolt forward and put another round into the tube magazine. "These shells are pretty light. What load are they?"

"Winchester double A's, 2 ⅔ dram of powder and an ounce and an eighth of number 9 shot."

"That's pretty light," he repeated. "If my shotgun won't cycle the shells, you might need to throw the pair as singles."

He wanted to ask what was bothering her, but experience had taught him that the best way to handle Rebecca was to let her take this kind of thing at her own pace. She'd tell him when she was damn well good and ready.

"Pull!" John yelled, again quickly shooting the first bird from the high house and swinging onto the second bird rising from the low house. He squeezed the trigger a second time, and the low house bird shattered.

Rebecca grinned. "The pellets can't tell if it's a Jeep or a Ferrari."

Then her grin faded. She handed the remote to John and they moved fifteen feet over to station number 2. She took the shotgun off her shoulder, dropped a shell into the bottom barrel and began talking. "I've been a cop for eight years… Pull!" She fired at the high house bird and it turned to black dust. "I've loved my time with the department, but I don't know if I can continue. The city didn't lift a finger when that attorney accused me of being a racist in open court. Now, it's starting again. I know they're going to turn my arrest of the bank robbers into something it wasn't. They'll put me on trial and let those two crooks go. I mean, look what they're doing to Mano. It's become unbearable. Pull!" She swung on the low house bird, breaking it as she pressed the trigger.

She loaded both barrels, preparing for the pair. "You know when you watch the History Channel and they're doing something on the war in Vietnam? Of course, the veterans had it rough and something like fifty-five thousand American soldiers were killed over there. Pull!" The pair of birds flew crossways, and she swung her shotgun smoothly, breaking each bird.

They switched positions, John in the shooter's box and Rebecca standing behind, holding the remote with her gun again balanced on the shoulder. Rebecca said, "After all these years, they say it's not the combat or the killing that haunts the solders, it's the way the country turned its back on 'em. They were treated worse than child molesters when they returned home from service."

John called, "Pull!" and a bird flew from the high house and exploded into a ball of black dust a few feet from the high house.

"Well," she said, "I know exactly how those guys felt. It's how I feel and I gotta do something about it. I just don't know what."

John didn't know either, but it seemed he and Blakesley weren't the only ones who'd had a craw full of the department's bullshit.

"Pull!" he said. The bird from the low house sailed across the range. He fired, and the bird kept going. A miss.

He stood upright, ignoring his missed bird. "I've been thinking about the same thing. But you need to really think about what you're saying. Once we cross the line, there may be no going back."

"Sarge, the old me died six months ago. I went to Stevenson Elementary School for a fifth grader with a switchblade knife. When I pulled up in my black and white, the principal met me in the parking lot. He told me to wait in my car, not to come onto campus because the police have a negative influence on the children."

Her eyes were watery. "I sat there in my patrol car and it felt like my soul left my body. I drove away from the school, not waiting for the principal to return. That day, my mind was made up. I'm gonna do something. What happened to me in court just made me more certain. If we don't do something soon, it'll be too late."

John called for the pair. "Pull!" He quickly fired twice, with Rebecca calling out, "Missed pair."

They shot the rest of the round in silence, except for calling birds to be thrown. When they finished, Rebecca unceremoniously hung up the remote control and they went back to the truck without commenting on her perfect score.

Driving back to the recruits, she said, "I don't know what to do."

John stared out the windshield. "Don't do anything. If we all head off in separate directions, we might not get very far. But if we strategize and come up with a plan, we might be able to do something big."

***

A few minutes later, John stood in front of the recruits. He asked recruit Sanders, "If you could have any car you wanted, what would it be?"

She said, "A baby blue Volkswagen Bug, convertible."

He pointed to another recruit. "Your dream car?"

"A Hummer."

"Would you believe anybody if they told you their favorite car would never break down? The battery would never die, a tire won't go flat, you'll never run out of gas or a taillight will never burn out?" A few of the recruits shook their heads. "In some ways, pistols are like cars, at some point they'll all stop working. You could get a high primer, broken parts or simply not seating a magazine properly, but all guns will malfunction."

He said, "The department allows you to carry a second gun if you choose. Some officers carry a second gun in case their first weapon malfunctions. Other officers carry a second gun because they fear someone could take their primary gun or they might lose it in a fight. I don't, because of the extra weight. But it's a personal decision and no one'll ever criticize you, one way or the other."

He looked directly at Blakesley, then to Rebecca. "Second weapon or not, you must always have a plan of action. A plan of how to overcome and conquer."

Blakesley held his gaze, then gave a small nod as Rebecca gave John a small but approving smile. They'd gotten his message, but John wasn't sure whether to be gratified or appalled that neither seemed to have reservations.

The recruits worked on clearing malfunctions the remainder of the afternoon. When the class was over and the recruits had been dismissed, John called the instructors together. With all their gazes on him, he took a deep breath and plunged in.

"Some of you are feeling betrayed by the department and are at a crossroads. Others are so far beyond the crossroads you can't even see them in your rearview mirror. I want everyone to come to my house for dinner on Thursday, after work." He gave them a stern look. "Spouses and girlfriends aren't allowed. Plan on making a decision that could impact the rest of your career. If we're not all on board, then we stop right there."

He paused and swatted at a couple of mosquitos circling in front of his face. "It goes without saying, I trust each of you and would give my life, without hesitation, to get any one of you out of a tight spot. But if we decide to fight the department or Gaston, we can't win by their rules. Which means we may not be the honorable people we think we are. Now, let's get outta here before the mosquitos eat us alive."

They ran to their vehicles, waving their hands around their heads in feeble attempts to keep the mosquitos at bay. Scott followed John to his truck. "I know you've been talking with Blakesley and Rebecca. I overheard them talking about wanting to do something. I've gotta tell ya, I'm not in the same place as you guys. I mean, sure, I'm not feeling the love from the department and I'm the first to admit, my morale sucks, but what you guys are talking about... I have no intention of doing anything that's gonna get me fired."

"We're not talking about getting fired. We're talking about going to prison."

Scott shook his head. "I'll be at your house, but I'm telling you, whatever you're planning, it's not happening."

John started his truck. "We'll talk about it Thursday. Who knows, maybe you can talk some sense into the rest of us?" □

□

16

Attempting to overtake a bicyclist...

Officers share a special allegiance with each other, similar to the bond felt by soldiers serving in combat. Policemen also swear an oath to uphold their duties and defend the Constitution against all enemies, both foreign and domestic. Scott had never dreamed the loyalty he felt toward his partners would jeopardize this oath to the department. He felt obligated to support his brothers in arms, but this time he couldn't. He wasn't sure what they were planning, but he knew it went against everything he stood for. He made up his mind that, after his shift, he would text John and say he wanted nothing to do with their scheme.

All Scott ever wanted was to be a policeman like his dad. Starting at age thirteen, his father would bring him to the department's pistol range, where officers would pay him two dollars to clean their revolvers. It was the best job a kid could have, hanging out with the officers, cleaning their guns, and making money.

His dad had managed to work his entire career without ever shooting anyone or getting shot himself. Scott had not even been officially sworn in as a police officer before his first shooting. He was still in the academy doing a uniformed ride-along when a fifteen-year-old in a stolen car led him and his partner on a pursuit into Los Alamitos. The teen crashed into a parked car and got out shooting at Scott's black and white. Scott and his partner returned fire, hitting the young man four times. Thankfully, he didn't die, but Scott had been in several shootings since, and not all had ended so well for the perpetrator.

Two months after his first shooting, Scott graduated from the police academy. Sergeant John Chambers presented him with a new Glock 17 at graduation for being his class's top shooter. When he walked on stage to accept the pistol, John said, "I pray you never find the need to fire this weapon in anger."

The audience had cheered, and Scott's mother had cried. Scott wondered what had happened to the Sergeant Chambers who'd said those meaningful words.

Scott drove north on Cedar Avenue from 4th Street. It was the middle of summer, yet being so close to the ocean, it was only in the high 70s with a constant breeze coming in off the water. He turned west on 5th Street and had to immediately slam on his brakes. A thin Hispanic man, about twenty-seven years old and riding a yellow beach cruiser, cut across the street and almost hit Scott's black and white.

The man on the bicycle had on a black and grey Pendleton shirt, buttoned up to the neck. The bottom four buttons were open, showing off a tattooed belly. His grey slacks were cut off just below the knees, and white socks disappeared under the legs of his shorts. He held something to his stomach with one hand and steered his bike with the other, which clutched a bulging white pillowcase and held it in place against the handlebar. The pillowcase appeared heavy, swinging back and forth as he pedaled. Its weight caused the handlebars to turn each time it swayed.

There was no doubt what this was. Most residential burglaries happened during the day while the homeowner was at work and the kids were in school. Usually, burglars stole things they could put in their pockets. However, when making a large haul, one of their favorite means of carrying out more than they could put in their pockets was to take the pillowcases off the bed and fill them with whatever they were stealing.

Scott muttered to himself, "Fucking parolee burglar."

The bike swerved toward Scott's black and white, narrowly missing the patrol car. The man jerked the handlebars, causing the bike to wobble awkwardly. It almost toppled, but the man kept his hand pressed to his stomach. He turned the beach cruiser north onto Del Rey Court, pedaling as fast as he could.

Scott picked up his car's microphone. "2 Lincoln 6 – northbound Del Rey Court from 5th, attempting to overtake a bicyclist, request assistance."

Dispatch came back. "2 Lincoln 6 – the want on the bicyclist and description?"

The beach cruiser sailed onto the sidewalk, then jumped off the curb going west on Cereza Way. It crossed in front of a gardener's truck, which screeched to a halt in the middle of the intersection, causing lawnmowers and leaf blowers to pile up against the cab. Three men in the front of the truck yelled at the bicyclist and, seeing Scott's black and white squealing around the corner, pointed at the bicycle.

He would have liked to track down the gardeners as witnesses later, but he was too busy driving to note the license plate of their truck. Right now, the guy on the bike was the top priority.

Scott spun the steering wheel, trying to match turns with the bike.

The bicyclist turned his head to see the patrol car pull even with him. Eyes narrowing, he yanked at the handlebars to maneuver through an open gate and shoot down the walkway into an apartment complex too narrow for a car to follow. He was going too fast, Scott realized, an instant before the bike crashed into the corner post. The bicyclist scrambled to his feet and bolted, leaving the bicycle and taking the pillowcase.

Scott picked up his microphone and shouted, "2 Lincoln 6 – out on foot, 530 Cereza."

Scott flipped the record button on his body camera as he sprinted from the car. He could hear dispatch. "Any unit in the area of 530 Cereza, 2 Lincoln 6 is requesting assistance, possible foot pursuit. Unknown suspect description or want."

"2 Lincoln 12," came Rebecca's voice on the radio, "ETA two minutes."

"2 Lincoln 6," Scott said, panting with exertion, "west through the apartment complex, male Hispanic wearing grey and black."

He picked up his pace, keeping his eye on the suspect.

Still frantically running, the suspect came to an eight-foot cinder block wall at the rear of the apartment building and stopped. He looked left and right, then threw the pillowcase over and stretched up to place his hands on top of the wall.

With a yelp of pain, he jerked them away. "Ow, shit!"

In many economically challenged communities, like the area around Del Rey and Cereza, residents were unable to afford barbed wire to keep thieves from scaling their walls. Instead, they found another way to discourage people from jumping onto their property. They'd collect glass bottles—and in this neighborhood, empty beer bottles were always in ample supply. They would break the bottles and leave glass shards on the tops of the cinder block walls. Police called this ghetto fencing.

The suspect moved a couple feet to his left and eased his palms onto the top of the wall. He flicked aside a large piece of glass, then pulled himself up and over.

Scott shouted their direction of travel into his radio, as the suspect disappeared over the block wall.

Scott was familiar with ghetto fencing around the neighborhood. He had plenty of scars on his hands and forearms as reminders, and most of his annual uniform allowance went to paying for pants and shirts it had ruined. As the suspect had done, Scott eased his hands onto the top of the wall. Avoiding any large shards of glass, and with his hands firmly atop the wall, he pulled himself halfway up. He stopped short to look over the wall, not wanting to rush over in case the suspect was waiting to ambush him on the other side.

Seeing nothing, he eased himself up, scraping his gun belt against the wall.

On the other side, a narrow concrete walkway separated the wall and the next apartment building. Scott looked right and left. To the right, towards the street, was a chain link gate with a lock on it. To the left, the walkway emptied into a parking lot.

Jumping off the wall, Scott saw two gold necklaces, several crumpled twenty-dollar bills, an empty canvas pistol case and the controller for an Xbox. Seeing the empty gun case, he drew his weapon. He grabbed his hand-held radio from his belt and ran toward the parking lot, shouting into the radio, "2 Lincoln 6 – northwest towards 6th and Chestnut, suspect's possibly armed."

The emergency radio tone sounded, limiting radio traffic to the officers involved in the chase.

Scott glanced down, putting his radio back into its holder. The last thing he wanted to do was lose his radio during a foot chase and have no way of letting other officers know his location. When he looked back up, the suspect was right in front of him.

Shit. He must have stopped behind the corner of the apartment.

The man swung the pillowcase, hitting Scott squarely in the face. The impact knocked him backwards, eyes watering, a burst of pain in his nose. The Glock tumbled out of his hand and clattered across the asphalt into the parking lot.

Flat on his back, Scott shook his head and rolled onto his stomach. He felt dazed, but he knew he needed to get to his feet as fast as he could. He shook his head to clear the haze and saw the man reaching into the pillowcase.

Instinctively, Scott grabbed at his holster. Empty. His pistol was gone. With a chill, he remembered it slipping from his hands.

Shit.

Climbing to his feet, he eyed the suspect. After swinging the pillowcase, the man had taken a few steps backwards and now stood ten feet away, his hand on the wooden grip of a revolver. He tugged to free the weapon from a tangle of cords in the pillowcase.

Scott's mouth went dry. He never said it, but he'd always considered officers who carried a back-up pistol a little too gung ho or maybe lacking in confidence with their primary weapon.

But right now, he would have given anything for a second gun in his back pocket.

It was too far to rush the man. But Scott knew he had to do something, or he was going to die. He pointed his finger, raised a thumb to form a pretend pistol, and pointed at the man. "Drop it or I'll shoot!"

The man stopped short and lifted his arms to surrender, dropping the pillowcase. The revolver spilled out of the pillowcase and lay at his feet. Cocking his head to the side, he lowered his hands and stared at Scott's.

"What the fuck?" he said. Then a vicious smile tugged at the man's lips. Damn. He'd realized Scott was unarmed. Moment of truth. Would he fight or run?

For a moment, he blinked at Scott's finger pistol. Then he bolted west through the parking lot, Scott close behind. At the west end of the lot, he approached another eight-foot cinder block wall. Without hesitation, the suspect leaped at the wall, grabbing the top at the same time Scott's hands closed on his legs.

They hadn't run far, under a quarter-mile. Scott was in decent enough shape, jogging four or five times a week. However, the adrenaline overload he felt from losing his gun and almost getting shot was starting to wear off. Suddenly, he felt exhausted, out of breath, and soaked in sweat.

From the suspect's gasp of pain, Scott knew slivers of broken bottles were cutting into the man's hands. Muscles quivering, Scott pulled harder at his legs.

Scott knew he didn't have to overpower the man, just hang onto him until help arrived. Judging from the traffic coming from his radio, assistance was only seconds away. But he was not going to let someone else handcuff the guy who'd tried to kill him. Scott wanted to hear his own cuffs ratcheting tightly around the man's wrists. He'd gotten himself in this situation; he could also get himself out.

The suspect pushed off the wall as Scott threw him to the ground. Their combined momentum sent both of them crashing backwards into the parking lot. Scott heard a cracking thud. Then the man lay still on top of him.

Scott took a deep breath, thankful for the brief respite, readying himself for the fight about to ensue. He kept his arms around the suspect's legs for a moment, waiting for him to start fighting, but he didn't move. Must be knocked out.

Scott rolled him off and fumbled for his handcuffs.

People were swarming out of the apartment complex. A man yelled, "Get off him. Why'd ya do that? Ya killed him!"

Scott looked down at the man's face. A single drop of blood glistened below each nostril. The suspect's eyes were open and unblinking, his mouth open and jaw slack. The back of his head rested awkwardly on a concrete parking bumper in a thick pool of blood. Scott stopped handcuffing the man.

He'd put the cuffs back on his belt when Rebecca ran up with her pistol in hand and Scott's Glock tucked inside her Sam Browne belt. She looked down at the suspect. "Fuck, this guy won't be running from us anymore." She reached into her belt and handed Scott his pistol.

The gathering crowd screamed, "Look, look, they're planting a gun!"

An anxious flutter settled in Scott's stomach. This was bad, very bad. Especially in light of the department's latest witch hunt.

Rebecca picked up her handheld radio. "2 Lincoln 12 – suspect in custody. Requesting a supervisor." She noticed the cuts on Scott's hands and again spoke on her radio. "Roll paramedics for 2 Lincoln 6 and the coroner for the suspect."

As the crowd became more agitated, Rebecca transmitted on her radio a third time, "2 Lincoln 12 – request additional units for crowd control."

Dispatch replied, "2 Lincoln 12 – paramedics have been notified and additional units are in route. Watch commander is responding."

Still out of breath, Scott turned to Rebecca, pointed to the far corner of the parking lot. "Go back over there, look for a white pillowcase. Find his gun."

She looked at the deceased suspect, then across at the seething crowd. "I'm not leaving you alone. As soon as the next unit arrives, I'll go get the gun."

Scott nodded. She was right, but every second they waited was a chance for the gun to disappear.

Three long minutes later, officers began arriving. Seeing Blakesley, Rebecca called out, "Come with me!" She grabbed him by the arm and lowered her voice. "We gotta find a gun and pillowcase somewhere in this parking lot."

Blakesley said, "We'll look, but the chances of 'em still being here are slim and none."

Rebecca caught Scott's gaze and said, "We've gotta try."

Again, she picked up her handheld radio. "2 Lincoln 12 - I need this crowd moved out of the parking lot and yellow crime scene tape put up."

John finally arrived and barked at Rebecca and Blakesley. "I'll take over here. Go do what you need to do."

Scott paced and watched as the others spent the next half hour double- and triple-checking the parking lot. They even had the paramedics put up a ladder, allowing them to climb over the wall Scott had chased the suspect over. But no matter how many times Rebecca and Blakesley retraced the route or how hard they looked, they couldn't find the pillowcase or gun.

A detective wearing a suit and wraparound Oakley sunglasses holding an iPad told Scott, "After you go to the station and give a statement, go home. Report to Captain Dickerson's office tomorrow at ten AM sharp. There's no need to be in uniform when you see the Captain."

Scott had been involved in three shootings in the course of his eight-year career. Two of them had resulted in fatalities. They'd all been righteous shootings, but after each one, he was ordered to take a week off and see the department psychologist. He knew the drill. But this time was different.

He thought again of his father, who had retired from the Long Beach Police Department six years before Scott started the police academy. He'd spent over thirty years working the same downtown beat as Scott and never fired his weapon, even though the department had a shooting policy far less restrictive than it was today. How could a city change so much, in such a short time?

He ran a thumb over the handle of his weapon, but it gave him no comfort. Now that the adrenaline had left him, he was aware of his scraped hands and throbbing nose. More than that, he knew he'd been hung out to dry. The order to report to the Captain's office in civilian clothes was the the giveaway. The department was distancing itself from him.

They were treating him the same as Rebecca and Manolito.

17

...you're not old enough

Gaston felt like shit.

Things were starting to go his way at the police department, but not fast enough. Getting any cops in front of a jury was still months away. At least he would be standing when it was over, not like what they did to Peter...

He parked his Audi outside the stables and ambled in, dust on the hems of his slacks and horse shit covering the bottom of his loafers. Several bales of hay were stacked in the aisle. He pulled three bales inside a stall, making himself a comfortable seat. After a moment, he went back out and retrieved a saddle and blanket. When he'd secured the stall gate, he loosened his tie, plopped down, and cracked the seal on his bottle.

Banjo, the bay roan he exclusively rented for his cowboy mounted shoots, whinnied and bobbed his head. Gaston took a deep pull of whiskey and looked up at the horse. "How's my only friend in the whole world, you old bag of bones?" He rubbed the horse's nose. "I thought you needed some company."

Banjo took a step forward and pressed his nose into Gaston's chest, trying to see if the bottle was another treat.

"We're not riding today," Gaston said. "I'm here to cheer you up." He pushed Banjo's head out of the way.

He was more than halfway into the bottle, now lying on his back, head resting on the saddle, with pieces of hay stuck all over his white button-down shirt. His elbow rested on one of the hay bales while he rubbed the underside of Banjo's chin. He looked into the horse's eyes. "Do you think Peter would have liked riding?"

Banjo didn't offer his opinion.

Gaston drank some more. "Well, I like riding, gives me a chance to talk with you. Even when I finish with those stupid cops and stick it to the gun idiots, I'm still gonna ride. Trail ride, no more cowboy bullshit."

The horse licked at the bottle and Gaston pulled it away. "Sorry, buddy, you're not old enough."

He immediately teared up and regretted saying those words. That was the last thing Peter ever said to him.

They were walking home from school and David had wanted to try smoking a cigarette. Peter tried talking him out of it, because no clerk would sell a sixth-grader a pack of smokes. That was what the other kids called them. They all had Marlboros.

The plan was to go into the corner market, have Peter distract the guy behind the counter by giving him the wrong change for a 3 Musketeers bar. David would be at the other end of the counter, reach around and snatch a pack of cigarettes off the display rack.

The whole way to the store, Peter tried talking David out of it, but David wanted to be cool. He wanted to be the Marlboro man, whoever that was. Finally, Peter went along with it when David promised to pay for the candy bar.

They saw the police cars parked around the corner, and one of the cops waving his arms at them, but they hadn't done anything wrong, not yet anyway, so they went inside the store. That's when they knew why the cop had tried to stop them. A man was holding up the store.

The robber wore a black ball cap pulled low and big sunglasses hiding his face. He had two customers sitting on the floor in front of the counter where David was supposed to reach for the cigarettes. He made the boys sit on the floor with the others, then forced the clerk to open the register and unlock the night deposit box.

The police had been staging, waiting for the crook to come outside, but when David and his younger brother got past them, the officers panicked and rushed into the store. Four officers made a dynamic entry and there was a brief exchange of gunfire. One of the officers staggered backwards, hit, and the robber fell dead.

Then David looked at Peter and saw the red dot start to spread from the center of his yellow happy-face T-shirt. As if in slow motion, Peter slumped sideways, his eyes already glazing. The doctors said he'd died instantly, and David hoped to God that was true.

He tipped up the bottle and drained it. His cheeks were wet, and he could hardly talk. "Imagine, Banjo, dying in a liquor store and never know what it's like to get drunk?"

Banjo rested his head on Gaston's shoulder and the empty fell to the ground. "Peter would have been a good rider." He wiped his face with his shirt sleeve. "Peter, I fucking swear. Those cops are going to pay for what they did to you."

He stretched out on the hay bales and pulled the horse blanket over himself. "Good night, you old bag of bones. Hope you feel better."

◻

18

…he just killed Jesus

For the first time since John could remember, it was a slow day, no major crimes and not too many radio calls. He parked his black and white and strolled along the pier, talking with tourists and fishermen along the way. Then he noticed the time and returned to his patrol car to call Scott. "Are you at the station yet?"

"Be there in ten minutes."

"I told Donna Fisher you'd be coming in and need her help. She'll be at Dickerson's office in a couple minutes."

Donna Fisher was one of three attorneys the Long Beach Police Officer's Union had on retainer to represent officers in criminal and administrative proceedings.

Scott cleared his throat. "I appreciate it, Sarge, but I don't want an attorney there."

John shook his head in disbelief. "What are you talking about? You saw what they did to Mano and Rebecca."

"Yeah, I know," he said. "I was talking with my dad and he said the best way to approach Dickerson is straight away—man to man. Dickerson hates when officers hide behind their attorney. He tries to give them the maximum discipline when they go into his office with a lawyer."

John said, "I hope you know what you're doing. I'm afraid you'll be walking into a hornet's nest without her."

Quickly, as if he wanted to get off the phone, Scott said, "I'm parking my truck now. Call Donna back and tell her not to come."

"You got it, buddy." Then, a little too casually, John asked, "Are you still planning on coming over for dinner tonight?"

***

Scott stood outside Captain Dickerson's office. Carol sat at her desk sipping coffee. She gave him a sympathetic smile. "You better go right in. The captain's expecting you."

He waited to be acknowledged before entering. Jason Dickerson looked up from his paperwork. "Come in, Scott, come in." He shook Scott's hand, guided him into a chair and closed the door. "How's that old man of yours?"

"He's doing fine. He and Mom have season tickets again this year for the Dodgers, and they're spending a lot of time at the stadium."

Scott had first met Dickerson when he was a teenager, hanging out at the Long Beach pistol range. Sergeant Dickerson would give him five dollars to shoot his monthly qualifying score and clean his gun. Scott thought he did it to be nice, but after he joined the department, realized Dickerson did it because he didn't like shooting and always cut corners. Dickerson would have been fired if his captain had known he went all those years without qualifying at the range. Still, he'd always been decent to Scott. Surely, that meant something.

Dickerson glanced at the papers on his desk. "That brings us to this messy business from last night. Internal Affairs and the chief's office have been going over your statement with a finetooth comb and frankly, it doesn't look good."

Scott recoiled in his chair. "What do you mean, it doesn't look good? My attorney prepared the statement. There shouldn't be any problems."

"Well, you're only seeing it from your perspective. The chief and I have to look at the big picture. Have you seen the news?"

"No, sir."

Dickerson reclined in his chair and pointed a remote control at a portable television at the far end of his office. "This is a little something the geeks in IT put together."

A blue screen appeared on the television and a DVD began playing.

"Happening Now News. We go live to Long Beach, where some residents are saying the police murdered another unarmed minority. On the scene, reporter Connie Jones has been talking with residents in Long Beach. Connie, what have you learned?"

Connie's layered blond hair was perfectly in place, and she looked concerned. "Thank you, Brad. Residents of this close-knit Long Beach community are saying Jesus Camacho was a quiet family man, poised for great things."

The scene on the television changed to Connie standing on a front porch, talking with a woman standing halfway in her apartment, holding open the security screen so she could be seen by the camera. The woman said, "Jesus had a job interview today. He was a little nervous, so he got on his bicycle to exercise. That's when the police saw Jesus and killed him for doing nothing. Jesus never did nothing."

Scott felt paralyzed. There was no way anybody could think he did anything illegal or out of policy. Why didn't this bleeding-heart reporter go interview the people whose house was burglarized? Ask them what a nice guy this Camacho was. Why didn't she show this guy's rap sheet? Two convictions for burglary, three for petty theft, one for assault, and he was awaiting trial on an auto theft charge...

And I'm the bad guy?

The scene on the television switched again. This time, Connie Jones was in a mahogany-paneled office. "I'm in the office of prominent civil rights attorney David Gaston."

Scott immediately recognized Gaston as 'Dusty Dave,' the cowboy action shooter who'd challenged John at the range.

Gaston said, "There's a custom and practice at the Long Beach Police Department of corruption, abuse, brutality, civil rights violations and assault under the color of authority. This is just the latest example."

Gaston puffed out his chest like a tom turkey in mating season. "My office has been investigating a string of assaults and killings by Long Beach Police Officers of unarmed minority members. We have uncovered some startling facts. Blacks, Hispanics and gays have become the favorite target of the Long Beach Police Department. And Connie, I use the term target, because the group of officers making these vicious attacks have collateral assignments at the pistol range, where they practice shoot-to-kill tactics. Furthermore, these same officers are teaching this culture of misconduct to new police academy recruits." He paused to let the implications sink in. "We need to break the circle of violence."

"Specifically, what have you learned about the Jesus Camacho incident?"

"Well, Connie," Gaston said, "the Camacho family has retained my services to represent them during this difficult time. I might add, this case is so horrendous, I'm representing the

Camacho family for no money upfront." Another pause. Scott figured this one was to give the audience time to register what a swell guy Gaston was. "This latest killing fits the pattern precisely. Here we see a young Hispanic family man out exercising, improving himself, when Officer Smith pursues him and immediately tries to run him down."

Gaston spread his hands in an expansive gesture. "Again, we have a lone minority member with no witnesses nearby, and that's when these officers are striking. Fearing for his life, Jesus tries to get away from this out-of-control officer. The officer puts out on the radio that Jesus is armed, signing his death warrant for any Long Beach Police officer to kill him on sight. And this is a very important fact. At the same time Officer Smith broadcast that Jesus was armed, Officer Smith turned off his body camera. Now, there's no witnesses and no video."

Connie looked aghast. To Scott, it looked like she was auditioning for a Hollywood casting agent. Cue concern. Cue righteous indignation. She shook her head as if she couldn't believe what she was hearing. "Are you saying Officer Smith turned off his body camera intentionally?"

"That's exactly what I'm saying. And the facts in this case are irrefutable. After chasing him down, Officer Smith pile-drove Jesus' head into a concrete parking bumper, killing him instantly. After he was dead, witnesses saw another officer—an officer who the city just paid out a large settlement for her racial profiling— handed Officer Smith a gun." He shook his head. Clucked his tongue. "This is one of the most egregious cases my office has ever seen. These are rogue lawmen."

A photograph of Scott in uniform standing next to his father filled the screen. Gaston said, "And this Officer Smith, he just killed Jesus."

He used the English pronunciation of Jesus, not the Spanish pronunciation. Scott felt his neck grow hot.

Scott's picture disappeared from the television, and Connie looked into the camera. "There you have it. Another killing of an unarmed man by the Long Beach Police Department. This is Connie Jones, Happening Now News, reporting live from downtown Long Beach."

Dickerson clicked off the remote. "He made some serious accusations."

Scott said, "Those are half-truths and flat out lies. It's crazy! I killed Jesus! I intentionally turned off my body camera. What a bunch of bull! I'm telling you, Captain, the guy had a gun. I lost mine when he hit me, and I never did pile-drive or anything else with his head. He kicked himself off the wall, fell on top of me and hit his head. It could have been me who died in that parking lot as easily as him."

Dickerson said, "We all know this attorney's a slime-ball, trying to make a name for himself. But I've gotta tell you, the chief's very troubled. This thing's not gonna go away by itself. The chief wants to get out in front of it. This whole thing about

Rebecca handing you a gun while you're standing over Camacho's body and calling this guy Jesus. The attorney makes a very powerful argument and a lot of people are listening to him."

Scott blinked. "You know I'm not a bad cop. I wouldn't do anything anyone else on the department wouldn't do."

Dickerson pointed back at the television. "The first thing we're gonna do is place all members of the range staff on paid leave while the investigation is underway. I'm also suspending your ancillary duties as range instructors at the academy."

Scott couldn't believe what he was hearing. "Are you talking about all of us, or just me?

He said, "All of you. I haven't told the others, but I've had them called to my office. You're all on suspension from your regular duties and from teaching at the range until this whole thing gets resolved."

Scott felt a fire building in the base of his skull, moving up the back of his head. "It was dumb luck his head hit the parking bumper. You can't possibly believe anything this sleazeball is saying."

"I've already asked the range staff from the Orange County Sheriff's Department to take over your duties at the range."

Scott wanted to scream Fuck you! at the top of his voice, but he knew this was not the time or place to contradict Dickerson and have a charge of insubordination leveled against him. He wished he'd listened to John and had the attorney with him.

"Sounds like it's a done deal," he said quietly.

Dickerson nodded. "Okay, there's one more thing. I'm gonna have a couple of our homicide guys follow you home. You're gonna let them look around and see if there's a second gun Rebecca gave to you during your scuffle."

Scott blinked. "Wait a goddamn minute. You think I'm gonna let you search my house?"

The captain's smug expression said he did indeed.

Scott took a breath. Sweat rolled from his armpits. He knew it was a mistake, but he couldn't take it any longer. "Captain, I came in here without an attorney as a sign of respect. It's evident I made a terrible mistake." Voice shaking with rage, he said, "If I'm on suspension and subject to discipline, I'm not talking without legal representation. You don't have permission to go anywhere near my house."

For a moment, Dickerson held Scott's gaze. Was there a message in the captain's eyes? A challenge? An ounce of regret? Then Dickerson averted his gaze. "I'm sorry you feel that way," he said. He stood up and opened the door to his office.

***

Driving home, Scott wondered why the department was treating him this way. He was a straight arrow, always had been.

He followed the rules. He was faithful to his wife. And the evidence clearly showed he'd done everything right, regardless of what that attorney and news reporter said.

Twenty-minutes later, he turned onto his street. Two Long Beach black and whites and a detective unit were parked in front of his house. A Crime Scene Investigations van sat in his driveway and Lieutenant Willie Jackson stood in front of his house talking with Scott's wife.

Lisa was visibly upset. Her breathing was labored, and a tear ran down her cheek. As Scott got out of the car, he heard her her say to Lieutenant Jackson, "Why couldn't you wait until Scott came home? It's not like we're hiding anything."

Scott slammed the car door.

Lisa looked up. "Thank goodness you're home!"

Scott walked over and put an arm around her. "Are the boys okay? What's going on?"

"Travis and Joseph are in school. The department has a search warrant, and they're going through everything. What's going on, Scott?"

Scott's eyes narrowed. To Jackson, he said, "I want to see that warrant. I just came from the captain's office and I told him he didn't have permission to search my house or take any of my guns."

Two crime scene technicians came out of the house, each carrying a cardboard box full of pistols. Each pistol had an evidence tag attached.

Jackson shrugged. Handed over the warrant.

Scott read it through once, then read it again, trying to reconcile the time and date written at the top. 8:10 this morning. Almost two hours before his meeting with Dickerson.

"That son of a bitch," Scott muttered.

He'd been a Long Beach policeman for eight years, and his dad had served another thirty. In all that time, the department had served search warrants at the homes of only two other officers. Once when an officer was caught in an FBI sting, agreeing to kill another man's wife. And once when an officer was recorded on camera stealing six kilos of cocaine from the property and evidence room.

It felt like a punch to the gut. The department thought no more of him than a hit-man or a junkie.

"Hey." Lieutenant Jackson stuck out his hand. "We're finished. I hope there's no hard feelings."

Scott turned away, ignoring the lieutenant's outstretched hand.

Fuck the niceties. He'd always followed the rules, and look what it had gotten him.

Maybe John and the others were right. It was time for a little pushback.

Arl Farris

19

Gee, thanks, Professor

Jenny had her mom take the kids to her house for the evening. At five o'clock, the range staff had gathered around their two backyard patio tables drinking beer, iced tea and water. Jenny made guacamole and set out two bowls of chips along with cut celery and carrot sticks, while John and the others discussed their dilemma. After Scott's fatal foot pursuit and the vicious spin by Happening Now News, their positions had worsened overnight. Dickerson had responded to the PR nightmare with predictable spinelessness, placing the whole team on suspension. If Gaston kept up his crusade, they might never be going back.

Blakesley said, "The captain tells me Gaston's filed a complaint for unlawful detention and assault under the color of authority for arranging a rookie to drive a wino for breakfast. Can you believe it?" His grip tightened on his beer bottle. "I've been with the department over twenty years, never been late for work, never even been written up for anything. I tell ya, the department's gone off the rails."

Mano grimaced, and Rebecca piped in. "Yeah, and you know what he tells me?" She lowered her voice and stuck out her chest in a mocking imitation of Captain Dickerson. "He goes, 'I don't need to remind you of our recent accusations of disparaging treatment of minorities. When you saw Scott's gun lying in the parking lot and he was on top of a dead Hispanic kid, why didn't you stop what you were doing and wait for your supervisor?'"

John shook his head, imagining the ramifications of leaving the gun unsecured. He took a sip of his iced tea and said, "Things are gonna get a lot tougher before this whole thing plays out."

There was a moment of glum silence. Then Jenny sat her glass of wine down and flashed a strained smile. "I'm gonna go inside and get the hot dogs and hamburgers, if you wanna start the barbecue?"

As the door closed behind her, Scott said, "I can't believe Jenny's recovery. If someone met her today, they'd never know we almost lost her a few months ago."

John looked towards the house. "She's quite a gal."

Scott dipped a chip in guacamole and said, too casually, "We all love Jenny and she is definitely one of us, but I thought you said no spouses?"

"I did." He looked at Blakesley and back at Scott. "I know Anita and Lisa could be trusted with anything we might say tonight. But for the sake of your kids, we should try and shelter your wives as much as possible. That's why I said they couldn't come. But Jenny... if we have any chance of pulling this off, we're gonna need her."

Blakesley raised his eyebrows. "Pull what off? What can we do while we're on suspension?"

"Let's just lay it all out first," John said. "This can play out one of three ways. First, they could say we did everything alleged in the complaints. We did it with malice and fire us."

Rebecca grabbed a handful of tortilla chips. "That's not gonna happen. There's not a single thing in those complaints that's true."

Blakesley shook his head. "It's no longer about the truth. Political correctness has taken the place of truth. The brass showed us the truth doesn't matter."

John continued, "The next thing they could do is keep us away from the department for a year. When this whole thing blows over, find the allegations in the complaints to be unfounded. Then bring us back as if nothing's ever happened."

Blakesley knocked back the rest of his Corona. "You're just full of good news, tonight. There's no way I could sit at home for a year, waiting this thing out."

"Besides," Mano added, "I don't think Gaston's the kind of lawyer not to follow up."

John ignored the interruptions. "The third option—and I think the most realistic—is they'll retire us. They'll have a doctor write a psych report stating we have PTSD and the department gets rid of us on a medical retirement. The chief has a big press conference where he announces the investigation's complete and all officers involved have been dealt with. He would say personnel rules prohibit him from stating what happened or what discipline has been handed down, but the officers have been separated from the department. That way, the chief can say he cleaned house and avoid any future claims of corruption."

Rebecca's fist clenched, crushing the chip in her hand. "Retiring us would be the most corrupt thing he could do."

John said, "You're thinking in practical terms. The chief lives in a political world. Getting rid of a problem, or I should say five problems, no matter what it costs the city to pay our pensions and settle with Gaston, is a real possibility."

Manolito added salt to the chips. "This is all mildly interesting, but we still haven't decided if we're gonna do anything. If the five of us aren't committed to working together, then this evening turns out to be just a nice night with friends. But if we commit, then this is the first day of a great adventure."

Blakesley dropped his empty bottle in the trash. The loud clank made Mano jump.

John pretended not to notice. He'd seen it take months after shooting incident for a cop to stop startling at loud noises. Sometimes it took years.

Blakesley glanced at Mano. "Sorry, man." He looked back at John. "It's gonna be hard to do much, since we don't have access to the department."

Jenny came out through the sliding glass doors carrying two platters of hamburgers, hot dogs and buns. "Honey, it's time for the manly job of cooking the meat."

John jumped up and met her at the barbecue. "About six to eight minutes and these beauties will be on the table."

"That's my man." He swatted her bottom as she turned to go back into the kitchen.

Rebecca came up to the barbecue and quietly asked John, "Has Scott said anything to you? The last time we talked, he wasn't having any of it. Quite frankly, I was a little surprised to see his truck here."

John said, "He's not said anything to me. I really don't know what he's gonna do. Whatever it is, we'll respect his decision."

Jenny carried out a basket of condiments and paper plates just as John brought the hamburgers and hot dogs to the tables. As if by mutual agreement, they set aside serious matters and ate and joked through dinner. When they finished, Jenny went into the house and returned with more drinks. The sun had set, and John turned on the gas fire pit. They moved their chairs around the fire. Rebecca brought the chips.

Scott said, "Ya know, I've been doing a lot of thinking. Yesterday, my mind was pretty much made up. But then a parolee nearly kills me, some civil rights attorney tells the world I killed Jesus and the department executed a search warrant on my house. They took all my guns."

Rebecca stopped eating mid-chip. "They what?"

Scott used his hands to emphasize his words. "When I was in the captain's office for a ten AM meeting, he had Lieutenant Jackson serving a search warrant on my house."

Rebecca looked like she'd been slapped with a dead fish. "Oh, my God, Scott! What'd Lisa do?"

"What could she do? It was a search warrant, she had to let 'em in."

"Did they take any of your pistols?"

"Every one of them, except for the one I had with me."

Manolito shook his head in disbelief. "Searching your house... That's a declaration of war."

Scott took a sip from his plastic cup. "I've never felt so humiliated. You bet, I am one hundred percent in, and Lisa stands by whatever we come up with tonight."

John gripped Jenny's hand and looked each officer in the eye. "Okay, there's no going back. We're a go." He let out a breath and lifted a glass of tea to his lips. Only the rattle of the ice in his glass betrayed his anxiety. He drank nearly the entire glass before setting it down. The others watched intently, and he wondered if they could see his nervous resolve.

Jenny reached around and rubbed his back to give him encouragement.

He looked around the circle of chairs again. "I know this may sound crazy, but we're gonna rob a bank."

All but Jenny broke out into hysterical laughter. Jenny made eye contact with John and imperceptibly nodded for him to continue.

"Wait a minute." Rebecca looked from John to Jenny and then back again. "You're joking, right? I almost had two bank robbers shoot me earlier this week and now you're saying we're gonna rob a bank? We should become like those guys?"

John shrugged. "You gotta break a few eggs if you wanna make an omelette."

Rebecca stopped laughing. "That's not a plan," she said dismissively. She turned to look around the group, then looked back at John, her expression disappointed and wary. "Don't tell me this is the best you've got?"

"Okay, you need to hear me out." He waited for them to stop talking. "If you don't like it, game over. But it's the only way we get this civil rights attorney off our backs so we can return to the department."

Scott said, "You know, a criminal conspiracy isn't committed by merely hypothetically discussing committing a crime. A criminal conspiracy is complete only if one of us takes an action towards the implementation of the crime discussed."

Manolito lifted his hands to express contempt at Scott. "Gee, thanks, Professor."

Scott replied, "I just want everyone to know where we stand. I'm pissed at the department, the city, the television news reports and the civil rights attorney, but I don't wanna go to prison."

John nodded. "Scott brings up a valid point. There's nothing illegal with a couple friends getting together and imagining doing something illegal. It only becomes a crime when and if we start taking action to commit it."

Blakesley said, "We're all veteran cops. We understand what criminal conspiracy is. I don't know about the rest of you, but I want to hear what John has to say."

"Thanks." John splayed his hands across his thighs and drew in a long breath. "I've been spending a lot of sleepless nights thinking about this. Any idiot can rob a bank, and we've arrested our share of bank robbers. However... all the people we've arrested for bank robbery have either been mainline drug users or some other kind of whack job. Given what each of us knows about law enforcement, how robbery cases are prosecuted, and the rules of evidence, I think we can get away with it. Not only that, but with a little luck we can pin the crime on our friendly neighborhood civil rights attorney, Gaston."

"But why rob a bank?" Scott asked. "Isn't that a little extreme?"

Manolito leaned forward. "No, it totally makes sense!" He looked around the group. "You know when you're driving around in your patrol car and nothing's going on? What are you doing?"

Blakesley restrained a laugh. "You're out collecting women's phone numbers, and the rest of us are hiding from the sergeant."

Mano chuckled. "No, really. We're imagining we're burglars, car thieves or bank robbers. We think how we'd go about robbing a liquor store or a bank. Then we look for people carrying out our plans and we arrest 'em. As policemen, I'm sure we've thought how to rob each bank in Long Beach, hundreds if not thousands of times."

Everyone nodded in agreement, and Jenny looked quizzically at John. "Officers hide from you? How sad."

John smiled. "We're facing a unique set of circumstances where people are going to be dressed in costumes and carrying guns, in a place where few people know each other's real names. Using our knowledge and skill set, we can get away with it."

Rebecca said, "Yeah, but why would we risk going to prison for a few thousand dollars, assuming we get that much?"

He said, "You aren't following me. We're not gonna keep any of the money. We're gonna give it all to Gaston and have him get caught with it."

Blakesley pulled the cap off another bottle. "Let me see if I understand this. Your plan's for us to rob a bank, so we can give all the money to the attorney who got us suspended from the police department in the first place?"

"Exactly." John nodded. They were getting there.

Blakesley gave a mocking laugh. "Well, if you put it that way…"

"Okay, listen," John said. "Gaston'll be only a few miles from our bank, dressed in a cowboy getup and carrying guns. If we rob the bank and people in the bank think they've seen Gaston, we're halfway there. We plant evidence from the bank on Gaston or in his car. He gets prosecuted and his trumped-up cases against us go away."

Manolito said, "There's two things all crooks think; they're smarter than the cops and they can get away with it."

John agreed. "That may be true, but we are the cops. And we're gonna try and get caught. Well, have Gaston get caught."

They were silent so long John was afraid he'd lost them.

Manolito grinned, and John let out a breath. Relief washed through him.

Mano said, "I don't know about the rest of you, but I'm willing to try it. We all know tactics and the rules of evidence. I think we know how to get away with it. Besides, the best policemen are always thinking like crooks anyway."

Blakesley said, "Half the people who see the police think we're crooks, not to mention the brass doesn't trust us. Might as well give 'em what they ask for. I guess I'm in too."

Scott looked at John. "What makes you so sure Gaston'll be near the bank on a particular day and time, armed and in costume?"

"That's the easy part. He'll be at the End of Trail shooting match."

He explained what he and Blakesley had learned from Hurricane Heather. When he'd finished, Rebecca turned to Jenny. "Do you think it'll work?"

Jenny nodded. "I'm not a policeman, so I don't know everything you guys know. But John's discussed it with me, and I think it has real potential."

Rebecca folded her arms across her chest. "If you're able to convince Jenny, I guess I'm in too."

Scott said, "Then it's unanimous. So, what now?"

John looked around the circle. "We're gonna turn the tables on Gaston."

***

They wanted to know the details. John assured them he had it all planned. "I've got individual jobs for each of us and things we've gotta do together. Since none of us have to go to work, there shouldn't be any reason we can't do everything. But we gotta act quickly. There's actually a timeline we can't miss."

Manolito asked, "When's all this gonna happen?"

John held up three fingers. "In about three months."

Blakesley said, "We could all be retired by then."

John dismissed the idea. "No, they won't retire us before Gaston's taken a shot at each of us in civil court. Also, the department actually did us a favor suspending us. Otherwise I don't think could pull this off."

Scott said, "Sarge, you're beginning to sound like the captain." He stiffened his back, raised his eyebrows and said, "I'm doing you a favor, Officer Smith."

Everyone laughed, but there was a nervous edge to it. Then Blakesley sighed. "I hope we're as smart as we think we are."

"We are," John said. "I know we are. Now, the first thing everyone needs to do is go on line and become a member of SASS."

Manolito tilted his head. "What's SASS?"

"It's the Single Action Shooting Society. I've been online doing a lot of looking into this group and I suggest everyone does the same. We need to become members, come up with cowboy names, and qualify for the End of Trail."

Rebecca scowled. "We've all won our share of shooting matches. It's not gonna change anything if we win another match while wearing a cowboy hat."

John said, "Gaston'll be competing at the End of Trail match, and we'll also be there. The only way to be able to shoot at it is to be a member of SASS and shoot in three qualifying matches. We're gonna rob the bank during the End of Trail. But, if we fail to qualify, our plan won't work."

Blakesley added, "I've been doing a little online research myself and noticed the last twenty years, End of Trail's been in New Mexico. Gaston's sure to compete in it this year, because it's being held in our own backyard, at the Santa Ana Shooting Complex."

Rebecca frowned. "What if he doesn't qualify?"

"He will," John said, with a cat-that-ate-the-canary smile. "He's done it before. Three years in a row."

Scott said, "I can't believe this whole cowboy thing's been going on at our range and we knew nothing about it."

Blakesley pushed aside his beer. "Obviously, there's lot of ranges out there and we have no idea what's going on at the majority of them. However, we'd have definitely known about cowboy action shooting when End of Trail comes to town.

They're expecting hundreds of shooters and thousands of spectators that weekend."

John said, "The first cowboy match is in three weeks. We need to buy our guns, holsters, ammo, hats and clothes, and get ourselves registered. But before anyone goes out and starts buying their gear, we need to get specific clothes and guns. For this to work, one of us needs to dress exactly like Gaston."

Rebecca held up her hands. "Don't look at me!" She turned to give Mano a speculative look.

Manolito said, "I hate to be the one to insult you, boss, but of all of us, you're the closest in size to him."

"Yeah, I thought the same thing."

Jenny rubbed John's back. "It's okay, dear. I still love you."

Everyone laughed.

John said, "On Saturday, Blakesley and I are gonna go back to the range. All the people who are gonna be shooting at the next match will be practicing. We're gonna find out more about SASS rules and photograph Gaston. That gives me three weeks to buy the same guns and clothes he has."

Scott asked, "What about the rest of us?"

"I need you and Jenny to follow Gaston. Find out where he eats, what cars he owns, where he lives. Get as much information about him as you can. He'd recognize you, so stay low, but he doesn't know Jenny."

Jenny said, "Why do you need to know all that about him? If you're gonna rob a bank and give him all the money, what's it matter the kind of car he drives or anything else?"

Before John could answer, Manolito explained, "The more we learn about him the better chance we have of using something against him." At her baffled look, he added, "Say if every Friday night, he played in a high-stakes poker game and he owes fifty-thousand dollars? Don't you think something like that would be useful?"

"I see what you mean."

Scott asked, "What's up with that guy, anyway?" His gaze swept the group. "Has anyone ever heard of a civil rights attorney owning a gun, let alone going to a range and being part of a shooting league?"

Collectively, they all said, "No."

"I'm telling you, this guy's up to something. Every civil rights attorney I've ever met would give their right arm to do away with the Second Amendment and eradicate all guns if they could. There's no doubt he comes from the same mold as the rest of 'em. If anything, he's even more extreme. There's no way a shyster like that's a real shooter. So what's he really doing at the range?"

John tapped the side of his bottle. "We're drifting off course. Mano, I need you to get red safety vests, and two-ounce spray bottles with water and twenty-five percent bleach solution. You'll also need to get Halloween masks to wear under our cowboy hats."

Manolito said, "I'm glad you brought that up." He took a hesitant breath, then said, "I've never told anybody, but when I get super stressed out, my eyes water and I get tears dripping down my face. It happened after my shooting. With DNA analysis, one tear could land us in prison. But that bleach solution would contaminate any blood, saliva or tears any of us might leave behind."

John hadn't completely formulated his plan, but knew the less time they spent in the bank, the better. "We should be in and out of the bank in two or three minutes. If we're leaving DNA samples behind, something would have gone very wrong. We're each gonna carry the spray bottles for insurance. Better to have them and not need them than to go to prison."

Rebecca asked, "And what about me?"

John said, "I need you to book riding lessons for us. We're gonna need to be efficient at riding horses for this to work. We're gonna have some extreme riding conditions to overcome and I can't have anyone falling off their horse."

Jenny looked in disbelief at John. "Do you have any idea what you're doing? When I was a kid, I spent a few summers on my uncle's farm. You can't learn to ride in a few weeks. It takes years to be good at it. It's not like one of your mule deer hunts where an outfitter puts you on the old grey mare and pulls a string of pack horses up a mountain trail. Riding a horse isn't easy."

John said, "We've got time."

Blakesley chuckled. "Did you know at one time, all Long Beach officers were required to know how to ride a horse?"

Everyone laughed, and Scott added, "No, it's really true. My dad remembered an oldtimer who said when he started, like sixty years ago, he used to patrol the wetlands on horseback."

Rebecca shook her head. "Could you imagine Dickerson on a horse?"

Jenny grinned. "I do think he's a jackass." Rebecca gave her a high-five.

Frustrated, John cut in. "Let's stay focused, guys. Does anyone have any other questions?"

"I do," Scott said. "Just to be clear, you said we have to qualify for the End of Trail match. Are we shooting in it, or are we robbing a bank?"

John pursed his lips. "We're gonna do both."

Rebecca raised her hands. "But I still don't know the plan. The exact plan."

John sighed. "All we need to do for now is register with SASS and complete our assignments. It's too early to worry about the details. I'll handle everything except what I ask you guys to do."

He glanced around the table. "There's one problem I don't have an answer to. We'll need to fire one or two shots from a pistol and not leave any rifling marks on the bullet. Does anyone have any ideas?"

When a firearms company makes a thousand 9mm pistols, all of them look identical. But in the manufacturing process, when the gunsmith is cutting the lands and grooves into the inside of the barrels, there are little machine markings that show up under a microscope. If a single round were fired through each pistol, a crime lab could probably tell what bullet came from what gun in nine hundred and fifty out of the thousand. Since bullets are just a little bit wider in diameter than the inside of the gun's barrel, when a bullet is fired and spiraling down the barrel, the bullet is being squeezed, and the lands and grooves, or rifling, are being cut into the sides of the bullet. The more a gun is fired, the more unique its barrel becomes. Let the same thousand pistols be shot a few dozen times, cleaned once or twice, and they would be able to match all thousand.

Rebecca said, "Don't use a pistol, shoot a shotgun. Shotguns don't have rifling."

Scott said, "I saw a movie where someone made a bullet out of ice and after they shot someone, the bullet melted and there was no evidence."

Manolito said, "I've been reloading ammo for years and there's no way that'd work. No ice bullet could survive the crushing pressure of when the bullet's seated into the brass casing. I don't even think an ice bullet would make it out of the barrel after being crushed again by the rifling."

Rebecca said, "Besides, you can't run around with an ice chest keeping your ice bullet from melting. You know, I don't understand why we're even talking about this." She looked at the others and said, "Before we go too far, let me be perfectly clear. I'm in for robbing a bank, but I'm not gonna have any part of this if we're planning on shooting anyone. That includes shooting Gaston."

Blakesley said, "I totally agree with Rebecca. If we're talking about killing someone, I'm out."

John said, "Absolutely not. No one gets shot, and if we're confronted by a security guard or an off-duty officer in the bank, we can surrender or try to run away, but under no circumstances are we gonna shoot anyone."

She said, "Then why are we talking about rifling?"

John said, "It's impossible to duplicate the rifling marks on a bullet fired from someone else's gun. Therefore, if we can get a gun to fire bullets without leaving any rifling, they could have been fired from any gun. At that point, the focus of evidence is not on the gun, but finding the ammunition."

Manolito said, "Ahh… and if Gaston has the ammunition on him while being investigated for the bank robbery, he wouldn't be able to explain it away. It'd link him directly to the bank robbery."

"Exactly. If it can be done?"

"That's where Jenny comes in." John turned to Jenny. "Sure you're up to this? The doctors haven't cleared you to go back to work, and if you aren't able to help, we can come up with something else."

She placed a hand over John's. "I already told you, I can do it."

Rebecca held a glass to toast. "Here's to us—cops, crooks and cowboys."

◻

20

…John Wayne, not Jeff Bridges

They rode in silence. John drove, and Blakesley thought back to being in high school at Long Beach Poly. Half the kids in his class were scholars and the others were junior criminals. He was bright, but he didn't like hanging out with the nerds. About the only one he could tolerate was Calvin Broadus; even then, they were not real tight. When they were seniors, Calvin started insisting everyone call him Snoop Dogg and that was one bridge too far for Blakesley. The two drifted apart and neither tried reaching out to the other after high school.

He'd come a long way from being a dweeb at Long Beach Poly.

The sound of their tires rolling over the gravel road to the range caused Blakesley to focus his attention on the task ahead. He looked over at John. "I hope you know what you're doing."

John steered around a pothole in the road. "I'm making all this up as we go."

"Nice try. Your nonchalant act doesn't play with me. Jenny told me how you're staying up nights until three and four in the morning working on this. "

John seemed to consider the enormity of his plan. "We've got a lot at stake, and I can't help but think I'm forgetting something. The last thing I want is for this to fail because I overlooked some minor detail."

Thinking of his wife and kids and the possibility of going to jail, Blakesley looked out the side window of the truck. "You can say that again."

John said, "Just get some good photos so we can see what we need to buy. I'll go look for your girlfriend."

Blakeseley rolled his eyes. "Don't even go there. I'm happy with Anita, and I don't need some psycho thinking I have the hots for her."

John parked outside of range 8. "Come on Blakesley, a lady on the side with a name like Hurricane Heather, what could possibly go wrong?"

Unlike their movie and television counterparts, most policemen were faithful to their wives. Blakesley didn't cheat on his wife, and as far as he knew, neither did John, but they never missed an opportunity to harass each other.

Inside the range, they saw several small groups of cowboy shooters on different stages. John pointed to a group of five shooters. "There's Gaston, get some good pix. And that looks like

Hurricane Heather heading to another range with different group. I'll meet you back here after I talk with her."

Blakesley took off and sat in the bleachers with several other people. He went unnoticed, clicking away with his Nikon camera. Using the maximum zoom on his 200 – 500mm lens, he filled each frame with different parts of Gaston's clothes, paying particular attention to buckles, snaps, buttons and any tears or repairs. He took several dozen pictures of Gaston's hat and boots, trying to photograph them from every angle. He took closeups of the attorney's guns—both .38 Specials—and holsters, making sure they showed the way he positioned the ammunition around his belt.

In an hour, he had all the pictures he needed. John returned to the bleachers and sat next to him. Blakesley asked, "Did you have fun with little miss Hurricane Heather?"

"Actually, I did. If you knock the dust off her, she's not so bad. She gave me some useful info."

Blakesley kept looking through the lens of his camera. "I'm sure she's a regular treasure trove of information."

John chuckled. "She told me, at End of Trail, the shooters don't actually compete against each other. They shoot one at a time against the clock, and the shooter with the fastest time wins. But here's the interesting part—"

Blakesley interrupted. "Don't tell me it can get any more fascinating than this?"

John ignored the sarcasm and kept talking. "Apparently, the big draw, other than the trophies of course, are the side matches."

"Side matches?"

"Remember when Hurricane Heather first met us and she made such a big deal about the river range being hidden somewhere out in the sticks?"

Blakesley checked his camera lens for dust. "Some. I think I lapsed into unconsciousness halfway through her description."

John nodded. "It was weird, wasn't it? But now I know why she made such a big deal about it. Different posses will challenge rivals to gunfights. They ride to the river range and shoot it out. I don't mean shoot each other, but they shoot parallel courses to determine who's the best under pressure of head-to-head competition. Any registered posse can challenge any other posse."

Blakesley asked, "And this is good news?"

"Absolutely!" John assured him. "I know how we're gonna do it."

Blakesley took out a cloth and rubbed at the lens. "The more you speak, the less I understand." He lifted the camera and looked back out at the range. The people on the range had finished shooting and started to put away their guns and gear.

John asked, "Are they any good?"

Blakesley shrugged. "There're a couple guys who can shoot, but mostly they're just your typical weekend warriors."

"How about Gaston?"

Blakesley said, "That guy's weird. He's a hell of a shooter, but it's obvious he doesn't wanna be here. He argues with the guys in his posse about everything. I don't know why they hang out with him."

John repeated what Hurricane Heather told him. "Apparently, he buys pretty much everything for the group: ammunition, holsters, range fees. Everything."

"Kind of like he's paying for them to be his friends?"

"Pretty much. She did say something about Gaston that doesn't fit."

"Yeah? What's that?"

Before John could speak, Blakesley held up his hand. "Hold on. This is interesting."

The Lead Bottom Posse had finished putting away their things and were leaving the range. John turned away and Blakesley lowered his head so Hurricane Heather would not spot them in the stands. Gaston remained behind, watching his comrades' retreating backs. When the others were gone, he reached into his range bag and removed two glass vials, each the size of a cigar.

John said, "I think we might be seeing the true Gaston and what he's really doing here."

Gaston bent down, scooped some dirt off the ground and put it into one of the vials. Blakesley refocused his telephoto lens and took another photo.

Looking through the camera, he said, "He's collecting soil samples off the range."

Gaston screwed the cap back on the vial and wrote something on it. He placed the vial back into his range bag and put the empty vial into his shirt pocket. He picked up the range bag and carried it, disappearing into the brush and trees leading to the Santa Ana River.

John said, "I'd sure like to follow him and see what he's doing, but I think we've pressed our luck as it is."

Blakesley snapped the cover on his lens. "I'm telling you, Gaston's a strange guy."

"No, he's devious," John said. "Let's get outta here before he comes back and sees us."

***

In the truck, John said, "It's been a pretty good day. How about I buy your lunch?"

Blakesley laid the camera on the seat next to him. "You're getting me sent to prison. The least you can do is buy me an iced tea and some onion rings."

Ten minutes later, they pulled into Farmer Boys restaurant. They ordered their lunch and waited for their food, placing a plastic number on the side of their table.

Blakesley said, "I'm having problems with my SASS application."

"How so?"

"Well, you know after you fill in your name, address, email and everything, it asks for your handle. I've put in Jessie James, Hop-along Cassidy, Wild Bill Hickok and it says all those names are unavailable. I can't think of a name."

John laughed. "Of course not. Those names were taken a long time ago. You need a name no one else has used." He leaned back and squinted at Blakesley as if he were taking his measure. "How about Typhoon Tom?"

Blakesley stretched his legs under the table. "Good as any. What name did you use?"

"Bighorn Buckaroo."

"Ha," Blakesely said. "Wishful thinking."

A group of men wearing khaki cargo pants, yellow polo shirts with "STAFF" embroidered across their backs and pistols on their side came in the restaurant. One of them called out, "Hey, John," and walked to their table.

John wagged a finger at Blakesley. "Now, be nice to these guys."

"What? I'm always charming."

John stood. "Gary, I'd like you to meet Tom Blakesley." John turned to Blakesley. "This is Gary Newhouse. He works for the Huntington Beach Police Department. They're our replacements teaching at the academy."

Blakesley's smile felt frozen. It wasn't Gary's fault, but the thought of being replaced still rankled.

Gary asked, "Where's Scott? I've gotta get a picture with the guy who killed Jesus."

John chuckled. "I don't know if I'd tease him too much right now. The wound's still pretty fresh and, as you know, we're all on suspension. It's doubtful the department will bring us back."

Gary said, "Well, that's a bunch of bull and we all know it. If you guys need anything, and I mean anything, we'll be there for you. All you need to do is ask."

"Thanks, Gary. There is something, but I don't know..."

Gary waved away John's objection. "What do you need?"

John lowered his voice. "I'm still working something on the QT. I don't have access to the department, and I could really use a vehicle GPS tracking device."

Conspiratorially, Gary looked around the restaurant and took a half step closer to John. "If you'd asked me last week, there'd been no problem. But one of our newer officers with girlfriend problems thought he'd keep an eye on her while he's at work. When the girlfriend discovered the device attached to her car, she drove straight to our station. I'm sure you can imagine how things blew up after that. Now, the captain keeps the trackers locked up in his office. To take a vehicle GPS tracker out of the station, we gotta sign 'em out with the captain and have a case number assigned to an investigation."

John sighed. "That's okay," he said. "I guess that rules out the use of your helicopter too?"

The three men laughed.

Gary stood up to leave, then turned back and said, "Hey, one more thing. What's the big joke in this academy class about a sink and a set of earmuffs?"

***

Jenny giggled. "You look like Rooster Cogburn in the movie True Grit, when he was drunk and about to fall off his saddle."

John grimaced and said, "I hope I look like John Wayne and not Jeff Bridges."

The group was inside a corral, each perched uneasily on a horse that looked a lot taller from on top than it did on the ground. And that was saying something. A woman by the name of Samantha Everhart stood in the center of the circle, glancing at each of them in turn with dubious appraisal. "The first thing you need to do before you can ride" she said, "is learn how to mount and dismount your animal. You all managed the first. Now we're going to try the second. Then we'll practice mounting and dismounting until you're comfortable with that."

Mounting was harder than it looked on TV. In fact, John was pretty sure they'd looked more like a slapstick routine than a John Wayne movie. Rebecca's horse had walked away just as she started to swing a leg over, and she'd landed on her backside with a grunt, her mouth half open in surprise and embarrassment. John's mount was a little more agreeable, but still he'd overestimated the necessary momentum and barely managed to keep from sliding off the other side.

Aided by gravity, dismounting proved to be easier, but no more graceful.

"A horse will do exactly what you want," Samantha said. "You just gotta let 'em know who's in charge."

Shifting in his saddle, Manolito told Scott, "I didn't realize how high up you are on a horse."

Scott's horse turned and began walking. Startled, he said, "Stop! Don't move! Hey, somebody, a little help here, please!"

Samantha called out to Scott, "Use your reins! He'll do what you tell him."

Talking over his shoulder, his voice rising in panic, Scott asked, "Where's the brakes?"

In disgust, Samantha looked at Jenny. "When do they need to be ready?"

After an hour, Samantha told everyone, "That's about it for today. My horses look exhausted and you can use a break. Let's go to the stables, where I can show you how to saddle your animal. After that, your first lesson will be complete, and I'll see everyone back here in a couple days."

Manolito muttered, "All we want to do is ride a horse, not become veterinarians."

***

The next day, with Scott in the passenger seat of her white Honda Accord, Jenny parked in the 330 block of Broadway, across the street from the law office of David Gaston. Fortunately, the law office was across the street from the farmers' market, so finding a place to park was not a problem.

She couldn't believe how giddy she felt at the thought of being a part of a surveillance. Finally, she was getting to see a glimpse of John's world. Of course, since they were planning a heist, she supposed she was seeing it from the other side. Still... she was getting a taste of what his job was like.

They carefully watched every car leaving the underground parking lot, and after two hours, Jenny had decided surveilling someone wasn't nearly as exciting as it looked on TV. She stifled a yawn. Then Scott nudged her. Still looking through his binoculars, he pointed to a two-door silver Audi A5 as it exited the garage and headed east on Broadway. "That's our boy."

Jenny started her car and pulled away from the curb.

"Not so close," he said. "I'm sure he gets tailed quite a bit. Give him plenty of room."

Gaston turned north on Pine and west on 3rd. Scott said, "He's making a big loop around the block to see if anyone's following him. When you get to Pine, turn right. I'm sure he'll go left. We'll cut down 4th, then go down Long Beach Boulevard and hopefully catch up with him as he crosses Broadway at the Boulevard. You better step on the gas so we don't lose him."

Jenny checked her mirrors. "I don't know these streets like you guys. Where do I turn?"

He said, "Just drive. I'll tell you where to go."

She gripped the steering wheel and pressed the accelerator down. She was not used to driving her Accord so hard, but she was up for it.

Scott said, "We're gonna pass Gaston. Don't look at him." He reached down, put his seat in a fully reclined position so he couldn't be seen as they drove past Gaston's Audi.

After turning right, she went north on Pine and right again on 4th. Scott raised his seat and said, "What I wouldn't give to have access to a GPS tracker on his car. We'd watch wherever he goes on my laptop."

Jenny wished so too. There were so many turns Gaston could have made. What if Scott had picked the wrong one? She entered the left turn lane and stopped for the red light at Long Beach Boulevard and Broadway. They saw the Audi go past, westbound on Broadway, and she let out a sigh of relief.

Scott said, "He's gonna drive past the department. This is his safe route. He thinks he can stop at the police department if anyone's following him and they'll leave. If he does stop in front of the police department, don't stop, just keep going."

Like he thought, the Audi pulled over in front of the police department. Scott quickly reclined his seat again and Jenny drove past.

Scott said, "Don't hit your brakes. If he sees your brake lights, he'll know we're following him."

She said, "Can you believe this guy? He's quick to sue the police, but look how fast he runs to them when he thinks he could be in trouble. What a little shit."

"He is special."

Jenny asked, "What should I do?"

"When you come to Atlantic, turn left."

"I'm at Atlantic now."

He raised his seat. "It's okay to use your brakes now. Get into the left turn lane. As soon as you turn left, make a right into the business area and park. We'll see if he goes down Broadway or turns on Atlantic."

They waited four minutes and Jenny said, "I thought Audis were kind of rare, but six or seven of 'em have gone past since we've been waiting. I think he's gone another way."

Scott said, "Give it a few more minutes. Don't forget, he rubs elbows with scum every day. He has reasons to be paranoid."

She ran her hand across the top of the steering wheel. "Somehow, he made us. How'd he figure out we're following him?"

Scott shook his head. "Don't give up. We still might be on him."

In another minute, the silver Audi came to a stop at the red light. Jenny lifted a finger off the steering wheel and pointed. "You're right, there he is."

"Can you see which way he's gonna go?"

"His left blinker's on, but he's not in the left turn lane. Maybe he just forgot to turn it off when he pulled away from the police department?"

Scott kept his seat reclined so he couldn't be seen. "He's a nervous guy, he could do anything. If he makes a U-turn in the middle of the block or takes off at a hundred miles per hour, just let him go. We can always pick him up tomorrow."

The light turned green and traffic started forward. Gaston remained stopped. Cars behind him honked, and he held his hand out the window and waved for them to pass.

Scott peeked over the dash. "He might prove to be a little more slippery than I first gave him credit for."

After all the cars went around, Gaston remained stopped in the center lane of Broadway. When his light turned red again, he went through the light and immediately turned into the same parking lot as Scott and Jenny. Scott said, "If this guy made us, I swear, I'll become a vegan."

The Audi parked three spaces from their Accord. Scott grabbed Jenny by the shoulders and pulled her close to him. "We need to be a loving couple if he looks our way," he whispered an inch away from Jenny's mouth.

She whispered back, "I'd hate to see what you'd do tailing someone when you're in the car with another guy."

"Oh, that's simple," he whispered. "We just wouldn't get caught."

She knew he was joking, but it still made her feel bad. Like she'd failed in her task.

Gaston stood outside his car and looked around. When he seemed convinced that no one had followed him, he hit the key remote locking his car and walked away.

Scott said, "You can sit back now."

Jenny turned to watch where he went. He didn't seem to know they were there, so maybe she hadn't failed after all. "I think he's gonna go eat at the Peppercorner restaurant. No, wait, he's going in the Shear Delight Barbershop. All this for a haircut!"

The two sat in Jenny's Accord for another five minutes. Scott said, "We can't be in your car when he comes out. Let's go into the Peppercorner and wait there."

As they passed Gaston's car, Scott took out his cell phone, leaned over the windshield and took a picture of the Audi's VIN number. He went around to the rear of the car and took another photo of the license plate.

Jenny asked, "What are you doing?"

"Better to have more information than not enough."

***

They sat in the reception area of the restaurant and the hostess asked if they wanted a table or a booth. Jenny told her they were waiting for a few others and would stay in the reception area until their friends arrived. They waited for twenty-five minutes before Gaston left the barbershop, got in his car and sped away.

Scott scrambled out of the restaurant to the barbershop. There were four red barber chairs inside. Three people were seated getting their hair cut and the fourth chair was vacant with brown hair clippings on the floor. He grabbed a broom and dust pan from the back wall and swept the hair clippings around the vacant chair.

The barber, who had stepped to the front of the shop to call the next person, called, "Hey, I'll do that."

Scott said, "I know, I just hate seeing hair on the floor. It makes me feel dirty." He made another big sweep with the broom, getting the remainder of the hair into the dust pan. Then he took it outside with the barber following.

"Now what do you think you're doing?" the barber demanded.

"Just emptying the pan."

A metal trash can was chained to a post. He reached inside, pulled out a crumpled McDonald's bag, opened it, and dumped out some stale French fries. He emptied the dust pan into the bag and returned the dust pan.

The barber went back inside, mumbling, "I see all types in here."

Holding the McDonald's bag like a trophy, Scott turned and grinned at Jenny. "That's enough for today," Scott said. "Ready to go home?"

"No way. Let's go up Atlantic and eat at the Bake 'n' Broil."

Scott said, "I love the Bake 'n' Broil."

He started for the car, carrying the bag of hair as if it were treasure.

***

Thursday morning, Manolito went to the bank and withdrew a thousand dollars. He went to Home Depot, Behind the Scenes Costumes, and the Broken Horn Saddlery. He spent the entire amount getting the things they would need. On the way home, he went back to the bank and withdrew another five thousand dollars. Tomorrow, they planned on going to a gun store in Anaheim that specialized in cowboy action guns and clothing.

He'd never realized robbing a bank could be so expensive. If he kept spending money like this, he was really going to have to rob a bank.

□

Arl Farris

21

…these are replicas not toys

Gathered by the pool at John and Jenny's house, Blakesley clicked his heels together and summoned his finest posture offering his hand to Rebecca. "My cowboy handle is Typhoon Tom. Who do I have the pleasure of meeting?"

She shook his hand. "I'm the Scattergun Girl."

Manolito laughed. "I don't feel so dumb now. I signed up as the Badland Bandito." He turned to Scott. "Let's hear it. What's your cowboy name?"

He grinned. "Two Shot Scott."

Rebecca said, "I wonder if the department psychologist heard these nicknames if he would think they are funny or some repressed alter egos coming out?" She looked at John. "I'm sure a shrink could spend days conjuring up all kinds of theories about your pseudonym, Bighorn Buckeroo."

John spread his hands, palms up in a gesture of innocence. "Whatever do you mean? But, while we're talking about names, we need to come up with something to call our posse."

Rebecca threw out, "Whaddya think about the South Side Longos?"

Manolito frowned. "Yeah, we'd go spray painting the name all over the range. What about Cop Lives Matter?"

Scott said, "I have an idea. When Gaston was on television, he called us a bunch of rogue lawmen. Why not that, the Rogue Lawmen Posse?"

John considered. "Gaston might get suspicious if we used that name. How about the Southland Regulators?"

The others looked at each other and collectively agreed. Southland Regulators it was.

John asked, "How did everyone do this week getting their tasks completed?"

Manolito said, "I have Halloween masks, latex gloves, two-ounce spray bottles, and bleach."

John looked at the group. "I don't need to remind any of you about keeping receipts or anything else at that could later be used as evidence against us. When you're buying things, make sure you're using cash. We don't want your purchases showing up on a credit card statement."

Rebecca said, "No kidding!" She ran her hands up and down over her bottom. "I'm really starting to understand what they mean by saddle-sore."

Manolito said, "I can't believe how much money I'm going through, and we haven't even started buying guns, holsters or the clothing yet!"

Making a point, Blakesley drew out his words. "We'll be lucky if this little adventure only costs us money."

Rebecca rolled her eyes at Blakesley. "Always the pessimist."

Scott recapped their surveillance, then said, "He made several counter-surveillance maneuvers when we were tailing him. If we're gonna follow him any more, we're gonna need to rent a couple cars and do it as a team. Of course, GPS trackers would be best."

John said, "That's a dead end." He looked at Jenny. "Great job following Gaston, by the way. When Jenny got home from your little rolling surveillance and barbershop hijinks, she kept me awake for hours telling me all about it. She's already telling me she needs a faster car if she's gonna be going on any more surveillances... Not!"

Jenny balled her hand into a fist and rubbed it in her eye, pretending to cry, then held up her hands like she was holding a steering wheel and started humming the sound of a racing car engine.

John looked at Scott. "See what you created? She was such a nice conservative driver when she left. Now she's ready for NASCAR."

Manolito said, "I've been thinking about how we can use Gaston's hair. We can put it anywhere we want, and after the crime techs from the lab match Gaston's DNA to the hair, they'll swear he was wherever we planted the hair."

Jenny said, "I see why it was so important to follow him around."

Manolito held up his thumb and forefinger as if holding a small bottle. "And speaking of DNA, don't forget when we do this, we're gonna be carrying those spray bottles with distilled water and bleach. So, if one of us sneezes or something, we can spray down the area and the crime lab won't be able to identify us."

John nodded, acknowledging the deeper issues under Mano's fixation on their "insurance in a bottle." It just showed how rattled he still was over the tears he'd shed in the aftermath of the shooting.

Blakesley changed the subject. "When John and I were at the range, we saw something unusual." They were quiet as Blakesley told them how Gaston had collected samples of dirt from the range. "He had a second vial," Blakesley finished, "but we couldn't see what he did with it. We last saw him going into the brush towards the Santa Ana River."

Rebecca asked, "What's this guy really up to?"

John said, "I've been thinking. What do civil rights attorneys do?"

Manolito answered. "They sue people."

"That's exactly right, they sue people. I think he's collecting evidence to sue the range, sue the Single Action Shooting Society, sue whoever."

Rebecca gave a low whistle. "So Gaston's gathering soil samples off the range to show what? Elevated densities of lead in the soil at a shooting range?"

"What else it could be?"

She rubbed the bridge of her nose distractedly. "What about the second test tube? Do you think he was collecting a second soil sample from the wooded area to compare against the sample taken on the range?"

John shook his head. "Maybe. Or maybe he's seeing how far lead deposits can be found from the range?"

Scott asked, "How far from the range is the river?

John pointed in the house where his computer was set up. "It's a half mile to a mile away, according to Google Earth. Depends on what route you take."

Scott said, "If Gaston's getting soil samples, you can bet he's also collecting water samples."

John nodded. "While Blakesley was taking his pictures, I had another talk with Hurricane Heather. She told me the Lead Bottom Posse has about twenty members and they mostly keep their distance from Gaston. Those four guys we keep seeing him with are about the only ones willing to hang with him, and that's the group that will be shooting at End of Trail. He's been a member of their posse a few years and always acted strange. Apparently, when he first started coming out, he would ask crazy questions. He'd ask other shooters if they'd rather be shooting people or targets? If carrying a gun made them feel tough and things like that."

Rebecca wagged her finger. "Those aren't the kind of questions a shooter would ask if they're trying to learn a sport."

"Right," said Scott, then took Rebecca's thought further. "Those are the kind of questions an attorney would ask if he's trying to gather witnesses in a law suit."

"Anyway," John said, "she told me he hasn't changed much, he's just not as clumsy asking questions. But she did say, anytime someone commits a safety violation, he's all over it. Not trying to correct the safety violation, but collecting as much information about the person involved as he can."

Rebecca frowned. "Whaddya mean?"

"During a match last month, a shooter from a visiting posse ran from one shooting stage to another with a revolver in his hand, rather than holstering it before running. It was considered a safety violation and the shooter was disqualified from continuing the match. Gaston demanded to know the shooter's name and make of his gun. The shooter told him his cowboy name and Gaston went nuts, demanding to know his real name. He was being such a jerk about it, the visiting posse left in the middle of the match."

Blakesley said, "I thought shooters never used their real names when shooting a cowboy action match and the whole point was to use cowboy names?"

Scott made a sour face. "An attorney wouldn't file a lawsuit saying Billy the Kid committed a safety violation, but he would file suit stating William Bonney violated safety protocol and endangered the lives of bystanders."

Rebecca said, "And he's been doing this for several years? Geez!"

"The more we learn about the guy, the worse he looks," Mano said.

John snapped his fingers and looked at Blakesley. He'd gotten so caught up in Gaston's skullduggery with the vial that he'd forgotten to mention something else he'd learned. "There's something else. Before the start of any match, Gaston bows his head and says, 'I'm doing this for you, Peter.' When Hurricane Heather first saw him do it, she asked what that was all about. He said it was none of her business but soon everyone would be giving Peter his due."

Manolito frowned. "Who the hell is Peter?"

Blakesley raised an eyebrow. "Could be important to find out."

John looked at Rebecca. "In good time. Now, this is important. We've seen the group from their posse that will be shooting at End of Trail. There's no women. When the time comes, can you disguise your voice so it sounds like a man?"

Doing the world's worst imitation of Forrest Gump, she announced, "Stupid is as stupid does."

They all laughed, and Mano punched her lightly on the arm.

***

John gave them the address to the gun store and in twenty minutes, they were all at Walker – 47. Inside, the man behind the gun counter said, "Can I help you fellas?"

Manolito asked, "Can you outfit us for cowboy action shooting?"

The clerk waved an arm, showing off everything in the store. "Cowboy action shooters make up about ninety percent of our business. The rest is from hunters looking to hunt with black powder rifles. You guys are lucky. We happen to have a lot of equipment in stock."

Rebecca replied, "Well, you're lucky too. We happen to have a lot of money in our pockets."

The clerk pointed to Scott and Manolito. "Do I know you guys from somewhere? Maybe from the news or something? Your faces kinda look familiar."

John's pulsed quickened, but Manolito looked resolute. "Yeah, we get that a lot. Reality TV. We were on television, the ninth season of Big Brother."

Proud of his powers of observation, the man grinned. "We always welcome celebrities into the store."

Rebecca laughed, then whispered to Mano, "You don't use that line with the women you meet, do you?"

"No, I just made it up, but it has potential."

John glanced at the clerk to see if he'd overheard, but he seemed too busy talking about the weapons on display.

There were well over a hundred single action revolvers in the glass display case the clerk was leaning on. Manolito pointed to a Cimarron, Single Action Army revolver with a 4 ¾-inch barrel. "Can I see that one?" He pointed to the chrome plated weapon.

The clerk said, "Sure," unlocking the display case. He removed the weapon and opened the loading gate to see there were no rounds in the cylinder before handing it over.

Manolito held the revolver in his hands, moving it back and forth. "Nicely balanced." He placed the revolver in his right hand, put his index finger in the trigger guard and twirled the revolver end over end three times before stopping the gun with barrel pointed forward.

The clerk reached out and grabbed the revolver, taking it back, "Ya know these are replicas not toys!"

"A thousand bucks for a replica! I'll pay another five hundred for an original." Mano pointed at a Colt revolver. "I'll take two of those in case hardened blueing .357 caliber. I also want a Winchester 1873 in .357 and a hammerless 12-gauge double-barrel coach gun shotgun."

Reluctant to get the weapons, as if fearing Mano might try twirling the revolvers again, the clerk seemed about to say no. However, when Manolito pulled out a half-inch thick stack of hundred dollar bills, any hesitation he had about letting Mano handle the weapons vanished.

"While you're writing up the gun sales," Mano said, "is there someone who can help me with western clothes and a hat?"

The clerk looked towards the back of the shop. "As long as you got money, we're selling."

An attractive woman in her early thirties approached. Her name tag said Sharon. "I can help you. Is there any Western celebrity, time period or event in history you'd like to reconstruct?"

Mano looked at Rebecca, winked and faced the woman. "Hi, Sharon. I'm Manolito Torres, reality TV star."

While off duty, policemen generally didn't tell people what they did for a living. As rookies quickly discovered, people were curious to learn if they'd ever shot anybody, been shot, had the ability to write a ticket out of their city and where could they buy the best marijuana. Off duty officers normally changed the topic or simply never answered the question. John had never known one to come up with something as crazy as telling someone he was a reality TV star.

Rebecca smirked and took a step back from Manolito.

Sharon said, "Hello, Mr. Torres. Whaddya need?"

He pulled his iPhone from his pocket and scrolled through several western photographs. "I want to look like this guy, from his hat to his boots and everything in between."

She studied the photos. "Clint Eastwood from 'High Plains Drifter.' That shouldn't be a problem. Does it all need to be the same colors as in your pictures?"

Manolito said, "All the way down to the sweat stains on the hat."

She reached over to his phone and enlarged the photo, looking closer at the hat. "Sweat stains aren't a problem. It just takes a few days to complete, and there's no returns on a hat once we stain it."

Rebecca said, "Only Nordstrom allows returns on clothes that get stained."

Ignoring Rebecca, Manolito turned back to Sharon. "For all your hard work, how about dinner tomorrow night? I know a nice little place where the fish is flown in daily from Hawaii. You'll love it."

Blakesley elbowed John. "I hope we get our cowboy clothes before he pisses her off."

Sharon lifted her chin, but her eyes sparkled. "I hate fish."

Without missing a beat, Manolito corrected himself. "Did I say fish? I meant to say pasta. Sabatino's in Newport Harbor, tables overlooking the water, a man singing Sinatra, it's al dente."

She looked him up and down. "You're kind of cute and I know you're full of shit, Mr. Reality TV Star. But I think you'd be a lot of fun on a date, as long as you can behave."

Manolito pointed to Rebecca. "Ask her. I kiss babies and help old ladies across the street."

Laughing and holding up her hands, Rebecca said, "I'm not getting involved in this."

Sharon said, "Kissing babies and helping old ladies, that'd make you either a policeman or a fireman? I get off at five. I can be ready by six-thirty."

With a large grin on his face, Mano moaned, "A fireman? You're killing me!"

Shaking his head, John showed Sharon the photographs of Gaston's clothes. She studied them for some time and said, "The J.

Chisholm boot company quit making elk suede cowboy boots about ten years ago, and the bone-handled skinner knife tucked into his boot might be a problem."

John felt a hint of despair creep in. "You can't let me down."

Looking again at the pictures on his phone, she said, "It'll cost you, but I could get a pair of Lucchese suede calf boots, cut the bottoms off and put a Tony Lama welt, outsole and heel on them. It'd be pretty close to what you want."

Squinting, he said, "Sounds expensive. What's it gonna cost me?"

Dragging out her answer, she drawled, "I could do it for maybe… five hundred dollars?"

"Five hundred dollars?! Jesus. And how about the knife?"

"That's a custom knife. You're never gonna duplicate it. I can give you the names of some custom knife makers who might be able to help, but I wouldn't get my hopes up."

"In for a penny…"

***

It took four hours for everyone to complete the paperwork on their guns and get fitted for their clothes, boots and hats. A few items needed to be ordered, but they were promised everything would be ready when they returned in ten days. California had a ten-day waiting period for purchasing firearms. Policemen were waived from the ten-day waiting period, but only when they presented a letter signed by their commanding officer on official police department letterhead. Today, though, they had no waiver letter from the department.

Leaving the store, Rebecca asked, "What's next?"

Manolito said, "A date with the sexy Sharon."

Rebecca inhaled. "One of these days, Mano. One of these women is gonna steal your heart and you'll be hooked."

"You know me. I'm a bachelor for life."

John said, "Other than adding to Mano's social calendar, we'll continue with our riding lessons and come back next week to pick everything up. I'm gonna call some custom knife makers and spend whatever's left in our kids' college savings account. Ten days from now is a Friday. Our first cowboy match is the next day, Saturday."

Blakesley asked, "We have to shoot a match without even practicing with our cowboy guns?"

John nodded. "It's probably a good thing if we show up a little rusty. Our goal for the first match is to show up and qualify, not to win."

Getting to their cars, John said to Scott, "While we're at the match next week, I'm gonna have you run a little covert operation."

"No sweat. Will Jenny be joining me again?"

"Hardly, and it's gonna cost you three or four hundred bucks. I don't really know if you can get away with it."

Scott said, "I'm the master of covert operations, but they usually don't cost any money."

John said, "It's gonna be critical, and dumb luck will have a lot to do with it."

Waving a hand in front of himself like a magician doing a sleight of hand trick he said, "No sweat."

John turned to Manolito. "I know you were distracted by little miss Sharon Goodbody, but in the gun store, I saw some .32 Long Colt ammunition. I asked the clerk what was the exact diameter of a .32 caliber round, and he told me it was .312 inches. That's a little over four-hundredths of an inch difference from a .38 Special, at .357 inches."

"So, what's your point?"

"I think I've figured out how to fire a bullet without leaving rifling on it."

"You've got my attention!"

"What if you take a bullet from a .32 Long Colt, put some grease or glue around the sides and attach little pieces of wood around the bullet. You could use an exacto knife to slice small slivers off flat toothpicks."

Manolito visualized it as he spoke. "The wood would fill the gap between the bullet and the brass casing and be strong enough for me to crimp the casing to the bullet."

"I think so," John said. "The wood shavings would come apart as the bullet travels down the barrel. The bullet wouldn't touch the inside of the barrel, so there'd be no rifling."

Nodding, Mano said, "It might work. I'm gonna go to a different gun shop to buy the bullets, though. I wouldn't want my new friend to tell a detective about me buying .32 caliber bullets."

John said, "Just make sure you aren't telling your dates about anything other than being a reality TV star."

"Give me a little more credit than that."

John took a breath. "More policemen have talked themselves into trouble than anything else. I'm just saying, we've got a lot riding on this."

Manolito ignored the lecture. "Sharon's last name," he said. "Is it really Goodbody?" □

22

…this just keeps getting better

John bought two sets of western clothing, one for End of Trail and another for practice. They did not want to risk Gaston seeing him dressed the same, become suspicious and change his getup. John kept the clothes for End of Trail folded in their original package and wore the lesser of the two costumes for the preliminary matches.

He hadn't realized how much everything would cost. Adding the price of guns, holsters, ammunition, riding lessons and custom boots, he was overbudget and spending from savings. That didn't count replacing the carpet and couch after he wore his new spurs in the house. But either he would be back at work soon, and getting new carpet and reupholstering the couch would be less painful then, or he would be in prison and it wouldn't matter.

He still needed a skinner knife like Gaston wore in his right boot. The knife makers he'd called did not have materials to duplicate the knife, but one hoped to have something for him in a few weeks. If he couldn't get one, maybe he could fake it by fabricating a sheath and handle. In the excitement of the bank robbery, how closely was anybody likely to look at the knife? Hopefully, it wouldn't come to that, but a plan could fly or fall based on such minute details.

As he scrutinized his costume in the mirror, Clara came in and asked if he would buy her a pony, now that he was taking riding lessons. He had a hard time explaining to his horse-crazy daughter that he would not be doing the cowboy thing after shooting in the big match.

Arriving at the range for their first cowboy action match, the Southland Regulators parked together, away from other contestants and spectators. They dressed at their trucks and put their pistols in their holsters. After signing in and getting the schedule of stages for the match, they made their way to Stage 1.

Stage 1 consisted of ten steel plate targets balanced on stakes in the ground fifteen feet from the shooter's box. A second shooter's box was twenty feet to the side of the first. For this course of fire, the shooter would enter the first shooting box and at the sound of a whistle, draw a pistol and shoot five steel plates. The shooter would then holster his first pistol and draw his second, shooting the next five steel plates.

For cowboy action shooting, shooters were only allowed to load five rounds into their six-shooter, keeping an empty cylinder under the hammer. The empty cylinder kept the revolver from accidentally firing, should something strike the back of the hammer. This avoided the possibility of an accidental discharge. If a shooter loaded six rounds into his pistol, it was considered a safety violation and he would be disqualified from continuing the match.

Having shot all ten rounds from his revolvers, the shooter holstered his empty pistols and ran to the second shooting box, where his rifle lay on a table. While standing in the shooting box, the shooter picked up his rifle and fired at seven additional steel plates from a distance of forty feet.

The courses of fire changed from match to match, and the shooters never knew what the courses would be until they entered the stage to shoot.

Scott was the first to shoot the course. With every shot, he knocked a steel plate off its stand, but his shooting was slow and John could tell the pistols felt awkward in his hands. As soon as he finished Stage 1, John clapped him on the shoulder and said, "Good luck. We'll stand in for you until you get back."

***

Scott left the berm area and took the phone from of his pocket. He scrolled through his photos until he found the pictures he'd taken of Gaston's car outside the barber shop. He placed a telephone call.

A pleasant woman answered. "Corona Porsche and Audi. How can I direct your call?"

"Audi service, please."

"One moment, sir."

A young man's voice quickly came on the line. "This is Chad. How can I help you?"

Scott said, "This is really embarrassing. I lost my car keys."

"No problem, sir. Are you with your car now?"

"Yeah."

He could hear Chad typing information on a computer as he gave directions. "I need you to stand next to the driver's side door and lean over the windshield. There's a seventeen-digit number. That's the vehicle identification number or VIN. Can you read that number to me?"

Looking at the picture on his cell phone, he recited the number. He then said, "I hope there's not gonna be any problems. I bought my car at Long Beach Audi and all the guys over there know me."

If he had been back at the police station, Scott could have easily gotten this information by running a registration check on Gaston's license plate or by asking another officer to do it for him. However, he did not want to ask another officer for fear they would recognize Gaston's name on the registration printout and realize he and his range buddies were planning something.

As paranoid as he was, Scott felt confident the Audi would be registered to Gaston's civil rights office. Most people who registered their cars to their business had an unrealistic feeling of anonymity and Gaston was no different.

You wanted our attention, Mr. Dave Gaston, Scott thought. Well, you've got it.

"I have all your information up on my computer," Chad said. "I just need to get a little more information before we get started. I see the telephone number you're calling in on isn't registered on your account."

Scott suddenly had a sinking sensation in the pit of his stomach. He'd forgotten to block the caller ID on his phone.

"No. I'm out here at the shooting complex in the Santa Ana flood control and my wallet and cell phone are locked in the car. I borrowed another shooter's phone. Don't add this number to my account. I won't be using it again."

"No problem, sir," Chad said. "Just tell me, who do I have the pleasure of speaking with today?"

Scott said, "David Gaston." He then gave Gaston's work address on Broadway.

He knew he'd guessed correctly when Chad came back, "Your information matches our account. If you can give me the telephone number assigned to your account, I can help you."

He gave Gaston's office number and Chad said, "Thank you, Mr. Gaston. All your information's correct. I can electronically unlock your car from here if you'd like."

Thinking how Gaston would act on the telephone with someone like Chad, Scott said, "Damn it, I want a new key brought to me, and if you aren't gonna do it, I want to talk with your manager."

"I can have your key ready in fifteen minutes and a courier deliver it in an hour."

"Finally, we're getting somewhere. As soon as the courier gives me the key, I can unlock my car, get my wallet and pay for it then."

Chad said, "That won't be necessary, Mr. Gaston. We have your credit card on file. I'll simply charge it to your account."

"No," Scott said. "I want to keep this expense separate. I prefer to pay cash for the key when the courier gets here."

"That won't be a problem, sir."

In a sharp tone, Scott said, "Before you hang up on me, connect me with your quality control department. I prefer to take their survey while I'm on the phone rather than keep receiving all the bullshit quality questionnaires in the mail. I swear, Chad, if you send me something in the mail, I'll personally come down there and have your job. I'm an attorney, and I know what I'm doing."

Chad's voice betrayed only a hint of exasperation. "Yes, Mr. Gaston. I'll connect you right away, and I promise, you won't get anything in the mail from today's transaction."

After he finished giving Chad directions to the range and the location of Gaston's Audi, Scott hung up and waited in his truck for the courier to arrive.

Sitting inside his Ford Excursion, he could hear shooting from the range and wondered how the match was going. After thirty-five minutes, he spotted a white van driving in his direction. He got out of his truck and stood next to the Audi.

When the driver opened his door, Scott said, "I'm sure happy to see you."

Stepping from van, the driver said, "Yeah, I get that a lot."

He handed Scott a white cardboard box, the size of a small shoebox, with "Corona Porsche Audi" printed in large black lettering on the top. Scott opened the box and the man said, "I just need to see your I.D. and get three-hundred-twenty-six dollars and eighty-four cents."

Scott said, "Didn't you talk with Chad in parts? I told him I lost my keys and wallet and needed a new car key. I have the cash under the car seat, but I lost my wallet. I don't have any identification."

The man looked at his watch. "We aren't supposed to give out keys without proper identification."

Scott said, "This has already been worked out with Chad and the parts department manager."

The driver squinted at him for a moment. Scott held his gaze until the man looked away and said, "Well, I guess it'll be okay. Just sign the clipboard. You said you'll be paying cash?"

Scott reached in the cardboard box, removed the key and opened the driver's door of the Audi. He made a show of reaching under the driver's seat as if retrieving a secret stash of money, then laughed to himself as he felt a pistol and two small plastic baggies under the seat. He slid the pistol and baggies out far enough to see a Glock subcompact .40 caliber and two baggies of cocaine. This just keeps getting better and better.

He tucked the pistol and cocaine back under the seat and held up the cash in his hand. He counted out three hundred and sixty dollars.

The man blinked. "I don't carry any change."

"I didn't ask for any."

For the first time, the driver grinned. "Thank you," he said, handing Scott his electronic clipboard. "You don't need a pen. Just use your fingernail to sign your name."

Scott had been practicing signing Gaston's name, using Gaston's signature from the complaint form in the Jesus Camacho case as a template.

"Thanks again, Mr. Gaston," the driver said. "Do you need anything else before I leave?"

He shook the key at the courier. "No, I have everything I need."

He waved goodbye as the van made a U-turn and drove away. Then he tore the lid off the cardboard Audi box, put it on the floorboard of his truck, and walked back into the enclosed berm where the cowboy action match was taking place.

When he met up with the others, John asked, "Any problems?"

"No, it went without a hitch. And by the way, our friend enjoys a little blow and keeps a Glock 27 under his seat."

"Nice." John grinned. "By the way, Mano's been standing in for you, shooting the stages while you were gone. Your scores have steadily fallen since Stage 1, and Badland Bandito's scores are picking up."

"Yeah, amazing how that works."

They were at the last stage of the match. It was a shotgun-only stage with twelve springloaded steel plates on the ground. After a shooter hit the steel plate, it would fall backwards, causing a clay bird to be thrown in the air. The event was scored based on time. The clock started with the beep of a timer and stopped when the shooter shot the last target. There was a five second penalty for each target missed.

No one was surprised when Rebecca had the fastest time of all the shooters and hit each clay bird.

After the match, they collected their gear and placed any leftover ammunition back into their range bags. As they were leaving, David Gaston and the other four posse members he'd be shooting End of Trail with, sauntered over and stood behind them.

Gaston said, "I heard there was a new posse out here, I had no idea it would be you guys. I'm surprised any of you rogue cops would be willing to step outside your house, let alone come here and shoot. Cowboy shooting's a lot different than shooting defenseless kids."

Scott and Manolito dropped their range bags, freeing their hands to ready themselves for a fight. Without saying a word, John raised an open hand a few inches from his side and ever so slightly shook his head no. Manolito and Scott took a half step back and let John talk.

"You're a lousy lawyer and an even worse shooter," he said. "You might be able to pretend you're some kind of a gunslinger when you're shooting against housewives and old men with beer bellies, but if you ever shoot against a real shooter, you'll find yourself sorely lacking."

"Let's go, asshole."

"That's not very gentlemanly," John said. "We have no interest in wasting any more time listening to you pretending to be something you're not. We're gonna leave so you can scare a few mousy women and fat old men."

Gaston said, "My posse can take your misfits anytime, anywhere."

The four men behind Gaston fidgeted, looking uncomfortable. They seemed willing to undergo a little embarrassment in exchange for free ammo and shooting supplies, but they hurriedly moved out of the way to let John and the others pass without obstruction. As the Regulators left, Gaston continued taunting them. "I don't know why you guys are even here," he said to their backs. "No one called the police. Oh, that's right. You're not police anymore. Not for long, anyway."

None of the Regulators answered.

At their trucks, Blakesley said, "It'd be so fun to plant a roundhouse in that guy's face while he's spouting off."

"It would," John agreed, "but that'd be playing into his game. Now, he's gonna be playing our game and we're gonna crush him."

Manolito said, "You have us out here dressed like nincompoops, shooting guns that were obsolete a hundred years ago, and you say he's playing our game?"

"Trust me, we're driving the bus and Gaston's going under it." He pointed to Rebecca. "I need you to confirm with Samantha that she'll trailer the horses to End of Trail. We need the horses starting on Thursday evening and through the weekend."

"No problem," she said. "I'm gonna stop by the range office on my way out and ask what they charge to keep a trailer and five horses here for End of Trail."

Manolito said, "If anybody needs more ammo, let me know. I've been busy in my garage reloading ammo for all of us and I've got plenty."

Rebecca snickered. "I'm surprised to hear you have time for reloading, with that new girl you've been seeing from the gun store. What was her name again... Ms. Goodbody?"

Manolito said, "You don't mean Sharon? That was so last week. Who has time to date a woman more than three times when there's so many beautiful ladies just begging for an evening out with a gentleman?"

John wagged a finger at Mano. "I hope you didn't break that girl's heart. I'm still trying to find someone to make a custom knife for me, and she's helping me find the right knife maker."

Manolito thumped his chest with a thumb. "Trust me sarge, she'll probably give you a big discount the next time you go into her store."

23

speak to me…

Manolito sat in front of the reloading bench in his garage. He had just removed the lid from a can of Hodgdon gunpowder to pour it into his Dillon 550 reloading press when the phone rang. Sighing, he set down the can and screwed the top back on. End of Trail was this weekend, and he still had a lot of ammo to reload.

"Hey, Mano," John said. "How's it coming?"

"We're all set. I just finished the project we talked about and I'm reloading another thousand rounds. That should be enough for practicing this week and leave us with plenty for End of Trail."

"That's why I'm calling. Tomorrow evening, I want all of us to meet at my house for dinner. We have a lot to talk about."

"Finally! We need some specifics. I was starting to second guess this whole thing."

John's tone was suddenly serious. "I don't think we should discuss any more of this on the phone."

Mano took a moment to consider the implications. "You don't think the department has a wire up on our phones, do you?"

"If they're alleging we colluded in some kind of criminal conspiracy, how else would they try and make a case?

"By tapping our phones, but there's no way…"

"I'm just saying when you talk to your girlfriends, don't say anything you wouldn't want to read somewhere down the road in an affidavit."

"Point well taken." Mano changed the subject, not wanting to consider the possibility of wire taps and affidavits. "Would Jenny like me to bring anything over for dinner, dessert, chips or whatever?"

"I'll check and call you back in a few minutes."

Mano returned to the reloading press and had just started to pour powder into the press when his phone rang a second time. He laughed and put the cap back on the can. That hadn't taken long. "Speak to me, boss."

The phone was quiet for a second before the voice on the other end began speaking. "Hello, Officer Torres, this is Captain Jason Dickerson. How are you?"

Manolito's mind raced. What if the phone really was tapped and the captain was trying to get him to say something incriminating or see if he called to warn the others?

Manolito took a gulp of air. "I'm fine, sir. I hope you're calling to tell me this whole thing's over and I can come back to work."

Dickerson said, "I know it's tough, waiting this out. These things take time, but we're making progress."

"Progress is good."

Dickerson said, "We're gonna need you to come in and clarify a few things from the parking garage shooting."

Mano frowned. "I don't get it, Captain. I gave a very detailed account of what happened. I was interviewed twice the day of the shooting and accounted for every shot."

"I'm aware of that," Dickerson said in a brittle tone. "It's just some routine stuff, nothing to sweat. I'll be expecting you in my office tomorrow morning at nine-thirty."

Manolito thought of what had happened to Scott. Would Dickerson have Lieutenant Jackson search his house while Mano was in the office "clarifying a few things"? Aloud, he said, "I wouldn't miss it for the world."

They hung up and the phone immediately rang again.

"Hey, Mano," John said. "Jenny says just bring your appetite. She's gonna have me grill some salmon steaks and sweet summer corn."

"Sounds great." Mano hesitated for a moment, then told John about the captain's call.

"That can't be good," John said. "Make sure Donna Fisher's with you."

Donna had met Manolito and prepared his formal statement after his shooting. She also knew Scott from his ordeal when the burglar hit his head on the parking bumper. After the range instructors had been placed on suspension, John had called Donna and she'd agreed to represent them if the department pursued cases against them.

"I'm gonna call her as soon as I get off the phone," Manolito said.

John said, "Let her do all the talking."

Manolito asked, "Hey, do you know if Donna's single?"

John laughed. "Seriously, that'd be a big mistake while she's representing us."

***

On Wednesday morning, Donna parked her metallic blue Porsche Cayenne on the second floor of the parking structure at the Long Beach Police Department. Manolito preferred parking on the top floors in parking structures because he took a lot more burglary reports from cars parked on lower floors than higher. He knew the cars were pretty safe in the police department parking structure, but officers developed a lot of quirky habits over the course of their careers, and this was one of them. Manolito saw Donna getting out of her car and pulled into the empty stall next to her car.

Donna was close to forty years old, a short woman with sharp muscle tone. Her makeup had been expertly applied to her fair skin, and Manolito guessed it must have taken her over an hour in front of a mirror, getting herself to look just right. He considered asking if she worked out using free weights, but remembering what John said about getting involved with their attorney, he didn't ask.

She wore a gray skirt with matching jacket, a turquoise silk blouse and navy leather pumps. She kept her strawberry blond hair pulled back with a tortoise-shell hair clip. Behind her, she pulled a black Samsonite expandable briefcase on rollers.

Manolito had to run to catch up with her as she neared the elevators.

Seeing him jogging up behind her, she said, "Hey, Mano, have you spoken with John or the others?"

"Yeah, he invited all of us to his house for dinner tonight."

"No," she said as they got onto the elevator. Two detectives squeezed onto the elevator behind them before the doors shut. Donna stopped talking, and all four stood facing the doors in silence.

The elevator stopped on the third floor, and Donna and Manolito got out. She said, "The captain called the others after he spoke with you. John, Scott, Blakesley and Rebecca are going to be here. They called me right after you did, and I asked them not to call each other. We don't want the department to think you guys are involved in some kind of ongoing conspiracy."

Suddenly, he felt sick to his stomach. "Conspiracy?"

She said, "Let's wait 'til everyone's here before discussing our strategy."

John was sitting outside the captain's office. He stood when he saw Manolito and Donna approaching.

Donna greeted John and asked, "Have you seen Rebecca or Blakesley this morning?"

He pointed behind her as Rebecca and Blakesley were getting out of the elevator.

Donna stepped over to Carol. "The captain's nine-thirty appointments are here. I just need five minutes with my clients before we're ready."

Carol said, "I'll let him know." She picked up her phone, spoke a few words and hung up. She put on a headset and busied herself typing on the computer, not meeting their eyes.

Donna retrieved a yellow legal note pad from her briefcase and walked to the end of the hallway with the officers following. Watching the sway of her hips from the corner of his eye, Mano suppressed a smile. Just because he couldn't act on his interest didn't mean he couldn't appreciate a good-looking woman.

In a hushed voice, she said, "I have to say, it doesn't look good, calling everyone up here. If the captain hands you notices of termination, accept the notices and don't say anything. Let me argue it on appeal."

Rebecca said, "There's no way I'm gonna sit there without saying anything while he fires us."

Blakesley nodded. "That goes double for me."

Donna looked at each of them. "Let's not get ahead of ourselves. We don't know if you're being fired, but the less talking you do in there, the better it'll be for everyone."

She jabbed an index finger in the air. "All of you are more than capable of taking care of yourselves on the streets, but in here, you're out of your element. There are very specific guidelines that must be followed prior to the discharge of an officer. It's all about following the most current case law, legal precedent, and judicial practice, and applying department disciplinary standards to those elements. The captain just needs to screw up one of these and I can get any discipline overturned on appeal with the police commission."

John said, "If the only way we can save our jobs is through legal gamesmanship, we should really think if they're worth saving."

Manolito knew what John was talking about and it had nothing to do with the meeting they were waiting to attend. But you could ask yourself the same question about their own solution. If the only way they could save their jobs was by robbing a bank, were those jobs really be worth saving?

Donna told the group, "Remember, no matter what happens in there, he can never take away who you are."

Rebecca said, "Yeah, we don't need his help for that."

Blakesley pointed back down the hallway to a woman wearing a lab coat and carrying a white plastic tray holding empty glass vials. The group stopped talking as she said to Carol, "I'm phlebotomist Nguyen from the lab. I'm here to see a Captain Jason Dickerson."

Carol removed her headset and escorted the phlebotomist into the captain's office.

Donna smiled and announced, "You guys aren't here to be fired. You're here for drug testing."

Under the California Police Officer Bill of Rights, police officers were not subject to random drug testing, nor could they be compelled to take a lie detector test. However, in cases where an officer used deadly force or a supervisor suspected an officer to be under the influence or by court order, an officer was required to submit to drug testing. Refusal to comply with an order to take a blood test under one of these circumstances would be grounds for immediate termination.

Donna said, "When we go in there, just roll up your sleeves and give them a sample. Easy-Peasy."

Carol came out of the captain's office. "You can see the captain now."

Captain Dickerson greeted everyone, then handed a stack of papers to Donna. "Counselor, I have a court order demanding the department take blood from each of your clients. They will be tested for opium, cocaine, THC, amphetamines, barbiturates and alcohol."

Donna sat in a chair reading the documents. In a few minutes, she said, "This order was issued yesterday, at the bequest of attorney David Gaston, at an ex-parte hearing. Why wasn't I notified of the hearing? My clients' right to due process has been violated by not notifying their counsel about this hearing."

Dickerson smirked. "Don't get uppity with me. I'm just following the judge's orders. If there was any way I could fight this, you know I would've done it." He gave a half smile, shrugged his bulky shoulders and said, "It's a court order. What could I do?"

"We'll comply with the order, but it was issued in error." She placed the documents in her briefcase. "I've never had the pleasure of going up against Gaston in court. He always settles before trial. What he's trying here is a big step up for him. I'd hate to see the department bullied by someone like him."

Dickerson said, "Before you dismiss Gaston as being a lightweight, he was able to convince the judge your clients acted with prejudice and malice against minorities. He also got the court to buy off on these officers having a possible drug problem and taking their frustrations of addiction out on minorities. No attorney has ever done that before. I think you'd be remiss to not take this guy seriously."

Shaking her head, Rebecca said, "That's one of the craziest things I've ever heard."

Manolito's jaw tightened. "You took my blood right after the shooting as part of the original investigation. Why do you need a second sample?"

Donna shot him a warning look and told the captain, "Our fight's not with you. Of course, we're happy to comply with the judge's order."

Rolling up his sleeve, John told the phlebotomist, "I'll be first."

Manolito said, "Everything Gaston's said about each of us is a lie. Rebecca's not a racist and giving away throw-down guns, Blakesley didn't assault anyone, John didn't refuse a complaint, and Scott and I are not murderers. This is just another one of his stunts. He's got nothing and after our results from the blood tests come back, he'll have even less."

Dickerson looked at Donna. "Based on these new allegations and since the other matters haven't been fully investigated, the chief feels we need to send a firm message. I am to collect all badges, credentials and department issued firearms."

Donna raised her voice. "Now, wait a minute! There are no new developments, and the court order was issued outside any representation on the officers' behalf. This court order doesn't change anything."

Dickerson said, "Your clients no longer have any police authority or police officer power. They're no longer authorized to carry a loaded weapon on their person."

Her eyes flashed. "You might be able to restrict their ability to carry a concealed weapon, but you can't take away their Second Amendment rights to bear arms in their private lives."

Scott was seated in the chair with the phlebotomist drawing blood from his right arm. Red-faced, he pointed at Dickerson, his voice shaking with anger. "You searched my home, frightened my wife, took my guns and now you're gonna tell me I no longer have police powers with a smirk on your face. You say we should kowtow to some lying attorney. You're so weak you don't even know what your job is anymore. Whatever happened to supporting the officers in the field?"

Phlebotomist Nguyen scrambled to release the tourniquet, pull the needle out of Scott's arm, and put a bandage on the stick.

Donna stepped in front of Scott, blocking Dickerson's view of him. "These officers deserve better than what they're getting," she said. "There's no foundation for the action you're taking against my clients. We'll submit to your authority and this trumped up court order, but trust me, you're going to have a very rough time explaining your actions to the police commission."

Dickerson put a finger in the knot of his tie and pulled it away from his neck. Then he forcefully jabbed his finger onto his desk. "Counselor, I won't have anyone coming in here threatening me or telling me what I can or can't do. You better listen to me. If any one of these officers is found to be in possession of a concealed firearm, I don't care if it's a BB gun, I'll fire every one of 'em. They're to place their department-issued weapons and credentials on my desk, or they can go to the office of personnel and submit their letters of resignation. I really don't give a shit which they do, but they're not leaving here as officers."

The captain's ears were blood red. Mano looked over at John, who slowly took the wallet containing his badge and department-issued identification out of his back pocket and tossed it on the captain's desk. He unholstered his Beretta and set it on the desk next to his wallet.

"Fine," John said. "You people are only doing this because you're afraid of your own shadows."

Dickerson didn't answer. Instead, he handed Donna the officers' suspension orders. She looked at the orders while the others set their wallets and pistols on Dickerson's desk. Then she handed the papers to the officers, and they all signed the orders.

Mano thought of how proud he'd been the day he graduated from the academy. He'd felt like he was part of something noble. There was nothing noble about this.

Dickerson spoke to Donna as if the five officers weren't in the office. "The order states they no longer have police officer powers. They can't carry a concealed weapon and are to submit to drug testing within two hours of being requested by any member of the department's administration."

In her most practiced, professional tone, she said, "Thank you, Captain. Will there be anything else?"

Dickerson shifted in his seat. "You can't say I didn't warn you. Gaston petitioned the court for an emergency hearing, for this Tuesday. He's told the court your clients represent a danger to the community, and he needs the case against them to move forward immediately. The subpoenas are attached to the back of the written orders."

As they left the office in stunned disbelief, Mano replayed the parking garage shooting. He'd handled it exactly right. Any differently, and he'd have left that building in a body bag. So how could this be happening?

In the parking structure, Donna said, "I know you guys are getting together for dinner tonight. Would you like me to stop by and go over anything from this meeting or talk about what to expect on Tuesday?"

Mano tried to suppress the jolt of panic that shot through him at the thought of their lawyer showing up for dinner while they went over the final details of the bank robbery.

Casually, John said, "Thanks, but I don't want to talk about this in front of my wife and kids."

"Okay, I'll call everyone before Tuesday to discuss our strategy." When she waved goodbye, Mano was pretty sure her gaze held his a little longer than was strictly professional. It might not be wise to get involved with their attorney, but the possibility made this whole awful situation a little easier to bear.

***

Gaston postponed his usual Wednesday morning meetings with prospective new clients to go to Wallace Laboratories, in the city of El Segundo. He was greeted by Pamela, an overweight, cheerful fifty-year-old woman wearing black slacks and a leopard print silky top with an inappropriate plunging neckline. The only thing making her top semi-passable were dozens of gold necklaces that somewhat covered her cleavage. Gaston thought the woman had enough gold around her neck if she were to fall—or better yet, were pushed—into a swimming pool, her chances of survival would be very much in doubt.

She said, "Hello, David. Have some more samples for us?"

He removed two glass vials from his inner suit pocket. "Yeah, I've got a couple more, and this time I'm wanting better results than what you've been giving me." In a sharp tone, he said, "Get me a lab technician."

Pamela glanced around the office. "I'll see what I can do. I'm not sure what they're gonna tell you that isn't in the reports already."

"Ive been coming in here every month for a year and a half and your reports all say the same thing. It wouldn't surprise me if you change the dates and send me the same report every month."

Her mouth tight, she picked up the telephone, punched in a couple numbers and spoke softly into the receiver before hanging up.

"One of our technicians will be right up. I can assure you, we make a full analysis of every sample we receive. We're a professional laboratory and our reputation stands with every finding we make."

She stood up and came around the desk to take the two vials.

He took a step back and held the vials out as far from his body as he could. It was no use. The overpowering smell of Liz Claiborne perfume smacked him in the face, and he coughed as the odor enveloped him. He thought, No one's tried drowning her because no one can get close enough without choking. When he'd managed to catch his breath, he said, "Where's that lab tech?"

Pamela held the two vials up to the light and laughed. "Honey, your soil sample's contaminated. You've got a .22 shell casing in there. With such a small soil sample, the brass casing's gonna distort the metal elements within the sample."

"Are you an analyst?" he snapped. "I'm not paying for your opinion."

A thin Indian woman wearing a lime green pants suit and a pair of glasses on a silver chain lanyard around her neck entered the lobby behind Gaston.

"Hey, Fatima," Pamela called out. "Do you have a minute to talk with David about a contaminated soil sample?"

"Sure, Pam." Fatima put on her glasses and looked at the soil sample. "Oh, my," she said. "This'll never do."

She looked over the top of her glasses. "So, you're David Gaston. I do the lab work on the samples you bring in every month." She stuck out her hand to shake.

He reluctantly shook her hand, holding his breath, afraid all the women who worked in the lab bathed in cheap perfume. "Why haven't you reported toxicants on your reports?" he demanded.

She took off her glasses and let them dangle from the lanyard. "My reports accurately reflect the samples you've brought us. The Wallace Laboratories can stand the test of any scientific scrutiny."

Pamela propped her elbows on her desk, fingers crossed under her chin, and rested her head on the backs of her hands, listening. Gaston starred at her. She stopped watching and busied herself with a stack of papers.

Fatima said, "You know we don't get involved in lawsuits and won't offer a legal opinion. We only provide analyses to optimize growth and ensure environmentally responsible nutrient enhancements for crops. We don't want to spend our time in court." She lifted the vials. "I am happy to analyze your samples, but unless something significant changes, the results are most likely going to be the same."

He said, "Every month, I collect samples from the shooting range where tens of thousands of bullets are fired every month. How can you tell me there's not been a rise in the lead content of my samples?"

She lifted the glasses from around her neck and placed them on her nose. Looking intently at the water sample, she said, "Don't forget lead is a natural occurring element and deposits are common in bedrock. Pollutants such as car batteries, wheel weights and old radiators will add to the lead content in the water. Up until 1972, most water pipes were made of lead and we still find lead paint on many old buildings. You could have any one of these factors in the water along the range site that would cause an abnormally high lead count in your water. We can tell you what the lead content parts per million are, but not the cause."

Gaston looked over Fatima's shoulder to make sure Pamela was not eavesdropping. He poked an index finger into his chest. "I've been paying you people four hundred and sixty dollars a month for the last eighteen months. I'm expecting a little more than what I'm getting."

She pursed her lips, as if formulating a response.

"What can I do to get a different result on the tests?"

Fatima tilted her head to the side. Cautiously, she asked, "What do you mean?"

"You know exactly what I mean," he said. "How much would it cost to get the lab result I need, showing the bullets from the range are polluting the ecosystem, contaminating the soil, the water or whatever? I'm willing to compensate you for a little consideration."

Fatima's cheeks reddened. She stuttered, "I... I don't even know what to say to that."

Pamela got up from behind her desk and took the vials from Fatima. She placed a hand on Fatima's shoulders. "Don't worry, honey, that's just David."

She looked across at Gaston. "You know it upsets our girls when you come in here and do that."

Not fazed or embarrassed, he said, "All I'm saying, you help me—I help you. It's a win– win, and we can all make a few extra bucks."

Pamela smiled. "The answer's the same this month as it was last month. I'm sorry, but no."

She set the vials on the counter and began filling out a 'Request for Analysis' form. "We'll do your water sample, but your soil sample's contaminated. I'll bill you for just the one sample this month."

Exasperated, he rolled his eyes, "Whatever!" He reached inside his jacket, pulled out a knockoff Mont Blanc pen and signed the form.

Pamela smiled and said, "I'll see you next month, David."▯

▯

24

...reprobate with an attitude

Jenny had cheese, crackers, grapes and celery sticks on floral patterned platters. The range staff were in the backyard, seated around the patio tables.

John had a manila folder on the table in front of him. He opened it and pulled out his subpoena and written order. "It's not as bad as I thought. I'd've guessed the order would have prevented us from associating with one another."

Rebecca popped a grape in her mouth. "They couldn't stop us from seeing who we want."

"Wanna bet? That's the norm when officers get suspended."

They almost always restricted officers from associating with other members of the department and prohibited suspended officers from setting foot at their place of employment.

Blakesley placed a slice of sharp cheddar on a cracker. "Why do you suppose Gaston didn't try to keep us from going to the range? After all, the range could be considered our place of employment too."

Jenny said, "He's gonna file an environmental class-action lawsuit against everyone at End of Trail. That's why he's been so interested in getting everyone's name who's been shooting cowboy action events. I think he's been waiting for End of Trail to come to the Santa Ana Shooting Complex so he'd have all the cowboy action shooters in one place and file his lawsuit in a court he's familiar with."

Plucking from a stem of grapes, Rebecca said, "I'm sure he has a judge in his pocket and wants to bring whatever he's doing in front of him. How else could he get a judge to sign off on an order stating we represent a danger to the community?"

"Listen to us," Manolito said. "Trying to figure out why the guy's a reprobate and coming up with logical explanations for what he's doing. Who cares! All we need to do is follow through with our plan, and whatever scam he's trying to pull goes to prison with him."

Blakesley said, "You didn't just make up that word, did you? Reprobate. I don't know what it means, but it describes him perfectly."

Everyone laughed.

Jenny leaned into Blakesley, and in a whisper said, "It means someone who..."

At the big smile on his face, she stopped talking. She playfully slapped him on the arm, which caused him to laugh even harder.

John sighed. "Remember what Hurricane Heather said about Gaston praying to Peter before each shooting match? Well, it really stuck with me. I was online thinking about it and Googled Peter, Pete's Dragon, Saint Peter, then Peter Gaston."

Blakesley stopped laughing, and Rebecca quit chewing grapes, listening carefully.

"A few years ago, a 501(c)(3) charity was created in the name of an eleven-year-old boy who was killed in a liquor store robbery. This nonprofit is dedicated in his memory and calls for the elimination of all private handgun ownership through legislative and judicial action. And I'll give you one guess the name of the boy killed on his way home from school way back in 1992."

"Oh, my God!" Jenny placed a hand over her mouth. "Peter Gaston. David is doing all this because he loved his brother. He's honoring his dead brother by fighting against guns, gun violence."

Manolito scratched at his jaw. "Shooting at a range is not gun violence."

Rebecca swallowed the food in her mouth. "You're right. Why would he be on such a tear to sue us? We didn't have anything to do with his brother's death."

Scott said, "We're cops and we carry guns. He wants to take down anyone with a gun. You, me, the whole department." He looked back to Jenny. "And he doesn't care who else he has to hurt to do it."

She nodded. "I think he's setting up something big for End of Trail, and he's planning on using the money he gets from suing you guys to fund his charity and somehow sue the range or everyone who shoots at End of Trail."

Blakesley bit into a celery stick. "The way he's coming after us, it makes sense. I actually feel kind of sorry for him, but there's no other way to get our jobs back. And if we don't turn the tables on him, there's nothing that will stop him."

John said, "I wouldn't be surprised if on Monday, we all get telephone calls from Donna Fisher, letting us know the court hearing's been postponed. There's no way he can be at End of Trail all weekend and be ready for us in court on Tuesday."

He stopped and looked at Manolito. "You didn't have anything to do with her wanting to come here for dinner, did you?"

Mano lifted his hands, palms up. "I don't know what you mean, Sarge."

Blakesley said, "Mano, if you screwed it up with our attorney, I'll show you what a reprobate with an attitude can do."

John said, "Not to change the topic, but did you bring the ammo?"

"Before we talk about ammunition, what are we gonna do about not having your boot knife? When we go into the bank, you have to look as much like Gaston as possible."

Disappointed, John looked across the table at his folder. "I know. I just can't find one."

Scott asked, "What are you gonna do?"

"When I walk in the bank with my mask, gloves and cowboy outfit, I'll be Gaston. I'm roughly his height and weight. I'll be dressed exactly like him except for not having the boot knife."

Blakesley said, "If Gaston's only defense is the robber didn't have a boot knife, then he's going to prison."

Rebecca finished the grapes and tossed the stem in the trash. "Any prosecuting attorney that's been outta law school for ten minutes can come up with a million reasons why he didn't have the knife with him in the bank."

Manolito said, "We don't even know if the resolution on the bank cameras will show the knife. How many banks have high definition cameras that'd show that level of detail, anyway?"

They all agreed.

John said, "I think it'll be okay without the boot knife. Now, what about the ammo?"

Mano reached into his front pants pocket and pulled out a single .38 round and handed it to John. John looked at it and passed it around.

Manolito said, "It's a .38 Special casing loaded with a .32 caliber bullet. It's held in place with tiny slivers of wood I cut from toothpicks. I melted paraffin wax around the crimp where the brass pushes into the wood slivers, holding the bullet. If there were any gaps, there would be a chance of losing the gunpowder out one of the holes or not getting enough pressure built up to actually ignite the round."

Scott looked over John's shoulder at the round. "Are they safe to shoot?"

Mano nodded. "Gunpowder will burn just like a piece of paper. But when that same gunpowder is put in a brass case and ignited by the primer, the gunpowder begins to burn, and gases build up until those gases explode. That explosion is the bang we hear when a gun is fired. That's what the paraffin wax is for, to ensure there are no gaps between the wood slivers."

Holding the round in his hand, Scott asked, "Have you tested these to make sure they work?"

"Yeah. They actually aren't too bad. The accuracy's good to about ten feet. Then they really start to hook off course, like a golf ball."

Rebecca asked, "What about rifling on the bullet?"

"I recovered several bullets I fired, and none had any rifling on 'em." Mano reached into his pocket and pulled out two bullets. "Here's two I dug out of the sand. See, no rifling." He passed them around for everyone to see.

Rebecca said, "Now tell me again why these bullets are such a big deal?"

John said, "We'll fire one of these inside the bank. When the crime lab examines the bullet, there'll be no rifling on it. They won't be able to match the bullet to one of our guns, or any other gun. Instead, they'll be looking for someone who has .32 caliber bullets loaded into ammunition. When they find Gaston in possession of that ammunition, they'll have their suspect." He looked again at the bullets. "These are perfect, absolutely no rifling."

Manolito said, "The wood shavings I placed around the bullet either peeled off in the barrel or caught fire and burned up, making a match of any rifling impossible. I've got thirty-four more just like this one."

Rebecca asked, "So, why thirty-five?"

John said, "We're all gonna load our pistols with these. If one of us winds up doing any more shooting inside the bank, we'll be shooting the ammunition that leaves no rifling, making more physical evidence that'll point to Gaston."

Blakesley said, "If we fire more than one shot in the bank, something will have gone very wrong."

Rebecca quickly did the math, six rounds in five guns. "That accounts for thirty. What are the other five for?"

Manolito smiled. "Those are for Gaston."

She thought for a minute. "Won't we have the same problem as him after we leave the bank? The ammo will be in our guns!"

John said, "Yes, but only for a little bit. We're gonna dump whatever ammo's in our revolvers in the river on our way back."

Jenny went into the house and came back a few minutes later with a platter of salmon and another of corn on the cob and asparagus. She nodded toward John. "It's time to start barbecuing."

He stood up and said to the group, "We'll finish our discussion after dinner."

He put the salmon, corn and asparagus on the grill. Jenny served a Caesar salad as John finished cooking. Everyone ate, but they were quieter and more sedate than normal.

After everyone had finished and the dishes had been carried into the kitchen, Jenny returned with a platter of freshly baked chocolate chip cookies. She returned to the kitchen for a gallon of milk and a pot of coffee. Then, with everyone munching on dessert, the talk returned to the robbery.

Rebecca said, "Something's bothering me. How are we gonna get the ammunition to Gaston? Will one of us walk up and say, 'Here, load your pistol with these'?"

Scott said, "You're forgetting, we have the key to his car. These rounds don't need to be in his gun. They just need to be found in a place only Gaston has access."

She nodded. "Like his car."

Again, John opened his manila folder and slid out three diagrams of the inside of the bank. He marked X's on the diagram where he wanted everyone to be during the robbery. He asked Rebecca, "Have you been practicing disguising your voice to sound like a guy?"

In a throaty voice, she said, "I'm ready."

For the next forty-five minutes, he spoke with little interruption. When finished, he asked, "Does everyone understand the plan and know what their roles will be?"

They looked at each other and nodded.

"Remember, whatever you do, don't shoot the Plexiglas windows inside the bank. Our bullets will ricochet off the Plexiglas and bounce back at us. Mano should be the only one who fires his gun, and that'll be into the ficus tree next to the teller door." He again pointed to the spot on the diagram.

Manolito looked at the others. "I think we have it." He wavered a moment and made a face. "I just thought of something—the horses! We're riding Quarter Horses, a couple of chestnuts, a red dun and two sorrels. I don't know what Gaston and his posse have, but our horses aren't going to be the same."

Blakesley shook his head. "Doesn't matter. As long as we don't ride through the drive-up window, they'll never be on camera."

Scott said, "I know horse people take better care of their horses than they do their own kids, but once their animals are fed, watered and groomed, they can be in the stables for hours. Who's to say Gaston and his posse didn't ride someone else's horses when robbing the bank? I mean, that would make sense, right? Covering their tracks?"

John turned to Blakesley and Rebecca. "When you're inside the vault, you'll be moving fast. I don't need to remind you how important it is to remove any dye packs or ETS devices from the money."

For years, banks had put exploding dye packs in stacks of money and called it "bait money." When a robber held up a bank, an electronic triggering device implanted in the bank door ignited the dye pack causing bait money to explode. A pinkish purple dye covered the money and the robber, making the cash unusable and marking anyone nearby. More recently, banks, jewelry stores and high-end electronic stores had been using an Electronic Tracking System, known as ETS. The ETS device was a small computer chip attached to something small, like a dollar bill. When the chip was removed from the bank, it was activated, much like the dye packs were triggered. Police cars and helicopters were equipped with receivers that pointed officers to the ETS computer chip and thus to the crook. Well over half of all bank robberies were successfully resolved as a direct result of deploying dye packs or ETS devices.

John did not intend for this to be one of them.

He collected the three pages of the bank diagrams and put them back in his folder. He stood up, placed the manila folder on the grill and watched it turn to ashes.

He turned away from the grill. "I can't stress how important it is to get rid of anything that could be used as evidence against us."

He told Manolito, "Toss your reloading dies into the ocean, off the Vincent St. Thomas Bridge and burn any receipts you may have kept."

Mano nodded. "Done."

"You know what can be used as evidence. Double and triple check everything. We know the department has no problem getting a search warrant and turning your house inside-out."

Scott said, "Trust me, they'll go through everything."

John reminded them, "They're having a few End of Trail events tomorrow at the range. It wouldn't hurt if we went and looked things over. Our first match is Friday, and it's game on for Saturday."

Rebecca said, "I can't believe we're really doing this. It's the first time in a long, long time I feel in charge of my own destiny."

Scott said, "Yeah, I just hope our destiny's not spending the rest of our lives in a federal prison."

◻

25

...like a Renaissance Fair with guns

The Santa Ana River Shooting Complex was owned by the County of Riverside. Because no permanent structures could be built within a designated flood control area, they rented the land out, cheap. The owner, who'd made a bundle on a fast food franchise and lost most of it in a divorce, had negotiated a fifty-year lease on the 8,000 acre site, then parked an old trailer on the property and called it the range office. He hired a couple young shooting enthusiasts to manage the range and once a week would come in to pick up his earnings. Other than his weekly trips collecting money, he couldn't care less about what happened at the range. The man didn't even own a gun, but he knew a golden goose when he saw one.

After paying his seven-dollar parking fee, John followed the line of traffic and parked in a large dirt field with a number 3. He asked a couple next to him how many parking fields there were. There were eight, they said, and they would be full all weekend.

He suddenly realized he'd overlooked a critical component of their plan. How were they going to find Gaston's Audi on Saturday? There would be thousands of cars scattered in eight fields. Without knowing where Gaston's car was parked, they could spend hours wandering up and down the parking rows. He grimaced, hoping there weren't other things he'd overlooked.

He followed the crowd into the main exhibition area. There were several hundred booths set up in long rows, allowing people to stroll up and down the aisles. Anything remotely related to western clothing, crafts, leather goods, cowboy guns and food was for sale. Western ballads blared from loudspeakers mounted on poles around the exhibition area. Between songs, a gravelly voice with a pronounced drawl made announcements: "For the next ten-minutes, Sarsaparilla on sale at booth 322, thirty-six ounces for a buck," and "Gunsmithing done while you wait, see Strong-arm Stanley at booth 141."

John veered toward a nearby booth when he saw Rebecca standing in front of it, talking to a man selling shooting spectacles, wire-framed safety glasses with clear plastic side shields and circular lenses for the authentic cowboy action shooter. He said, "Well, if it's not the Scattergun Girl."

She thanked the man for his time and said, "Can you believe this place? It's like a Renaissance Fair with guns. You said it was gonna be big, but I had no idea. I bet I saw license plates in the parking area from all fifty states."

"Yeah, we've got a slight problem with that. We're gonna have to find where Gaston's car's parked by eight-thirty in the morning. Any suggestions?"

"Short of placing a GPS tracker on the bottom of his car, one of us is gonna need to be waiting near the gate and follow him into the parking area."

"I was hoping you could be a little more creative."

Rebecca stopped talking and looked at several old U.S. Marshal badges displayed for sale. She flipped over an Arizona Ranger badge and set it back down after seeing the price. "It'd cost us a couple hundred bucks, but I might have another way."

John asked, "Whaddaya thinking?"

"Give each of the parking attendants forty or fifty bucks and the description of Gaston's car. Have them direct his car to the VIP lot. Promise to give them more when you see his car in the VIP lot." She shrugged her shoulders. "That might work?"

"With Gaston's grandiose sense of entitlement, he would never question why he was being directed to the VIP lot."

She looked at her cell phone. "I just got a text from Samantha Everhart. She's here with the horses."

It took five minutes to get to the stable area and another five to find Samantha.

She told them the combination to the horse trailer and in which stable their horses would be kept. They thanked Samantha and returned to the exhibition area, looking at all the western gear.

When they finished, Rebecca asked, "Whaddaya want to do next?"

John replied, "I gotta get a bunch of fifty-dollar bills."

She laughed with surprise. "Are you really gonna do it?"

"Absolutely," he said. "It's a brilliant idea. I just hate leaving something so important in the hands of some part-time, temporary workers. But a fifty-dollar bill makes a big impression to someone making minimum wage."

Going back out to their trucks, they ran into Scott, Manolito and Blakesley.

Scott asked, "Did you guys see Gaston?"

John looked back over his shoulder at the crowd. "No, I'd be surprised if he were to show up today. He's thinking as soon as we see him, we'll confront him and maybe one of us'll take a swing at him. He's hoping for that kind of drama tomorrow when there's lots of witnesses and video cameras rolling."

Scott asked, "How do you see it playing out tomorrow?"

John said, "Gaston will show up feeling cocky, thinking he has us over a barrel. It'll be interesting to see how he acts when the tables are turned. But make no mistake, he'll do everything he can to provoke one of us into a fight. Or a dream come true would be if one of us were to draw and point a revolver at him."

Blakesley said, "That'd win his case against us without ever going to court."

John said, "Yeah, and get all of us fired at the same time, but that's never gonna happen. We're gonna do everything we can to stay as far away from him as we can. Gaston and his posse'll come looking for us, and the more time he spends trying to find us, the more prone he is to making a mistake."

Manolito looked around at all the cars and trucks parked in the fields. "How much cash do you think the range is gonna be depositing from parking?"

John said, "I tried adding it up in my head. Between parking, exhibition and stable fees plus participant fees, conservatively, they should be depositing better than half a million dollars Saturday morning."

Blakesley said, "That's a lot of money. You realize how much space and weight that much money takes up, especially when it is in ones, fives, tens and twenties?"

Scott said, "It'll be quite a haul."

They all laughed.

John said, "Rebecca and I are gonna take care of a last-minute detail. After you guys look at all the booths, go check on our horses in stables 17C through 17G. All the tack is locked up in the trailer, and the combination to the trailer is 30-8-26."

Manolito said, "By this time on Saturday, we'll either be celebrating or in jail."

Scott added, "Or dead." □

26

She's the perfect man for the job…

On Friday morning, John stood in front of the bathroom mirror and looked up and down at himself. He was dressed in his new western clothes and felt confident they duplicated Gaston's, except for lacking the skinner knife tucked inside his boot. Thanks to a dozen stone washings, the slate grey cavalry bib shirt that had been crisply packaged in the box only a few days earlier now appeared tattered and frayed. His brown canvas trousers were equally worn, including a small tear he made on the inside left knee resembling a similar rip they discovered with the help of Blakesley's telephoto lens. Completing the getup, he had black Y-back braces, a black silk neckerchief and a brown slouch hat with sweat stains around the brim.

Perfect. He gave the regalia one last careful check, then changed into his Bighorn Buckaroo outfit for the day's competition.

Going downstairs, it took him a couple trips back and forth to get his things in the truck. On his second trip into the house,

Jenny had come downstairs wearing black Spandex exercise clothes and said, "Don't forget, you're just like a civilian. You're not allowed to keep your guns and ammunition together in the truck. "

He kissed her. "Don't worry, honey. We're not about to give the captain cause for claiming one of us had a concealed weapon, not when we're so close to making this happen."

She took a step back and looked at his western get-up. "I can't believe End of Trail's finally here."

He said, "We're just shooting a cowboy action match and sparring with Gaston today. Tomorrow's when everything happens."

She hugged him. "Just be careful. I don't trust that attorney and wouldn't put it past him if he tries something today. Where's the money?"

He pointed into the kitchen. "The envelope's on the breakfast counter. You should only need half of it today and the rest tomorrow. What time's Crystal gonna be here?"

She looked at her watch. "In another twenty-minutes."

He said, "We're gonna have to do something special for your mom for taking the kids for the weekend."

"I know." She grinned. "What do you think about all of us going to Hawaii for Christmas?"

John lifted his eyebrows. "You realize we're not keeping any of the money we steal from the bank?"

She said, "Christmas in Hawaii. We should really do it."

He considered airfare, hotels, car rental and the cost of eating out and wanted to change the topic. "We can talk about it after this weekend. And not that you needed to tell her, but did you let Crystal know to dress so she'll get the attention of the parking attendants?"

Jenny laughed. "Don't worry, that's one thing she does quite well."

"She's the perfect man for the job. I just hope she doesn't do anything dumb."

Jenny shook her head. "Nothing ever goes the way it's supposed to when she's involved. Remember the time we had her watch the kids for us when we went to the movies, and she showed up ten minutes after the show started, sitting in the row in front of us with Patrick and Clara?"

"I recall we still paid her for babysitting, but there's no way she can screw this up. You'll be right there with her." He pulled her close. "Try to stay out of sight as much as you can. Those guys'll be trying to get an eyeful of you in your sexy workout clothes."

She pushed him away. "Go shoot 'em up, my Bighorn Buckaroo."

"Text me if you have any problems." He gave her a final kiss and left. Over his shoulder, he said, "Keep an eye on Crystal."

***

Thirty-minutes later, she got a text. 'I'm here, r u ready?' She grabbed the money and climbed in the passenger seat of Crystal's Jeep Wrangler.

Crystal had on skin-tight black Spandex shorts, a loose-fitting sleeveless exercise top cut out far too much around the arms, tennis shoes and no socks.

Jenny flinched when she looked at Crystal. "Wow! When did you dye your hair? You're so… blond!"

"I think I'll make a lot more money like this." Looking at herself in the rearview mirror, Crystal asked, "Whaddaya think? Like it?"

"I don't think the guys who go to Hooters look much above your neck."

A flash of hurt crossed Crystal's face, and Jenny was instantly sorry she'd made the crack. But Crystal had already moved on. "I only got three hours sleep last night. You're really gonna owe me for doing this for you guys."

"Thanks," she said. "John and I really appreciate your help, but you know we're running a few minutes late."

"Okay, I'm late, but it's five-thirty in the morning. You know I'm not a morning person. And before you say anything, I'm stopping at Starbucks."

Jenny said, "All I was gonna say is, I'm buying and I can use a mocha." Pulling into Starbucks, Crystal accidentally drove one of the Jeep's front tires up onto a concrete parking bumper. Jenny held onto the dash and roll bar until the jeep stopped moving. "Watch where you're driving, will ya?"

Crystal took off her seatbelt. "Stop being so dramatic. It's a Jeep. It can do things like that."

With their morning coffee secured in their cup holders, they were on the freeway and headed towards the range. After a few minutes, Crystal said, "Now, tell me again, why is this so important?"

"One of John's friends wants to play a practical joke on another guy. We can't let him find out who's responsible for making him park in the farthest field."

"What's the big deal?"

Jenny wanted to be as vague as possible. "It's for a couple guys at the police department. If we don't do it right, it'll look bad for John."

Crystal's hands tightened on the wheel. "It's not for Mano, is it? I won't do anything for that jerk. Did I tell you on our first date, he tells me I reminded him of ice cream? I thought it was cute, Mint Chocolate Chip, Rocky Road or some exotic flavor. I didn't realize he was talking about Baskin-Robbins flavor of the month. When the month's over, the flavor goes away."

Jenny felt a flash of annoyance at Mano. He never pretended to be anything but a player, but she still felt bad for her little sister. "We tried to warn you about him, but you wouldn't listen."

A dreamy smile crossed Crystal's lips. "He's just so good looking."

Jenny swirled the mocha in her cup. "You still aren't over him, are you?"

"I'd like him to see me now." Crystal rolled her hair between her fingers. "He'd beg me to take him back. And you watch, I'd make him beg."

Jenny said, "You know, if this goes well, I'm sure Mano will hear about it. It might make him a little bit jealous when he finds out John asked you to do something important and not him." She hesitated, realizing she was adding one lie to another. But it couldn't be helped. If Crystal knew what they were doing, she'd be even more of a liability. Jenny took a sip from her cup. "I'll make sure John tells him all about it."

She went over the details again until Crystal blew out an exasperated breath. "All right, already! I'm not an idiot."

Jenny lapsed into silence.

After a moment, Crystal extended a peace offering. "It must be important if your friend's willing to pay all this money to play a practical joke."

Jenny averted her gaze. "Trust me, it's important."

Fifteen minutes later, they stopped at the gate in front of the shooting complex. The parking attendant said, "Seven dollars, please."

Crystal smiled one of her girly smiles and stuck out her chest as far as she could. "Can I park here?" she chirped. "I have something to give you."

The parking attendant said to Crystal's chest, "Lady, you can do anything you want."

She reached in the envelope and took all the money. Jenny grabbed her hand. "There's only six attendants."

Crystal smiled. "You've always gotta make them think they can have more."

Jenny nodded. "I can see where you'd be good at that."

Crystal tucked the bills into her exercise bra and bounced out of the Jeep. All six men stopped what they were doing to watch. "Hey, guys," she said. "It's your lucky day. I've got something for everyone and I promise, you're gonna like it. I just need one tiny little favor."

Jenny rolled her eyes and muttered, "Men."

The parking attendants worked in teams of three, one group for each lane coming into the shooting complex. Crystal first spoke with the attendants closest to the Jeep, quickly describing Gaston's car and what she needed them to do with it. Going to the second group, she wielded all her talents. The gravel and tumbleweeds were her runway and the attendants her paparazzi. The stage was all hers. She took her time reaching into her top and pulling out three fifty-dollar bills. When she gave each the money, she leaned forward and kissed them on the cheek.

After giving the last one his money, she took a brochure and pen from him. She scribbled something on it and handed it back. She called out to all six, "I can't wait to see you boys tomorrow."

They watched her sashay back to the Jeep. She made a show of dropping the car keys. She giggled and bent over from the waist with her butt in the direction of the men. Her audience stared. One whistled and another asked if he could take a smoke break, as she took her time picking up her keys. Standing up, she turned and blew a kiss back to them.

Getting in the Jeep, Jenny asked, "What was all that about? What did you write on the paper?"

Crystal tossed her hair. "Why are you always trying to get in my business?"

She started the Jeep and shifted into gear.

"Swear to God, Crystal. If you wrote your phone number on that piece of paper..."

"Why don't you have a little faith in me, sister? Besides, people don't write their phone numbers down. That was so 2010!"

Jenny said, "Stop the Jeep. I'm gonna get the paper unless you tell me what you wrote."

"I made a happy face on one of the brochures. Is that all right with you? Geez, give me a little credit!"

Still looking at Jenny, she made a U-turn across the road.

Right into the path of a silver Audi.

It skidded on the gravel and slammed into the front driver's side of Crystal's Jeep. The force flung Jenny hard against the seat belt and spun the Jeep halfway around. It ground to a stop in a cloud of dust.

Jenny blinked. Then she looked over at Crystal and grabbed her sister's arm. "Are you hurt? Are you okay?"

"I think so. I'm not sure."

Crystal's hands were shaking, and her hair fell in front of her face. Her lower lip quivered, and tears rolled down her cheeks.

"I hope you've got insurance, lady," a man's voice said from outside the window.

Jenny looked up, and her mouth dropped open in shock. Gaston was standing at the door. It was his silver Audi Crystal had smashed into. Of all the wretched luck.

Crystal whimpered, "My Jeep, it's not hurt, is it?"

The parking attendants ran over to the Jeep. Ignoring Jenny altogether, they vied for position, trying to get in and as close to Crystal as they could.

"Are you okay?" one asked.

Another elbowed him out of the way. "Is there anything we… I mean, I… can do for you?"

Gaston, wearing his cowboy hat and clothing, pushed the parking attendants aside. "You stupid bitch. I don't have time for this. I'm late as it is."

Crystal blinked back her tears. "Just because our cars crashed is no reason to talk like that."

Looking at the two cars, one of the parking lot attendants asked, "Is this the car we're supposed to be watching for?"

"Watching for?" Gaston's eyes narrowed. "What do you mean by that?"

Jenny realized the entire plan was about to unravel if she didn't take charge of the situation. She had to think of something and get him away from the parking lot attendants and from Crystal.

She slid out from the Jeep and hurried around to Gaston. She grabbed his arm, pulling him away and to the front of the Jeep. Without any idea of what to do or say, she started talking. "I'm so glad nobody's hurt. It would've been so embarrassing if someone got hurt because of us." She could see there was no real damage and each car only had a few scratches.

He looked around and asked, "Why? Who are you?"

Dammit. She'd walked right into that one. Better come up with something quick. Jenny hesitated a moment and stuttered, "Well... we're part of the awards committee with End of Trail." She put her hand over her heart, stalling for time. "Excuse me while I catch my breath. I'm not use to this sort of thing."

Gaston leaned forward, staring at her.

Trying to appear flustered and giving herself a few more seconds to come up with something to say, she patted her chest. "In addition to the usual awards for the top shooters in all the events and overall best shooter award, we're gonna be giving out cash prizes for the most authentic dressed cowboy and cowgirl. Also, this year, in an attempt to reach out and get more people involved in our sport, we've asked the parking attendants to let us know if they see anyone dressed in an outfit that best represents the gentleman cowboy and exemplifies the cowboy lifestyle that we all cherish."

Gaston looked confused.

She went on, "We drove to the gate this morning and asked the parking crew to look for a true cowboy gentleman—and I think we found him. We'll publish your name in our paper and present you with the 'Gentleman Cowboy Award."

She could tell he liked that.

He said, "I've been shooting Cowboy Action for a couple years. How come I've never seen you two before?"

She said, "Well, obviously we're not in our western clothing right now. I'm always behind the scenes." She pointed at Crystal. "We just hired her. I'm sure you can tell she wasn't hired for her brain. She's our awards presenter."

Crystal called out from the Jeep. "You're not gonna report this to my insurance company, are you?"

Jenny tried to shush Crystal by waving her hand, but stopped when Gaston caught the movement. She said, "If I can get your cowboy handle, I can make my recommendation to the committee. I'm sure you'll want to stick around after the matches tomorrow night for the awards ceremony. You won't be disappointed."

He picked an imaginary piece of lint from his shirt collar. "I always do my part to help whenever I can. I'm Dusty Dave." He gave her a big smile.

Crystal walked up from behind them. "Can I give you three hundred dollars not to report this to my insurance company?" She gave him the remaining fifty-dollar bills.

He shoved the money into his shirt pocket and wagged a finger at Jenny. "Just make sure my picture gets in the paper."

Jenny said, "You can count on it, Mr. Dusty Dave."

Gaston got in his car and rolled down his window. He drove alongside the parking attendants and yelled, "It's all your fault. You're responsible." He stepped on the gas, hit the button automatically rolling up his window, and sped away, kicking up gravel as he left.

Jenny said, "What an ego!"

Crystal nodded. She looked proud of herself. "At least I talked him out of reporting this to my insurance."

Trying to regain control of the situation, Jenny tugged at Crystal's arm. "Come on, we're gonna talk with the parking attendants again."

Crystal said, "Yeah, but I was just in a crash. Shouldn't I be recuperating or something?"

"With all the excitement, I want to make sure these guys don't forget what to do." She looked at Crystal, bottle-blond hair mussed and mascara running. Did she really want her sister talking to the attendants again? "Yeah, maybe you should wait in the car."

It only took a few minutes. As she was climbing back in the Jeep, Crystal asked, "Should I drive out and find John?"

"No. Let's go home. You've done enough for one day." Jenny pulled out her phone.

Crystal asked, "Are you texting John, so Mano will know what I did?"

Jenny thought about throwing her phone at Crystal. "Yeah, something like that."

Crystal smiled. "Read me what ya sent him. No, wait. Forward it to me so I can read it."

Jenny shifted her eyes toward Crystal without turning her head. "I'll send it to you after we get home. We don't want any more accidents because you're reading a text."

She put John's name in the recipient box and tapped in, 'Crystal crashed, but it went fine.'

***

John and the rest of the Southland Regulators Posse were watching Manolito, AKA the Badland Bandito, using his lever action rifle to shoot five plates off a spinning Texas Star target. John felt the phone vibrating in his pocket. He read the text. Crashed. What the hell did that mean?

He texted back. 'Crashed—as in she failed or crashed—as in traffic accident?'

She texted back. 'Fender-bender with Gaston's Audi. Everything's fine.'

Gaston's...

John sucked in a sharp breath and fumbled at the keys. 'OMG! Tell me everything!!!'

The pulsing dots that meant she was typing seemed to pulse forever. Then the message popped up. 'We'll talk tonight. Everything's okay.'

Rebecca said, "That isn't your good news face. What's going on?"

"I don't know. It looks like things didn't go quite as we planned with the parking attendants."

"How's that possible? A sexy woman handing out fifty-dollar bills, what in the world could go wrong?"

He put the phone back in his pocket. "Crystal, that's how."

Rebecca shook her head. "She doesn't know Mano's out here, does she?"

"I hope not. I told Jenny to keep a close eye on her and not let her do anything too loony."

Rebecca said, "If she knows Mano's out here, we could be in for a little drama. Of all the women you guys know, why'd you use her?"

Looking at the ground, he said, "You go to war with the army you have."

After finishing shooting the Texas Star shooting stage, the Southland Regulators Posse walked to their last shooting stage of the morning. At their final stage, they were to start the match lying on a cot, with their boots and hats off and holsters hanging on a hat rack. At the whistle, they were to jump up from the cot, put on their boots and run to the hat rack. At the hat rack, put on their hat, strap on their gun belts and shoot ten targets off a plate rack. The plate rack was a wide metal stand that looked like the letter A from its side. Plates were attached to the top of the stand and when the plates were shot, they would fall over backwards. The fastest time from the whistle to shooting all the plates won. A five-second penalty was added to the time for every target missed.

Rebecca said, "I think this stage is prejudiced against women. Everyone knows it takes us at least an hour to get ready after getting out of bed."

After shooting the stage, they walked from range 11 to the exhibit area for lunch. Food trucks were parked in a large circle with picnic tables inside the circle. John said, "Let's stay together. The last thing we need is for Gaston to take a run at one of us. If we're all together, he might not do anything."

They settled on barbecued beef sandwiches, chips and sweet tea for lunch. Over their meal, they discussed how they'd shot earlier in the day. Mano said he thought they might be in first or second place.

Scott said, "Yeah, we did pretty good, but I've heard several people talking about the Monument Springs Bushwhackers out of New Mexico and the Nevada Rangers from Las Vegas. They say they each have some guys who can really shoot."

Blakesley said, "The match is the least of our worries, but I must admit we are doing pretty good."

"Speaking of pretty good," Rebecca said. "How about these sandwiches?"

"Look what we have here." A voice sounded from behind the table. They turned to see Gaston with his four compatriots behind them. "I'm surprised your captain let you come to the range."

Rebecca said, "You're such a pathetic little man. Why don't you just leave before someone mistakes you for a piece of dog shit?"

A little surprised at Rebecca's quick come-back and afraid she was about to launch herself at Gaston, John stood. "I've got this."

Rebecca sat farther back on the picnic table bench, and John sat back down. Maybe he was the one who was over-reacting.

Gaston and his followers looked at Rebecca with suspicion. After a brief pause, Gaston said, "You assholes think you're better than anybody on the range. I have news for you. You're going down."

Holding up an empty water bottle, John said, "Hey, Gaston, why don't you make yourself useful and get me another bottle of water?"

"I'll piss in it before I become your water boy."

John tossed the water bottle at Gaston's feet. "Go ahead, fill it. I wanna see if you sit or stand when you pee."

Blakesley leaned over to John and whispered. "You might want to take it down a notch, Sarge."

Blakesley was right, he needed to calm down. He could only imagine, if Gaston had gotten under his skin like this, the frustration the others had to be feeling. He leaned over to

Blakesley and whispered, "You talk to him."

Gaston took a step to his right and crushed the water bottle with the heel of his boot. "You guys don't get it. I'm gonna take your house, your cars, your job and any savings you might have."

Blakesley smirked. "Yeah, you've got us shaking in our boots, crushing a plastic water bottle like that. I bet you didn't have many friends growing up, did ya?"

Gaston pointed his finger at them. "I've been waiting for this. Right now, let's go out to the river range and see who can take who. My posse against you assholes."

He raised his voice, and the other shooters in the food court stopped what they were doing and watched. "Come on. I'll show ya, you don't need to be an elite Long Beach police officer to be good with a gun."

John held up a hand and motioned for him to lower the volume. "Trading insults back and forth isn't going to solve anything. Tell ya what, Gaston, tomorrow morning at nine o'clock, let's do this. Meet us at the river range and bring your horses. If you really like losing and being humiliated, we're happy to accommodate you."

Rubbing his leather-gloved hands together, he said, "You're on, asshole. Nine o'clock."

Gaston turned to leave. One of his spurs pierced the water bottle he'd smashed, and it stuck to his boot, ruining any chance of a dignified exit. He cursed and began hopping around on one leg trying to shake off the bottle. In frustration, he told one of his posse members, "Get this damn thing off me!"

Rebecca chuckled. "The price of a barbecue sandwich, five bucks; water, two bucks; watching Gaston getting a water bottle caught in his spur, priceless."

Finally, Gaston yanked the bottle off his boot and stalked away, trailed by his sheepish-looking posse.

Blakesley looked at John. "I'm impressed. For our plan to work, we needed Gaston and his posse at the river range in the morning and they practically volunteered to be there."

John said, "Sorry for losing my cool."

Rebecca shrugged. "It was a little refreshing to see you're human, after all. But I think it's really gonna hurt his feelings when we don't show up in the morning." ❑

Arl Farris

27

...it's time to ride

They were up at the same time. Jenny had her hair woven into a single French braid and had on jeans, a long-sleeved white button-down shirt and cowboy boots. She carried a straw cowboy hat in her hands. John had on the clothes that matched Gaston's.

Jenny said, "I'm really nervous. By now, Gaston has to know everything I told him was a lie and there's no Gentleman Cowboy Award."

John shook his head. "I'm not so sure. His ego's pretty big. He'll want to believe it as long as he can."

Jenny fanned herself using the cowboy hat. "Of all the cars on the road, I still can't believe Crystal crashed into his."

"You're sure the parking attendants will make him park in lot number 8?"

She said, "I'm not sure which made a bigger impression, getting a fifty-dollar bill or watching Crystal parading around in front of them. Trust me, they'll do it. I'll be there first thing this morning to make sure everything goes according to plan."

He agreed. "They're gonna be disappointed not seeing the Crystal show today."

Jenny looked into the distance. "I told you it was a bad idea using her."

"Yeah, but what were the odds she'd crash her Jeep into Gaston's car?"

She hugged John. "I know you'll be great today. Please be careful and look out for the others."

He gave her a squeeze. He loved having her arms around him. "We're gonna be fine. Are you sure you're physically up for this?"

She said, "There's no way I'm staying home while you guys are taking such a big chance. I know if Lisa and Anita knew what Scott and Blakesley were doing, they'd be out there too. Please tell me you'll be careful."

He kissed her on the forehead. "I will. And you'll come visit me in prison if we get caught?"

She snuggled into him. "I'll be in the cell right next to yours."

He cleared his throat. It felt tight with emotion. "I love you too." He leaned forward, bending her backwards, and gave her a deep kiss.

When he released her, she said, "You better go or I'm gonna take you upstairs and you'll really be late."

They drove to the range in separate cars. John paid for parking and Jenny pulled off the gravel road where Crystal had parked the day before. Three minutes after passing through the gates, he received a text from her. 'Call me ASAP! We have a problem.'

He called from his hands-free car phone. "What's going on?"

"Apparently, our gentleman cowboy came through here a half hour ago, didn't stop and drove through without paying. They called for a tow truck and are looking for his Audi right now. When they find his car, they're gonna tow it."

"That entitled bastard," John said. "Pay for his parking and tell 'em you'll pay the towing fee. We can't let them tow his car. We need his car here, and we gotta know where it's parked."

She spoke rapidly into the phone. "I'll do what I can, but these guys are really pissed. They know they're not getting the rest of their money from our deal."

He said, "No, you gotta pay 'em, right now! Give them the seven dollars for Gaston's parking and tell them you'll pay all expenses for the tow truck. They can't tow the Audi. It wouldn't hurt if you give 'em each another twenty bucks. We need those guys on our side."

The phone went silent for a second. "I don't have that much cash with me, and I don't have time to go to the bank."

Using an authoritative tone usually reserved for criminals, he said, "Do not go to the bank!" He angrily muttered, "I can't believe I didn't withdraw more money from our savings account yesterday."

Forcing his voice under control, he said, "Do what you can. I don't need to tell you how important what you're doing is. If it falls apart now, we got nothing. We gotta know where his car is by nine o'clock."

She let out a breath. "I'll do what I can."

John's mind was racing. He needed to come up with an alternative plan or call off the whole thing. He considered putting the money from the robbery in Gaston's office or in the stable where his posse kept their horses, but rejected those ideas as quickly as he thought of them.

He followed the stream of cars and trucks into parking lot number 4. There were a lot more cars than there had been yesterday. Was that a good sign or a bad one? Both, he guessed. More chances for someone to notice an unfortunate detail, but also more opportunities for confusion.

He had to come up with something. Everyone was counting on him.

He made his way into the stables where Manolito and Scott were already saddling their horses. Mano looked like a Hollywood cowboy in his tight jeans and red shirt. Scott, in his long duster, looked like he'd just stepped out of a spaghetti western.

He glanced around. "Where's Rebecca and Blakesley?"

Scott said, "I got a text from Blakesley. He's in lot 5 and..." He stopped talking, pulled out his cell phone. "Rebecca's getting off the freeway. It'll take her another fifteen minutes."

John turned to Manolito. "Is everything here?"

"Yeah, our stuff's in an olive drab duffle bag, locked up in the horse trailer."

John looked back and forth at their revolvers. "You guys loaded with the ammo?"

Scott tapped the revolver in his right holster. "Loaded and ready to go."

John nodded. "As soon as you're saddled, I need you guys to ride out and see if you can find Gaston's Audi."

They stopped what they were doing and stared at John. After a moment, Manolito said, "I thought you paid those guys at the gate to take care of that?"

He told them about Gaston running the gate and a tow truck being dispatched. He said, "Jenny's doing what she can to fix it, but we still need to find his car."

Scott tightened the cinch firmly but without jerking it, then gave the horse a moment to release its breath before tightening it the rest of the way. "What are we gonna do if we don't find it?"

John pushed back the brim of his hat. "I'm coming up with a plan B. But right now, we need to try and find his car."

In a few minutes, Manolito and Scott were saddled and on their horses.

In the three months they'd trained with Samantha Everhart, they had gone from novices without skills and afraid of their horses to accomplished riders with decent horsemanship abilities. They looked calm and natural in the saddle.

John looked at his watch. "You've got twenty minutes to find his car."

Scott looked at Manolito. "I've got parking lot number 1. Why don't you check lot number 2?"

They spurred their horses and galloped out of the stable, narrowly missing Blakesley and Rebecca, who were stepping in.

Dusting off his shoulders, Blakesley asked, "What's up with those guys? Where are they going in such a hurry?"

John filled him in, then added, "We gotta find Gaston's car."

Blakesley pointed toward the parking lot. "There's ten thousand cars out there. It'll be like finding a small ball in a field of tall weeds."

Rebecca looked like she had been punched in the gut. "It's over. Without the car, our plan won't work."

John said, "If Mano and Scott don't find the car, I have a plan B."

His cell phone rang and he looked at the screen, then accepted the call and put the phone to his ear. "Tell me you have some good news."

***

Scott and Manolito came back into the stable leading their horses. Manolito said, "No luck. We looked through each aisle in lot 1 and 2. The Audi's not in either one."

John slid his phone into a pocket. "Jenny just called. She paid for his parking and the tow truck fees. At least we don't need to worry about his car being towed." He looked at his watch. "Time to load up and get going."

Rebecca frowned. "Isn't this a no-go if we can't find his car?"

Sounding more confident than he felt, John said, "Jenny'll find it while we're gone."

Scott said, "I'm not so sure. It's like forgetting where you're parked at Dodger Stadium.

It'll take her hours, if she can find it at all."

Rebecca said, "Tell us about plan B?"

John's eyes shifted from one to the other. "We'll move forward as planned, except we bury the money at the river range."

Scott frowned. "The idea is for the police to find the money and incriminate Gaston. If we bury the money, we won't accomplish anything."

Pointing his finger at John through a leather riding glove, Blakesley said, "Up until now, your ideas have been pretty solid." He shook his head, which made his chin strap sway back and forth. "We're gonna have to come up with something better than burying the money."

Frustrated, John looked at each of them. "If anyone can come up with a better idea, this would be a good time to share it."

Manolito said, "Hold on just a minute." He quickly turned and walked away. A few moments later, he returned, holding an old military surplus folding spade. "Plan B sucks. But until one of us comes up with something better, we're going with it." He lifted the spade. "I'll strap this to the back of my saddle and hope we don't have to use it."

Rebecca said, "I'm not giving up. Jenny'll find the car." John knew her words were meant as encouragement, but she couldn't disguise the defeat in her voice.

Trying to build their confidence back up, John said, "I've never let you guys down, and I'm not about to start now. If it's humanly possible, Jenny'll find it. We're gonna do this and it's gonna work."

Manolito dragged the olive drab duffel bag into the stable and handed everyone their equipment and new shirts to change into after the robbery. Then they each loaded a revolver with the ammunition Manolito had cobbled together. They put the rest of the things into their saddlebags, and Scott double checked the straps that would secure the money sacks behind Mano's and Rebecca's saddles.

"Eight-forty," John said. "It's time to ride."

[]

[]

Arl Farris

28

…game on

Upon first joining the Single Action Shooting Society, Gaston had made a tactical error calling the Sierra Club's legal research department. The mistake wasn't telephoning the Sierra Club. His lapse in judgement came from giving more information than he received. He knew the Sierra Club had teams of lawyers who were more than eager to file a litany of lawsuits to protect a river's ecosystem. However, he did not want the competition from other attorneys cashing in on the environmental calamity he had so carefully cultivated.

He'd asked the Sierra Club paralegal what they were doing to protect the area from a range along the river and dealing with excessive lead from the shooting. The legal assistant told him they were unaware of any issues and wanted additional details. He gave a long history about the range and emphasized lead ammunition being shot within the flood plain. The legal assistant thanked Gaston and assured him they would get right on it.

Gaston longed to see the range shut down, but not to protect a stupid duck that was too dumb to stop eating lead bullets. He wanted the range closed and the land turned into open space with a couple of picnic tables and maybe a few barbecues. They could rename it the Peter Gaston Memorial Park. The fact that there were no adverse environmental impacts occurring from the range was a problem he was trying to work through. If only he could get Pamela or Fatima at Wallace Laboratories to see the greater good and change their findings. Armed with the right environmental reports, he could be done with this entire charade.

Or maybe they were already falsifying their reports. Maybe someone with deep pockets, like the NRA, had gotten to them first. Yeah, that was probably it. The thought made him queasy with anger.

He understood it would take years to compile enough facts, evidence and expertise to put together a case that would bring down the firearms industry, but he was done waiting and ready to take these gun nuts to court. He had put in the time, done his research and paid his dues. He wanted to cash in.

He felt something big was about to break in his favor with the water and soil samples or with all the shooting at the range this weekend. At the least, he expected a large payday coming from his cases against the Long Beach Academy range officers.

Either way, it was time for a big win.

***

It was a ten-minute ride from the stables to the river range, if you knew where you were going, which Gaston did not. With his loyal crew of four trailing behind in single file, he rode to the river, turned left and followed the bank. Not only did he go the long way, but the closer to the river, the denser the vegetation, undergrowth and tangle of trees became, making travel on horseback extremely arduous. Twigs and saplings pushed aside by one rider would snap back at the next, swatting at horse and rider alike.

After finally arriving at the range, he was angry John and the rest of the Long Beach range staff were not waiting for him. They dismounted and tied their horses to some nearby saplings. He looked at his watch, "Ten after nine, those assholes are late."

***

In the center of the exhibition area stood the public announcers booth, a 20 x 16 green army tent. It had carpet attached to its inside walls for soundproofing and was located far enough away from the shooting venues to keep the sounds of gunshots being broadcast over an open microphone, although attendees preferred hearing gunfire to advertisements.

Jenny lifted the tarpaulin door flap and went inside. The odor of rotting canvas hung in the air and a single 100-watt bulb dangled precariously low from the center of the tent. The glare from the naked bulb caused her to squint while looking at the man operating the sound system. In his late fifties, he was unshaven with a pot belly. He wore cowboy boots, a Henley long sleeved shirt with food stains on the front, dirty Levis and three-inch wide suspenders. She wasn't sure if this was his cowboy costume for End of Trail or if he dressed like this every day. She suspected the latter.

She asked, "Do you take requests?"

He looked happy to have a woman in his tent. Flashing a big smile of crooked yellow teeth, he said, "As long as it's something by The Sons of the Pioneers, Marty Robbins, or Tennessee Ernie Ford, I can probably help you out. Otherwise, not so much."

She laughed. "No, not that kind of request. The Southland Regulators want to call out a couple members of the Lead Bottom Posse to a shoot off at the river range, and we'd like it broadcast over the public address speakers."

He scratched at his belly. "As soon as Johnny Cash stops singing about Ghost Riders in the Sky, I'll be happy to put that out for ya."

She shook her head. "No, the Southland Regulators are still shooting in a match and won't be done for another fifteen or twenty minutes. I hoped you could make the announcement sometime between nine-thirty and nine-forty."

Looking her up and down in the piercing light, he said, "Anything for a pretty lady."

She told him exactly what to say. "Do you want me to write it down or do you have it?"

He frowned, pursing his lips. "I've got it. I'm always happy to help a lady, but this isn't a very friendly message. Sure ya want me to put it out there like ya said?"

She nodded. "It's not meant to be nice."

"Well, I suppose you know what you're doing. I don't know who these boys are in the Lead Bottom Posse, but I kind of take it they're not your friends." He chuckled. "Leastways, they sure aren't gonna be after they hear this."

Jenny flashed a mischievous smile. "If you could singe their ears when they hear it, so much the better."

Taking a page out of Crystal's charm book, she leaned forward and kissed him on the cheek. "You're a sweetheart."

As she turned to walk away, he held a hand to his cheek where she'd kissed him and muttered, "Oh, to be twenty years younger and fifty pounds lighter..."

Hmm. Maybe Crystal was onto something after all.

***

They left the stables and headed north, opposite the river and around the fields of parked cars. John had butterflies in his gut and suspected the others felt the same. His confidence waned, and he didn't know if his growing doubt was from losing Gaston's car or knowing what awaited him if they got caught. No matter what prison sentence the others might receive, as their superior, his would be double. Not that it mattered. He had seen what life was like for police officers in custody, placed in protective isolation until another inmate managed to get close enough to run a shank between their ribs. He couldn't live like that, not for twenty years.

Leaving the range and before hitting the street, they stopped to put on orange safety vests. A few weeks earlier, John had been online reading about urban sprawl around the Santa Ana flood control, and the article happened to mention a county ordinance requiring equestrian riders to don high visibility safety vests when on paved streets. The last thing they needed was to be stopped by a bored patrolman for violating some inconsequential ordinance.

They rode single file along the right side of the street, in the bicycle lane. In a mile, they turned onto River Road and entered a designated horse trail paralleling the highway.

Rebecca led with Scott behind. Scott looked around her and stiffened. Following his gaze, John saw a Riverside County Sheriff's patrol car approaching from the opposite direction. He felt the bottom of his stomach sink and his arms seemed to weigh fifty pounds each. He closely watched the black and white, ready to make a run for it if the police car tried to stop them. The patrol car motored by, showing no interest the riders.

Manolito let out a breath as the black and white went past. "Now you know what a crook feels like when we go by 'em in our patrol cars."

Scott laughed, but it sounded forced. "Man, I'm still shaking."

In a couple blocks, they went from behind a residential tract to the front of shops and convenience stores. The horse trail ended, forcing them back into the bicycle lane.

John's cell phone rang. Blakesley, last in line and behind John, said, "If that's Captain Dickerson, I don't think I'd answer it."

He looked at the phone. It was Jenny. "You've gotta talk fast. We're almost there."

"I found his car! I was going back to the stables from the announcer's booth and for whatever reason, I took the long way back."

"I don't have time. Just tell me where's the car?"

"That's what I'm doing. He drove his car behind the stables and put bales of hay around it. He must have known they were gonna tow it for not paying the parking fee. The car's inside the hay bales behind the stables."

John felt like a tremendous weight had been lifted from his shoulders. "You're the best, honey. We'd've never found it. I've gotta go." He shouted, "Forget plan B. Jenny found the car."

They collectively sighed with relief. Their chances of success had just gone way up.

***

Rebecca remained in the lead and waited for a break in traffic. She crossed the street and the others followed. With everyone safely across the highway, she gestured at the bank with a nod of her head. "There it is. Game on."

The Wells Fargo Bank had red brick sides with white concrete accents and tempered glass windows. Like most buildings in Southern California, it supported terra-cotta colored Spanish roof tiles. A parking lot wrapped around the building to accommodate two drive-up windows.

Surprised to count thirteen cars in the lot, she thought, That's a lot of people we're gonna have to control.

They stopped and removed latex gloves and Halloween 6 Michael Myers masks from their saddlebags and put them on. They adjusted their hats and tied the neckerchiefs so no skin showed beneath their masks. Rebecca turned her horse around and rode past the others, critically inspecting everyone's mask for any giveaway details that could identify them. She stopped and leaned into Blakesley, lifting up his neckerchief. "We can't have any of your skin showing."

"Thanks."

Scott left his leather gloves on and put on a Lone Ranger eye mask.

Rebecca looked at him. "You need to raise your bandanna over your mouth."

"Geez, I can't believe I forgot!"

John struggled with his mask. In frustration he said, "The holes don't line up with my eyes. I can't see outta this stupid thing!"

She reached out to help adjust his mask. After tugging and stretching it, she said, "Take it off. I'll cut new holes for you to look through."

"No," he snapped. "We can't alter any of the masks, especially this one."

Holding her knife in her hand, she asked, "Ya sure?"

"Yeah, we don't have time to fool with this. Come on!"

She looked at the others one last time. "Let's do this."

***

Their excitement was palpable, but John knew not to rush the approach. "Take it easy. Go slow until we get there."

Rebecca turned her horse back towards the bank and the others followed. Pulling his mask to one side so he could see out

332

of the eye holes, John rode alongside Rebecca. "Remember, use your big boy voice."

"Got it." She turned her horse into the parking lot, rode on the sidewalk and dismounted next to the front door. The others did the same, handing Scott the reins to their horses. He stayed outside with the animals and to make sure no one else came in. The others drew their revolvers and went inside.

◻

29

…don't pet that end of the horse

Gaston kicked at a clump of dirt. "Those bastards aren't coming. Let's go back. I'm gonna rip those those guys a new ass. Making me wait, this is gonna cost 'em, big time!"

They mounted their horses and left the range with Gaston in the lead. He went in a straight line away from the river, retreating from the jungle of brush and trees. After five minutes of plowing through the tangles of vines, sticks and saplings, the vegetation thinned and they were able to make better time. Eventually, they came out near parking lot number 8. They turned their horses and headed in the direction of the stables.

They could have blended into any frontier town of the 1870's. They looked every bit the part of cowboys from their clothes, guns, holsters and saddles. They may have lacked the calluses and were better fed than the men they were trying to emulate, but in every measurable way, they were cowboys.

As they rode into the exhibition area, Marty Robbins had just finished singing about a cowboy dying in a west Texas town when the announcer took to the loudspeaker and recited the massage Jenny had given to him.

"This is for the lowdown, yellow-bellied posse led by Dusty Dave. You called out the men of the Southland Regulators Posse then failed to show for the shoot off. The honorable men of the Southland Regulators are waiting for you at the new river range. The Santa Ana Flood Basin isn't big enough for both posses. If you yellow-belly Dusty Dave Posse cowpunchers don't show your faces at the new river range, you'll be branded as cowards. This next song is dedicated to you. You can decide which you are, but it's definitely not good."

The theme song from The Good, The Bad and The Ugly began playing.

Gaston stopped, a slow rage building as he listened. Those arrogant, murdering bastards. He was worth ten of any one of them. Hell, he was worth ten times all of them put together. Damn it, he was getting the Gentleman Cowboy Award.

When the announcer finished, he turned to the others, his voice rough with emotion. "Where the hell's the new river range? Were we at the old one?"

Walter, a clerk at the Los Angeles Transit System during the week and a member of the Lead Bottom Posse on weekends, said, "They make a new river range every year. Maybe we're at the wrong one?"

Gaston said, "Of course we're at the wrong one. Where the hell's the new one? I do everything for you guys. You took me to the wrong fucking range! Just once, I wish you'd do something for me. Stop fucking around and find the goddamn new river range!"

George, a 43-year-old Hispanic man, who was a sales manager at the Long Beach Ikea store when he wasn't participating in cowboy action shooting, pointed back the way they'd come. "I guess it's back there somewhere?"

"Of course it's back there, you idiot. Come on, we're gonna find those assholes!"

He spun his horse around. The others exchanged glances, then followed single file, back towards the river.

***

Inside the bank, bulletproof Plexiglas windows extended from the counter tops to the ceiling, shielding the tellers from their customers. Tellers talked through speakers set into the windows at chest height. There was also a pass-through in the countertop allowing them to exchange checks and money back and forth. On each end of the teller counter were Plexiglas doors that were kept locked during business hours. The tellers and branch manager had keys to individual cash drawers, but none had keys to the doors. While the bank was open for business, the only way to gain access through the doors was by having a teller from behind the Plexiglas unlock the door with one of the remote access buttons located at the teller windows.

Rebecca entered first and went directly to the branch manager's desk. The manager, a blond woman in her early forties, sat at her desk talking with a young Hispanic couple. Rebecca grabbed the manager's arm and, in a raspy voice, said, "You're needed in the vault."

The manager started to pull away, then looked up and saw the mask. She let out a yelp.

Customers turned to see what caused the commotion and saw three menacing robbers pointing guns and taking tactical positions.

While Rebecca controlled the branch manager, John and Blakesley stepped in front of the teller line and aimed their revolvers at the tellers. Calmly, John said, "Raise your hands. Don't press the alarm."

He knew the bullets from their revolvers would not penetrate the Plexiglas and, truth be told, they would be in more danger from a bullet ricocheting off and coming back to hit one of them. He hoped the tellers would be stunned by the sight of two masked men pointing guns at them long enough for Blakesley and Rebecca to get behind the Plexiglas partition before the tellers realized they were perfectly safe.

Mercifully, the tellers did as they were told, raised their hands and avoided the alarm.

Manolito stood between the Plexiglas door and a potted ficus tree. John hoped there would be plenty of soil to allow the crime technicians to recover a fired bullet with no rifling. In a voice just louder than a conversational tone, Mano said, "We're sorry for any inconvenience, but I must insist: Lie on the floor. Put your cell phones in your pockets. You won't be hurt."

The customers stood frozen in disbelief. He cocked the hammer on his revolver and fired into the soil of the ficus tree. At the sound of the shot, the customers immediately dropped to the floor.

Mano said, "Thank you. We'll be gone in a minute. But for now, no talking. No cell phones."

Holding her revolver to the bank manager's head, Rebecca walked her to the Plexiglas door and said to the closest teller, "Let us in, please."

While in the backyard at John's house, they'd discussed the tone they would take while committing the robbery. They knew from working other robberies, if a customer became frightened, had a heart attack and died, they would be charged with murder. Wearing masks was scary enough; they didn't need to yell. Besides, when Mano fired a shot, that would convince everyone to cooperate.

The teller closest to the door lowered her hand, and the door buzzed. Rebecca opened it and went inside; Manolito and Blakesley followed. They ordered the tellers to step back from the windows and to put their hands in their pockets, so they wouldn't be tempted to reach for the alarm.

John remained outside the Plexiglas with the customers. He tugged at the side of his mask, trying to realign the eye holes. He pointed his revolver at the couple still seated at the branch manager's desk. "On the floor, please."

The man dropped to his knees, but his wife reached into her purse and pulled out a can of pepper spray. "I'm not afraid of you!"

She extended her arm and depressed the plunger. John was still pulling at his mask and adjusted it just in time to see a stream of pepper spray coming through the eye holes. An instant later, his eyes were on fire. Involuntarily, his eyes clamped shut. Tears streamed down his face, his body's pathetic attempt to eliminate the chemical irritant. He twisted around and dropped to his knees to avoid any more repellent.

Best-laid plans.

Crap.

***

From behind the teller windows, Manolito saw the woman squirting pepper spray and John go down. He ran out to the customer lobby to see the woman taking aim, preparing to fire again. Focused on John, she didn't see Manolito running towards her. As Mano stretched his hand out to knock the spray out of her hand, he saw the man climb to his feet and fumble beneath his shirt. A glimpse of the concealed handgun was all it took. Manolito shoved the woman to the ground and charged the man.

The man yanked upward, pulling the weapon from his waistline. His cheap clip-on holster had come off his belt, still attached to the gun. He stripped the holster away from the gun as Manolito crashed into him. The force knocked the man backwards onto the bank manager's desk.

The pistol fired.

Mano felt like he'd been punched in the shoulder. He pushed away from the wide-eyed man, who dropped the pistol and held up his empty hand as if he could call the bullet into it.

Holding the small automatic in his right hand, Manolito reached down with his left, grabbed the front of the man's shirt and threw him off the desk and onto the floor. Then he stood over the man, panting, momentarily stunned.

The pain was beginning to seep in, a deep throb with a burning at the center. The shoulder of his shirt felt warm and wet.

***

With one of the robbers on his knees and another shot, several customers raised their heads off the floor. They looked at one another, not knowing if they should get up and run or were about to pay the ultimate price for someone trying to foil the robbery. Before they could decide what to do, Blakesley ran out from behind the teller area and the customers knew any chance they had to run away had vanished.

***

Holding the horses' reins, Scott jumped when he heard the second shot. Their plan called for Manolito to fire one round in the bank, allowing a crime tech to recover the bullet. They'd discussed what they would do if confronted by an off-duty policeman. They all agreed they would try to disarm any off-duty policeman but if the officer refused to drop his gun, they would holster theirs and try to flee without robbing the bank. Under no circumstances would they shoot another policeman.

The second shot told Scott things were spiraling out of control. He readied himself in case whoever or whatever obstacle the others encountered might be coming out to challenge him.

The horses were skittish and pulled against the reins when he attempted to push them aside to look through the front doors of the bank. He figured the animals could sense his anxiety and decided he would not try to force them back and risk one bolting.

His hand instinctively jerked to the revolver on his hip when he saw a figure next to their horses. It was a boy of about seven standing directly behind the horse closest to the bank. The boy's mom held his left hand while he petted the rear leg of Rebecca's horse. Scott stopped his draw, took a breath and relaxed his arm.

He said, "Don't pet that end of the horse."

Seeing Scott's mask, the mother asked, "Why are you dressed like that? What are you doing?"

"Oh, you know Wells Fargo. They're filming a commercial. You might want to go to the other side of the parking lot. Our stagecoach is about to come through here."

He wanted to scream at the woman to take her kid and get the hell out of here. Couldn't she see? They were in the middle of an armed robbery!

The mom asked, "Can I put Trevor on one of your horses and take a picture?"

"When the commercial's over, I'll give Trevor a ride. But right now, we need you to go to the other side of the parking lot."

Still holding the boy's hand, she went to the other side of the parking lot. "I don't see any cameras," she said. "Where are the cameras?"

Scott pointed behind her and said, "Over there."

***

"It's broken!" the woman screamed, lifting her twisted right arm.

Hearing the second shot, Blakesley ran out from behind the Plexiglas, spurs clanking on the tile floor. He saw John on the floor, writhing in pain. Manolito had blood spreading on the right side of his shirt, and bank customers were getting off the floor.

"What the hell!"

Assessing the situation, he pointed his revolver at the customers, expecting a revolt from one or more. Seeing no resistance, he looked across the lobby. Manolito held the barrel end of a compact semiautomatic pistol, and a man lay at his feet, pleading for his life. Manolito's posture slacked and he began to wobble. Quickly, Blakesley put an arm around his waist and sat him in the bank manager's chair. Then he reached inside Manolito's orange vest and looked under his shirt. "Fuck!"

He took the neckerchief from Manolito, folded it into a rectangle and stuffed the makeshift bandage around the front and back side bullet wounds. He grabbed Manolito's left hand, placed it over the front wound. "Keep pressure on it, and hope it stops bleeding."

Incredulously, Manolito said, "Give me a minute. I'll be fine."

Blakesley pointed his revolver at the man at their feet. "Don't do anything stupid."

Holding his hands palms up, the man gasped, "I'm sorry. Please! Please don't shoot me!"

Blakesley thought the way the man gulped for air, he would either pass out or vomit. Either way, he was no longer a threat. He told the man, "Shut up. Crawl over to the others."

Not sure what to do, the man sat motionless.

Blakesley jabbed the air with the revolver. "Go over with the others."

He wondered if any other customers were armed. He wanted to tell them if they liked shooting bank robbers, come to Long Beach; this sort of thing happened three or four times a week.

Blakesley looked at the woman with the broken arm and back at the man. "Is that your wife?"

The man looked at her, then back to Blakesley and retched.

Avoiding the mess on the floor, Blakesley said to the woman, "You can help him, or he can help you. Just don't…" The man vomited again. Blakesley said, "Geez!"

Blakesley turned to Manolito. "How you holding up?"

"I'm good."

Their situation wasn't good, and their options were limited. Blakesley said, "Then cover these people while I check on the boss."

Mucus dripped from under John's mask. He coughed and hacked as Blakesley bent over to see what was wrong. He immediately smelled the distinct odor of pepper spray. "Son of a…"

Blakesley kicked at the shoes of two men on the floor. "Get up. Get the Sparkletts bottle from on top of the cooler. Go!"

The two hesitated, looked at each and stood. Cautiously, they went to the water cooler, keeping their hands in the air, swiveling their heads back and forth, looking between Blakesley and the cooler. They set the jug at Blakesley's feet, then lay back down on the floor.

Blakesley grabbed John's shoulder. "Get up. Follow me, Gaston."

He told the two who carried the water to him, "Get up. Bring the jug."

The men sprung up, grabbed the five-gallon jug. "Wherever you want it, mister."

Blakesley thought, As eager as these guys were, must be Stockholm syndrome. Well, for once, he was grateful for it.

He guided John into the closest restroom and told the two men to set down the jug. He ordered them to get back and lie down with the others.

***

Still disguising her voice, Rebecca asked the branch manager, "Where's the money from End of Trail?"

"End of Trail?" the manager repeated. "What's that?"

"The cash deposit from the Santa Ana River Shooting Complex."

"It's in the vault."

"Let's get it."

The manager looked at the keys on a lanyard around her neck. "I only have one key. It takes two."

Rebecca pointed her revolver at the tellers. "Who's the commercial teller?"

A woman in her mid-fifties raised her hand, with keys jingling around her wrist. Rebecca nudged the manager to walk forward and told the commercial teller, "Come with us."

***

Trusting Mano to control the hostages, Blakesley pulled off John's mask and tossed it into the sink. He turned the faucet all the way on, soaking the mask and causing water to splash onto the floor. Then he positioned John in front of the toilet, picked up the jug and slowly poured it over John's head.

The cool water on the sergeant's face would lessen the stinging, but it would take a good ten minutes before John could even begin to function.

That was longer than they could afford.

***

Still holding the man's automatic, Manolito fumbled to remove its magazine and lift the slide off the frame. His fingers weren't working right. These gloves. It had to be these damn gloves. He took the barrel out of the slide and winced as he reached to open one of the desk drawers. Awkwardly, he dropped the barrel in a paper hanging folder and plunked the slide into the waste paper basket. The frame slipped from his hand and fell to the floor. He raised his hand in front of his face, opened and closed it. Nothing. He had no feeling in his hand, arm or shoulder.

In frustration, he kicked the pistol frame across the floor.

The motion pulled him off balance, and he stumbled forward, caught himself. The room did a slow spin.

A splash of red caught his eye. Red on the floor, red on the desk. So much red. He needed… needed…

Bleach.

Unsteady on his feet, Manolito used the bleach solution spray bottle on the chair and desk, wherever he might have bled. When the bottle was empty, he let it tumble to the floor.

He needed more.

Who had more?

Blakesley. Blakesley was with John. Dealing with the pepper spray. Right.

There was something he was supposed to be doing. He'd ask Blakesley about it.

Had to find Blakesley.

***

Blakesley looked up at the spreading stain on Mano's shirt and knew things had gone seriously sideways. He grabbed the dripping mask and pulled it down over John's head. "Time to go."

He tugged John and Mano back to the main lobby and turned to look at the teller line. A 19-year-old teller stood at the window with her right arm under the counter. Shit.

He drew his revolver and fired into the ceiling. The teller screamed and jumped back from the window, joining the others.

"Alarm!" Blakesley called. "We gotta move—now!" He switched hands holding the revolver and pulled out his spray bottle.

Using his right hand, he pumped the spray bottle as fast as he could on the floor. His left held the revolver, covering the room. After ten seconds of spraying, he unscrewed the lid with his teeth and poured the liquid on the floor, spreading it around with his boot and mixing in some of the vomit. Then he tossed the empty bottle aside.

No sign of Rebecca. He stepped behind the Plexiglas door. As he passed the tellers, the young woman who pressed the alarm sobbed. "I'm sorry. I'm so sorry. Please don't hurt me!"

"Don't worry about it." He wanted to tell her how brave she was and should be proud of herself. However, he didn't have the time, nor would she understand it coming from him.

He went past the tellers and into the vault. Rebecca had two canvas bags on the floor that came up to her waist. She looked up and said, "What's going on out there?"

"Alarm's hit. Gotta go!"

"Almost done."

"Leave it. Let's go!"

She closed both bags, keeping out two stacks of cash held together with paperclips and two single ten-dollar bills. She said, "Bait money and ETDs." She pointed to a red furniture dolly in the corner of the vault used for wheeling coins in and out and said to the branch manager and the commercial teller, "Put that sack on the dolly. Then roll the dolly and follow him."

The two women labored putting the money on the dolly.

Rebecca walked backwards, watching the two women and pulling the other sack behind.

Her stomach clenched when she stepped around the counter and saw the spreading stain on Mano's shoulder. Quickly, she used her spray bottle to give the blood between Manolito's feet a few squirts.

"Go," she told him. "We'll be right behind." Keeping one eye on the women with the dolly, she stayed close behind Mano, making sure he wasn't leaving a blood trail.

Manolito stopped at the front door, holding it open with his uninjured hand as the two bank employees wheeled out the dolly. In a voice strained with pain, he told them, "Set it next to the horses."

After setting the money down, the women waited for direction. Blakesley pointed. "Back inside, join the others."

***

Scott stared in disbelief as Rebecca led Mano out the door. He didn't know what happened inside, but knew this wasn't part of their plan.

Rebecca came out, dragging the second sack. Blakesley followed, guiding John out the door.

Scott said, "So much for us being smarter than the average bank robber."

◻

30

...why are you all wet?

John felt like a red hot poker was pressed against each of his eyes. They'd clamped shut, tears trickling from the corners, and he still couldn't open them. His nose and mouth felt seared; all he could smell and taste was the chemical spray.

He fumbled for the saddle horn, silently cursing his helplessness. Then someone— Blakesley, he guessed, from the strong hands at his back—lifted John's foot into the stirrup and pushed him up onto his saddle.

"Thanks." John tilted his head in what he assumed was still Blakesley's direction. He was anxious to start riding, knowing the wind in his face would quickly dissipate the effects of the pepper spray.

He needed to get his wits back as quickly as he could. There was still a lot to do before they were safe, and he didn't want to let his guys down any more than he already had. With a rising panic, he wondered what else they hadn't accounted for. But he had seen his team in tough spots before, and there was no one else he'd rather be with in a jam.

Breathe.

He drew in a painful breath. How had everything gone so wrong?

***

Scott held the horses' reins, trying to sort them out the best he could. His companions' identical masks slowed his progress. He looked at John, then looked again. "Why are you all wet?"

He got no reply, but John's swollen eyes and the miasma of pepper spray around him told the story.

Not good. From the time policemen began the academy, they were exposed to chemical spray. After years of frequently using and being around the irritant, rather than building up a tolerance or resistance, many officers became more sensitive and vulnerable to its effects. John was apparently one of them.

Rebecca got on her horse next and used her normal voice, "Little help here." She pointed to a canvas sack.

Blakesley helped Manolito onto his horse, then grabbed a sack of money, swung it up and secured it behind Mano's saddle. Then he moved to Rebecca's horse and did the same with the second bag. To Mano, he said, "You okay to ride?"

Manolito swayed in the saddle, then steadied himself with the horn and grunted, "Look after the boss."

Scott took in Mano's dangling right arm and the bloodstain at his shoulder. His voice rose. "Are you shot?"

Blakesley hurried back to Scott. "It looks bad, but I think he can sit a saddle. Alarms been pushed, we've gotta leave!" He took the reins of Oh, a stocky chestnut, and Utah, a tall, rangy sorrel.

Scott jumped on his horse and shouted, "Let's go!" He maneuvered his horse beside Mano's in case he needed to reach out and steady his wounded partner.

Rebecca led, setting the pace at a steady trot. Leaving the parking lot, the others rode nose to tail behind her. The horses' steel shoes made a loud metallic clip-clop on the pavement.

The woman Scott had told to wait on the other side of the parking lot waved as they rode past. "Trevor, look for the cameras. Wave at the pretty horses."

***

John had his hand under his mask, allowing air to flow up and onto his face. The midmorning temperature was close to 80 degrees, but the warm air felt cool against his cheeks. He could now breathe through his nose and could finally open his eyes to slits. Through the misaligned eyeholes, he caught occasional glimpses of light and shadow, but for all intents and purposes, he was riding blind.

"Damnit!" He wanted to go back to the bank, but it was too late. The plan called for him to leave two strands of Gaston's hair on the branch manager's desk when the customers were on the floor. Nothing was going right.

***

They were in the bicycle lane. Horns honked as they rode through a red light. In a few minutes they came to the start of the horse trail. Without breaking stride, they entered the dirt path and Rebecca pushed them a little faster.

She gestured toward a patrol car on the street racing towards them, eastbound with its overhead lights flashing, and yelled over her shoulder, "Put your heads down."

Scott quickly complied. Blakesley followed suit, then reached over and tipped John's hat forward. Scott did the same for Mano. With luck, the wide brims of their hats would shield their masks from the passing officer.

Traveling at twice the posted speed limit, the black and white nearly went past them before going into a four-wheel locked skid and coming to a stop in a plume of blue tire smoke. The police car sat motionless, except for its overhead lights rotating. Rebecca knew what was going on inside the Dodge Charger. The officer was advising dispatch he'd located the bank robbers.

Funny how life happened. A few months ago, she'd been putting the cuffs on a couple of bank robbers. Now she was one. She knew the rest of her life would be determined by their riding skills and by what was about to happen next.

The officer activated the siren, made a U-turn and crossed the painted double yellow centerline for west-bound traffic.

Shit.

***

John heard the car skidding past them and, against all odds, hoped the screeching tires were not from an officer's car responding to the robbery. But there was no time to ask. As he took his hand out from under his mask, his horse bolted, jolting him off balance. With a stifled curse, he grabbed for the horn and struggled to pull himself upright in the saddle. Did Blakesley have the reins? Or was his horse completely out of control?

He could feel the other horses around him. Either Blakesley still had Utah's reins, or the other horses had spooked too.

Finally, his horse found its stride. He found his seat again and put his hand back under the mask, welcoming the additional wind on his face.

Then the siren screamed behind them, confirming his worst fear.

Beside him, Rebecca slapped the flank of her horse, and they shot off at a full gallop. Even so, he heard the black and white draw parallel to them in seconds. The horses shied and snorted, skittish at the sound of the siren, but thanks to their acquired riding skills, the Regulators were able to adjust to the animals' erratic strides.

Thank God for riding lessons. For all the good it would do them. A horse, even a fast one, couldn't outrun a patrol car on a highway.

John dropped the edge of the mask and leaned forward, lifting his seat off the saddle a fraction to help the horse lengthen its stride. Giving up was not an option.

***

Manolito couldn't remember ever being in so much pain. He was in a cold sweat. At least he hoped it was sweat and not blood dripping down the center of his back. If it didn't mean giving up the others, he would have gladly stopped and let the officer take him into custody, to end the pain. He spurred his horse and winced as it bounded forward.

He felt that gray haze slide over his mind and teetered in the saddle.

No. Hang on.

He bit his cheek hard, and the new, sharp pain brought his brain back into focus.

A hundred yards farther, the double yellow centerline gave way to a raised center island with trees and river rock. The officer in the pursuing black and white would have to make a decision: should he stay on the right side of the road and contend with the stop-and-go traffic, or drive on the wrong side of the divided roadway, trusting no oncoming cars would crash head-on into him?

The officer made the wrong choice, taking the safe route and staying in the westbound lanes of traffic. The horses thundered onward, and shortly after the roadway split, traffic came to a stop, blocking the black and white.

The horses slowed to a canter, pulling away from the pursuing vehicle. Mano took a deep breath, and the earth spun. He grabbed the saddle horn again and gasped at the wave of pain that shot through him.

Just a little farther.

***

Their escape was short-lived. Another police car, going the wrong way in the eastbound lanes, rapidly accelerated towards them. From fifteen feet away, the officer turned off his siren and shouted into his loudspeaker, "Riders. Stop your horses!"

A horse can't outrun a car, but a car can't go where a horse can. While they remained on the street, the advantage went to the black and white. But Rebecca knew if she could get in a field with some good-sized rocks, they would be home free.

She glanced back over her shoulder. John seemed to be getting stronger by the minute. Mano, on the other hand, was looking bad. As he started to slump off to the side, Scott reached over and steadied him. Mano's breath came in ragged gasps, and he clutched at the saddle horn as if it was all he could do not to lose consciousness or cry out in pain. Mano was no quitter, but she didn't think he could last much longer.

Behind them, the officer gave up on using the loudspeaker and flipped the switch, turning on his siren. The horses spooked at the sound, but they wanted to run, and all the riders had to do was nudge them in the right direction. For another quarter-mile, the patrol car and horses paralleled each another.

The horses' sides heaved, and their nostrils flared. Rebecca's horse stumbled, then recovered. She squeezed her legs, pushing it onward, hoping the animal could maintain the pace. Its neck was drenched in sweat, but they couldn't afford to stop.

Come on, baby. She willed it forward. Just a little farther, and you can have all the peppermints and carrots your big old heart desires.

At the end of the raised center island, traffic cones were set, allowing westbound traffic to cross into the eastbound lanes. Stopped by the traffic in front of him, the officer turned off his siren and picked up the microphone to the loudspeaker. In a voice tinged with desperation, he shouted, "Riders—Stop or I'll shoot!"

She knew the officer's commands were a hollow threat. They were all quite familiar with the legal parameters authorizing the use of deadly force. Simply running away from a bank robbery was a long way from meeting the threshold allowing the officer to open fire.

Rebecca pulled up on the reins, going from a hard gallop to a slow trot.

She bent forward to give the horse's neck a pat. If they'd had any time to waste, she would have kissed it.

Thank you, baby. You guys really saved our bacon.

***

John had nearly recovered from the pepper spray and couldn't wait to rip off his mask. He tugged at it until he could see out of one of the misaligned eyeholes.

Ahead of them, Rebecca maneuvered between the cars, trying to get into End of Trail. The others stayed bunched up behind her while snaking through the stop-and-go traffic.

John turned his head to scan the rest of his team through half an eyehole. Manolito's shirt was soaked with blood. Before John could speak, Scott reached over and pulled Mano's coat across his chest to hide the blood.

John turned his gaze forward, his stomach queasy. When had Mano been shot?

The officer chasing the horses tried to squeeze his Charger between the cars parked along the curb and those lined up for End of Trail. Another bad decision. The police car brushed against a slow-moving pickup and slammed into the row of parked cars, clogging the entrance behind them.

John let out a breath. They just might make it after all.

Soon, the horses loped through the gates and past the parking attendants entering the shooting complex. Rebecca turned her horse to the left, through a field of sage brush and small trees towards the Santa Ana River. They could no longer hear the siren from the black and white, and a police car couldn't drive through the field.

She slowed her horse to a fast trot.

Fully recovered from the effects of the pepper spray, John took off his mask and said to

Blakesley, "I can take it from here."

Blakesley handed him Utah's reins just as Rebecca turned in her saddle and shouted, "Looks like we're gonna make it."

The rumble of a helicopter flying low and fast proved her wrong. John looked up to see the chopper heading directly towards them. "Let's go. Hurry up, to the river!"

John dropped back to end of the line and watched as the others passed him. Manolito had bowed his head and tucked his arm into his chest, clearly struggling to remain upright. Scott took Mano's reins and looped them around his own saddle horn, then rode with one hand and steadied Mano with the other.

They spurred their horses again and were off at a full gallop with the helicopter in pursuit.

☐

☐

31

…who said pigs can't fly

The Riverside County Sheriff Office's aviation division operated two Hughes 500D and two M D 500E model helicopters. All four helicopters were equipped with a Forward Looking Imaging Infrared system or FLIR. The FLIR system worked exceptionally well at night, being able to identify people hiding in the darkness or in vegetation. The infrared spectrum image appeared on a small computer screen in the cockpit. Images looked like a negative on black and white film. The FLIR system picked up heat radiated from people, animals or cars.

If a person were to lie down, hiding in a flowerbed or clump of bushes at midnight, the FLIR system would have no problem finding them. However, on hot days when the sun was beating down and there was less difference between a person's temperature and the temperature on the ground, the FLIR system was of little value. The value of using a helicopter in law enforcement, be it in a high-speed vehicle pursuit or responding to emergency calls, was its ability to have a clear and unobstructed view from above and to direct ground units into the most advantageous position to make an arrest.

Fortunately for the Regulators, it was unusual for more than one of those four helicopters to be flying at any given time. If there was a need to have a helicopter assigned for a search and rescue mission, a second helicopter would be put into service, but on a typical day, only one was flying at a time. Even with additional helicopters in reserve, it took about thirty minutes, with all the pre-flight inspections and safety checks, to get a second helicopter in the air, assuming a flight crew was ready and standing by.

That knowledge was some consolation as the green and gold Hughes 500D flew over the five riders, tracking their progress as they galloped across the broken terrain.

In the sixteen years John had been with the Long Beach Police Department, he had never worked in the aviation division. However, being a sergeant in downtown, he had enough experience coordinating with the helicopter pilots on searches, responding to crime scenes and joining pursuits, he knew how they would react and how to exploit any shortcomings with the technology on board the aircraft.

Rebecca rode hard with the others following. They could hear the thump, thump, thump of the rotors cutting into the air. The dry sage brush started to give way to more green brush, taller plants and trees the closer they got to the river.

John rode as fast as he could, passing Blakesley, Manolito and Scott. He caught up with Rebecca and signaled for her to stop. They came to an abrupt halt with the horses breathing hard and in a circle with the helicopter hovering overhead. He pointed at the helicopter and shouted, "The pilot'll be calling for ground units to go into lots 8 and 2. Our only chance is the river."

He yelled to everyone, "The horses can't take much more, but we've got to get to the river. Come on!"

They were off at a full gallop again with Rebecca leading and John behind her. Scott and Manolito ran a dozen yards behind, Mano leaning precariously in his saddle. Blakesley slowed until he and Scott flanked their injured friend. Mano sat up straighter. "I'm not dead, yet," he said. But he swayed in the saddle and didn't protest when they each put out a hand to steady him as they galloped on.

***

Even with their overhead red and blue emergency lights flashing and sirens blaring, the police cars were having difficulty getting inside the entrance gates. The cars and trucks trying to enter the shooting complex had nowhere to pull over allowing the police to pass. Adding to the congestion, the black and white that crashed into the parked cars blocked one of the lanes.

One of the officers pounded his fist on the steering wheel. "I swear, I'm never watching another western again."

***

After a quarter-mile, the trees and brush were too thick to permit them to travel in a straight line. John felt certain the pilot would lose sight of them as they disappeared under the canopy of trees.

As the vegetation along the river made forward movement increasingly difficult, Rebecca slowed her horse to a walk. In another couple hundred yards, they arrived at the river. She turned her horse west to follow the river back to the stables.

John yelled, "No, follow me," and rode into the river.

In the months preparing for this day, John had spent a considerable amount of time on the internet reading everything he could about the Santa Ana River and studying satellite images on Google Earth. He'd read several articles referencing stories about foolhardy individuals trying to ride rafts down sections of the river after heavy rainfalls. Those with any degree of whitewater rafting skills were lucky to survive five minutes. Those without skills didn't make it fifty feet.

When it rained, the river was an unforgiving torrent not to be messed with. However, this was early October in Southern California and there hadn't been any rain in months. The river was diminished to twenty-five feet across and three feet deep with a gentle flow.

He stopped in the center of the river with the others circling him. The helicopter had gained altitude when they entered the trees and now hovered two hundred feet above. The helicopter began descending towards the river. Scott removed a Yellowboy carbine from his scabbard and fired two shots in the air, well in front of the helicopter. The pilot immediately reversed course, regaining altitude.

John shouted over the noise of the rotors chopping into the air, "Don't hit the chopper."

Scott shook his head. "Not even close. Just giving us space."

John said, "We're gonna split up. Mano. Rebecca. With me. Scott. Blakesley. Cross the river and work your way back to the stables. Stay under the trees as much as you can. The horses are spent. Keep 'em cool so they won't stand out on the FLIR."

Scott handed Mano's reins to John and turned his horse around. Then he paused for a moment, shrugged out of his duster, and handed it to Mano. "Put this on. It'll cover that shoulder."

He helped Mano pull on the leather coat and arrange the tails over the horse's haunches. Then he gave John a two-fingered salute and said, "Good luck, see ya on range 12." He and Blakesley took off across the river to the south side. John, Manolito and Rebecca doubled back to the north.

As they rode up the river bank, Manolito's eyes fluttered, and he slumped over his saddle horn. John leaned over, pulled back the coat, and saw the wet sheen on Mano's shirt.

Manolito opened his eyes and mumbled, "It's all the riding."

John knew it was his fault. If he had tried on the mask ahead of time, they could have fixed the misaligned eyes and none of this would have happened. His officers deserved better and he wouldn't blame them if they stopped listening to him.

Manolito roused himself and waved a bloody hand. When he spoke, his words were slurred. "I'm a.... always been.... big Second Amendment guy. Ya know?" He shifted his weight. Grimaced in pain. "People got a right to, to carry a gun. Only... Yeah." His eyes fluttered back, then cleared. He shook his head as if he could shake himself fully conscious. "Never thought I'd be... shot by some goof... some city... citsuz... citizen... lawfully pro... tecting themselves."

Rebecca and John exchanged a glance. She seemed as at a loss for words as John felt. Finally, she asked, "Shouldn't we get rid of the masks and ammo now?"

John shook his head. "We might run into Gaston, and he could identify us. Besides, if they search the river, this'll be the first place they look."

She pointed to her mask and asked John, "Shouldn't you put yours back on?"

He blinked. "No. I can't see outta the damn thing. I'll put it back on if we see or hear anyone coming."

They backtracked about seventy-five yards before turning west. They could hear the helicopter flying up and down, east and

369

west along the river, trying to locate them through the trees. Their horses were still sweating, and John knew they needed to keep them cool.

He stopped his horse and asked Rebecca, "Is any of the money wrapped in bundles?"

"All of it. That's what took so long in the vault. I had to go through it looking for the stupid dye packs and Electronic Tracking Devices."

He asked, "Wasn't Blakesley supposed to help with that?"

She snickered, "Yeah, he got a little distracted."

Another pang of guilt shot through him as he realized what she meant.

Pointing at the money sack behind her saddle, he said, "Give me one of the bundles."

"No problem." She reached into the bag and pulled out a bundle of one hundred five dollar bills. "That enough? Ya want any more?"

He put the paper bound stack of five-dollar bills under his orange safety vest. "No, that's plenty."

They wound their way through the jungle of vegetation that both concealed them from the helicopter and slowed their progress. After five more minutes of painstakingly picking their way through the thickets, John said, "The horses are too hot. Plowing through all this underbrush is making 'em sweat. The helicopter will pick up our heat signature if we keep pushing 'em."

He turned his horse south, and in a few minutes, they were back at the river. They rode into the water, with John and Rebecca dismounting. Manolito stayed on his horse. If he got off, it was doubtful he would ever get back up.

John said, "We're getting too close to End of Trail. We need to get rid of everything here before someone sees us."

Rebecca took off her mask, wrapped it around a softball-sized rock and tossed it into the deepest part of the river. She collected Manolito's mask and orange safety vest and wrapped them around a rock the size of a cantaloupe. They made a large splash when she dropped them in the water.

John also sank his mask and vest using more rocks.

In the unlikely event their masks or vests were ever found, who could say who hid them there? The police would say the robbers did it, but who exactly were the robbers, anyway? The constant flow of water from the river would have long ago washed away any traces of DNA.

John said, "I thought we'd've run into Gaston and his posse at the river range. I guess we missed 'em?"

Rebecca looked at Manolito's shoulder and sighed, "Probably for the better."

John reached in his shirt pocket, removed the two-ounce spray bottle and tossed it in the river, peeled off his latex gloves, put a tennis ball size rock in each and let them drop into the river. He said, "Get rid anything you don't want to get caught with."

Manolito said, "You and Rebecca are the only one with spray bottles."

He looked at Manolito's shoulder. "I guess so."

Rebecca helped Manolito with his latex gloves, sinking them with more rocks.

John reminded them. "We better do our ammo while we're at it."

Wincing in pain, Manolito drew his revolver, pointed its barrel upward and opened the loading gate. He rotated the cylinder, letting five live rounds and one empty casing fall into the river.

Rebecca asked, "Ya think we should load up with our regular ammo?" Before he could answer, they heard the helicopter approaching and rode hard for the cover of the trees. The helicopter flew by from nearly a thousand feet above without spotting them.

Rebecca looked towards the sky. "I guess they haven't found Blakesley or Scott or they wouldn't keep flying back and forth."

John said, "Come on, we still have a lot to do."

***

After riding around in circles for nearly forty-five minutes, Gaston and his posse made their way back to the river range. They were worn out from fighting through the brush and their horses were lathered in sweat. Gaston dismounted Banjo, his bay roan, and let it wander untethered. His posse dismounted, grabbed his Quarter Horse and tied the animals to saplings at the far end of the range.

George, the Ikea sales manager, told Gaston, "We've ridden every inch of this river bottom and there's only one river range."

Gaston brushed leaves and twigs off himself. "We're gonna sit here and wait for 'em. We're not going back so they can say we never showed up."

After a few minutes, they heard the sound of a helicopter passing up and back along each side of the river. Gaston looked up. "Who said pigs can't fly?"

George said, flippantly, "I'll bet ya someone fucked up and shot somebody. That's why we've been hearing all those sirens and the helicopter's flying around."

Gaston's eyes widened, and a shiver of excitement ran through him. This was it. This was what he'd been waiting for. Finally, he was going to be able to sue the fucking NRA and this goddamn range.

Almost frantic with anticipation, he said, "Really? Did you see something? Quick, tell me what you know!"

George's eyebrows lifted, and he took as step back, as if disturbed by Gaston's overreaction. "Well, I mean, all the cops and stuff. What else could it be?"

"You're right. We've gotta get back. This is fucking righteous!"

Suddenly, Gaston had another thought. What if it was one of those assholes from the Long Beach Police Department, the Southland Regulators who shot somebody? This could be even bigger than he'd ever dreamed!

Gaston's excitement was palpable. George looked worried, as if he wanted to take back what he'd said. "Someone could have fallen down and twisted their ankle, ya know, something like that?"

"No," said Gaston. "There's been a shooting, and I think I know who caused it."

***

Leaving the river, they headed northwest, in the direction of the stables. After a short distance, John found himself riding into a clearing the size of a tennis court. He saw a group of five cowboys sitting at one end, their horses tied at the opposite.

Realizing he'd just ridden into the river range, John slipped the bundled of five-dollar bills out of his pocket and into his hand. He slapped his horse's flank, and Utah broke into a full gallop. Rebecca, holding Manolito's reins, rode right behind. Seeing the horses running at them, Gaston and his cohorts scrambled trying to get to their feet and out of the way of the charging horses.

***

Gaston stood as John passed four feet from him. John threw the money at Gaston as they thundered past. Gaston raised his hands an instant too late, and the bundle smacked him square in the face. He fell over backwards, mouth gaping in surprise. Two of the Lead Bottom Posse members ran for the protection of the trees. George and Walter stayed behind, reaching out to help Gaston.

Gaston had been so fixated on the idea of someone being shot at one of the shooting events, it took him a moment to comprehend what happened. All he knew for sure was that something had hit him in the face, he was lying flat on his back and what the hell was going on with all those horses?

John stopped at the far end of the range, untied three of the posse's horses and rode off with them in tow. Rebecca untied the remaining two, and she and Manolito followed John into the woods.

An equestrian could easily distinguish Gaston's bay roan from John's chestnut and a sorrel from a red dun. Some of the horses were lighter, a few darker, and others had a different color tail and mane, but at this point it didn't matter. The horses had not been seen on the bank's CCTV, and the only thing that mattered now was getting away.

Gaston saw the riders making off with their horses and shouted, "Get those guys! They're stealing our horses!"

George and Walter ran after the horses as they were being led away.

Still on the ground, Gaston picked up something near his hand to throw it in disgust. Raising his arm back to throw, he noticed he was holding a stack of money. "What the hell?" He stopped to look at his hand. Then a grin spread across his face, and he jumped to his feet to look for more money.

He wasn't sure if it was the money that had hit him in the face or if it had been hidden under a branch. Gaston decided it had to be the money that hit him, but that couldn't be right either. No one goes around riding a horse in the middle of this crap throwing money at people.

He made one last look around his feet, then shoved the cash into his shirt pocket. "Let's get those guys!"

***

The helicopter flew over the river range. The pilot could plainly see Gaston and his crew. He watched the five cowboys run out of the clearing and into the vegetation where he could no longer observe them. The pilot began to circle, making large loops, trying to see the five again. In a minute, the pilot noticed five riderless horses standing in the middle of the river, a quarter-mile west of the river range. Next, he saw the five cowboys run into the river, mount the horses and ride away as fast as they could.

He got on the radio. "I've got a visual on 'em in the river about a mile south of parking lot 8, possibly headed northwest to the exhibition area."

***

John kept the Lead Bottom Posse's horses long enough to ensure they wouldn't be immediately followed and left them close enough where Gaston would be able to find them. After turning the horses loose, they rode away from the river. It took ten minutes to reach the back side of the exhibition area, and "Running Gun" was playing over the loudspeakers.

When they reached the hay bales, John and Rebecca dismounted. John helped Manolito off his horse and looked at Mano's shoulder. The bleeding had slowed, but it hadn't stopped.

They needed to get him some help, but they couldn't have him bleeding all over the car. And Mano was proud. He wouldn't want to be sidelined.

"Why don't you stay here and keep watch?" John said. "We'll get you taken care of."

Keeping his arm to his chest, Manolito said, "No doctors. We can't risk it."

He was right, but John didn't want him to be right. He unfastened the straps and lifted the money sack off Manolito's horse, then went to Rebecca's horse and did the same. He carried one of the sacks to the trunk while Rebecca dragged the other one back. He removed a leather glove, reached into a pocket and took out the Audi key Scott had delivered to them two months prior. He pressed the button on the key and held it until the trunk popped open. Then he pressed the other button twice, unlocked the two front doors and put his glove back on.

Rebecca opened one of the canvas bags. "I've got it from here. You go up front and do the rest."

He said, "Be fast. Not sure how much time we've got."

John hurried back to his horse and removed a black trash bag from one of the saddlebags. He sat in the passenger side of Gaston's car, leaving the door open and his right leg outside the car. He took a plastic sandwich baggie out of the trash bag and emptied five rounds of the no-rifling .38 Special ammunition into the cup holder on the center console. He reached back into the black trash bag and pulled out a Halloween 6 Michael Myers mask and an orange safety vest still wrapped in cellophane.

He took the mask out of its wrapper and intentionally dropped it on the ground outside the car. He rolled the mask on the dirt, having it appear dirty and worn. He placed it face down in his lap, reached into the trash bag and removed another plastic sandwich baggie containing clips of Gaston's hair from the barbershop floor. John's fingers were clumsy with the leather gloves and it took a couple of tries to pick up a few loose strands of hair from the baggie. He placed Gaston's hair inside the mask and stuffed it under the passenger seat. Next, he took the orange vest and, like the mask, kicked it around on the dirt with his boot. He put more hair from the baggie around the collar and stuffed it under the seat next to the mask.

While John planted evidence inside the car, Rebecca worked in the trunk.

She removed a clear plastic storage box with cowboy clothing and four boxes of .38 Special ammunition. She placed the plastic box on the ground and lifted the carpet, exposing the spare tire, first aid kit and jack. Using both hands, she shoved bundles of cash around the spare tire. She emptied the first bag when John came back to the trunk and he lifted the second bag into the trunk. "Make sure the empty bag gets in here."

She threw it on top of the spare tire. "Got it."

He said, "Great. Let's button it up and get outta here."

Rebecca tried to put the carpet covering back over the spare tire, but it wouldn't fit. "Damn it! There's too much money."

John flipped the carpet off the spare tire. "Let me try."

It took a minute to rearrange the money around the spare tire. "Try it now."

Together they folded the carpet over the spare tire and it fell into place.

Rebecca said, "Good enough for government work."

John slammed the trunk and they went to where Manolito and their horses were waiting. John double clicked the key, locking the car. He removed his black neckerchief and used it to clean Mano's wound. Then he changed into a new shirt and handed Mano the one he'd worn during the robbery. Since the rest of Mano's regalia was different from Gaston's, it shouldn't arouse suspicion. "Put this on. It will hide the blood."

Rebecca pushed up her sleeve and looked at her wristwatch. "Our match starts in thirty- five minutes. What are we gonna do about Mano? If he doesn't shoot, we'll be disqualified."

No one said what they were all thinking: without an alibi, the police would start to look at them for the robbery.

Manolito said drowsily, "I can shoot better with my... with my left hand than most of these guys can with... two."

John got on his horse. "I'll take care of it. You're not gonna be doing any more shooting today."

Manolito said, "I can't go to… hospital with… with… a gunshot wound."

Hospitals were required by law to immediately report when they treated anyone entering their facility with a gunshot wound.

John said, "I'll get you some help, just try not to open your wound any more than it already is."

He looked at his iPhone, scrolled through his contact list and called Gary Newhouse. Gary picked up after the first ring. "Gary, remember a couple of months ago in Farmer Boys restaurant when you said if I needed anything—anything at all—to call you? Well, I'm kind of in a bind…"

32

…like smoking in the bathroom

They helped Mano back into the saddle, careful not to re-open the wound, then rode three across, north along the dirt perimeter road. There were not as many trees this far from the river, but the sage and tumbleweeds were thick enough. They watched as the helicopter flew over them. It continued past and turned back towards the river. Going by a particularly thick area with weeds and sagebrush, John reached into his pocket, took out the Audi key and threw it as far into the brush as he could.

An overflowing trash dumpster sat in parking lot #3, twenty feet from the dirt road. John broke away from Manolito and Rebecca and, leaning out of the saddle, shoved the black trash bag deep into the dumpster.

A sheriff's patrol car sped towards them, leaving a large dust cloud in its wake. Its overhead red and blue lights were on, but not its siren. Rebecca looked to John, and he said, "Take it easy. If they knew it was us, the helicopter would be hovering. I'm sure they're checking all riders."

He looked at Manolito. "Keep your shoulder covered."

Mano tugged the right edge of Scott's duster farther across his chest, and grunted, "Easy for you to say."

They stopped and let the police car come to them. The officer got out, one hand on his pistol. He told the riders, "Keep your hands where I can see 'em."

Rebecca asked, "What's going on, officer?" She grinned and gestured to her horse. "We weren't speeding, were we?"

"We had a robbery not far from here and the suspects got away on horseback."

Turning halfway around in his saddle, trying to hide his shoulder, Manolito pretended to look off into the distance. "I don't see any robbers."

The officer followed Mano's gaze, then tracked back toward the group. "Have you seen anything suspicious, this morning? We're looking for five guys on horseback who might have come out near the river."

Rebecca emphasized, "Five guys, huh? No women?"

The officer got her point and shrugged. "We're checking everybody."

John shifted his weight in the saddle. "We've been shooting all morning, haven't seen a thing. We always cooperate with the police, but can't help you today."

The officer got back in his car, shut down his overhead lights and drove away. John pulled out his iPhone and texted Jenny. 'Come to range 12 ASAP!!!!'

***

Jenny spent the morning prowling around the exhibition booths. Several times, she saw a helicopter flying overhead and it made her nervous. In the last twenty minutes, she saw groups of officers on foot near the displays. They were obviously not there to be social and carefully eyed the men dressed in cowboy outfits, which was practically every man there. Every few minutes, she looked at her cell phone, waiting for the go-ahead from John, but hadn't gotten anything. When his text finally arrived, she texted back. 'Doing it now.'

John texted, 'Hurry!!!!'

She went towards the stables and saw a black and white parked at the end of the crafts area. An officer sat inside, focusing a pair of binoculars in the direction of the river. The windows of the police car were up, the engine running. She stood at the driver's door for a minute, without the officer acknowledging her. Then she tapped on the window, startling him. He dropped his binoculars and pressed the button, allowing the window to roll a fraction of the way down. A blast of cold air slapped her face, and through the crack in the window, the officer scolded, "What do you want?"

He was an overweight man with a scowl that said he was annoyed to be talking with her. Leaning in towards the car and trying to sound as friendly as she could, she said over the roar of the air conditioner, "I don't know what's going on, but I saw—"

He cut her off. "Look, lady, I'm in the middle of something. Go over there, they'll help you." He pointed back to where she had come, rolled up his window and returned to scanning the trees with his binoculars.

Disappointed with the officer's inept response, she hurried away, going back to the crowds of people around the exhibits. She spotted two sheriff's deputies slowly making their way through the spectators. The deputies were wearing dark green military style battle dress uniforms with darkened Riverside County Sheriff shoulder patches and dull-colored cloth badges over their left shirt pockets. They were not mingling with the crowd, but clearly looking for someone. Five someones, Jenny thought.

Both deputies appeared to be very fit and each had a Colt M4 rifle with close-quarter combat EOTech optics slung across his chest. She guessed these were SWAT officers called in to look for the bank robbers. She had known several Long Beach Police SWAT officers and knew them to be highly motivated and anything but lazy.

Not like the officer in his air-conditioned car.

She approached them and said, "I don't mean to bother you, but I just feel like I need to tell someone…"

One of the deputies, with Peterson embroidered over the top of his right shirt pocket, turned to her. "How can we help you, ma'am?"

The deputy, with Fleming on his name tag, glanced at Jenny, then resumed scanning the crowd as she spoke.

"Well," she said, "not five minutes ago, I was walking my dog, Lucky, over behind the stables." She pointed to the area, but the deputy kept looking at her without turning where she pointed. "Anyway, these guys rode out of the trees and got off their horses next to the hay bales."

Like she had done after the collision in Crystal's Jeep, she took a breath and placed a hand over her chest. "My heart's pounding so fast. I don't know why I'm so nervous."

Deputy Fleming rotated his sunglasses off his face to the top of his head and took a small notebook from his pocket. Both deputies were now looking directly at her.

"They took a bunch of stuff out of their saddlebags and made several trips. They were carrying stuff back and forth from their horses into the space with all the hay bales."

Deputy Peterson asked, "How many were there and what were they wearing?"

She gestured with her hands. "Not really sure. Maybe four or five? They were wearing cowboy clothes and had guns."

Deputy Fleming asked, "Did they appear wet or out of breath?"

She half smiled. "That's the thing. I really wasn't paying attention until I heard one of them say, 'That's all the money.' I think they were carrying money from their saddlebags and hiding it in the hay bales. What they were carrying could have been stacks of bundled cash. They were carrying it in their arms. Like this."

She bent her arms at her elbows and raised the palms of her hands to her chest, showing how someone would carry bundles of cash pressed to their chest.

Deputy Fleming watched Jenny demonstrating how the men carried the money, then returned to writing in his notebook.

"If I didn't hear them say that about the money, I wouldn't have noticed them." She looked from Deputy Fleming to Deputy Peterson and shrugged. "I know you have more important things to do, but ya know what they say: see something, say something."

Deputy Fleming stepped aside and spoke on his handheld radio, letting his sergeant know they possibly had a material witness and were gathering additional information.

Jenny said, "I really wasn't paying attention. I'm a little embarrassed to even tell you about it. I know they use a lot of western props in their shooting matches and maybe it wasn't even real money, but these guys seemed like they didn't want anyone to see what they were doing."

Deputy Peterson asked, "Whaddya mean, they didn't want anyone watching?"

Lying again. "I'm an elementary school teacher. You can tell when boys are up to something and don't want anyone watching 'em, you know, like smoking in the bathroom. Anyway, these guys were definitely up to something."

Deputy Peterson asked, "Could you tell if they were wearing masks?"

She faked a laugh. "Masks? You're making fun of me."

Deputy Peterson said, "No, ma'am. We had a robbery near hear and the robbers had on masks."

Jenny pretended to think that over, then said, "I'm not surprised. They had a lot of money."

Deputy Peterson repeated his original question, "So were these men you saw wearing masks?"

She stopped talking, tilted her head to the side and pretended to recall something from memory. "I never really saw their faces. When they finished, they got back on their horses and took off in that direction." She pointed towards the river.

Deputy Fleming scribbled in his notebook. "Why do you suppose they went that way?"

She replied dismissively. "To get more money or maybe hide. How would I know?"

Deputy Peterson said, "These guys robbed a bank in town and got away with a lot of money. There were several shots fired during the robbery and one of them's been shot. Did any appear injured?"

She nearly collapsed from the news. Not John, she thought. It couldn't be John. He'd just texted her. But you could be shot and still text, depending on where the bullet hit you. A sharp, searing pain shot through her leg, shoulder and side of her head where she'd gone through the sliding glass doors at the hospital. She thought she might throw up, but somehow she managed to find her voice. "That's terrible, someone getting shot."

While Deputy Fleming called on his radio asking for two additional deputies, Deputy Peterson snickered. "Not that terrible, when a crook gets hammered."

"Oh, my God!" Jenny gasped.

Deputy Peterson looked around. "Where's your dog?"

Reeling from the news of the shooting, she momentarily forgot her story. "What dog?"

Deputy Peterson pointed at the ground. "You said you were walking your dog. I think you called him Lucky? Where's your dog?"

For a moment, her mind went blank. She thought she might faint if she kept talking with the deputies, but she had to say something. Looking down to her left side, where her imaginary dog should be, she said, "I... I gotta go. I knew I shouldn't let him off his leash." She took off into the crowd, calling, "Lucky, where are you, boy? Come here, Lucky."

Deputy Peterson shouted after her, "Hey, lady, I need your name."

Deputy Fleming told Peterson, "We can catch up with her later. We need to check out her story first."

◻

◻

Arl Farris

33

…my pulse is 87

Jenny sat crying in her car. She texted John. 'r u ok?' She started the Honda and turned the radio to one of the twenty-four-hour news stations. She listened to the stock market report, followed by traffic and the weekend weather forecast. There was nothing about a bank robbery or shooting. She turned off the radio and Googled 'robbery at Wells Fargo' on her iPhone and scrolled through the results. Man shot in leg near Wells Fargo Arena: Woman shot at Wells Fargo ATM in Fayetteville: Body found in front of Miami Beach Wells Fargo Bank: She couldn't find anything about a shooting at a Wells Fargo bank today.

She scrolled through the earlier texts from John and everything seemed like it was going as planned. Jenny thought, What if John's hurt and someone else is texting me from his phone?

She put her car in reverse and backed out of her parking spot. She stopped when a text came in on her phone. It was John. 'Where r u?'

Jenny texted. 'r u ok?'

'Range 12 – ASAP. NO MORE TEXTS!!!'

She got stuck behind a slow-moving pickup truck and the pain from her injuries made her nauseous. She slapped at the steering wheel and shouted, "What did we do?"

It took ten minutes to get to range 12, but it felt like a lifetime. When she arrived, she saw a dozen horses tied to hitching posts outside the range. John and the rest of the Long Beach range staff sat in the spectator bleachers. They appeared normal, but she knew something had gone terribly wrong.

It was all she could do not to run into John's arms. However, not wanting to attract attention to herself or the others, she casually sat in the bleachers in front of them. Almost whispering, so no one else could hear, she asked, "What's going on? The deputies I spoke with said someone…" She stopped talking, noticing Manolito's ashen complexion and the perspiration on his face. She thought to herself, my God! Mano's going into shock and they're just sitting here doing nothing!

John said, "Mano's feeling a little sick. You wouldn't mind driving him home?"

On the shoulder of Mano's duster, she saw a blood spot the size of a softball. "Get him to my car."

They stood, and Scott caught Manolito as his knees buckled. With a weak laugh, Mano slurred, "I'm feeling kinda puny."

They got him to the passenger side of Jenny's car and took off his gun belt. John removed his hat as they buckled him in. Jenny pulled the trunk lever and told John, "Get the blanket from the trunk and bring it up here. We've got to do something for shock before his body starts shutting down."

She looked at Blakesley. "Move the seat all the way back and put the backrest down flat. He needs to lie down with his feet up."

By the time Blakesley adjusted the passenger seat, John was back with the blanket.

Jenny turned to John. "I can't believe you guys were letting Mano go into shock. Put the blanket over him and prop his feet up on the dash."

"We couldn't do anything without people noticing," John said. "Especially with all the police around here." He finished tucking the blanket in around Manolito.

She reached over the top of Manolito, took hold of John's hand, and squeezed it firmly. John stopped, and she looked into his eyes. "I love you," she said. A tear rolled down her cheek.

Manolito opened his eyes, looked left at Jenny, right to John. "I love you too, man," he said, and chuckled.

Jenny let go of John's hand and shook her head. "I'm surrounded by idiots."

She rolled down the passenger window and told John, "If he doesn't improve, I'm taking him to the hospital."

Knowing full well the ramifications, John nodded.

Driving as fast as she could without drawing attention, Jenny took off, trying to see around the boots propped up on her dashboard. "Geez, Mano, I didn't realize your feet were so big."

He didn't answer.

***

They stood watching Jenny and Manolito go. Rebecca looked at her watch. "Our match starts in five minutes. Does anybody have any ideas?"

Scott said, "Should we turn ourselves in or—?"

Just then, someone behind them called out, "Hey, John, there you are! I didn't recognize you with your hat and cowboy outfit."

It was Gary Newhouse. John said, "Gary, I can't tell you how happy we are you're able to come down here. You've already met Blakesley. This is Rebecca and Scott."

They shook hands, and Gary said, "So, I finally get to meet the guy who killed Jesus." He looked towards the road coming into the range. "It's a good thing I made it through the entrance before you called. Apparently, there's been a bank robbery, and the suspects were last seen on horseback coming this way. The sheriff's department has quite a manhunt going on, and the gates coming into the shooting complex are all but shut down."

"We heard something about that, but we've been too busy to pay much attention. I can't imagine someone robbing a bank and thinking they'd get away by coming out here. Do you know if they caught 'em yet?"

John rubbed his forehead with the back of his hand. Besides working the range for the Orange County Sheriff's Department, Gary worked robbery-homicide for the Huntington Beach Police Department. It wouldn't take much for him to start connecting the dots. They'd better change the subject, or he'd put this whole thing together.

Gary said, "I'm sure it's just a matter of time."

"Yeah, we can only hope," John said.

Gary asked, "So, what do you need?"

Happy to not be discussing the robbery, John replied, "We've been practicing to shoot End of Trail for several months and this morning, our fifth team member, Manolito Torres, got sick and had to go home. If we can't find a replacement, we'll be disqualified. I hoped you could stand in as Mano and shoot with us. All our registration fees have been paid. You just need to shoot and have fun."

Gary looked skeptical. "I don't have any cowboy guns, and I've only shot a single action revolver a couple of times."

John shrugged. "It's just like any other pistol—watch the front sight and gently press the trigger."

"If only I had a dollar everytime I told that to a recruit."

John held up Manolito's gun belt and cowboy hat. "You'll be perfect. When we sign in, use the name Badland Bandito."

Gary laughed. "I don't know. Are you sure about this?"

Gary had on a blue long-sleeved dress shirt, jeans, boots and a leather dress belt. Blakesley took off his neckerchief and handed it to him. "They're not so keen on poly-cotton blends out here. Put this over your shirt and you'll be good to go."

Rebecca cut in. "They're calling our posse. Time to start or we forfeit."

Gary put on Manolito's holster and shook his head. "Something doesn't feel right about this."

Trying to divert Gary's train of thought, John said, "I know what you mean. It's weird. Wearing all this stuff and shooting these old guns… it's like being in another time."

***

Leaving the shooting complex, Jenny reached in her purse and took out a bottle of Vicodin. She handed Manolito a water bottle. "Here, take two of these. They're major pain killers I had after my accident. Don't drink too much water when you take the pills, or you'll throw 'em back up."

She used the car's hands-free dialing to call her mom. "Hey, Mom, I hate to ask you, but something's come up and we're on the way home. We need the house to ourselves for a few hours. If it's not too much trouble, can you take Clara and Patrick to your house?"

Barbara teased, "All right, you two lovebirds."

"Thanks, Mom," Jenny said and hung up.

Manolito took a sip of water. It seemed to clear his mind a little. "Your mom's pretty sharp. She'll be gone when we get there?"

"You won't need to worry about that, Mano. In about five minutes you'll be lucky if you can hold your eyes open. I just hope I'll be able to get you out of the car once we get home."

Manolito closed his eyes and Jenny thought about carrying him into the house. There was no way she could do it alone.

She sighed and reluctantly called her sister.

***

The two SWAT deputies returned to their car and drove around to the area where the hay bales were stacked. They were surprised to see another car parked inside, hidden from view.

They called in the license plate number of the Audi and dispatch came back with the registered owner as David Gaston and his address in Long Beach. They did a quick wants and warrant and DMV check on Gaston. His driver's license photo showed a handsome man in his late thirties with brown hair combed straight back and a scowl for whoever snapped the picture.

They put on tight fitting black leather gloves and ran their hands under and around the hay bales without finding any money. Stepping back, Fleming said, "It's gotta be in the car."

Peterson brushed a few pieces of straw off his uniform. "That's what I'm thinking. We gotta get hold of that lady who lost her dog. Without her name, address and phone number, I don't think we'll be able to get a search warrant."

A few judges would issue a search warrant based solely on an officer's sworn statement, but they were the exception. Most judges required some form of corroborating statement, evidence or a set of facts independent of the officer's statement that supported the request for a search warrant. The deputies knew that without the contact information of the woman who'd told them about the men hiding the money, there was little chance they could get inside the car.

Fleming cupped his hands against the passenger window to see inside. "There's always the possibility of getting a consent search."

Peterson said, "I have no idea who the owner of this car is, but if he's already hiding the car, there's no way he'll let us look inside it for evidence."

Unable to see anything in the car, Fleming pushed away from the window. "We can always ask."

Peterson asked, "What'd ya think of that lady's story?"

Fleming wrinkled his upper lip. "It sounded legit to me. Well, except for her dog. I can't understand why she'd lie about having a dog?"

Peterson said, "I thought the same thing. It was also kinda weird how she suddenly took off."

"Yeah, now that ya mention it." Fleming took out his cell phone. "I'm gonna call the sergeant and let him know what's going on." He spoke for several minutes. When he finished talking, he said, "Sarge wants us to back off and see if anyone comes back to the car. He's sending a couple more guys to help out."

Shortly, they were joined by four additional SWAT deputies. They were in the shade of the horse stables and Peterson briefed the others on the woman's statement and finding the Audi parked inside the hay bales.

He told two of the deputies, "I need Tomlinson and Smitty to go back through the exhibition booths and look for a lady in her late thirties wearing a white long-sleeved button-down shirt, hair in a braided ponytail with a straw cowboy hat, maybe with or without a dog named Lucky. When you find her, get her contact information ASAP and let me know. I want everyone to stay on frequency five."

Deputy Tomlinson said, "Finding the right lady wearing a white shirt and a cowboy hat in this crowd? I can see two women fitting that description from here."

Deputies Tomlinson and Smitty left the stables and were about fifty yards away when they saw five riders emerge from the woods, riding toward the stables. Tomlinson got on his handheld radio. "These could be the guys riding in now."

Tomlinson and Smitty unslung their rifles and lay on the ground in a prone shooting position. They watched through the red dot sights on top of their rifles as the cowboys got closer. Tomlinson told Smitty, "If they start shooting, I've got the three on the left."

Smitty felt for the safety on his rifle. "I've got the two on the right. All suspects are armed with multiple weapons."

The two remaining deputies unslung their M4s and stood at the low ready position: rifle butt stocks against their right shoulders, muzzles down and across their left knees, left hands on the forearms of the rifles and their right hands on the grips, thumbs on the safeties and index fingers resting just above the triggers. The deputies would practice shooting from the low ready position because it could be an extremely fast shooting position and a general bystander, seeing a deputy standing in the low ready position did not feel as threatened and therefore was least likely to complain about overly aggressive SWAT officers.

Softly, Deputy Peterson told the deputies, "Easy. We don't want to shoot these guys if we can help it."

The riders came to the entrance of the stables and dismounted. Peterson recognized Gaston from his photo. He still had the scowl. When they were off their horses, Peterson and Fleming walked out of the shadows. "Hello, gentlemen. Please, keep your hands away from your guns."

The helicopter circled overhead, advising Sergeant Pham the deputies had made contact with the five suspects they'd been tracking from the river.

"What do you think you're doing?" Gaston asked.

Peterson said, "We're investigating a shooting. Keep your hands where I can see 'em, away from your guns. Don't make any sudden moves or you'll be shot."

***

Gaston assumed the shooting they were investigating was the one George had mentioned while they were at the river range. Wanting to get to the scene of the shooting before another attorney beat him to it, he said, "We were at the shooting earlier. I'm negotiating for representation in the matter."

The deputy who had spoken—Peterson, according to his badge—lifted the rifle off his chest, pointed it at Gaston and shouted. "Hands in the air, drop to your knees then onto your stomachs. Anyone's hand goes near a gun, you'll be shot!"

Gaston's men immediately complied and laid on their stomachs. However, Gaston stood in defiance. "Do you know who I am? You can't tell me—"

Another deputy—Fleming, Gaston noted, already mentally preparing the complaint he intended to file—took two quick steps forward, grabbed Gaston in a front arm bar hold and took him to the ground, turning his wrist hard to the left. Gaston yelled out in pain and rolled over onto his stomach. Then Fleming cuffed Gaston with his hands behind his back.

The two deputies who had been standing at the low ready position stepped forward and handed Fleming additional handcuffs. He handcuffed the others and collected their guns.

Seething with rage, Gaston couldn't believe he was being treated like a common criminal. He deserved respect. After all, he represented the poor downtrodden in the court of law. Suddenly, he erupted, "You people've pissed me off! I'm gonna sue you, sue your department and have your badges! By the time I'm done, I'm gonna own the Long Beach Police Department, this Sheriff's Department, half the County of Riverside and this fucking range! Let me go, right goddamn, now!" Spittle sprayed from his mouth as he shouted.

Peterson said, "That's pretty big talk from a guy who just confessed to robbing a bank."

Gaston's head recoiled off the ground. "What? Bank robbery! What the fuck are you talking about?"

Peterson said, "Didn't you just say you'd been at the shooting and were gonna get representation?"

Gaston blinked twice. "Yes. Well, no. I mean, what? I'm representing a party at the shooting on the range. I don't know anything about a bank robbery."

Peterson cocked his head. "I don't know what you're talking about, pal. The only shooting's been at the bank."

Gaston pulled at his handcuffs and tried twisting his head to look at George. Why would George make up something like someone being involved in a shooting if it wasn't true? He replayed the conversation in his mind. *I'll bet ya someone fucked up and shot somebody.*

Gaston shook his head at his own mistake. He'd let his excitement at the thought of finally achieving his goals shade his interpretation of George's words.

He looked back at Peterson. "Well, it couldn't have been us. We were at the river for the last hour."

Peterson said, "Yeah, and ya stashed the money in the car."

Gaston took a breath. "That's fucking pathetic. Now, uncuff me and let me go."

Peterson asked, "Does the silver Audi belong to any of you guys?"

"It's mine. What's it matter?"

Peterson looked towards the car. "I think it's full of money from the bank."

"You people are all the same, city cops or county sheriffs, it doesn't matter. You're all fuckin' liars."

Peterson looked back at Gaston. "You can clear it up. Give us permission to search your car for the money and if it's not there..." He shrugged to complete the sentence.

Gaston knew he had a loaded Glock under the driver's seat, but he was at a shooting range. No problem. However, he couldn't remember if his stash of cocaine was under the seat or if he'd snorted it with the ladies at the Spearmint Rhino. Regardless, he wasn't about to give these stupid cops permission to search his car. He glared at Peterson. "You can bite me."

***

Sergeant Pham arrived and took Peterson aside to ask for an update. He listened for a minute, then said, "I watched the surveillance tape from inside the bank, and one of the robbers definitely got shot. Is one of these guys wounded? As long as they're still talking, ask if they were in the river and if any of them admits to being in the bank."

"No problem, Sarge."

Sergeant Pham looked at the handcuffed men. "Who's the car belong to? Why don't ya try getting permission to search it?"

Peterson pointed to Gaston. "It belongs to the loudmouth, and he doesn't want us anywhere near it."

Sergeant Pham folded his arms across his chest, raised his right hand to his face and tapped the tip of his nose. "Go back and talk with 'em. I'm gonna call the on-call deputy district attorney, see if we can get a judge to sign-off on a telephonic search warrant."

On weekends and after business hours, most District Attorneys' offices had a prosecutor available to law enforcement twenty-four hours for legal questions and to act as a liaison with judges in order to obtain search warrants.

Peterson told Fleming, "Pat 'em all down again and see if anyone's been shot or has been in the river."

Fleming said, "They're all soaking wet."

Peterson nudged Gaston with a toe. "Hey, why are your clothes all wet?"

"If you'd been doing your job, we wouldn't be." Gaston sneered. "While we were at the river range, three people rode up and stole our horses. We had to go into the river to get 'em back."

Peterson nodded. "So you were in the river? Anyone been shot?"

Gaston blew out an annoyed sigh. "Which is it? Was there a shooting here or not?"

Fleming patted down the four others and started searching Gaston. He tried to jerk away, but Fleming's grip on his arm held him fast.

"Keep your grubby hands offa me!"

Fleming plucked a wicked-looking knife from Gaston's boot, then patted up Gaston's body until he felt something in his shirt. "What do we have here?" Reaching inside, he pulled out a paper-bundled stack of five-dollar bills. For the first time, Gaston looked like he might be sick.

Fleming called out to Peterson, "Hey!" and showed him the stack of five-dollar bills with the bank wrapper.

At the sight of the currency, Sergeant Pham smiled as he spoke with the deputy district attorney on the telephone.

***

Gaston seemed to sink a few inches into the dirt. "Hey, that's not mine. What's happening? What are you doing to me? When those guys stole our horses, one of 'em must have dropped that or something. I just picked it up. You can't pin anything on me!"

Peterson looked at the pile of weapons they'd removed from Gaston and the other riders. "You expect me to believe the five of you, with all these guns, let someone steal your horses, then gave you a bank roll of money?"

"It wasn't like that. They stole our horses and left 'em in the river. They must have dropped the money when they took our horses."

Peterson looked at the other four. "Does anyone have anything else to say?"

Gaston interrupted. "I'm an attorney and I represent everyone here. I'm advising my clients not to talk with you."

Peterson asked, "Any problem with us searching your horses?"

Gaston rolled his eyes. "Knock yourself out. Ya gonna stick your hand up my horse's ass?"

Peterson gestured at the two deputies who had been providing cover to search the horses.

Deputies Tomlinson and Smitty looked inside the saddlebags. After a few seconds, Tomlinson said, "We have a bingo!" as he removed two paper bank-bundled stacks of one hundred twenty-dollar bills from one of the saddlebags.

Gaston couldn't believe it. This had gone from the day he imagined would be the focal point of his legal action against the County of Riverside and the range, to him being set-up for something. He couldn't understand who would do this to him or why?

"I've never seen that before. It must have been put there when our horses were stolen."

It sounded lame, even to him.

***

Jenny saw Crystal sitting in her Wrangler in front of the house. She pulled into the garage, leaving the door open, and Crystal walked into the garage, enthusiastically chomping on a wad of gum. "Did you know if chewing gum gets in your hair you can rub peanut butter on it and it will…" She saw Manolito and stopped.

His head was tilted awkwardly to the side, and drool ran from the side of his mouth. She stuck a hip out and twirled her blond hair between her fingers. "So, Mano, you heard John needed my help at the range?"

"Give it a rest," Jenny said. "He's medicated and can't hear you."

Crystal bent forward and peered through the window. "What's his problem? He looks weird."

"He's been shot. I need help getting him upstairs."

Crystal's face paled. She looked at Mano, lips quivering. Then she rushed around to the passenger side of the car, flung open the door and knelt beside him. "Hang in there, baby. Mama's here for you."

Jenny lightly backhanded her shoulder. "Spin him around, pull off his boots and help me get him in my bed."

Crystal's face turned pouty and her eyes watered. "He shot himself because he didn't think I'd take him back. Right?" The hope in her eyes made Jenny want to both hug her and shake her. Crystal rubbed Manolito's hand. "You can have my kidneys or heart, whatever you need. Just pull through so we can be together."

There was so much wrong with that statement, there was really nothing Jenny could say. She pushed her sister out of the way. "Why don't you close the garage door while I get his boots off?"

With Mano turned sideways in the seat and his boots cast aside, she tapped his face with the palm of her hand. "Mano, come on, wake up."

Crystal ran back to the car and jumped into Manolito's lap. Jenny choked back a cry. "Crystal! Are you trying to kill him?"

"He needs to see my face first thing out of a coma."

Jenny regretted calling her sister and made a mental note to ask her mom which one of them was adopted. "He's not in a coma. Get under an arm and help me get him into the house."

The blood on his shirt had spread, and there was more on the seat back. A little scrubbing with hydrogen peroxide and the stains would come out. Jenny silently prayed she could treat Manolito's wound just as easily.

With considerable effort, the sisters were able to get Manolito upstairs and onto the bed. Jenny laid him on his back and tore his shirt getting it off.

Crystal took her phone from her pocket. "You go wait for the ambulance while I stay with Mano."

Jenny lunged at the phone. "Tell me you didn't call 911?"

"I'm just getting ready to."

Jenny placed Crystal's phone in the nightstand drawer where John used to keep his pistol before Dickerson collected it. "We are going to care for him ourselves, not the hospital. Just you and me."

Crystal blinked as if she couldn't quite process what she was hearing. "Yeah, but..."

Jenny spoke over her. "Remember when I taught you how to take a pulse? I need you to do that for me while I collect a few things. Don't do anything else until I get back."

Jenny hurried into the bathroom and came out with a first aid kit and a roll of dental floss. She went downstairs, got a sewing needle, turned on the stove, and held the needle in the flame until it glowed orange. After sterilizing the needle, she stopped at the sink and made the water as hot as she could without burning herself. As she scrubbed her hands, she tried not to think of all the things that could go wrong.

She went back upstairs to find Crystal lying on the bed next to Manolito, holding her wrist. "My pulse is 87."

Jenny bit her cheek to hold back the frustrated diatribe on the tip of her tongue. She'd never thought of Crystal as stupid— scatterbrained, sure, but not stupid—but today was beginning to test that conviction. "They say there's someone for everyone, but I don't know. Help me clean his shoulder with Betadine."

Crystal sat up and rolled Manolito onto his side while Jenny did the work. "Can Mano still work with John if we get married?"

Jenny threaded the dental floss onto the sewing needle and stitched the front and back of where the bullet went through his trapezius muscle. "I think you should see if he wants to date again before worrying about that."

Crystal watched, teary-eyed, her hands in her lap. "I know I'm being an idiot," she said. "I know that. It's just..." Her voice broke. "I'm still crazy about him. How dumb is that?" Without waiting for an answer, she stood up and hurried from the room.

Jenny watched her go, then turned back to the patient. When she'd finished closing the wounds, Jenny taped gauze pads over the injuries and took Manolito's pulse. Feeling confident he was out of danger, she laid her hand on Mano's heart and said to the still unconscious patient, "I can only help so much. The rest is up to you."

***

"Let me see if I got this straight." Deputy Peterson read from his notebook. "Someone comes along, gives you a stack of money, steals your horses and leaves more money in your saddlebags. He then leaves your horses in the middle of the river, where you swim out to retrieve them?"

"That's right," George said. "Well, we didn't swim. The river's only three feet deep."

Peterson crossed out a line in his notebook. "Thank you for clearing that up."

George, who had been handcuffed and staring in wide-eyed disbelief, said, "I don't know what kind of shit he's mixed up in, but the rest of us don't know nothin' about any money or why his car's parked in there. You can search me, search my car and my horse, but we don't want anything else to do with this guy!"

Gaston flared his nostrils, took a breath and tried to roll over so he could look at George. Fleming stopped Gaston from spinning around. Gaston yelled at George, "After all I did for you! It was you! You're the one who's trying to set me up!"

Sergeant Pham disconnected his phone and said to Peterson, "The deputy D.A. says you have more than enough probable cause to search the Audi without a warrant or the owner's consent."

Peterson asked Gaston, "Where's your car keys? Or would you like me to break out your windows?"

Dejected, Gaston said, "My right front pants pocket."

Deputy Tomlinson removed the keys from the pocket and Sergeant Pham called Peterson back over. "We might have plenty of probable cause to search this guy's car, but I watched the video from the bank. One of the suspects got shot during the robbery. None of these guys has a gunshot wound, and we still haven't found the masks or vests they wore in the bank. I'm not convinced we have the right suspects."

Peterson looked back at the men handcuffed on the ground. "These have to be the guys. Gaston has money from the robbery. I'm sure everything else will be in the car."

Peterson went to the driver's door and Tomlinson to the passenger side. Tomlinson clicked the key remote and unlocked the doors. He looked under the driver's seat and Tomlinson looked first in the glove box, then under the passenger seat. Peterson said, "I've got a Glock and it looks like some coke under here."

Tomlinson smiled. "Looks like your buddy's gonna have a hard time explaining this mask and orange safety vest."

Peterson said, "Make sure you don't touch that stuff. Our crime techs are gonna want to check it for DNA."

He looked in the cup holder on the center console. "Look at these. Have you ever seen ammo like this? I don't know a lot about cowboy shooting, but it looks like the wrong bullets have been loaded into the casing. I wonder why he'd do that?"

Tomlinson took a pen from his shirt pocket and moved the ammunition around inside the cup holder. "That is strange. I've never seen anything like these before. I'm sure our lab geeks will love looking at them."

Peterson shrugged. "I still don't see any money."

Tomlinson said, "I'm betting it's in the trunk."

They left the two front doors standing open, went to the rear of the car and popped open the trunk. Seeing only a large clear plastic storage box and a couple boxes of ammunition scattered on the carpet, they couldn't believe there was no money.

Peterson stared into the trunk. "The way our witness talked, I thought for sure we were gonna find the money from the robbery."

Tomlinson had a thought. "The spare tire!"

He reached inside, took out the plastic storage box and lifted the carpeted spare tire covering. "Voila!"

Surprised by the amount of money, Peterson started counting then quickly gave up.

Tomlinson asked, "Didn't the guy who owns the car say he's an attorney?"

"Yeah."

"Looks like he's gonna need his own attorney."

They closed the trunk, shut the car doors and set the alarm. Peterson spoke to Sergeant Pham in a low voice so Gaston couldn't overhear.

"We found a mask and an orange safety vest under the front passenger seat and some weird looking ammunition in the center console. There's a loaded Glock and some cocaine under the driver's seat. And I almost forgot, there's about seven or eight hundred thousand dollars in wrapped currency in the trunk."

Sergeant Pham nodded. "Yeah, the bank estimated the loss to be nine hundred thirty-six thousand dollars and change. Are ya sure there's only one mask and orange vest?"

He said, "It's possible we missed a few things, but that's all we found."

Sergeant Pham folded his arms in front of his chest, placed his right hand in front of his face and tapped the tip of his nose. "Okay, we definitely have enough to arrest the owner of the car, but unless you come up with something else, we don't have anything on the others."

"I know it," Peterson said. "Gaston's the only one who had the bank notes in his possession and in his horse's saddlebag. Not to mention, everything in his car."

Sergeant Pham spoke slowly, thinking as he spoke. "The resolution of Wells Fargo's surveillance tapes isn't worth a crap, but you can clearly see one of the robbers got shot. If one of these guys doesn't have a gunshot, we don't have any evidence tying 'em to the robbery."

Peterson asked, "So, what do ya want me to do with 'em, Sarge?"

"Take all their guns and issue a receipt. There were several shots fired and maybe we'll be able to match ballistics with their guns. If the bullets fired inside the bank don't match up with any of their guns, that'd prove they had nothing to do with this."

"And what about Gaston?"

Pham raised a thumb and flipped it over his shoulder like an umpire calling a runner out at second base. "Impound his car, arrest him for robbery, aggravated assault and possession of cocaine. Before you take him to the station for booking, ask him about the robbery again. Start by asking about the loaded gun in his car. If he's still talking, ask about the coke. Maybe he'll tell ya he's an addict and did it to feed his habit."

Peterson snickered. "Yeah, like all the other bank robbers."

Sergeant Pham got into his Tahoe. "Our lab techs are at the bank, processing the scene for evidence. I want 'em to process the Audi as soon as they can. One more thing. Get a couple guys and look for the female witness you let walk away."

Peterson bit back a retort. Pham was right. Letting the woman go had been shoddy work. He pushed it from his mind and headed back toward Gaston. When questioning a suspect, Peterson liked to start with small talk and build rapport before getting to the investigation. However, he guessed with Gaston, attempting to develop a mutually respectful conversation was pointless.

He put on his don't-fuck-with-me face and took a moment to savor the anticipation of matching wits with the sleazy little attorney. He was going to enjoy taking this guy down.

***

Gaston stared at Peterson without saying a word. He was being set up, he just didn't know how elaborate the ruse was or how many people were involved. He knew George must be in on it. Probably Walter and the entire Lead Botton Posse as well. No matter; they were all idiots. He was smarter than all of them put together and besides, he knew the legal system. They didn't.

Peterson said, "I'm curious about the ammunition in the front of your car. Tell me about that?"

Damn. They'd found his gun under the seat. Well, screw them. He could lie his way out of this and, then he'd be free to go. And then he'd show George and the rest of these assholes they'd picked on the wrong guy. He put on an innocent expression. "Damnit, did I leave ammo in my car? I certainly wasn't going to drive outta here with it in there."

Peterson wrote in his notebook while talking. "Yeah, but what's it for?"

Gaston suppressed a snort. This must be amateur hour if this big galoot thought he was going to get me to say I keep the Glock loaded so I can shoot people. Peterson must be even dumber than George or Walter.

He said, "I was gonna shoot that ammo before going home."

Peterson kept writing. "Ya wanna tell me about the coke?"

Gaston's stomach sank. The California Penal Code still had possession of cocaine listed as a felony. However, the courts sentenced all first-time offenders to diversion, and as long as an offender made it to all six counseling sessions, any narcotics charges would be expunged from their record. Therefore, if he played it smart, this would not impact his ability to practice law. The best thing he could do for himself now was to stop talking.

He said, "We're through. I'm exercising my Fifth Amendment right and choose not to talk any more."

"Thank God!" George exclaimed. "Finally, somebody's found a way to shut this guy up!"

For a moment, Gaston felt hurt. He knew sometimes the guys lashed out because they felt threatened by his superior intellect, but beneath all that, he'd thought that on some level, they liked him. Then the hurt gave way to anger. These assholes. They'd only pretended to tolerate him because he was best shooter on the team.

Peterson closed his notebook and put it in his pocket. "I suppose you don't want to talk about the mask, vest and nearly a million dollars in stolen currency we found in your car?"

Gaston rocked back, stunned. Mask? Vest? A million fucking dollars? That couldn't be right. How could anyone have broken into his car and left that kind of incriminating evidence? Who was George working with, anyway? And why?

But then he knew. Those cops. Those fucking Southland Regulators. "Hey, wait a minute..."

Peterson raised both hands in front of his chest, palms outward. "No, Gaston. You wanna exercise your right to not incriminate yourself, you got it. You'll have to live with the consequences. I hope you enjoy the next twenty years in a federal prison."

▢

Arl Farris

34

...policing's a young man's sport

Manolito opened his eyes feeling sore, unsure where he was, constricted and unable to move. Seeing Crystal snuggled around him and staring at his face from three inches away, he flinched. She squeezed him tighter, sending a jolt of pain through his shoulder. "You've been asleep for a long time."

He tried to flex his arm, but it was tangled in blankets.

She gently patted his bandage. "You are going to need to take it easy. We can't have you pulling out the stitches."

Seeing a picture of John and Jenny on the night stand, he realized he was in their bed. He looked down toward his shoulder. "So, Jenny was able to sew me up."

Crystal combed his hair with her fingers. "Sure, she helped…"

He caressed the side of her face. How had he ever compared her to the flavor of the month ice cream? "You have always been good to me. I…" He looked away. "Do you think we could start over?"

She nuzzled into him, and he grimaced as her head came to rest on the wound. "I wish we could stay like this forever."

He lifted her head. "I don't think life would ever be boring with you."

***

John poured cold cereal for the kids and threw together their sack lunches. Jenny made sure the lunches got in the right backpack, along with their homework, before sending Patrick and Clara off for school. When they were alone, Jenny sat at the table, sipping a mocha and scanning her iPad. She looked more beautiful than ever. He still couldn't believe what she'd risked for him.

She said, "I don't understand why this article has nothing about Mano getting shot. It says authorities believe one of the robbers may have injured himself during the heist."

She set down her iPad. "Why wouldn't they just say one of the suspects got shot? Is that the police trying to control the flow of information, or did the reporter get his facts wrong?"

John put their breakfast on the table and sat down. "You'd be surprised how much they get wrong. The police department wouldn't have any reason to hold that detail from the public."

She blew on the top of her mocha. "Yeah, but it's so lame. It makes it sound like Mano tripped or scraped his shin."

John spread jelly on a piece of toast. "The only good thing was that the guy in the bank panicked. If he'd kept his cool, he could've killed both Mano and me."

"Well, who wouldn't be afraid of five guys wearing masks in the middle of a hold up?"

John took a bite. "No doubt we were intimidating, but you still gotta respect the guy for standing up to us." He tried not to think of all the ways it could have gone wrong. If the bullet had gone in a little to the right. If the man had been a little more cool-headed or a little better shot. If the police had investigated their alibis a little closer.

"I guess so."

John's cell phone was on the counter behind them and he got up from the table when it rang. He listened for several minutes before he said, "Next Saturday? Absolutely. I'll be there." He hung up and sat down grinning.

Jenny set down her cup and smiled back. "Give it up. Who was it?"

"Captain Dickerson. Evidently, with Gaston's arrest, all proceedings against us have been dismissed. The department's concluded their investigations, and we can all return to work next week."

She beamed with delight. "That's great news, honey."

"Captain Dickerson said Gaston claimed he had nothing to do with the robbery and he'd been framed." He laughed. "When first being questioned, he blamed his own posse for setting him up and now he's telling detectives we did it."

She shrugged dismissively. "Desperate people say desperate things."

They made eye contact and laughed.

Then, in a more serious tone, John said, "Speaking of desperate people, I'm feeling ambivalent about going back to work for Dickerson. Believe me, if I could have come up with a way of getting Dickerson rung up at the same time as Gaston, I'd have done it in a heartbeat."

She reached a hand across the table and placed it over his. "You don't work for the captain. You work for the people of Long Beach. Besides, your officers are counting on you. They aren't going to look at Dickerson for leadership, they'll come to you."

He smiled, though he wasn't sure bank robbery was the best qualification for law enforcement leadership. "When did you get to be so smart?"

She took another sip from her drink. "What else?"

He was about to take another bite of toast, but set it down before answering. "Dickerson's been on the phone with the guys from the sheriff's department and they told him whoever robbed the bank were real professionals. Their crime lab hasn't been able to recover any usable DNA, despite all the blood and other fluids left behind by the suspects. They've called in the FBI and ATF to take over the case."

Jenny pulled her hands away from her drink. "The ATF and FBI! How do you feel about that?"

He shrugged. "I'd be lying if I said it didn't make me a little nervous, but if there's no evidence… I just hope they live up to their reputations; Famous But Incompetent and Assured To Fail."

Jenny chuckled at the acronyms. "Not so incompetent if they knock on our front door with a warrant in their hands."

"I don't think they will. They matched Gaston's DNA to hairs found in the mask and on the vest in his car. They also identified the ammunition in his car as the same fired in the bank. It would have been a lot stronger case if I'd left a couple of his hair clippings in the bank." He closed his eyes for a moment, reliving the pepper spray coming inside his mask. He shook off the thought. "On the other hand, he does have four witnesses who were with him all day. He should beat the robbery charge, but with the cash in his car, the possession of stolen property is a solid case."

She cocked an eye and lifted her coffee mug. "I can't believe how well your plan worked. But don't you feel a little bit bad for Gaston? I mean, he's a narcissistic sociopath, but he didn't rob a bank."

Surprised by her comment, he pushed his breakfast aside. "One of the first lessons a policeman learns is people are almost never convicted of the crimes they commit. Drunk drivers plead guilty to reckless driving and rapists plead down to assault. Al Capone committed countless murders but served time for tax evasion."

"Yeah, but still..."

He said, "Gaston stole from every client under his no-fee-up-front scam. You can't tell me he wasn't robbing the City of Long Beach every time he filed one of his phony lawsuits. He would settle out of court because it cost the city too much money to defend the case. He's as crooked as they come."

She finished her drink. "I guess you're right, but still..."

His jaw tightened. "The guy was a few days away from taking everything from us in civil court. We didn't deserve to have our future and the future of our kids stolen."

He got up and took the dishes to the sink. "He didn't rob a bank, but he's definitely a one man crime wave. If we didn't stop him..." He let the sentence hang in the air. Maybe he was rationalizing, but that didn't mean it wasn't true.

Jenny seemed about to reply, but stopped when her iPad chimed. She held it up for him to see. It was a photo text from Crystal, showing Mano framed with red roses.

He was grateful for the chance to change the subject. "Yeah? What's up with those two, anyway? They're acting like a couple of kids at senior prom."

"Don't ask." She closed her eyes for a moment, and he wondered if she was worried Mano would break her sister's heart again. "So, what did Dickerson say about next Saturday?"

He grinned. "The academy graduates on Saturday, and they want me to present the top shooter award."

She stood, walked behind his chair and hugged him. "That's so nice, honey. You love doing that." She moved her lips a little closer to his ear. "And I've got some good news of my own. I was gonna wait until we were all together at dinner to tell you and the kids, but this seems like the right time."

He placed his hands on the table and braced himself for what she was about to say.

"I got a call yesterday evening. They cleared me to come back to work at the hospital. We're going to get our lives back!"

He let out a sigh of relief. "Don't ever tell me you have good news like that again. I thought you were going to say you're pregnant."

***

The academy graduation took place inside The Walter Pyramid at California State University Long Beach. The range staff attended, wearing their class A uniforms, complete with hats, ties and white gloves. John thought they never looked better.

Scott said, "I feel strange, coming back to work like nothing happened."

John noticed a slight wince as Manolito plucked a piece of lint from Scott's collar, but Manolito carried on as if he was never hurt. "I'm not really sure we changed anybody's minds or the way anyone looks at policemen. If anything, I bet Captain Dickerson despises us more than ever."

Blakesley said, "I'm not sure I'm gonna go back. I have enough time on, I'm thinking about retiring."

John looked up, surprised. "You can't be serious? There's a lot you can teach these rookies." He couldn't imagine the team without Blakesley. Somehow, he'd thought they would go on together until they were all ready to retire. All for one, and one for all, like the Three Musketeers. He shook his head at his own naïvete.

Blakesley broke eye contact, adjusting John's badge. "I'm getting too old. Besides, policing's a young man's sport. I'd really like to stay on and work the range, but I'm not sure I can go back out on the streets." He made an expansive gesture. "I mean, we risk our lives working for the department, and for them to just stick us on the shelf like we're an unwanted gift at a birthday party, it's... it's outrageous. And it's not like the public's any better. My own daughter unfriended me on Facebook when I told her I'd been suspended."

Disappointment etched across his face, Scott said, "Not a day goes by my dad doesn't wish he could come back on the department. Don't retire just because you're feeling let down by the department."

Rebecca grimaced. "It's a little more than that. The department violated its promise to us."

John looked around to make sure she hadn't drawn any unwanted attention. "What promise?"

"To support and defend the officers who put their lives on the line every day. I'm not saying two wrongs make a right, but I haven't felt so good in a long, long time. We didn't solve all the city's problems, but we took care of one of the guys behind the scenes who was corrupting the system."

John said, "You know Gaston will never serve any time, certainly not for robbery. He's got four solid witnesses who were with him all day. I'm sure he'll be convicted of possession of stolen property, and that's good enough for him to be disbarred, and lose his law license. He'll most likely get probation and who knows where he'll turn up after that?"

John let that sink in for a minute, then said, "What about the next time an elementary school principal doesn't want you on campus or someone accuses you of being a racist?"

"I've come to terms with that, and I'm gonna be okay," she replied with conviction. "I mean, we took control of our own destiny. We called the shots, not the captain or a corrupt attorney. I'm not suggesting we ever do something like this again, but at least I know whatever happens in the course of my career, it'll be because I made it happen."

John nodded. "I think the only way to change the culture of the department is to promote. If Captain Dickerson would have stood up for us, maybe Gaston wouldn't have become so brazen or powerful. And no, I don't think we should come up with another plan to get rid of the captain, no matter how much he deserves it."

They stared at him for a moment, as if trying to understand if he was suggesting they should go after Dickerson or not.

Manolito said, "There'll always be Gastons, and I'm afraid there'll always be a Captain Dickerson. The only thing that'll really change is their names. We made our point. Now it's time to turn the page and move on."

Rebecca held up her hand for him to stop. "If it was Captain John Chambers and Lieutenant Manolito Torres, things would have never gotten so out of control."

With the ghost of a grin, Blakesley said, "Well put, Chief Rebecca Wells."

John glanced toward the podium and gestured the others toward their seats. "The graduation's about to start."

Everyone stood as the color guard posted the flag and for the Pledge of Allegiance. Then Chief Buckley addressed the audience, expressing gratitude for the community partnership between the police, community residents and the businesses. How the police department reflected the community and the community believed in the department.

John and his team exchanged glances. It was all John could do to keep from rolling his eyes when Buckley talked about unity between the police department and the community, and he could tell the others felt the same. The hypocrisy was staggering.

Finally, Buckley stepped down and the certificates were handed out. John felt a swell of pride in the recruits he'd worked with at the range. Every one of them had surpassed the department's marksmanship proficiency standards. Class sergeant Michael Flores, graduating with honors, made a half-bow toward the range staff as he returned to his seat with his certificate.

When Buckley had handed out the last certificate, John took the stage. He began by awarding the top shooting award to Michael Flores. Then he put a hand on each side of the podium and addressed the crowd.

"What drives someone to commit a crime? Some might steal a loaf of bread because they're hungry, others commit crimes to feed a drug habit, and a terrorist commits crime to bring about social change. I might offer another possibility as to why someone might commit a crime.

"If the system's corrupt and there's no legal way to bring about change, a person might go outside the law. Our history is full of examples of people who stood up and broke the law to make this a better place. Each of our founding fathers who signed the Declaration of Independence acted outside the law. Martin Luther

King, Susan B. Anthony, Rosa Parks just to name a few, acted outside the law, and we're a better country because of their courage to do so.

"You've probably heard the term extreme prejudice. It means to pursue something with single-minded action. You never falter. You never waiver. That's how each of those people I mentioned pursued their vision of a better world."

He looked into the audience at the range staff and felt proud to work with such extraordinary officers. A little voice inside him said, You did it to save your own ass, and that was true. But it was also true that they'd done it to save each other and to neutralize a threat to the whole department and the community they served.

"As new officers of the Long Beach Police Department, you'll be called upon to enforce the law. You'll be required to do it fairly and without bigotry toward anyone. But you'll also be expected to use your best discretion, be compassionate, and always do the right thing.

"Every day, you'll make decisions that affect people's lives. Do you drag a single mom to jail for a petty traffic warrant, or do you help shepherd her through the system? Do you throw a homeless veteran with PTSD to the ground and cuff him just because he's sleeping off a bender on a park bench? Or do you give him a chance to get his head together and ride in the back of the patrol car with a little dignity? Do you know when to shoot? More importantly, do you know when not to?"

He looked out across the audience. The Regulators were sitting with rigid posture, hanging on his every word. The newly minted officers were fidgeting and reading their certificates. He closed his eyes for a second thinking of the tough choices he made over the last few months, and went on. "There may come a time when you find yourself in an extreme circumstance. A situation where your survival—or someone else's—hinges on the choices you make. When that happens…"

He paused, meeting Rebecca's gaze, then Scott's, then Blakesley's, and finally Mano's. "You make your best choice, the one that best fulfills your oath to protect and serve. And then you execute that decision with extreme prejudice."

The End

☐

☐

Arl Farris

435

ABOUT ARL FARRIS

Arl began his career as a police officer in Orange County, California. He worked uniform patrol, investigations and crime task forces. He promoted up the chain of command, becoming one of the youngest Chiefs of Police at a municipal police department in Los Angeles County.

Arl has been a police academy firearms instructor, docent at the Simon Wiesenthal Center Museum of Tolerance Los Angeles, volunteered countless hours on habitat projects in the Mojave National Preserve, and is a frequent competitor at the US Police and Fire Games.

He draws on his knowledge of policing and the love of the outdoors for inspiration in writing his novels. Learn more about Arl and his upcoming books at www.AuthorArlFarris.com

52517406R00269

Made in the USA
Columbia, SC
10 March 2019